LEVI

BRYNNE ASHER

Text Copyright
© 2022 Brynne Asher
All Rights Reserved
No part of this book may be reproduced, scanned, or distributed in any printed or electronic form without permission from the author. Please do not participate in or encourage piracy of copyrighted materials in violation of author's rights. Only purchase authorized editions.

Any resemblance to actual persons, things, locations, or events is accidental.

This book is a work of fiction.

LEVI

A Killers Next Generation Novel

Published by Brynne Asher
BrynneAsherBooks@gmail.com

Keep up with me on Facebook for news and upcoming books
https://www.facebook.com/BrynneAsherAuthor

Join my Facebook reader group to keep up with my latest news Brynne Asher's Beauties

Keep up with all Brynne Asher books and news. Sign up for my newsletter http://eepurl.com/gFVMUP

Edited by Hadley Finn

ALSO BY BRYNNE ASHER

Killers Series

Vines – A Killers Novel, Book 1

Paths – A Killers Novel, Book 2

Gifts – A Killers Novel, Book 3

Veils – A Killers Novel, Book 4

Scars – A Killers Novel, Book 5

Souls – A Killers Novel, Book 6

The Tequila – A Killers Novella

The Killers, The Next Generation

Levi, Asa's son

The Agents

Possession

Tapped

Exposed

Illicit

The Carpino Series

Overflow – The Carpino Series, Book 1

Beautiful Life – The Carpino Series, Book 2

Athica Lane – The Carpino Series, Book 3

Until Avery – A Carpino Series Crossover Novella

Force of Nature - A Carpino Christmas Novel

The Dillon Sisters
Deathly by Brynne Asher
Damaged by Layla Frost

The Montgomery Series
Bad Situation – The Montgomery Series, Book 1
Broken Halo – The Montgomery Series, Book 2
Betrayed Love - The Montgomery Series, Book 3

Standalones
Blackburn

CONTENTS

1. Tutor — 1
2. My Mission — 11
3. Scandal — 29
4. A Price for Everything — 41
5. Dumbass Mode — 53
6. You're Mine — 65
7. Popular Recluse — 75
8. Arctic — 83
9. Buried Deep — 97
10. A Real Winner — 105
11. Chickens and Zingers — 111
12. Little Jailbird — 121
13. Desperation and Strength — 129
14. Survival — 139
15. Commotion — 149
16. Power — 163
17. Be Prepared to be Kidnapped — 179
18. Snake Charmer — 193
19. Random My Ass — 203
20. Big, Fat, Burning Lava Pit of Drama — 213
21. Fuck Over Levi Hollingsworth — 225
22. Skip — 237
23. Gauntlet — 249
24. Bullets — 265
25. Rhetorical Bullets — 273
26. Parole — 279
27. Memories — 285
28. Yes — 295
29. Long Week — 309
30. Unsafe — 315
31. Birthday Girl — 329
32. Bonded Forever — 343

33. No More Lies	357
34. Declarations	367
35. Reindeer Games	373
36. FBI, CIA, NCAA, Elvis, or the Russians	381
37. Louise Has a Heart	389
38. The Love Machine	397
39. You Know What They Say...	407
40. Over	419
41. Just The Way You Are	425
42. Are You Ready?	431
Epilogue	443
Acknowledgments	453
Also by Brynne Asher	455
About the Author	457

*To the magic of young love.
Never forget.*

1
TUTOR

Carissa

Change is brutal.

This is also a new development. I never knew change could be a rusty knife to the soul, but the last thirty days proves it. This conversation from hell is the stinging tetanus shot proving all the recent changes in my reality could not suck more.

I never had issues with change until the weight of the world landed on my shoulders.

"We need to discuss your grades while there's still time for you to turn them around. This isn't in line with your transcript from your school in Phoenix. How are you settling in, Carissa?"

Settling in?

I fist the cuffs of my oversized cardigan where my arms are crossed. I don't want my white knuckles to give away what I'm truly feeling. "Fine."

I wonder if Mrs. Bradley is going to enroll me in a

theater class, since there's no way I could convince anyone that I'm anywhere in the universe of *fine* at the moment.

She fingers the polyester scarf tied at her neck as she studies me—more intently than I can say for myself when it comes to studying since we landed in the Commonwealth. "I have an appointment tomorrow with your grandmother about Cade. When your mother enrolled you, she gave me permission to talk to you about him. How is he settling in at home?"

There's not much in life that steels my spine, but the topic of my brother is at the top of that list. "I had no idea our grandmother has a meeting scheduled with you. Why? Cade's grades are better than mine. No, they're perfect. And if you really need to know, things aren't great, considering this isn't our home."

She pauses as her eyes narrow on me. "The meeting is a formality—protocol for the program. Our meeting tomorrow is nothing more than a prescheduled visit with Cade's teachers. But let's talk about the latter. Your grandmother gave me the impression you and Cade are transitioning well. If you'd like to share something else, it would help me a great deal before our meeting."

There's so much more to know, but my new school counselor has no power to fix the damage already done.

Instead of telling her that, I stand and sling my backpack over my shoulder. "Everything is great. I'm sure my grandmother will tell you how great things are at your meeting. I don't want to be late to my next class."

That's a lie too. I'd rather sit through another meal with Louise before getting to class on time. That says a lot about how much I want to sit here and talk to my counselor.

"Wait." Mrs. Bradley picks up a piece of paper from her cluttered desk and hands it to me. "Tutoring. You're scheduled three days a week after school in the library until you bring your grade up to a C."

My face warms immediately, and I'm forced to bite back the stinging that prickles my eyes. I've never needed a tutor in anything. I might hate science, and my grades in general are barely above average, but I certainly have never had a failing grade.

My words come out rushed. "I'll turn it around—I promise. I can do it on my own."

"If you'd like me to talk to your grandmother about this tomorrow I can. We can include your teachers, if you think that would help."

I clutch my backpack, and the panic starts to simmer. "Trust me, that would not help."

She gives me a sad smile. "Then you have two choices. Meet with one of our peer-approved tutors after school, or we can set up a schedule with Mr. Stance—"

"No!" I interrupt, spitting the word with too much emotion. Mr. Stance is what's wrong with public education. He's the worst teacher I've ever had. He's older than dirt and smells like an onion salad from two weeks ago—if onion salads are even a thing. If so, he would definitely be the kind of guy to eat them. "I'll take the tutor. I guess. I mean, that would be better than..." I bite the inside of my cheek before finishing. "Bothering Mr. Stance."

"I think that's a wise choice." She nods in agreement, and I wonder if her offering me a peer tutor is her idea of an olive branch, saving me from sitting too close to the stinkiest teacher on the face of the planet. "Your tutor schedule is listed here. Report to the library at your assigned study room."

"What about Cade? We have a schedule. I can't change that on him."

Mrs. Bradley softens her voice, and I decide I don't dislike her as much as I thought I did when I was called into her office fifteen minutes ago. "I know how important a schedule is for Cade. Your mother explained that. It's wonderful you're helping him with it. But your grades are important too. When I spoke to your grandmother this morning, I explained the situation."

Shit. Of course she called Louise before talking to me. Adults can be such dumbasses.

"Don't worry." Mrs. Bradley has no clue what she's talking about as she tries to assure me she didn't just stir up a shit show. "Your grandmother will pick up Cade after school and return later to get you."

I try not to roll my eyes.

My grandmother doesn't lift a finger to do anything for herself besides prepare dinner. There's no way she'd get behind the wheel to pick us up. She'll send someone who Cade is even less familiar with than Chuck.

"Fantastic." My response is tight and relays anything other than fan-fucking-tastic as I reach out and snatch the paper with my assigned tutor's information on it. When I glance at it, all I see is a long list of dates. Shit, she really has me scheduled three times a week for the next month and a half. I need to get my shit turned around quick so I don't have to deal with this nonsense longer than I have to.

"Carissa," Mrs. Bradley calls for me as I reach for the door.

I exhale before turning. "Yes?"

"I have confidence this will turn things around. I want nothing more than for you to settle in and make friends."

"Sure. Friends. I'll get on that." Louise would chastise me for being rude to any adult, let alone my school counselor, but I don't care. I have no time to worry about friends if Cade is miserable, and Cade currently being miserable is an understatement. It's hard enough moving across the country, but dealing with the changes thrown at us is too much for him. I'm doing my best to balance that for both of us. But from the state of my grades—and the current conversation—I'm doing a shit job at it.

"We have student volunteers for this sort of thing." Mrs. Bradley continues to hold me hostage in this office and won't stop talking. "If you'd like, I can pair you with someone with similar interests."

Wow. Assigned friends. Just when I thought my life couldn't get more depressing on the east coast. No matter the threats from my grandmother, my manners just flew out the window. "Thanks, but no thanks. I don't want anyone forced to spend time with me just to rack up their National Honors Society hours. I might look like a lost cause, but I'm not that hard up."

"That's not what I meant—"

I hold up the paper fisted in my hand. "This is plenty. Not sure I can handle any more mandatory interaction in one day."

I turn on my combat boot to hurry out of her office and the counseling center as fast as I can. The bell rings when I hit the hallway. I pull out my phone to text Cade.

Me – The damn counselor called me in.

Cade isn't obsessed with his phone, but he is obsessed with information, and his phone gives him direct access to that.

Big Bro – Did you get in trouble?

I sigh as I jog up the steps to my next class.

Me – Not completely, but I do have to stay after school. Louise said she'd pick you up, but I'm sure she'll send a car. I won't be too late, but I need to work on chemistry. When I get home, we'll hang out.

I don't tell him Louise has a meeting with our counselor and his teachers tomorrow. I'm not sure there's much more he hates than meetings about him. If he finds out, he'll lose it.

***Big Bro** – Fix your grades, Rissa.*

Cade might be in a program to make sure he's not struggling socially, but he's brilliant. His grades are always stellar.

***Me** – I've gotta go. See you later.*

I stuff my phone in the deep pocket of my cardigan. I'm about to do the same with my new tutoring schedule when something catches my eye at the top of it. I smooth out the wrinkled paper.

Levi Hollingsworth.

What?

We moved to BFE Virginia on New Year's Day. Mrs. Bradley was right—I've been here long enough to screw up my Chem grade something bad. I eat lunch with Cade every day, and my only friend is the child genius I sit next to in trigonometry.

Fine, Mason is not a child. He's a freshman—even though he seems younger than fourteen. However old he is, he's damn smart since he breezed through every math class I've ever hated, and did it before he officially started high school. I think he feels sorry for me since I'm new. Either that, or he pities me since I'm barely hanging onto a C in trig. Whatever it is, he's nice, so I'm calling him my only friend in Virginia.

Even so...

I know who Levi Hollingsworth is.

Everyone knows who Levi Hollingsworth is.

He's only the hottest guy in school.

But he's not hot the way most guys are. Levi is different.

He's a jock, but I overheard at lunch he's also in the running for valedictorian.

He also doesn't beg for attention. He just gets it everywhere he goes.

He's not quiet, he's stoic.

He's not cagey, he's mysterious.

He's definitely not social. If I were to look up aloof in the thesaurus, Levi Hollingsworth would be its number one synonym.

And I know all of this because I have a vagina and twenty-twenty vision. I also pass him in the hall everyday between second and third periods. I can further support my theory that he's all that because he eats lunch two tables over from where Cade likes to sit, and I have to try really hard not to stare at him because the last thing I need is everyone in the Commonwealth knowing I'm a freak.

I'll keep that secret as long as possible, thank you very much.

This is why I know that Levi is a man among boys—tall and broad with a full head of dark wavy hair. I've wondered more than once, or maybe twenty times, what color his eyes are. I've never been close enough to tell.

But that's all about to change.

Today.

After school.

At the library.

In a fucking study room!

"Carissa Collins?"

My head pops up, and I fist the paper in my sweaty hand. "Sorry. Yes, I'm here. What? I mean, did you ask me something? Sorry."

I wonder if these teachers are immune to idiot teenagers.

Ms. Riley doesn't look surprised I was daydreaming and gets back to her agenda. "Let's turn to where we left off yesterday in *Hamlet*."

I think I might be sick, and it has nothing to do with Shakespeare.

I have two hours to prepare.

Or run away.

I'm thinking the latter is a better bet.

I'm not sure how I can do that when my mom wouldn't let me bring my car from Phoenix. I'm stuck with Louise's driver or the bus. And who wants to ride the school bus their junior year?

I grab my book and open it to where we left off yesterday. I didn't review what we went over last night because Cade was in the mood to rearrange his room so it would look like his old one back home. By the time he felt good about it, it was late, and all I wanted to do was watch shit TV.

I stare at Shakespeare's words, and despite lit being my favorite subject, I don't comprehend any of them. Not a single one. All I can think about is chemistry hell, and how I'll finally get to quit wondering what color Levi's eyes are.

2

MY MISSION

Levi

"Sorry, man. I've got a tutoring gig in five minutes. I'll catch you next time."

"You and your service hours. Some of us barely passed the SAT with a high enough score to get into a shitty college. Your perfection makes me want to puke in your shiny, new Jeep after a field party." Jack is the goalie on our varsity lacrosse team, and there are days I think he's been hit over the head too many times with a stick. He slams his locker shut and turns to me. "But that'll never happen since you refuse to be my DD. Wait—they should give you service hours for being my damn DD. We'd both benefit, and you'd be making the world a safer place."

I tip my head and glare at him before turning to leave. I've known him forever. There's a fifty-fifty chance he's serious. "You're a fucking idiot."

His stride falls into a steady tempo next to mine. "I know you love me, Hollingsworth. There's no need to try and hate me for who I am. The bully bromance might work with some guys, but I'm not like them—I see through those walls you've built around yourself. You're hurting inside, and you're taking it out on me."

I roll my eyes and don't even bother glancing at him. "Is your mom still forcing you to watch Hallmark movies?"

"She wants me to get in touch with my sensitive side." When I hear the shit-eating grin in his tone, I look over. I'm not wrong, but along with the fucking grin, he brings his hand up and makes the universal sign for jacking off. "It's amazing what my imagination can do to a goody-two shoes who runs a stationary shop in small-town Vermont. You should try it. It's hot. Might help you release some of that pent-up, negative energy rolling off you. I can actually feel it. I worry about your aura."

"My aura is just fine, Jackie."

"See, that's what I'm talking about. We have a history. We've been tight since we were shitting our pants together. It's why I accept you for who you are—the high-maintenance, wounded hero who needs saving." He grabs my biceps and stops us in the crowded hall as teenagers of all shapes and sizes move around us, trying to escape after a long Monday. We're an island of rushing hormones. "Let me save you, Levi. You've got your scholarship locked up, signed and sealed. You tied down the mid-fielder position for Johns-fucking-Hopkins University. You'll soon be dripping in national championship jewels. But we have half a semester left before the universe tries to tear us apart like an abusive ex-husband at the eighty-percent mark. Let me save you from your boring-ass self before you die a tragic death of normalcy."

I hitch my backpack up my shoulder and stare at the moron I call my best friend. "Do you practice this shit at home in the mirror?"

Levi

13

The guy is a boomerang. "It's a gift I was born with. Try not to be jealous. You're in the running for Valedictorian—hang onto that like a lifeline. I do think after watching all these dumbass movies, I missed my calling. Should've tried out for the school play. Anyway, ditch your lame tutoring date, and come with me to Ben's house. His parents are out of town, and he's firing up the hot tub. His girlfriend is bringing friends from her school. They're on the dance team, Levi. Maybe they'll, you know..." Jack's eyes widen, and he wags his brows. "*Perform.*"

I shake out of his hold. "I'm going to be late. Call me later if you want to lift weights, but there's no way I'm going to that party. You're on your own."

"Come on, man," he complains. "Don't make me fly solo with the dancers."

I turn for the library.

"Levi, come back. I need you! You're the defect to my perfection. The night to my dawn. The ... the..." I'm two steps away from the library entrance when I hear him yell over the chatter in the halls, "The broody firefighter to my plucky cupcake bakery owner."

I turn back one more time and he's standing in the middle of the hall, unbothered by the slew of highschoolers, as if he's a boulder in the middle of a river. His backpack has fallen to the floor at his feet, and he looks like he was last to be picked for recess games on the playground.

I flip him off.

"Dude." His shoulders sag, and right before the hushed whispers of the library swallow me up, Jack hollers through the halls, "I still love you, best friend!"

The door clicks behind me, shutting out the bullshit and the guy who's been a constant in my life since before preschool when we were neighbors. He's the most likable idiot in the senior class, and he knows it. He plays the part well and has stuck with me over the last couple years when I gave the *fuck you* to everyone else.

People suck. I have proof and will stand by my conclusion until the end of time. I have no desire to give anyone else the opportunity to prove me wrong.

Not again.

Not ever.

I glance at the time and pick up my pace as I head to the back of the library to the group study rooms. When I turn down the long hall lined with closed rooms with big glass windows so kids can't fuck around in an enclosed space, I stop as soon as I get to the window.

I look down at the piece of paper Ms. Lockhart gave me. When she asked if I could tutor someone in chemistry, it was the last thing I felt like doing. I might have no desire to jump into a hot tub with the dance team from our biggest rival, but that doesn't mean I'm not sick of school. Senioritis is a real thing.

Hell, I had a month of sophomoreitis and an entire year of junioritis. Going through high school social hell will do that to anyone, and I was sure dragged through the pits of it.

But I had no good reason to say no. Ms. Lockhart said it didn't sound like it would take much to get the student back on track.

I double check the room number to make sure I'm in the right place. The door is wide open and a blonde is standing with her back to me, her backpack still flung over her shoulder. She's wearing a sweater that swallows her whole and hits the back of her knees. She's shifting her weight back and forth, like she might implode at any moment.

I look down at the paper again.

Carissa Collins.

Junior.

Chemistry with Mr. Stance.

Well, that's probably half of the reason she's failing. But hell, even Jack passed that class last year with a low C, and I didn't have to help him.

I reach out and put my knuckles on the open door and knock twice.

She jerks right before spinning in a half-circle on her boot. Her eyes are as dark as the earth, framed in lashes darker than the night. Her sweater might swallow her in the back, but hangs open in the front. She's in tight-ass leggings that disappear into her winter boots, and her T-shirt that barely hits her waist professes her love for the Arizona Diamondbacks.

She says nothing.

I break the silence. "Hey."

She catches her bottom lip between her straight, white teeth.

I look down at my paper and try again. "Carissa Collins?"

"Yeah, sorry." She shrugs her shoulder, bearing the weight of the bag. "That's me."

I step into the room and drop mine on the table. "Levi. I'm your chem appointment."

"Appointment," she echoes. "That's a nice way to put it. Thanks."

I cross my arms and look down at her where she stands no taller than five-five, if that. Her long blond hair falls over her shoulders in a messy heap, but on her, it fits. And she's not like most of the girls who try to run in my circles. She wears no makeup. She's not dripping in designer labels. And if she gives two shits what anyone thinks about her, then whack me over the head without a helmet.

I toss the piece of paper on the table with her name and the chapters we're supposed to work on, and pull out a chair. "It's no big deal. Lots of people need extra help in chemistry."

She doesn't take a cue from me and stands there unmoving. "I've never needed help with anything."

"Are you new?" I change the subject. Our school isn't small, but it's not big like some of them closer to the District. I've lived here my entire life. I know for a fact, I would have seen this chick before.

She crosses her arms and shifts. "Yes. Since the beginning of the semester, but it's not permanent. We'll be going home as soon as possible."

I relax back in my chair and nod to her shirt. "Is home Arizona?"

"Pretty much. We used to come to D.C. more often but haven't in the last few years." She sighs and finally drops her bag from her shoulder, but only to let it dangle by her side in one hand. "Look, I've never needed a tutor before. Can we just say we did this if I promise to study?"

"Study harder, or study, period? You're a complete stranger, and you expect me to lie for you?" I pick up the paper sitting on the table next to me and hold it up between my pointer and middle finger. "You're not the only one needing something from this. I get volunteer hours for being here, hours I need to get in with lacrosse starting soon."

She exhales, and her shoulders slump an inch. "Oh."

"Yeah." My expression turns to granite. "And I don't lie for my life-long friends, I'm sure as hell not telling my counselor I fulfilled my hours when I didn't. You want to leave, that's up to you, but I'm not signing off on shit."

Her brow puckers. "I didn't ask you to lie—"

"Saying we did this when we didn't, is what then?"

She shakes her head and backpedals. "That's really not what I meant. I'd never ask anyone to lie. I've had enough of that. It's just I need to get back to my gran—I mean, home. My brother is waiting for me."

"You know, we probably could've been halfway through your chapter review by now."

She pulls her phone out of the deep, saggy pocket of her sweater and stares at the screen as she mumbles, "You underestimate how far behind I am. If I didn't hate high school so much, I'd drop the damn class."

"That makes no sense."

I watch her sigh as she types something into her phone, and I wonder who she's talking to. The phone lands on the table before her backpack. "It means before my mother dragged me across the country to the middle-of-nowhere Virginia so she could get her life together, I was set to graduate a semester early. But now I'm here, forced to live with my grandmother." She rolls her eyes and yanks the chair out across from me. "I'm not going to get out of this, am I?"

I stare at the girl across from me.

There's something about her...

And it has nothing to do with her pure, natural beauty that she clearly doesn't have to try hard to pull off. In fact, if she gives two shits about what she looked like when she left the house this morning, I'd be surprised.

No.

She's gone from deer in the headlights to something so familiar, if I weren't looking at a chick who was so very fucking female in every way I like on the surface, I'd think I was looking into my own soul.

I learned a hard lesson when I was a shit judge of character, but not anymore. And I'm almost positive Carissa

Collins loathes the prison walls of high school almost as much as I do.

I don't move a muscle besides the slight tip of my head. "How bad is your grade?"

"Are you going to tell the entire lacrosse team what a failure I am?"

My expression hardens. "You're new here, so I'm not going to let that piss me off. But if you knew me, you'd bite your tongue before asking that."

Her teeth find her lip again.

"Well?" I press.

Her small chest rises and falls dramatically under that damn sweater, but she finally gives it up. "I'm below fifty percent."

I frown. "Seriously?"

"If you think I'm a lost cause, please, go do your lacrosse sporty things. I'm sure I can figure this out on my own well enough to pass the class."

I'm not sure what's gotten into me. I normally don't give a shit about anything when it comes to anyone, but for some reason, I want to know. "No one's on schedule to graduate early by failing classes. Stance is a shit teacher, but the class isn't that hard. What's the issue?"

"If you knew me," she tosses my words back, and they land like a sharp jab to my jaw, "you wouldn't ask that."

"That's fair." I'll give her that, but what I don't ask is what I really want to know—what's made this girl not give a shit about chemistry or graduation. Hell, what I went through made me care even more. "Did moving here fuck up your plans to graduate early?"

She fidgets in her seat. "I have no idea. It hasn't really been a priority since I got here."

I nod and lean forward, resting my forearms on the

table. "Let's get your chem grade straightened out, and then you can ask Mrs. Bradley. I'm a big fan of flipping off high school and moving the fuck on. If I can help you do that, then I've somehow done my part to make the world a better place."

That doesn't win me a smile, but it does soften her frown a touch.

"What do you say, Carissa Collins? You going to let me help you win that *Get Out of Jail Free* card?"

Her full pink lips roll inward, and I can tell I've gained her attention. The only confirmation she gives me is reaching for her backpack and pulling out her notebook and tablet. I nab the notebook and flip it open. Her handwriting is crisp and clean, there's just not much of it. For some reason, she either doesn't give a shit, or she's trying to fuck up her GPA and any chance at graduating early.

I look up and catch her staring.

I hike a brow.

She wraps her sweater around her small frame.

What in the hell is up with this girl?

Carissa

HYPNOTIC SWIRLS OF GOLD, brown, and flecks of green. They remind me of Virginia in the summer.

I always loved being here when the colors were thriving. We don't get that in Arizona. Being surrounded by green. The endless number of emerald hues are calming.

Even so, there's nothing calming about the hazel eyes that have been weighing on me the last hour. I've had to work hard not to allow them to hold me hostage and fall into a mesmerized pile of mush that has nothing to do with chemistry.

Not that kind of chemistry anyway.

I've tried not to stare. I've tried to focus on anything other than those piercing eyes.

When he first walked into the room, I thought they were merely light brown. Then I thought they were golden.

Boy, was I wrong.

When he sat down in front of me, the green flecks glistened in the harsh fluorescent lights. They might as well have handcuffed me to my chair.

Beautiful.

Soulful.

And, still, pensive.

My assumption about Levi Hollingsworth was not wrong. He hasn't smiled once since he made me his focus. He might be the picture of an all-American-boy-becoming-a-man, but there's something simmering beneath the surface. There's not one normal thing about him.

I was right to be nervous about my first ever tutoring session, and it has nothing to do with the fact I should not have gotten myself into this situation to begin with.

It's not like I would've been considered for valedictorian if I weren't failing chem, but I was closer to first than the last in my class. At this point I don't care what my grade is at the end of the semester, I just don't want to take it again or be forced to do summer school. I have more important things to worry about.

And before this afternoon, none of them were making it through a tutoring session with Levi Hollingsworth.

I tried to throw attitude for about two seconds in hopes he'd waltz his very fine ass out of the library, but he made it clear he wasn't having it. So, here I am, allowing the rumble of his deep voice to pour over me and trying to comprehend what he's saying.

"Do you understand why you're failing?"

Because I hate science seems like a lame answer. I take this opportunity to memorize every single green fleck. "Yeah. Though I'm not sure that was ever in question."

"You can't memorize this stuff, not when it comes to chem. If you don't have a grasp on what you learned five chapters ago, you'll never get this." He points to my notebook that contains very few notes from the semester. "I've made a list of sections for you to reread that should help with the next few tests. Learn the vocab, review the elements and equations. This is topic progression. You're lost because you can't apply prior lessons to the current one."

I can't remember the last time I sat down to study anything. I'm lucky to be skating by in my other classes. I haven't truly focused since before the beginning of the end.

Christmas Day.

I toss my pen on the notebook, lean back in my seat, and press my fingers to my temples. "I'll work on it. I'm sure you have better things to do than hang around school longer than necessary. I mean, you're about to graduate. Do you even need the volunteer hours?"

"No, I'm already in the lead. I've already claimed the title for most volunteer hours."

I frown. "Then why are you doing this?"

"I was wondering the same thing before I walked in here. I know nothing about you, but if you want out of this hellhole a semester early, that's something I understand. The only reason I'm still here is because I need my senior year of lacrosse. I'm committed and have a scholarship. My college coaches want to see their prospect perform. But you..." He shakes his head and pauses a moment. "I'm going to make it my mission to get you out early."

My breath catches. "You are?"

He doesn't answer, but he reaches for his cell. "Give me your number."

"Why?"

His soulful eyes narrow, and I lose sight of the emerald flecks. "To communicate. What if you have questions?"

Oh, I will not be bothering Levi Hollingsworth with chem questions outside of this room. "Google. YouTube."

"Give me your number, Carissa." His tone is demanding. Insistent. *Final.* "You've stopped what we were doing three times to message other people. I know you're capable of communicating."

My expression falls, but my defenses are strong. "I wasn't Snapchatting my friends back home. It was my brother. And when it comes to him, I never hesitate to answer. I'm sorry if I offended you, but he's a priority."

The man-boy, who's had my undivided attention besides the three times Cade texted me about Louise, relaxes into his chair. I'm gifted with his full hazel eyes again, and his voice hits me low and smooth—so much so, goosebumps prickle my arms under my cardigan. "Give me your number."

There's something about him. Besides the harsh impression that radiates off him when he stalks down the hall, I had no idea what to expect when I walked into the library this afternoon.

But Levi Hollingsworth wants my number.

You know, for chemistry.

I spout off the ten digits that will connect me to him.

Besides a lift of his chin, he doesn't move.

Something short of a mini-panic rises within me. "Aren't you going to write it down? Add it to your contacts?"

For the first time, Levi gives me something new. His lips tip north. Though just on one side and only by a fraction.

A hint of a smile—a satisfied one.

My panic isn't mini any longer. I've never been picked on or bullied, but that doesn't mean Cade hasn't. I recognize it a mile away. "Seriously? You just wanted to see if I'd give it to you?"

This wins me a full smile, and he leans forward on his forearms. "I thought we've been through this, but you don't know me, remember? When I get a piece of important information, it's burned on my brain. I don't need to write your number down. But now I want to know why that freaked you out."

Well.

Shit.

"Oh." It's the only thing I can think to say.

Levi stands, towering over me. "I'll get with you soon, and you'll have my number in case you have any questions. I'll be here Wednesday after school."

My chest rises and falls. "Wednesday."

I get a chin lift again before he slings his backpack over his shoulder, but he doesn't say another word.

He's gone.

My phone vibrates in my pocket again. When I pull it out to look at it, it's Chuck, Louise's helper. I don't even know what to call him, because he does everything from mop the floors to maintain her property. I'm surprised he doesn't cook for her. He's her yes man—if Louise barks an order, he's there. She doesn't even add a please.

I'm going to remind her of that the next time she throws our manners in our faces.

Chuck – I'm waiting in front of the school, whenever you're ready.

Because I like Chuck—and I'm not a total bitch—my manners come out in spades.

Me – Thank you. I'll be right out.

Chuck has worked for my grandmother for as long as I can remember. My grandpa died before we were born, and she has proven that she doesn't lift a finger other than to cook boring, tasteless meals.

I stuff my things in my backpack and make my way out of the library. I'm almost to the front door when my phone vibrates again.

Unknown – See? I'm a microchip. Now we can ... communicate.

I stop in the middle of the commons.

A microchip.

Communicate.

Well, I've never seen a six-feet-plus microchip who looks like a powerhouse dressed in athleticwear that could be couture, they're that nice and stamped with the priciest of logos.

I would know. My mom buys me anything I want.

Or, she used to.

My fingers hover over the unknown message.

I need to be chill. To not try *too* hard. You know, be ... not awkward.

Me – Which is why you're the tutor, and I'm driving the struggle bus.

There. I gave him kudos for being a brainiac, while being a little self-deprecating at the same time. Who doesn't like that?

I move to the front doors. Chuck is parked front and center in my grandmother's shiny, new Cadillac sedan.

Unknown – No more struggle bus. You can ride with me from now on.

A chill rolls over me, and it has nothing to do with the frigid Virginia winter. I have no idea how to respond. But I don't want to make Chuck wait, so I move to the car and climb in the front next to him.

"How was your day, Carissa?"

I buckle up and tell him the truth. "More interesting than it has been since I got here. How is Cade?"

Chuck pulls out of the snow-lined parking lot. "Pretty good. Not very talkative, but I tried."

"Thanks for that. That's more than Louise does."

My comment silences the car. I know I should bite my tongue, but I don't care when it comes to my grandmother. She sure doesn't care about us and hasn't done my mom any favors. And my mom could use a few right now.

"Oh, I was going to ask if you're working this weekend? It's been long enough that I want to see Mom. It would be good for Cade too. Will you take us?"

Chuck glances at me when he pulls onto the county highway that leads us farther out of the small town. "You'll have to talk to your grandmother about that."

"She'll say no," I spout.

He keeps his eyes on the road. "Maybe your mom isn't ready. If your grandmother says no, I'm sure there's a reason."

"I doubt it," I mumble and look down at my phone to read my uber-smart, hottie tutor's message again.

Life has turned to shit. Besides making sure Cade is as happy as he can be, I'm going to do what I want for a change. I'm not going to worry about my dad's demands, how my mom wants me to act in public, or what anyone thinks of me—especially my grandmother.

Fuck them all.

Me – I might take you up on that.

I get immediate bubbles, followed by a quick response.

Unknown – I'll hold you to that.

I smile and make it official, typing in the name of the most mysterious guy at school.

I officially have a direct line of communication to Levi Hollingsworth.

3

SCANDAL

Levi

I pull a towel down my face and catch the bottle of water flying through the air at me. I twist the lid open and chug half of it before saying, "You were slow."

"I'm fucking hung over." Jack is downing his own bottle as he sucks air.

"Practice starts next week. Coach will have your ass if you show up like you did today."

"You know, you weren't always such a goody-two-shoes. I remember a time at the beginning of high school you were actually," he pours half the bottle over his head before shaking like a dog, "fun."

"We both know where *fun* got me."

Jack isn't wrong. My grades are perfect because I work hard. The only reason I didn't fuck up my GPA the first year and a half of high school was because my classes were easy, and I wasn't old enough to drive yet.

I check my phone as I head to the locker room. Three

calls from my mom. My sister, Emma, texted twice—no doubt about our mom. And the most recent is from my dad.

I don't open any of them. Talk about fucking up your grades—Emma is doing a bang-up job of it. Apparently, my parents expect me to know what's wrong with her. I have no clue.

Instead, I scroll down to the subject of my newest tutoring assignment. I checked in on her last night to see if she had any questions.

She hasn't answered my texts. Not even one of them.

It seems Carissa Collins has ghosted me.

I toss my sweaty towel in the basket and open my locker. Jack leans next to where I'm pulling out my gym bag. "Fine. I'm willing to be boring with you until you leave for Hopkins. I might be able to party with anyone, but you're my person. I think I'm the only one who doesn't want high school to end."

"It's in Maryland, asswipe. You act like I'm going on tour with a band." I pull a hoodie over my head before gripping my duffle and slamming the locker. The old men are starting to file in after work, and I promised Dad I'd get home as soon as I could to check on the hermit—also known as Emma. "You killed too many brain cells last night if you don't want high school to end. I've got to get going. You still have a chance at a scholarship, but not if you're hacking like a chain smoker during workouts."

"This is all you think about, isn't it? You have a one-track mind, Hollingsworth, and it does not fit the eighteen-year-old strapping stud that you are."

I slap him on the shoulder. "I've got tutoring again tomorrow, but after that, we're here. We've got to get your ass in shape."

What I don't tell him is he needs the scholarship ten

times more than I do. My full-ride to Hopkins lets me use the college fund later for medical school, when I'll need it more.

"If I promise to become at least twenty percent Levi, will you promise to at least come to one party with me? Just one."

I turn and stop in the middle of the locker room. "Fifty percent, and I pick the party."

"Fifty?" He grabs his bare chest like I just shot him. "You're literally killing me. Thirty-five."

My cell vibrates in my pocket, but I ignore it. "Fifty. You can do it. I believe in you."

"I can't believe you're doing this to me. I feel dirty and used, but I'm desperate enough that I'll take your boring-ass, lame, kill-me-slowly, Mary Sue deal. Are you planning on running for President someday? Is that why you're dead set on protecting your digital footprint?"

"If I wanted to be President, I'd be out fucking up my life like you to give the media something to talk about when I'm old."

My friend grins like a fool and flexes, proving he might've been sucking air earlier because he hates to run, but he can kill it in the weight room. "Jack Hale for President. I like it."

I give him a low wave. "Don't get arrested before tomorrow."

The cold air hits my hot muscles as I make my way to my Jeep. We ran sprints, lifted, and ran hills on the treadmill. It's still muddy from the snow melt, so we're at the gym until practice starts for spring sports at the indoor facility.

I'm backing out when my phone rings over the Bluetooth. Shit, it's my mom again.

My parents divorced when Emma and I were young. It's

never been ugly, and they make it easy. Even my step-dad is pretty cool, but he was transferred to California not too long ago.

I hate high school more than anything, but I wasn't about to start over my senior year. Plus, my coaches and trainers are here. I'm committed to college only two hours away. Emma throwing a fit saved me from having to do the same. In the end, Dad does what he does best and fixed that shit for us fast.

But that means we're in a new house, and Mom is three time zones away and calls us nonstop when she knows we're not in school.

The sooner I get this over with the better and touch the screen to answer. "Hey, sorry. I've been at the gym."

"I just got off the phone with your dad. He says he's keeping a close eye on Emma, but I need to know if that's true. She's not herself. I can hear it over the phone, but that's only when she bothers to answer—which isn't very often."

"Mom, in her defense, you call a lot."

"Levi..." My name is drawn out the way I'm used to when she's irritated.

"What do you want me to say? You asked me the same thing two days ago. Mom, I swear, he's home when we're home. He's not even working full-time right now. Trust me, Emma's no different than every other girl at school. She needs to find new friends. Hers turned into bitches when they got to high school."

"Watch your mouth."

"Well, they are," I mutter, turning into the new neighborhood where my dad bought a house just so we could stay at the same school. "I'll try and talk to her again, but she doesn't want anything to do with me either."

"I should have brought you two with me. I should've put my foot down and insisted."

"Trust me," I bite. "That would not have been the answer."

Her sigh is heavy, cutting through the speakers of my car. I know that sigh. She's giving in.

"Her grades, Levi. She's struggling. Even with all you went through, you never had a problem with your grades. She's falling behind so fast."

That reminds me of a certain new girl from Arizona. "I'll see if she'll let me help. But Dad is doing everything he can. She's never at home by herself."

"I guess that makes me feel a little better."

"I'm home. Gotta go. I'll text you if Emma says anything about ... anything."

"I can't wait to see you next month. I miss you both so much."

It's hard to miss her when she calls constantly, but I don't say that. "Yeah, miss you too. If Em spills all her secrets, you're my first call."

"Thank you." She's grateful, as if I'm serious, which I'm not. Emma and I have always been close. If she tells me her secrets, there's no way I'm spilling them to anyone.

I pull into the garage next to my dad's truck as Mom makes me promise all kinds of things before I manage to hang up. When I walk through the mudroom and into the kitchen, my dad looks up from where he stands in front of the fridge with the door open. "Hey."

He shuts the fridge and leans a hip on the island with his arms crossed. "How was your day?"

I toss my gym bag on the counter and shrug. "Like every other day—somewhere between lame and prison. One day closer to Hopkins. Workout was decent."

His lips barely tip on one side. "Between you and your sister, I'm getting a complex. You both come to live with me, and life is miserable. I can't seem to fix shit with her, and all you want to do is leave. What am I doing wrong?"

I know he's giving me shit, but that makes me feel worse about telling him how Mom wants parenting reports every other day. I push past him and open the pantry to dig out a couple protein bars. "You're not doing anything wrong. What's for dinner?"

He shakes his head and motions upstairs to where I assume Emma is holed up in her room like she usually is. "I'm trying to figure that out. Em says she's not hungry, while you could eat a whole chicken. I hate to cook, and the grill is covered in snow."

I open the fridge and pull out a sports drink. "Chinese?"

"Sounds good, bud." He pulls his cell from his back pocket and keeps talking while he types. "Your mom get hold of you?"

I take a drink, but don't say anything.

He looks up. "Levi."

I lift my chin. "I told her the truth—that you've got this, because you do. She's worried about Emma."

He sighs and taps his screen a few more times before looking up at me. "I am too. I'll get her straightened out. I'm close to scheduling meetings at school with her teachers and told Crew I'll be at camp even less. I can coordinate Carson from here, so I can keep an eye on her—not that there's anything to see. I'm doing my best to be patient, but if it comes to it, I'll drag her ass out of the house."

"Good luck with that." I pick up my bags when I get a text and pull my cell out of my pocket.

It's her.

Fucking finally.

Shit.

I stare at her text, even though I shouldn't care.

I never care. I'm in the home stretch. Just a few months until I'm out of here.

"Bud," my dad calls for me. "I don't need to worry about you, too, do I?"

I stuff my phone back in my pocket, even though I'm itching to hit her back. "Never."

I start to leave so I can do just that when Dad calls for me. "Levi."

I stop and turn.

"I feel like I just got you back, and we only have a few months left. I can't say it enough ... proud of you. You've been through it, and it hasn't been easy. I want to make the most of the time we have before you leave."

And just like that, his *going through it* comment snaps at me like a wet towel on bare skin.

A reminder.

One I didn't want, but one I'm sure I needed. Especially with the impending message waiting for me.

"I want to make the most of it too."

Dad huffs a small laugh and smirks. "I know how bad you want to be done with high school and get the hell out of here. It's nice of you to humor me."

I bite back a smirk and shrug.

"Go." He waves me off. "Do your thing. I'll yell when dinner's here. I ordered you a buffet."

"Thanks."

"Say hi to your sister," he orders as I make my way up the stairs.

I take them two at a time, stop at Emma's room, and knock on her closed door. She doesn't answer, but I know she's in there. Unless Dad makes her come down to eat and force her to spend time with us, she's here.

I bang on it this time.

"What?" she clips.

I try the handle—surprised it's not locked—and push the door open. She's in bed, flipping through screen after screen on her phone. "What's up?"

She doesn't make a move to look at me. "I heard him tell you to stop and say hi. You can move on."

"Mom called. She actually called four times until I answered."

"Join the club," she mutters.

"Maybe you should talk to her."

"Maybe you should mind your own business."

"Em."

"Levi."

I push her door all the way open and lean on the door jamb, but say nothing.

She finally turns to me. "What do you want?"

"Why are you doing this?"

"Doing what?" Her hair, the same dark color as mine, is a mess, and she's more pale than she should be, even if it is in the middle of winter.

I look around her room. It's a pit. I'm no neat freak, but she didn't do this when we lived with Mom. My gaze focuses back on her. "Doing nothing. You don't go anywhere. Even if they were annoying, you don't hang out with your friends anymore."

"Why do you care?"

I throw my hand out to motion around us. "You're setting the vibe, Em, and it's a dark one."

Her eyes glass over, and she rolls back to where she was when I came in. "You're such an ass."

I sigh. "Do you need help with your homework?"

"Get out of my room."

"Emma—" I barely get the word out when a pillow flies through the air. I catch it with one hand and toss it back.

"Get out, Levi."

I give up and shut the door, wondering if she'll even come down for dinner.

I dump my shit on the floor and shut myself in my own room that's almost as much of a mess as Emma's. I ignore the clean clothes that are piled in a chair in the corner and go straight to the message I've been more curious about than I care to admit, even to myself.

Carissa – Sorry. I've had some ... stuff.

She's had some stuff? That's all she has to say?

Me – Does any of that "stuff" have to do with chemistry?

Carissa – Unless a day in the emergency room counts as chemistry, then no. Like I said, stuff.

Me – Are you okay?

Carissa – It wasn't me. It was my brother, and Louise doesn't know what she's doing or how bad it was.

Me – Damn. Who's Louise?

Carissa – You know this is a lot, right? You're only supposed to be helping me with chem, and I haven't done anything to study yet. Trust me, you do not want to know about my drama.

I stare at the screen and realize I didn't even look her up. Not on social media, not the internet ... nothing.

She could be a shit show.

I know what a fucking shit show is.

Been there.

Done that.

Don't need an Act II.

This time I leave her hanging, pull up my browser, and type in her name. The internet does not leave me wanting.

I scroll.

And scroll and scroll and scroll.

Sure, there are social media hits. She's a teenager, most of us are desperate to put ourselves out there. I say most, because, aside from my lacrosse shit that I had to post for recruiting, I have very little. If I've learned anything from my dad, it's that I do not need the world knowing everything about me.

But there's also every cable news network, national newspaper publication, and a million of the hits are in Arizona alone.

Carissa Collins is the daughter of Senator Cillian Collins from Arizona. The Chair of the Senate Appropriations Committee—the most powerful senator aside from the Majority Leader himself—and one who sits with the movers and shakers of D.C. and on more committees than I've heard of.

A career politician.

I click on images, and my screen immediately populates with pictures that look nothing like the makeup-free girl I'm trying to help graduate early. Most are of her and her family at political events. Some election rallies. She's always sandwiched between one of her parents and a boy, taller and with dark hair, as opposed to her blond.

I scroll farther. That's when I get to the good stuff.

The ones I'm sure she doesn't want on the internet. Pictures of her from afar, with friends, or with the boy she was standing next to with her parents. I hover too long over the ones of her at the pool with friends. Or laying out on a boat. Coming and going from the gym. Being dropped off at school in a chauffeured SUV.

Never would I have guessed the new girl who's failing chem would be the daughter of a prominent politician.

Levi

I go back to my original search and click on Cillian Collins.

This time I don't just get news and political outlets. I also get a slew of cheesy-ass sites, but TMZ is at the top. I click on it.

Holy shit.

Seems the good senator is in the middle of a scandal.

A sex scandal.

"Levi! Emma!" Dad bellows from downstairs. "Dinner's here."

I'm starving. My dad was right—I could eat a whole chicken. But I don't get up.

Instead, I open another app.

4

A PRICE FOR EVERYTHING

Carissa

Well, it seems Levi Hollingsworth—the lacrosse god who's as smart as he is hot—took my word for it.

As he should.

No one in their right mind would want anything to do with the Collins drama. And the last twenty-four hours didn't have anything to do with our drama. The last twenty-four hours was just life.

But life didn't have to heat up to the levels of summer in the desert.

I should know, we were born and raised there, even though we were forced to travel with my parents to official congressional events. Washington D.C. is our second home.

Like, literally.

We have a home in Alexandria—but most career politicians do. It's weird to know my dad is living his best life only forty-minutes from here, even though we haven't seen him since Christmas Day when our world blew up.

The pieces still haven't settled.

We were never forced to spend time with my mom's parents. Sure, we would see them at random political or charity events and eat the obligatory Christmas meal together.

Louise sure didn't spoil us with attention like my friends' grandparents did. My mom always complained about her mom and never made her a priority.

So last night when Cade had an asthma attack, she had no idea what to do or how bad it could get.

It was so bad, I almost called my dad last night.

Almost.

Instead, I called 9-1-1. That's how bad I don't want to talk to my dad.

I've hardly slept and assume my tutor will no doubt dump me for being a failure. Why should he waste his time when I can't manage to put in the work?

I'm about to throw my phone to the floor and take a nap when it rings.

I jump to pick it up, because no one calls me but my parents. I'm desperate to talk to my mom. As much as I don't want to talk to my dad, after the last twenty-four hours, I'll take it if he has any information about my mom.

My body turns to stone when I see the screen. It's not my mom or my dad.

It's Levi.

No one calls anyone. What the hell?

I swear, the phone vibrates through my fingertips and goes straight to my gut. There's more than an ounce of desperation bubbling inside me laced with guilt for wasting his time since I haven't cracked open my chemistry book.

I press answer. "Hey."

There's a pause. "Yeah, hey."

Listening to those two one-syllable words hit me in his deep voice makes my insides squishy.

I fall back to my pillow. "Look, I'm sorry I haven't had time to study. I'm going to take a quick nap and hit it hard tonight. Promise."

"That's not why I'm calling. What happened to your brother?"

I stare at the ceiling and picture his hazel eyes focused on me. "He has asthma. It wasn't horrible to begin with, but he got agitated when Louise tried to tell him what to do. She wouldn't listen to me, then it got worse, and that led to a hospital visit, which made it a full-blown attack."

"Shit," he mutters. "Is he okay now?"

I roll to my side and hug my pillow. "He's better. The cold air triggers it. Thank you for asking. But I missed school today so Cade didn't have to stay with Louise by himself. I'm sure this isn't going to help my chem grade."

"It's one day. You'll be fine. Who's Louise?"

"My grandmother. She's not exactly unicorns and rainbow sprinkles. Cade doesn't like her—I'm not far behind. After last night, I'm sure he hates her, and I don't blame him. Louise blamed me for blowing it out of proportion, which agitated Cade, and made it worse."

He doesn't say anything, and the silence starts to pang in my chest.

"Are you there?" I ask.

"I'm here. I want to ask a million questions that have nothing to do with chem, but they're none of my business."

"Join the club. I'm me, and I have a million questions."

"I looked you up." It's a statement, and not one he sounds embarrassed by. He owns it like he does the halls when he moves from class to class, the lunchroom, and probably the lacrosse field.

"Great." I cringe. "I used to get mad when people Googled me. Now that you have, you know why I've done my best to fly under the radar."

"So you and your brother live with your grandmother?" he probes.

"Louise," I correct him. "She doesn't deserve the title of grandmother."

"Sorry." There's a smile in his voice. I relish it, because I think it might be rare. "This living arrangement with Louise, is it a permanent thing?"

"If this is a permanent thing, then I'll definitely flunk out of high school."

"That hurts, Carissa. You have no confidence in your tutor."

"Trust me, it's not you, it's me."

"Wow. You hit me with the *it's not you, it's me* so soon into our arrangement?"

"Arrangement," I echo. "But, yes, I did. Trust me, Levi. It's for your own good."

"You underestimate me. I might not've known what was good for me once, but I'm no idiot. I don't need to learn a lesson twice."

Well, that's ... interesting. "What lesson is that?"

"You haven't earned that yet."

"There's a price?"

"There's a price for everything. The most expensive are those without a dollar amount attached to them."

I think about the last couple of months. Then I decide I might need to do a search on Levi, just like he did on me. "You're right. Name your price, because now I really want to know these lessons you've been forced to learn."

He pauses. "You've got a test on Friday. You pass with a C, I'll tell you."

"Are you serious?"

"Carissa, it's only a C."

"But—"

He interrupts. "I'll make sure you pass."

"This isn't fair."

"Nothing is fair. You're in Virginia, living with Louise, instead of at home in Arizona. If anyone knows life isn't fair, it's you, right?"

I close my eyes when they sting. At least he didn't mention the shit my dad has stirred up making headlines all across the country.

He's more right than he knows. Life isn't fair.

"What's your address?"

My heart catches and my eyes fly open. "Why?"

"Just give me your address. You can trust me."

"I don't trust people who tell me to trust them. My father is a politician, so I know this to be a fact."

"But I'm your tutor." All of a sudden, his voice is smoother than before and dips an additional octave. "You're trusting me to teach you things you don't know. You won't regret giving me your address."

I sigh and tell him the truth. "I don't even know Louise's address."

"Share your location with me."

"What? Are you deranged?"

"Not at all, which is why you can share your location with me."

All of a sudden, I'm not tired anymore. "You must take me for the stupid chick in a horror movie."

"I know you're not stupid. I saw your expression at your father's last fundraiser. You were thoroughly irritated to be there. If that doesn't say smart, I don't know what does."

I groan. "Please don't talk about that. I got raked over the coals by the media, my dad's campaign manager, and my mom for not being a team player."

"You looked miserable."

"I was miserable," I tell him the truth. "But Cade was more miserable, and I was worried about him."

"Cade?" he asks.

"My brother. My twin."

"You're a twin. I didn't learn that from skimming headlines," he admits.

"You're not a good skimmer."

"I'm not. I prefer to take my time and be thorough in everything I do." He lets that thought hang between us before getting back to the creepy topic at hand. "Carissa, I swear to you ... on my lucky lacrosse stick, that I will not show up at Louise's door uninvited. Not that I don't feel like I can't handle her—I'm good with old people, but that's beside the point. I might be an asshole some days, but I'm never a creep. There's a big difference."

There is a huge difference. And Levi might come across standoffish, but I don't think he's a creep. And I've never seen him be an asshole.

I bite my lip, but don't say a word. Instead, I pull my phone away from my face and tap on my screen.

Then, I wait.

I hear him move before a smiling voice comes across the line. A satisfied one. "Carissa Collins, you will not be sorry."

"Just for your information, I'm going to write a note and leave it somewhere you'll never be able to find that I just shared my location with Levi Hollingsworth. If I end up dead, you're the first person they'll look for."

"You just made it my life's mission to make sure no one unalives you. That and make sure you pass chem. Grab a nap, then get after it. I'll see you tomorrow in the library."

I finally ask the question that has been circling my brain like a merry-go-round. "Are you this nice to everyone you tutor?"

"Fuck no." He doesn't elaborate.

"Oh."

"Study. I'll see you tomorrow after school."

I roll to my back and stare at the ceiling again. "Tomorrow."

He doesn't say goodbye, and the line goes dead.

I should get up, open my backpack, and catch up from being absent today. And I should really open my chem book.

But we were in the emergency room all night. I never left Cade's side and barely got any sleep.

I'll just close my eyes for a few minutes...

"Carissa!"

I drag my eyes open. It's dark outside. I have no idea how long I was out.

"Carissa, get down here!"

Damn, Louise. Why is she yelling?

My bedroom door flies open, but it's not my grandmother. Cade storms in. "Why is she yelling at you?"

I roll to my ass and stand as I grab my phone. It's still early. I think I only passed out for thirty minutes. "I don't know, but it's almost time for your breathing treatment."

Cade turns toward my open door, and each word gets louder than the previous. "I'll do it if she quits yelling!"

I go to the top of the grand stairway that looks down to the entry. My grandparents owned this estate before my mother was born. It sits on over one hundred acres. No wonder Chuck works here full-time. There's enough work for two of him.

Louise is standing there holding up a huge sack with handles. She looks as angry as Cade is over her yelling.

Louise demands, "Did you order this?"

I frown. "No, I ... wait."

I run down the stairs as fast as I can. When I get to her, I tear the bag out of her hand and peek inside. There's a drink carrier with three cups—two hot and one cold. Just so they aren't lonely, and the sender from heaven doesn't skimp, pastries and cake pops fill the rest of the huge bag.

I feel the first smile spread over my face in a long time that isn't fake.

"Did you order this?" Louise repeats. "Because if you refuse to eat the dinner I've provided, you're not touching this."

I ignore her and rip off the note.

Carissa,
Study fuel. See you tomorrow.
LH

Wow.

I reach in, grab a fudge cake pop, and stuff the whole thing in my mouth. It's more fudge than cake. And because it's the first thing that's given me any happiness since before Christmas when life turned on its head, I look at my grandmother and do my best to smile when I yank the stick out of my mouth and start to chew.

Louise gasps. "What do you think you're doing?"

I level my eyes on the woman I've never seen happy about anything in my entire short life. Maybe she needs a cake pop.

But there's no way I'm sharing these with her.

I take my buffet in a bag and turn for the stairs. "I'm going to study."

"You're not taking that up there! I told you both there will be no food in the bedrooms."

I ignore her and start up the stairs. Cade is waiting for me on the landing, staring down at me with eyes bigger than the cake balls I plan to eat for dinner.

"Carissa!" My name bounces off the marble floors and hits the dome, stained-glass ceiling. "Come back here!"

I hit the landing and turn for the second staircase.

"If you don't come down here this instant, I'm going to-to ... call..." she stutters, because she doesn't know who she'll call. "I'll call Chuck!"

I don't stop moving. "Good luck with that. Chuck actually likes us. Feel free to call either of my parents and let them know I'm eating chocolate over your perfect, white carpet. Be my guest. While you're on the phone, tell them you almost killed their son last night, too, because you refused to listen to me."

Louise's gasp hits a new octave.

Cade actually barks a laugh.

When I get to the landing on the third floor where my twin is watching the show, I reach in the bag and hand him a cake pop of his own.

"Cade and Carissa Collins!" She yells. If she keeps this up, Cade might be immune to loud noises by the time we get out of this place. "If I didn't know better, I'd think you were both doing drugs!"

My smile is fake. "Cade is, and it's time for his breathing treatment, no thanks to you. And I know my mom warned you about the yelling."

I grab Cade by his shirt sleeve. "Come on. I think there's a hot chocolate in here. You can have it."

"You ordered that?" he asks once we shut ourselves in my room that used to be our mom's.

"No. It's a treat from my tutor." I pull out the thick chocolate drink that's still steaming. "Just don't spill on the carpet, or I'll eat shit for days."

5

DUMBASS MODE

Levi

When I told Carissa I understood why she wanted out of this hell hole they call high school, I wasn't kidding. I was ready to be out of here my sophomore year.

Just when you think you're living your best life, you get the figurative sucker punch to the balls when you're least expecting it.

While not wearing a cup.

And trust me, I've been caught in the balls plenty of times for real on the field. It fucking hurts with a cup. But when someone you trust—or thought you could trust—rips your world apart, it fucking sucks.

I don't need to learn a lesson twice.

I was sixteen and stupid for more than one reason.

I'm the big man on campus. I know it, but that doesn't mean I like it. My D1 athletic scholarship is as big a deal as my grades, even though I don't give a shit about my grades or being valedictorian or the accolades that come with it. But I'm not only competitive on the field. You place a dare at my feet, and I'm all over it more than I was my girlfriend my sophomore year.

But that's back when I was a dumbass—just not in the classroom. That part of school has always come easy, and when Ms. Lockhart told me I was tied for the number one spot in my class, it was a race I intended to win.

My dumbass came out when I was sixteen and dating the hottest girl in school.

Isla Perry.

If looks alone have anything to do with how hot a girl is, she'd be at the top of the pack. Actually, I thought she was. But since she turned out to be a lying, backstabbing bitch, she's nothing better than a rat.

And a hungry one. She's skin and bones.

Isla is the reason high school sucks. I've given up my social life, and because of that, will probably have the best grades in the graduating class in a few months.

After *it* happened, I decided I was done with chicks until I got out of this shit hole. No way would I trust anyone again until I got a fresh start.

But it seems when you become a social recluse and only speak to four and a half people in the building outside of teachers, it makes you mysterious.

I don't want to be popular or mysterious.

I just want out.

And I sure as fuck have never sent an enormous order to anyone by Uber Eats'. Ever. Not even when I was being a dumbass and thought I knew it all.

I don't know what's come over me.

Even though I've sworn I'd never allow myself to fall into dumbass mode again, there's something about her.

Maybe it's that she's new.

Maybe it's that I know she's smarter than she's coming off.

Maybe it's just that she wants out as much as I do.

Maybe it was the internet search...

So many fucking things cross my mind as I sit here and stare at her across the table in the library's study room. We've been here for twenty-one minutes. I've been counting since I'm willing time to slow down.

I also refuse to think about why I booked the room at the end of the hall, or why I closed the door after I held it for her to enter first. There's still a window to keep people from smoking pot, fucking around, or just plain fucking. Even with the window, we're still very much alone.

Carissa is cradling her forehead in a hand, staring down at the mock test I convinced Mr. Stance to give me before school for my latest tutoring gig. Her pencil taps—tap ... tap ... tap—slow and methodical as she stares at the paper and ignores me.

No one has ignored me in a long time.

Other than Isla. Thank God.

I pick my foot off the ground and give her furry boot an easy kick under the table.

Her head jerks out of her hand, and her dark eyes land on me. "What? I'm sorry. I am trying, I swear. I even studied last night. Like, for real studied. Not like I've pretended to since I got here."

Besides a shrug, I don't move from where I sit, reclined in the desk chair with my arms crossed. "So the caffeine helped."

Carissa tucks her blond hair behind an ear and bites back a small smile. "I think so. I haven't thanked you for that yet, sorry. It was such a surprise." The smile I almost got disappears. "I don't feel like myself here. I'm all," she shakes her head, "off my game."

"You have game?" As soon as my words hit her, she rolls her eyes.

"I'm pretty sure it's nothing compared to your game, Mr. Lacrosse King."

I don't argue that.

Her pencil lands on the table, and she mirrors my position, only she's a fraction of my size when she leans back and crosses her arms. "I might not be on my game, but it's hard to ignore the rhetoric. You won State last year, and I've heard all about your scholarship." This time she shrugs and gives her head a little shake. "I didn't have to look you up on the internet, either, but I can't help what I hear in the lunchroom."

"So you're an eavesdropper," I note.

Her smirk swells. I can't not focus on her pink lips. "People talk loudly. It's impossible to block out the chatter."

I don't want to know what else people say, so I change the subject. "How's your brother?"

That wins me another small smile. "He's better. He loved the hot chocolate, and I shared the dessert. It was a treat for him since Louise has done everything she can to limit our sugar since we got here."

"Louise sounds like she needs to take a walk."

"To the woods," Carissa adds.

"For some self-reflection," I keep on.

"And meditation."

"Maybe I need to send her a cake pop next time."

Carissa loses her playful expression. "Don't you dare. She doesn't deserve it. I mean, she almost killed Cade."

My eyes widen, but she doesn't give me a chance to ask if I need to kidnap her and her brother.

Her head tips. "Fine... Not really. I tried to tell her to chill with Cade. She has so many damn rules, and he was getting agitated. When I tried to intercede and calm him down, she made me leave because she wanted to handle it. In his own way, Cade is as protective of me as I am of him. He didn't like her sending me away, and his regular asthma led to an attack. We couldn't get it under control. It freaked me out, and she wouldn't listen to me when I tried to tell her what to do. I called 9-1-1, because I knew he was going to need more than his inhaler and a simple breathing treatment. I've seen my mom deal with it my entire life, and Louise doesn't know shit. We were at the hospital all night."

"Damn."

"Damn is an understatement. Anyway, your surprise was the best thing that's happened to me since we got here."

I don't recognize myself when I lean forward, rest my forearms on the table, and lower my voice. "If hot chocolate, a dirty chai, and an iced latte are the best things that have happened to you since you got here, I may need to do something about that."

She freezes.

"Carissa?"

Her gaze shifts around my face and I swear, her breaths come quicker. Not that I can see for sure since her hoodie with another high school's name scribed across her chest swallows her like *Moby Dick*. "This doesn't make sense. You don't know me. I asked you this last night and I really want to know, why are you being so nice?"

I pause a moment, but I don't bullshit her. "I don't know."

That doesn't help the situation. Her arms tighten around her chest. "In the world I grew up in, everyone wants something. Ulterior motives, posturing, agendas. They're everywhere."

"I don't have an agenda, Carissa." I didn't think I did, but maybe I do. Right now, my main goal in life is to make time stand still and not let her out of this musty room, and it has nothing to do with making sure she passes chem.

"You sure had an agenda when you dangled information in front of me in exchange for a C on my next test."

Shit.

I lean back in my seat. The last thing on my mind right now is making sure she passes her test on Friday. "I didn't mean it that way."

Her expression is tight and laced with hurt. "But that's what you did. You know all about my parents with one simple internet search—how my dad has been fucking his Chief of Staff for who knows how long. You've asked me question after question about my brother and Louise. And I've told you, even though I'm not sure why. Everyone else at this school ignores me. They ignore us, and we prefer it that way."

The room grows more and more stagnant with every word that falls from her lips. The text books and notes that are strewn on the table separating me from her have nothing to do with the real chemistry bouncing off the walls.

Electric.

Magnetic.

Energy ... but not the positive kind.

And that's on me.

She doesn't let up—the negative charges roll off her in waves. "I can ignore the news by choosing not to look at it, but not if it's thrown in my face. Despite the fact I hate it here, at least I'm invisible. We're invisible. I need it to stay that way for as long as possible—if not for me, then for Cade. He's having a hard enough time here as it is. So despite your caffeine and baked goods, you have to understand why I might question your motives. I don't trust anyone right now. Not my father, not the media, and least of all Louise."

"I was curious about you, and I haven't been curious about anyone in a long time. I thought I'd be able to scroll your Instagram and see what your coffee of choice is. Isn't it an internet rule for girls to post pics of themselves with a coffee at least once a week? That's all I wanted. I get it when shit that's not your fault is thrown in your face. That wasn't what I meant to do."

"What kind of grade am I going to have to get for you to tell me about you?"

I drag a hand down my face and pull in a deep breath. I need to turn this around fast, or I have a feeling she'll never give me the chance to fix it. "What do you want to know?"

She drops her arms and leans forward. "Levi, how am I supposed to answer that when I don't know what there is to know? Unlike you, I don't search people on the internet because the thought of anyone doing the same for me and my family makes me physically ill. I have not typed your name into my search bar, nor do I intend to. The shits I have to give about what the world thinks are just that few."

I don't break our connection as her deep browns try to penetrate a place in me I've had locked up for a long time. "I like that."

"Like what?" Her clipped words are laced with confusion and muddled with pure irritation. I don't blame her.

I reach forward and push her book and papers to the side. I haven't been desperate for much in the last few years other than everyone and their dog to leave me the hell alone. Now I find myself wanting nothing between me and the new girl from Arizona who is absolutely not invisible. I see her ... maybe more than I have anyone. "I like it that you don't care what people think. I like that in the short time I've known you, you put your brother ahead of everything else. I like that you don't trust anyone. I really like that you're not taking my shit, even though I didn't mean to dish it out to you to begin with."

She shakes her head. "You're as hard to figure out as section ten of my chemistry book."

"That's because you didn't learn section nine." Her eyes narrow, and it's hard not to smile. "And if you want to get technical, seven."

Her glare turns as dark as her eyes.

The thought of touching anyone after Isla has been about as appealing as rolling around in poison ivy, but fuck if I don't want to touch Carissa. And the desire gets stronger as the seconds tick by.

Instead of reaching out for her over the table, I slide my foot forward, but this time I give her more than a kick. With my long leg and only three feet separating us, it's not hard to fit mine to hers. She stills when I press the inside of my leg to the outside of her thigh.

She's lean and slim compared to me.

But I want more. I hook her leg with mine at the knee and hold her there.

This time she doesn't jerk in surprise, but I watch her fair skin warm.

And knowing it's from my touch makes me more than warm. I'm fucking hot. It starts in my gut and runs south.

She tenses but doesn't pull away.

I'm six-three and just hit two-hundred pounds, none of it being fat. I could snap her leg in two with barely any effort.

Power.

It comes in so many forms.

I watch her swallow, followed by her tongue sneaking out to wet her lips. "You're an odd guy."

I tip my head the other way. "I accept that assessment."

Her leg presses into mine. "I want to know why. And I want you to give it to me freely. I don't want to search for it or earn it with a passing grade."

"None of this is going to help you graduate early."

"I suppose not. But I still want to know."

"I'll tell you." I force myself to look away from her to catch the time. "We have thirty minutes. What are you doing after this?"

"Chuck will be here to give me a ride back to Louise's."

I tense. "Who the hell is Chuck?"

"Louise's only employee who basically does everything for her, including shuttle Cade and me around. And Cade is expecting me home right after this. I don't want to change that at the last minute if I don't have to."

"What are you doing tomorrow after school?"

She says nothing and shakes her head.

I move my leg on hers, and the friction makes me want more. I want to see her outside of this damn room. I don't know what's going on with her brother, but she's protective. They might be a package deal.

Right now, I'm desperate enough, I'll take what I can get.

"If you're going to pass the test Friday, we need more time together than the next thirty minutes. We'll go somewhere. Your brother can come if he wants."

Her leg instantly holds mine tighter in this weird thing we've got going on under the table when I mention her brother. "You're inviting Cade?"

I lift my chin. "Sure. I'll give you both a ride back to Louise's. Whoever this Chuck is can have the afternoon off."

She chews on her lip, and her gaze drifts to the side.

"Carissa, it's just you, me, and your brother. We'll all get our shit done, and I can make sure you're ready for your test."

Her brown eyes land on me again. "Okay. I'll see if Cade wants to go."

"What will Louise say?"

"I lost a night's sleep and Cade sort of died because of her. Louise can kiss my ass."

"Cool." I feel my lips tip up. "If I do those things, can I kiss your ass too?"

Those pink lips do their best not to smile. "When are you going to tell me all the things you promised if Cade is with us?"

"My dad curses our generation because we've lost the art of conversation. Answer your phone when it rings."

She nods.

I nod at the papers I pushed out of the way. "Finish your practice test, and I'll check it before we go."

She tips her head to the side. "It's really hard to focus while you're staring at me."

"I'll…" I pick up my phone and unlock the screen. "Scroll."

"Thanks." She sits up straight and picks up her pencil. When she tries to pull her leg free, I pull it back with my foot. I stare at my phone but hear her sigh. "Levi."

I don't look up at her. "Carissa."

"I can't focus when you're doing that either."

I flip the screens over mindless shit that other teenagers my age eat up like fast food, and mutter, "You're fine."

I feel her shift and sigh again.

This time she settles.

It's all I can do not to look up at her. I finally hear her pencil scratching on the paper.

It takes her thirty minutes to finish. I check it in under ten. She got almost forty percent wrong.

But that means she got sixty percent right.

Then I walk her to the front of the school and see that Chuck is almost as old as my grandpa on my mom's side. I prove to her I'm good with old people and talk to him through the window for at least five minutes about the Farmers' Almanac's summer forecast, and I know jack shit about the Farmers' Almanac or the weather tomorrow, let alone months to come.

Old people love me.

I bump her shoulder through the window. "I'll call you later."

She smiles. "I'll answer."

I lift my chin and look at my new, elderly friend. "Good to meet you, Chuck."

He gives me a wave, and Carissa smirks as she rolls up the window.

I move to my Jeep.

I've got to hit the gym before I go home, and I'm starving.

6

YOU'RE MINE

Carissa

Levi has called twice.
Twice he's been sent to voicemail.
And not intentionally.
I only know this because it's come across my watch, and Louise is technically illiterate. But I'm not pulling my phone out of my bag now. Not after what she just did.

It started when she found out Cade has been trying to call Mom for the last week.

Not that Mom has answered. I haven't even tried to call her because Louise told us Mom doesn't have her phone.

But Cade has been trying. A lot.

Louise found out about it today and confronted him while I was with Levi after school. When I got home, Cade was throwing a brutal fit because Louise took his phone.

I've always wondered if it's this way with all twins, for parents to claim favorites. Dad prefers me. I'm the easy kid. I have to be.

But Cade has always been Mom's. She's the one who

manages his environment. I think she does it to a fault, because he can handle more than she gives him credit for. The last few months have proved it.

I've always been okay with being number two when it comes to Mom. I've never known any different. As I've dug deep and really evaluated myself over the last few months, guilt plagues me. I'm not sure if I'm more worried about her or pissed at her for dumping us here and ripping us away from our lives.

There's nothing I wouldn't do for my big brother. And in his own way, I know he'd do anything for me too. We're connected and always will be.

Which is why the nightmare Dad put us through hurts even more.

Dad betrayed us.

And now Mom can't take care of us.

Cade and I are left to bear the brunt of their issues, but Cade even more so. He only has me, and he misses Mom.

We haven't seen her since our chartered jet landed in Manassas. That was the only day I've seen Louise get behind the wheel of a car since we've been here. After an emotional goodbye, Chuck loaded up our mom, and Louise drove us to her house. We don't know where Mom is since no one will tell us.

Now we're in the kitchen. Cade and I are side by side, in a standoff against Louise.

"If she doesn't have her cell, what difference does it make if Cade tries to call her? Give him his phone back," I demand.

Louise shakes her head, and her eyes are dazed with something that looks like panic. "How am I supposed to trust you two if I tell you not to do something and you do it anyway? First the coffee order and now this. We have to be discreet. What will people say if they find out about your mother? The public will have a field day if they know Cillian Collins' wife is in the middle of a breakdown after what he did. And what will my friends think?" She becomes agitated as she fists Cade's cell in one hand. "No one can know! This will all die down, and everyone will forget about it. We just need to give it time."

The hell it will.

Nothing will ever be normal again.

"Give him his phone," I repeat and take a step to close the distance between me and my grandmother. "He's worried about her—we both are, and no one will tell us shit."

She's horrified. "Don't talk to me that way!"

"Then don't treat us like toddlers and don't act like this is just going to go away." Louise's features contort as she white knuckles Cade's cell in her boney hand. I take another step and lower my voice. "If you don't give him his phone back, I'll call Dad."

"You wouldn't," she hisses.

"It's okay, Rissa—" Cade starts, but I turn and interrupt him.

"It's not. You did nothing wrong. Neither of us have." I turn back to Louise. "I haven't talked to him since we left Arizona, and I don't want to. But for this, I'll make the call. You can't cut Cade or me off from the world. And I know this might be a crazy notion to you, but we actually need our phones for school. I keep notes on mine, and Cade needs his calendar."

"I *need* my calendar," Cade stresses from behind me.

"Do you want me to call Dad?" I ask Louise. "I can tell him about our trip to the ER, while I'm at it."

My watch vibrates again. Dammit. That's three times.

I'm sure it's my tutor who likes to be touchy-feely from the thigh down. I had no idea playing footsie could be hot.

But it was. I can't stop thinking about how it made me feel. It's a miracle I finished the practice test with a sixty percent with him touching me, even if it was only with his leg.

Louise's glare shifts between me and my brother.

I've had about enough.

I reach forward, and before she realizes what I'm doing, I snatch Cade's phone from her hand and swing it back to him. The moment he takes it from my hand, I hear him turn and move up the stairs.

Louise watches him until he gets to the third floor where our rooms are connected with a Jack-and-Jill bathroom.

I wait for his door to slam and lower my voice. "He misses her. I mean, I do, too, but he *really* misses her. And if you haven't picked up on it after all these years, he deals with things just a little bit differently than me. If you can't be sensitive to that, then I'll do everything I can to be a barrier between him and you."

"Your mother is working on getting through this, but she needs time, and she's not allowed to speak to anyone. I'm doing my best, Carissa."

"*This* is your best?" I spit.

Her eyes narrow to slits immediately.

"Then don't bother," I say. "Chuck takes us to and from school, even though Cade or I could drive if you'd let us. Cade and I can handle dinner without you. There's no need for you to try to parent us—we're fine on our own."

A text comes through on my watch. Two of them actually. That could be anyone, but if it's Levi, he's really not a patient guy.

"You're my responsibility. I'll be the one to cook in this house."

I roll my eyes. She's too young to be stuck in the fifties, yet she sure acts like she is. "Just don't take his phone."

I turn to run up the stairs, so I can grill Cade on what happened when she calls up to me. "Dinner will be in ten minutes. I expect you to both be at the table tonight."

I don't look back. "I can't promise Cade will sit at your table after what you just did."

She tries to call for me one more time, but I'm already in my room and click the door shut on her demands. The last thing I need is to piss her off further by slamming it.

I tag my cell out of the side pocket of my backpack, drop the bag on the floor, and fall to my bed.

I hold the phone above my face and skim through notifications.

Three missed calls and one text from Levi.

The last text is from Cade, which I don't even bother to read since he barges into my room through our adjoining bathroom.

"What did she say about me?" he demands.

"Nothing." I let my phone drop to the bed and roll to my side to talk to him. "It's just like always. Why were you trying to call Mom?"

He shrugs but doesn't look at me when he speaks. He sits in my desk chair and starts to swivel back and forth. "Why not? She might have her phone back. You never know. I don't understand why she can't call us."

I fall to my back and stare at the ceiling. "I know. I still can't believe it happened. Adults are stupid. And the one cooking for us wants you at the table for dinner tonight." I look up at him. "Will you come?"

He's busy swiping at his phone and mutters, "If I'm hungry."

"If you do go down, don't bring your phone. Don't give her a reason to take it from you again. I might not be able to wrestle it from her next time."

That actually wins me a smirk. His wavy, dark hair is overgrown, and I think he likes it that way. There's no way Dad would allow him to wear it that long. "That'd be funny."

I grab a pillow from behind my head and launch it at him. "You would think that."

"Dinner and a show." He reaches up to deflect it, but it doesn't even make it that far and lands on the floor at his feet. "Are you still flunking chem?"

"Jeez, it's only been a few days. Yes, I'm still flunking." I pick up my phone and talk as I open my most recent text. "Speaking of, do you want to come with me tomorrow after school to study with my tutor?"

Cade frowns. "Why would I want to do that?"

"To escape Louise's fortress," I say as I read the text.

Levi – It only took an hour for you to officially ghost me.

Me – Sorry. I'm here. I had a Louise issue when I got home.

Levi – I'm headed into the gym. I can't live up to my end of the bargain if you don't answer your phone. You had your chance. Now you're going to have to wait a couple hours.

Me – You work out for hours?

Levi – Since I don't want to get my ass kicked on the field, yes.

"Where are you going to study tomorrow?" Cade asks.

I frown. "Does it matter?"

"Yes. Am I going to have to sit in a library or can I get a burger?"

Me – Cade wants to know where we're going to study tomorrow.

Levi – Wherever you want.

Me – Cade wants a burger. Since we got to Virginia, we haven't eaten anywhere but Cafeteria de Louise or the school lunchroom. Louise is a hermit.

Levi – You don't have to ask me twice to eat a burger.

I look up at Cade. "We'll go somewhere with food. You in?"

He doesn't look up from his phone. "Sure, I guess."

I smile.

Me – We're in. You're officially breaking the Collins twins out of prison.

Levi – Is Louise going to send out search and rescue? They'll try me as an adult, you know.

I don't think he's serious, but I put him at ease anyway.

Me – She's afraid of the media. Like, wants zero attention and is afraid of anyone finding out we're here. She wouldn't even take Cade to the hospital the other night.

I see bubbles play at the bottom of our text thread. They stop and then reappear again.

Levi – You're mine tomorrow. Talk in a few hours.

I roll to my side and stare at the words that just appeared.

You're mine.

It doesn't matter that the word tomorrow sits after them. Or that Cade will be with us. Or that I'll be studying a subject that I hate more than anything.

It might be stupid and sappy and totally something a girl would do in a trivial teen flick. I don't care. I do it anyway.

I take a screenshot. Then I edit it down so only those two little words appear and save it to my photos.

I've felt alone for a long time.

Since Dad became more worried about his approval numbers than us.

Since the moment the limo picked us up at home in Phoenix to take us to the airport.

And since Chuck took off with our wreck of a mom, and she never looked back.

You're mine.

"Dinner is ready! Don't make me walk up those stairs to get you!"

Cade groans. I roll my eyes.

Then I pull myself from my bed and realize I don't dread dinner quite as much as I usually do.

Because tomorrow after school is Levi and fast food.

Louise will just have to deal with it.

7

POPULAR RECLUSE

Levi

"You late for something?"

I scrape my plate and jam it into the overfilled dishwasher before looking back to my dad. He's sitting at the new kitchen table in the house we just moved into a couple months ago. Emma is slumped in her chair next to him, leaning on one hand, and pushing pasta around her plate with a fork. I didn't go for seconds so Emma isn't the first to run off from dinner, which has become the norm since we moved in full-time with Dad.

I don't tell him what I'm late for. There's no point. I don't need the lecture, the talk, or the reminder.

There are fucking reminders everywhere I look. I still question what the hell I'm doing, but I can't make myself stop.

And I've tried.

I grab my bag and backpack that I dumped when I came in. "I've got an AP Stat test tomorrow."

Dad pushes his empty plate back and reclines in his

chair. "You know, I pictured spending more time with my kids when I got you two back."

Emma rolls her eyes, and no one in the room misses it.

"Maybe this weekend," I offer.

"Great. Consider your weekend booked. I'll come up with something. The weather is warming up." Dad throws a glance at Emma and keeps talking. "Maybe we'll get outside."

This time my younger sister groans.

"I might not be home for dinner tomorrow. Tutoring." Vague and not a lie.

"Of course the golden boy is racking up his volunteer hours," Emma mutters without looking up.

Dad gives her a playful nudge, but it pisses me off. "What the hell is wrong with you?"

Emma's brown eyes angle to me, and I wonder what happened to my sister who used to be cool at least seventy percent of the time. "I guess your perfection hasn't rubbed off on me since I got to high school."

"Maybe you should snap out of it," I say.

"Maybe you should mind your own business," she bites back.

"How about we all chill?" Dad butts in to put a stop to it, which he doesn't usually have to do. Emma has just developed the pain-in-the-ass chip on her shoulder that's making life at home not at all enjoyable. He pins me with intense eyes. "Block your day on Sunday. Family shit—it's nonnegotiable."

"Are you not going to ask if I have plans on Sunday?" Emma balks.

Dad hooks her around the neck, and she turns into a wooden statue when he presses his lips to the side of her head. "Love you, Em, but you haven't had plans in months.

Sunday is family day. Be ready to leave the house and pretend to be happy."

That's going to be fun.

"I've got to get started." I turn to leave, but not before I hear my dad asking Emma about school, homework, and the friends she used to hang with but now wants nothing to do with. I wasn't kidding when I told her she needed to snap out of it.

I go straight to my room, dump my bags, and pull up the newest contact in my cell.

It's been hours. Surely she's handled her Louise issues by now. If I were a selfless tutor with her best interests in mind, I'd leave her alone to study chemistry.

It's not that I don't want her to pass. Hell, at this point if I could take the test for her, I might consider it. But Carissa needing a tutor only means I get to spend time with her. Case in point, burgers tomorrow with her and her twin. But at least I'll get to see her.

Which leads me to what I'm about to do.

Instead of calling her, I take a chance.

I fall to my back into my messy, unmade bed and wait.

It rings and rings and rings. Just when I think she's going to ghost me again, her face pops up on the screen.

Her smile is small. It says she's surprised but not pissed. "If you told me you were going to FaceTime me, I would've waited to shower."

A grin spreads over my face. A fucking grin. Who am I? "Then I'm glad I didn't tell you."

It's not like she's naked. I try to force that thought from my head and reach down to adjust my junk that's bigger than it was two minutes ago. She tucks her wet hair behind her ear, and I'm jealous. I wanted to touch her hair during our entire tutoring session this afternoon. Instead of tangling her hair in knots around my fingers, all I could manage from across the table was our legs.

And she didn't stop me.

"Did you kill it at the gym, like any decent DI athlete would?"

"I'm more than just a tutor. What can I say? But unlike you, I haven't bothered to shower yet. It's a good thing you can't smell me."

"I could've waited, Levi."

I shake my head. "I couldn't. You made me wait this long."

She flops to her side on a pillow. She's in bed, like me, sideways on my screen. "You're the one who made me wait. You've been teasing me with information that caused you to be broody and grumpy, but something tells me you're not really that way. Even though I think I have the right to be broody and grumpy, seeing as I'm dealing with Louise on a daily basis, I'm very anxious for you to tell all."

"What happened with Louise?"

"When I got home from school, she and Cade were in a standoff. She took his phone because he was trying to call our mom. It was stupid, but most things are when it comes to her. She doesn't deal with either of us well."

"Louise sounds like the evil stepmother in a kid movie."

"She is. Thank you for including Cade tomorrow. That doesn't always happen."

"Why? He's your brother."

"He doesn't always connect with people. Or maybe not everyone connects with him. And Louise definitely doesn't connect with him. I think the longer we're here, the worse it gets."

I think about Emma. And the longer the school year

goes on, the more withdrawn she is. Now I feel bad for being an ass earlier.

She keeps talking. "It's been harder for him. He has a couple friends at home, and he misses Mom. Not to mention we're trying to fly under the radar here. No one pays any attention to us."

"So I'm a no one." I shake my head and grip the rhetorical knife she just thrust in my heart. "That hurts."

"You're hardly a no one. I can't figure you out. You're, like, the most popular guy in school, but you're not popular the way I'm used to."

I shake my head. "I'm hardly popular. But you were in Arizona, right?"

Her pinched expression says it all. "Don't hold it against me. I can't help who my dad is."

"I knew it. But it's easy to see. Why do you want to fly under the radar here?"

"Why are you still grilling me with questions when you've told me nothing?" she demands.

"What's the hurry? I've got all night. You've been at this high school for about two point five seconds. I'm not popular. If anything, I'm infamous—that's very different. I don't want anything to do with anyone. My only friends are holdouts from before or teammates who are forced to spend time with me because I'm the captain. Tell me why you want to be invisible."

She pauses, and I wonder if she's really going to hold out or make me spill first. At this point, I'll do anything to get her to talk, including throwing up my ugly past first if that's what it takes.

"Why are you so persuasive?"

"It's my winning personality," I deadpan. "Ask anyone."

"The six-foot berth surrounding you at school does not scream *winning personality*."

"You've been watching me," I note and roll to my side to prop my phone on a disheveled pillow. It's like we're side-by-side, with Carissa facing me in bed. My bed. "How long has that been going on?"

"I'm not going to answer that since you haven't been watching me, which makes it that much more embarrassing."

"I'm watching you now. You're on my radar—there's no more trying to be invisible, Carissa. I still want to know why that was your goal to begin with."

She takes a second to prop her own cell before settling back into her pillow with a hand tucked under her cheek. "Levi, you're supposed to be smart. If your parents' names were plastered all over the headlines because of a torrid affair that ripped their marriage and family apart, would you feel like being the center of attention?"

It's my turn to pause. "You have no idea how close to the sun you're flying, Icarus. You're so hot, you're flirting with fire."

She frowns. "What is that supposed to mean?"

"It means I just might understand you more than you ever thought. It means you and me..." I let that thought dangle between us for a moment and wonder if I'm really going to do this. If she had one I-give-a-fuck bone in her body, she could find out in a nanosecond during any random passing period. "I never thought I'd be in the position to tell anyone this, let alone want to. But, right now, there's nothing more I'd rather do, and it's not because you want to know. I want to tell you because it might make you feel ... less alone. And I don't remember the last time I was selfless enough to jump off the plank for anyone."

She shakes her head. "Levi—"

"No, Carissa. Now I want you to know why I'm the most popular recluse in school. And only then maybe you'll realize why I get you."

She pulls in a big breath and on an exhale says, "I'm sort of afraid, but now I want to know more than ever."

I can't believe I'm about to do this, but there's something about her.

For her, I'll dredge up the shit I buried deep the middle of my sophomore year.

8
ARCTIC

Carissa

His hazel eyes have never been more intense. That's saying something since he reeks intensity. We're resting on our sides, gazing at each other through our screens. I wish I could touch him. Touch him in a way that is so much more than what went on in the study room this afternoon.

I want to touch his face.

Thread my fingers through his thick, wavy hair.

Run my fingertips over his bottom lip...

Shit. I squeeze my thighs together from feelings that are new and overwhelming and raw.

"Do you know who Isla Perry is?"

Wow. Talk about a bucket of water from the Arctic. Isla Perry is a senior who oozes beauty and demands attention by simply existing. She's tall with long, dark hair, darker eyes, legs that go on forever, and the perfect amount of curves. If she wore her underwear in public, she'd be mistaken for a Victoria's Secret Angel.

And she's not just pretty or basically beautiful. She's stunning in a way that kind of hurts my eyes since I'm short with very few curves and look nothing like an Angel in my underwear.

"Um, yeah. Who doesn't?"

If Levi Hollingsworth gives off a don't-fuck-with-me aura, Isla Perry emanates the exact opposite. I know her kind. She's the I-want-everyone's-attention-and-I'll-do-anything-to-get-it mean girl who wears her wicked crown proudly.

I'm good at reading a room.

Especially a high school cafeteria.

I can tell Levi would rather be tortured in any other way than tell this story. "We got together at the end of our freshman year. Feels like forever ago, but the aftershocks are still nipping at my heels wherever I go. Seems I'll never escape it until I leave this fucking school for good."

"Was it that bad?"

"Worse."

I pull a pillow to my chest and wait.

"We got serious." Levi pulls in a breath and shakes his head. "Too serious."

I can tell this is painful for him, and I'm ashamed that I haven't tried to make him stop talking—to spare him dredging up his ugly past. It's not like I want to talk about why I'm stuck across the country in Virginia with Louise.

But I don't.

Curiosity makes me selfish.

Guilt pangs gnaw at my insides knowing I could put a stop to this but don't when he keeps talking. "I was obsessed, and it made me stupid. So fucking stupid. For fear of sounding like my parents, I was too young to be doing the shit I was doing. But instead of doing what half my friends were doing and drinking and getting high, because getting caught doing that was the best way to fuck up my chances at playing D1, I was busy fucking around with my girlfriend. In every sense of the word."

I'm not sure what I expected, but I guess that doesn't surprise me. I mean, what teenage girl with raging hormones wouldn't want to jump Levi Hollingsworth? He's just that hot.

Kids sleep around all the time. My best friend from back home swears she's in love every time she dates someone new. Every time, I try to convince her it's nothing remotely close to love and that she needs to get a grip. Those dumbasses do not love her, they're talking about her.

I, on the other hand, never date anyone longer than a couple months because guys get bored with me. I'm not a goody-two-shoes or some better-than-you purity princess.

No.

I'm a girl with a healthy fear of having my private life being leaked for all to know. And in my case, *all* means much more than the walls of a high school. When I say all, I mean look at what my parents have done to themselves.

His words come out with efficiency and such grit, I'm sure he's ripping the band aid off only because he promised me the information. "She got possessive. In a bad way. Pissed when I had to go to a workout. Pissed when I wanted to spend time with my dad. Pissed about anything if it didn't mean bowing to her wishes. I got sick of it. She was controlling and demanding, and I realized I'd made the biggest mistake hooking up with her in the first place."

"Why do I feel like that isn't the worst of it?"

"Because that was a fucking walk in the park compared to what happened next."

His anger seeps through the screen. Like it was a trauma I'm making him relive all over again. I can't take it.

I try to stop him, but he keeps on.

"Levi—"

"A week after I broke things off with her, she showed up at my house when we were still living with our mom. She told me she was pregnant."

My eyes widen and I whisper, "No."

"Yeah. We were careful—I was careful. She was supposed to be on the pill, and I used a condom every single time. I mean, I know it can happen, but the chances..."

"What happened?" I ask. I mean, it's not like he's talked about a little Levi running around. And I'm pretty sure if he were a dad, I would've heard about it at school.

"It was hell. For two weeks. I've never been so pissed at myself. Pissed for hooking up with her to begin with. Pissed for fucking up my life. Pissed for being the dumbass teenager society warns you not to be. All because I thought with my dick instead of my brain and was blinded to what a suffocating, controlling bitch she really was."

"But..." I pause before going for it. I need to know how his hell ended. "What happened?"

"She wanted to get back together ... begged me to try and make things work ... *for the baby*. I'd just turned sixteen. I was freaked. I hated her but hated myself more. I was numb for a week. We agreed not to tell anyone. She was back to her normal shit, but all she did was make plans. It wasn't just for the weekend or homecoming, it was the rest of my freaking life. I was in knots and everyone around me could tell. I finally told Jack. He might be my best friend, but he's also a douche, and the news got out. The entire school knew I knocked up Isla Perry. That's when I finally broke down and told my dad. No way could I tell my mom. She's drama with a capital D. There are benefits to having divorced parents."

He stops talking while I'm over here tiptoeing on pins and needles waiting to find out how his nightmare ended. "I hope your dad isn't like my dad. It would be a public relations nightmare for him, on top of him being pissed."

"My dad's cool. Even so, everyone has their threshold. He's also in the business of fixing problems, so when something like this comes up, and he can't easily fix it, it makes him less cool. But what happened next proves I should have told him right away. It would've saved me two weeks in hell."

My palms are sweaty, and my heart races. "What did he do?"

Levi's expression hardens. "He told me to man the fuck up, accept the consequences of my dumbass choices, and dragged my ass to Isla's house. When her parents opened the door and found out why we were there, let's just say she hadn't told her parents, and I'm pretty sure I would've gotten my ass kicked if my dad weren't there. Not that I didn't want to kick my own ass. I did—every minute of every day."

My teeth sink into the flesh of my bottom lip as I watch him relive the torment and traumatic experience like it was just yesterday and not two years ago.

"Isla is drama central, but when we showed up at her house that day and her parents found out they were about to be grandparents, she freaked. I'd never seen anything like it. She was frantic in a way she hadn't been before, not even when she told me. That day in her house with her parents and my dad trying to manage our shit show, Isla turned into someone else. The more agitated she got, the more calm my dad was. That's when *he* started making plans. I'll never forget how the next ten minutes of my life played out."

"What did he do?"

"He ignored Isla and only spoke to her parents. Calling the baby their grandchild. Making plans even Isla didn't go so far as to make. Talking about college funds and commitments and responsibilities. As the moments clicked on, Isla's tear stained, swollen face panicked even more. But when the three parents in the room—and I'm not talking Isla or me—decided the next step was to take Isla to the doctor for her own health and well-being, that's when she snapped."

"Snapped?"

Levi sneers. "Yeah. She admitted she wasn't pregnant and never was."

My jaw goes slack, and I whisper, "No."

"Yes. She made the whole thing up so we'd get back together. Eventually, she was going to say she lost the baby or some shit like that. I'm not sure if her parents were more shocked than they were when we knocked on their door an hour earlier announcing I'd knocked up their daughter, but I'll tell you this, my dad was more pissed than he was when I told him what I'd done. He demanded bloodwork to make sure she was telling the truth, and we were out of there faster than I could blink. Let's just say it was a stressful ride home, but the weight of the world wasn't heavy on my shoulders anymore, so I was prepared to take whatever my dad handed me. I deserved it."

"I can't believe she did that. Who does that?" I'm pissed for Levi. Emotional distress is the worst, and to have it be manufactured just to be a manipulation? "I'm glad your dad was cool."

Levi sighs and drags a hand through his thick hair that's more of a mess than I've ever seen it. I wonder if this is what he looks like when he opens his eyes to a new day. It's not lost on me that this is one of the most personal conversations I've had with someone who was only a stranger a few days ago. And it's happening face to face in bed, even if we aren't in the same one.

"Dad was cool, but he was also pissed. We drove home in silence, which is probably worse than if he'd screamed all the way. But he's not a screamer. He could've been an asshole, but he wasn't. He took the shit I created and juggled it for me without it ever hitting the ground. When we got back to my mom's, we sat in the driveway for what felt like forever. When he finally spoke, he asked if I learned my lesson. Then he told me to make sure I never gave anyone that kind of power over me again."

"Your dad sounds intimidating in a whole other way than mine."

His answer comes quickly. "My dad is the shit, and that day cemented it. He's stealth in a way that's low-key. With him, you don't know what's coming."

I smile. "He took down Isla Perry."

The intensity finally dissolves from his features. "Fuck yeah, he did. I'm pissed I didn't see it myself. But that'll never happen to me again. I might've done it to myself once, but that's it."

I think about my mom and what my dad has put her through—what he's put us through. "So this is why you look pissed all the time?"

A smile tugs at his full lips. "I don't look pissed all the time."

"Not that I blame you. But the intensity ... that explains it. I guess it explains a lot of things. Thank you for telling me."

"It's not a secret. I feel like people are still whispering

behind my back. Hell, I'm surprised you didn't already know."

I snuggle deeper into my pillow. "I told you I wanted to fly under the radar. I have one friend, and I'm pretty sure he just feels sorry for me."

Levi frowns. "Who is it? I thought I was your only friend?"

I smirk. "Why so frowny again? It's Mason Schrock. I guess you could say he's my unofficial tutor. Thanks to him, I'm not failing trigonometry."

"What the fuck, Carissa. I don't even know who that is, but I can help you with trig too."

I pick up my phone and roll to my back. "Of course you can. Are you an expert in every subject?"

"Unfortunately, yes. I basically study and work out."

"And tutor," I add.

"And tutor," he confirms. "But I haven't spilled my secrets to a student before. Volunteer hours never turn out like this."

"Thank you for telling me."

"It was the least I could do since I felt like shit for a simple internet search."

"I'm glad I heard it from you and not anyone else."

I win another smile from the broody, intense Levi Hollingsworth. "Now you have to pass your test on Friday."

"I guess I should study."

"I'll meet you and Cade in the commons tomorrow after school."

"Levi?"

His frown returns. "You're not bailing on me, are you?"

"No. But you trusted me tonight. That means a lot to me. But tomorrow..." I shake my head. "Well, Cade struggles with social situations. He's autistic, really high functioning.

Don't treat him differently, he hates that. Just don't take it personally if he's not talkative sometimes, especially before he gets to know you. It's just who he is. He tries really hard and has had a lot of demands put on him because of our dad's job. But I'll never do that to him. I only want him to be himself."

"That doesn't surprise me about you. It'll be cool to meet your brother. My sister is a freshman and seems lost since she started high school. It can be brutal."

I roll back to my side. "Which is why I want to graduate early."

"Then you should study. I'll see you tomorrow."

I don't want to hang up. I want to look at him for hours and stare into his hazel eyes and figure out what he's thinking...

If he thinks about me.

Or—after our time in the library today—us.

Because the last thing I want to think about right now is chemistry out of a textbook.

All I can think about is the science of how he makes me feel, from the inside out.

But he's already dealt with one freak in high school, so I say goodbye. "Tomorrow."

He pauses.

Then he licks his lips.

My exhale comes out in a rush.

"Yeah," he agrees, his tone is low as his gaze burns through the phone. "Tomorrow."

I'm forced to clear my voice, but when I speak, I feel like an idiot. "Yeah. Okay. Well, bye."

And because I'm an idiot, I reach forward in a rush, push the button to disconnect, but I miss it.

My cell flies off the bed.

"Shit!"

It's face down on the floor. When I grab it and turn it around, my face flushes when Levi's amused expression is still staring back at me. "You okay?"

"I'm good. All good." The words rush out of my mouth. "I've got to go ... you know ... study."

He grins. "Just press the button, Carissa."

"Sorry. Okay. See you ... tomorrow."

"We've both said that already."

Damn him. "There's no need to make this awkward."

His grin shrinks to a smirk, and if I didn't know any better, I'd think he was proud of himself. "I'm not making anything awkward."

"Then disconnect."

"You disconnect."

I flop to my back again. "Why do I have to be the one to disconnect?"

"Because I'm not going to."

"But, I have to study."

"Then I'll watch you. It won't be a hardship."

"No way. You're not watching me study."

"Then hang up." It's almost a dare.

"I knew you were intense, but I didn't know you were maddening too."

Unlike me who's flipped and flopped around like a fish out of water, he's hardly moved a muscle. Until now. He stuffs his arm under his head, forcing his bicep to bulge front and center for me to stare at. And since he's only ever worn a hoodie since I've met him, the first time looking at his naked arm is ... a lot.

A lot-a lot.

"I've gotta go," I say in a rush. "For real, I'm going to have to hang up on you if you keep this up."

"How old are you?" he asks out of the blue.

"Seventeen. Why?"

"When is your birthday?"

"Now you're purposefully trying to keep me on the phone."

He shakes his head. "When is your birthday?"

"In a couple weeks. Cade and I are always the oldest. My parents waited to start us so Cade could have an extra year to adjust."

"I'm always the oldest too. But it's because I have a helicopter mom."

"Well, I don't even know where my mom is right now, so a helicopter mom isn't such a terrible thing."

And with that, the conversation goes from playful right back to tense. "Seriously?"

"Sorry. Didn't mean for that to take such a sharp turn. I just meant you're a priority for her, and that's good."

He doesn't let it go. "You really don't know where your mom is?"

I shake my head and try to push away the sinking feeling that has been settling into the pit of my stomach way too often. "The whole thing with my dad and how it played out publicly ... she, um, didn't deal well. I don't blame her, but I'm also pissed I don't know where she is. My dad said that she needed to be hospitalized. I guess that's what happens when you have a mental breakdown and end up checked into a facility because you threaten to harm yourself. It's hard, but I think it's harder on Cade. No, I know it's harder for him."

"Shit, Carissa. I had no idea. I feel like an ass."

"Why?"

"Because you've been dealing with that. No wonder you're miserable and your grades are shit."

I smile. "That should offend me, but it just doesn't. My grades are shit right now."

"Then you're lucky I'm your only friend in Virginia."

"You're not my only friend. I have Mason," I amend.

Levi's hazel eyes narrow. "Do I have competition?"

I roll back to my side. "I can have more than one friend, Levi."

His tone dips an octave. "You know what I mean."

"Mason isn't the footsie playing kind of friend, if that's what you mean."

"Footsie," he spits.

I bite back a smile. "You really don't want me to graduate early, do you?"

Levi sighs. "Tell Cade to decide where he wants a burger. And, again, I'll see you after school tomorrow."

"Thank you."

"Hang up, Carissa."

"Okay, Levi. I'll see you tomorrow."

He says nothing, but I do get a teeny-tiny chin lift.

And this time I don't make a fool of myself. I prove I'm more than capable of touching the screen like a cool and collected, totally chill human.

I disconnect myself from Levi Hollingsworth.

9
BURIED DEEP

Levi

Apparently Louise is somewhat of a prison guard, because when I asked Cade where he wanted to go, he had no clue what was around here. That's when I found out they go from home to school and back home again.

And they've been here since New Year's Day.

Or Louise's house. Cade was quick to correct me that this is not home.

I took them to a local restaurant that's a step up from fast food, even if that step is small. We ordered at the counter and found a booth. That's when I waited for Carissa to sit and slid in behind her letting Cade take the seat across from us.

Cade hasn't said much since we got here. He answers if Carissa asks him anything and adds to the conversation when necessary. Otherwise, he's focused on his work or his phone.

I scored another practice test for Carissa today. Last

night after I crammed, I found an online test with the same material. If Cade is efficient and focused as if the rest of us weren't here, his twin—and the central focus of all my thoughts for the last few days—is the opposite.

She must have actually studied after we got off the phone last night. She and I went through the section review before she started the test.

I'm checking her work as she goes. It's easy since she's working so fucking slow. Slower than yesterday in the library. She's doing her best not to fidget, but her best certainly is not great, and I wonder if this has anything to do with her lack of focus or her ability to sit still.

I know all this because when I sat down, we became glued to one another.

That was almost an hour ago, and we haven't moved.

Well, she has. She's moved a fucking lot. But she hasn't moved away from me.

I can only assume why she's having trouble focusing. As her tutor, I should be ashamed of myself.

But since she's gotten most of the questions right, I'm not moving away from her. She can fidget and stir anytime as long as it's against me.

She sighs, reaches for her drink, and sticks the straw between her lips.

My eyes dart to her brother to make sure he's not watching me study Carissa sucking on a straw in more detail than anyone has studied anything since we got here. Thank goodness he's too busy to notice. Cade is turned sideways in the booth with his back against the wall and his legs stretched out with his feet dangling off the end. He's not as tall as me but he's much taller than his sister. He's also brunette to her blond, but they share the same dark brown eyes.

I don't know what I expected from Cade Collins, but if Carissa hadn't told me about his disability, I might never have known. He looks and acts like any teenager who's irritated with life.

Which, from what Carissa shared last night, he deserves to be.

She starts to move once more, but this time, I reach under the table and wrap my hand around the top of her thigh.

Her gaze turns to me, and her eyes widen.

I smirk.

Then I lift my chin to the unfinished test sitting in front of her.

Carissa glances at her brother who's still focused on his iPad.

I give her a squeeze and don't let go. "You only have three questions left. Finish."

Cade doesn't look up as he says, "Louise has called me three times. I haven't answered and don't want to go back. Take as long as you want."

I keep my grip on her leg. "See? Relax and finish."

She narrows her eyes. "Relax? Sure, let me get on that."

I smile and tuck my foot around hers. "You can do it."

She rolls her eyes and drops her forehead to her hand like she did last night in the library and scribbles on the paper I printed out at home last night. Even with my hand on her thigh, my foot tucked around her calf, and our bodies glued together from the hip down, she finds a way to finish.

With my free hand, I swipe the paper when she drops the pencil and flip through it with one hand. I look down at her and smile. "A low B. An impressive turnaround from Monday."

Without looking up from whatever he's busy with, Cade mutters, "Good. Dad will kill you if you flunk a class."

Carissa picks up her pencil and tosses it at her brother. "We can't all be brainiacs."

"I can't help it." Cade rolls the pencil back across the table and turns his frown on me. "Are you into my sister?"

My hand instantly constricts around her slim thigh again at the same time Carissa tenses. I look from Cade to his twin, and I can't deny the fact I'm absolutely into her.

Even so, my lips tip on the side when I answer him but stare down at her. "Maybe."

"You know what our dad does, right?" It's the most conversation Cade has initiated with me since we met.

Since I have no idea if an internet search is as much of a trigger for Cade as it is for Carissa, I don't admit how I learned about Senator Cillian Collins. "Yeah."

Cade's expression doesn't change, nor does his inflection, when he delivers me a warning. "Then you should know that being into my sister means his staff will do a background check on you, your family, your friends, and your skeletons. Good luck."

"Cade," Carissa seethes.

My eyes narrow. "What the fuck?"

Cade turns back to his iPad. "Not just one. All the fucks."

The girl who I can't tear myself away from warns her brother. "You can stop talking now."

I turn to Carissa. "Seriously?"

She shakes her head, but her answer doesn't match the action. "Sort of. I mean, it's happened. But it's not like it always happens."

"That you know of," Cade mutters.

The first thing I think about is my dad. Then the shit that went down with Isla. Not that my sophomore year drama is a threat to national security, but it is enough of a reason for any random dad of a female to hate me.

But the guy cheated on his wife. Pictures of him and his Chief of Staff escaping into a hotel together when it was clear as day they weren't going to their separate rooms or discussing the national debt are plastered all over the internet.

Talk about throwing stones in glass houses.

"It's not a big deal," Carissa tries to assure me.

But she has no idea what my dad does for a living. Especially what he used to do.

If anything, that's a really big fucking deal.

I pull my hand away from her leg. The moment I let go, her foot nudges me. "Really, it's not a big deal. He's got enough to worry about right now anyway. We haven't talked to him since we left Arizona.

"We haven't talked to anyone since we left Arizona," Cade adds.

"Right," Carissa keeps on. "The last thing he has time to do is vet people we're hanging with in Virginia. I mean, there's nothing to vet anyway, so it doesn't matter."

That's what she thinks. Her dad might be an asshole senator, but mine was an assassin who contracted for the same government her dad works for. And now he trains people to do what he did only ten minutes away from our house.

My dad's shit is buried deep. It's never touched our lives —not once. He's not only made sure of it, but now his boss, Crew, makes sure their work stays far away from the families. Security clearance is a real thing, and my dad's goes straight to the top of the CIA.

But the Senate Appropriations Committee Chair?

I have no fucking idea what kind of clearance that position has. And since her dad is a douche by nature because he's a politician and a douche canoe because he's a cheater … I have no idea what he'd do if he actually ran my name, and that's not counting my family.

I push back in the booth and am already dreading the conversation I'll be forced to have when I get home, and lie, "Let your dad do his worst. I have nothing to hide."

"That's what they all say," Cade mutters.

Shit.

10

A REAL WINNER

Levi

My dad sits at his desk across from me, contemplating what I just told him.

Contemplating me.

As the heavy, silent moments go by, my gut starts to churn.

"Well?" I break the silence. "I need to know what you think, and I really need to know this won't be an issue. Tell me it won't be."

He shakes his head once, before he swivels to the side and stares out his office window to the street.

"Dad." I can't help it. The quiet is making me crazy.

When his gaze angles to me, it's sharp. "You've got a few months left, Levi. Graduation is literally nipping you in the ass. I'm not just going to ask if this is worth it, but is she worth it? She's not only a fucking senator's daughter, but one with a hell of a lot of clout. What are you thinking?"

I've wondered that same thing since Monday.

But I'm not about to admit that.

"Just tell me what's going to happen if the Senator decides to vet me. You've always told me your work is buried deep. I took that at face value because it never mattered. Now, it matters."

"I want to know why it matters," he demands.

I stare at him for two beats and decide to push past the shit that has haunted me for more than two years. I'm not sixteen. I might still be in high school, but I can fucking make choices for myself. "Because I've decided it matters enough to explore. I respect you and will do anything I can to protect our family, so I came to you about this. I don't need you to give me grief about my past choices. Tell me, how deep is your shit buried?"

He tilts his head an inch and narrows his eyes. "I'm not worried about me. I'm worried about you."

"Do you think I'd let what Isla did to me happen again? Or anything close to it?"

"I hope not."

"I'm not going to," I assure him. "So you're good? Her dad shit where he lives, and her family is a mess because of it. There's a chance I'll be so far off his radar right now, this won't even matter. But if he does look into me because I've shown an interest in his daughter, I need to know you're good—that Crew's organization is good."

Emma escaped to her room an hour ago, and we haven't seen or heard from her since. Once we were old enough, Dad stopped bullshitting about what he did for a living. Traveling the world as a contract killer for the CIA and our allies is no joke. Now he works for Crew Vega, a man I've known all my life. Dad is retired ... in a sense. Just a few miles from our new house, they train others to do what they did. It's not hard to understand the gravity of their work, which is why we're having this conversation.

He shakes his head and rests his forearms on his desk, lowering his voice. "My *shit* is buried so deep, it's lost in a black hole. The Senator might know of people like me, but he'll never know who we are. And I know who Cillian Collins is. If I'm a nameless, faceless asset, he's just an asshat. I don't think you're going to make another mistake, son, but that doesn't mean I want you on that man's radar, and that will happen if you're involved with his daughter."

I'm finally able to relax into my chair. My mom might be a helicopter parent, but my dad is cool. He's always got my back, and I know I can be real with him. "I thought you were worried about me fucking up again."

"You've laid low for two years. I'm just surprised at the timing."

I shrug and tell him the truth. "I'm curious."

"Shit." His lips tip north on one side. "Curiosity? Why am I more worried now than I was before?"

"What? You've never been curious about anyone?"

He leans back in his chair. "Not in a very long time. Also, nice deflection. But really, of all the girls at your school, you're curious about the daughter of Cillian Collins."

"What's wrong with him?"

"Besides the fact he's a politician? Everything, as far as I've heard. But if this curiosity of yours is something I can't squash, then you can be sure I'm going to dig into him. Let me make some calls."

"I'm not worried, Dad—"

He picks up his cell and starts tapping on the screen. "I told you I'll always have your back as long as you're open with me. I want to know what my son is walking into. You know me well enough, I need to know everything."

I stand and move for the door. "Like I said, I'm not worried, but I appreciate it."

"Levi." He calls for me before I leave as he sets his phone down. "What makes you so curious about this one?"

"Honestly? I don't know." I stuff my hands in my pockets and shrug. "She's new. She was set to graduate early before she moved here, but now her grades are shit, even though they shouldn't be. She's pissed at the world and doesn't give a shit."

Dad hikes a brow. "She sounds like a real winner."

"It's refreshing."

"If I didn't trust you so much, I'd be worried." His smirk melts into a somber expression "I appreciate you making sure we're good by coming to me with this. You've got my back too. Can't lie, it feels good."

I turn to leave when he calls after me one more time. "Don't forget, family day on Sunday. We're going hiking."

Hiking with my sister who complains about walking to the kitchen to eat dinner. I can't think of anything less fun as I head for the stairs and mutter, "Emma's going to love that."

11

CHICKENS AND ZINGERS

Carissa

"But when the bidding started, I couldn't do it. I birthed them myself, from day one, right from the incubator. I was the first face they saw when they pecked themselves from their shells. I mean, I know they're just chickens, and they were high maintenance when they were little. I had to clean them and keep the poop cleaned up in their coop and make sure they didn't get lice."

My yogurt cup hits the table in front of me, but Cade keeps shoveling cheese puffs into his mouth. Neither of us take our eyes off him. Mason followed me from trigonometry, talked my ear off through the lunch line, and sat across from me at what has become our spot.

Mason is a talker, and it seems Cade and I are here for it.

Mason lives on a farm that's been in his family for generations. I'm not sure how we got on the topic, but we're learning about how his 4-H experience went south once he got to the state fair.

"After I gave them a bath, I always used my mom's hair

dryer so their feathers would be fluffy and they'd be used to it for showtime. It was a lot—times fifteen. I was basically their chicken mom—or dad. Whatever. When I got to the fair, I made it to the finals. And that's when it happened."

"What happened?" Cade asks. He usually has little interest, but today he's hanging on every word.

"I couldn't do it."

I'm waiting with bated breath to find out what Mason couldn't do.

"What couldn't you do?" Cade demands.

Ironically, Mason takes a big bite of his fried chicken sandwich and talks with his mouth full. "Couldn't auction them off at market, so I pulled them from the competition, even though I could've won. My chickens are just that beautiful."

Cade shifts his gaze between Mason and his ironic sandwich. I'm thinking the same thing, but who am I to judge? "What happened to your chickens?"

"We still have them. I had to build them a bigger coop, but they're happy and thriving." He takes the last bite of his fried chicken patty, tosses the last piece of stale bun to his tray, and licks his fingers. "You can come over anytime and meet them if you want."

Cade's gaze shifts to me, and I wonder if he's desperate enough to get away from Louise that he's willing to meet Mason's chickens.

Either that, or he's telepathically begging me not to make him hang out with chickens.

I turn to Mason. "We don't have a car. Louise will never let us borrow her Cadillac. We're basically prisoners."

"Huh. I don't even have my learners permit yet, but I know how to drive. I could steal my dad's old truck to bust you from the clink if you can sneak out."

Cade's eyes widen. He doesn't do spur of the moment, and he sure doesn't do things like climb out a window and run through the night to a strange truck just to meet some chickens who were spared from being made into fried sandwiches in the school cafeteria.

I, on the other hand, would be down for some sneaking out. Louise isn't only technologically challenged when it comes to cell phones, watches, and laptops, she doesn't have a security system. She and my grandfather bought their estate as a weekend getaway. My grandfather was a prominent attorney in the District. Lord knows, with that many politicians and businesses trying to get a piece of Uncle Sam's pie, he had plenty of work. But they always thought they were too far out for crime to touch them, so no security system.

I could totally sneak out.

Just ... not for chickens.

I answer for both of us. "I'm not sure that's a good idea. If we got caught, who knows what Louise would do."

I feel a finger swipe my shoulder before my hair is tugged and swing my head around.

When I do, I'm perfectly in line with a pair of jeans—above the legs but below the waist.

Talk about a deer caught in the headlights.

I can't breathe, and I really can't look away.

That same finger that just yanked my hair, sending a zinger down my middle and to parts I shouldn't think about while sitting with my brother and Mason, lands on my chin and nudges my face up. My gaze moves away from ... things ... and follows the path up to the hazel eyes I'm used to studying when he's not making me work on chemistry.

His lips tip on one side, but only a touch. "Hey."

"Hhhe—" I force myself to clear my throat. "Sorry. Hey, yourself."

"You ready for your test after lunch?"

His thumb and index finger are now holding my chin hostage, and the last thing on my mind are chickens—alive, in custody, or fried and stuffed in a stale bun. "I think so."

He narrows his eyes, and I lose the green flecks. "You're not reviewing."

I try to shake my head, but he holds tight. "No, I'm not. I'm talking and eating. Do you know Mason?"

He doesn't look up. "No."

I've had enough. I reach up and pull his hand from my chin, but don't let go of it. "Are you sure? Mason Schrock."

He gives my hand a squeeze. "Pretty sure."

I look back to our table. "Mason, this is Levi Hollingsworth. Levi, Mason Schrock. We're in trig together."

Mason is wide-eyed, shifting his gaze between my tutor, Cade, and me. "Ah, hi."

Levi lifts his chin before looking back down at me and pulls out the chair to my right, flopping down in it closer to me than necessary, which I don't hate. "What's up?"

Mason proves he's not only the friendliest guy in school but cute to top it off. "I was telling Cade and Carissa about my chickens."

"I've never known anyone who's lived on a farm," I note. "We've lived in the same house our entire lives. It's in the middle of Phoenix. Rocks, succulents, and swimming pools. No chickens."

"Welcome to the country," Levi says.

"Wait, do you live on a farm too?" Mason asks.

Levi shakes his head. "Nope. But my dad's friend lives on a vineyard. They have cows, but they're more like mascots."

This gets Cade's attention. "Mascots?"

Farm animals have nothing to do with my skin heating when Levi relaxes back into his plastic chair and stretches an arm across the back of mine. He's more focused on my lock of hair he's winding around his index finger than cows when he mutters, "Yeah. They're always around when we're there."

"Huh." Mason crosses his arms as he sits back and stares at Levi and me. But when my gaze extends beyond him, I realize my new freshman friend isn't the only one staring.

I look around.

Shit.

I might've flown under the radar since I walked through the doors of my new prison, but I have a feeling the captain of the lacrosse team just changed that.

I have no idea how big the radius is, but we've garnered the attention of the tables in our general vicinity. At least the ones I can see.

Though, I have a feeling it's not *we* who are the subject of the lunchroom.

More like *he*.

I turn my attention to Levi and whisper, "What are you doing?"

He doesn't whisper. "I came to see if you wanted to review before your test."

"That's not what I mean." I look around. The chatter ... it's low and hushed and I feel the judgmental vibes roll through the vast space. "I mean everyone is staring ... at you."

Levi leans in closer—closer than he ever has. And doing it in front of every critical teenager in this neck of the woods is...

I don't know what it is.

It's nerve-wracking.

Maddening.

It feels like a declaration.

And, holy hell, when the tip of his nose brushes the top of my ear and his lips hover close, I think I might pass out. He smells like spicy spearmint mixed with arrogance when his breath tickles the side of my face. "Pretty sure they're staring at you."

My breath catches, and my eyes fall shut.

Shit. He's right. I'm an idiot.

"It's cool." I turn to Mason when he starts talking, and I'm thankful for the interruption until I hear what he says next. "You didn't tell me you were dating the scariest guy in school. Not that I thought I really had a chance, but you never know."

"We're not—" I start, but Levi interrupts.

"I'm not scary." Levi leans back in his chair, and his finger continues tormenting the ends of my hair.

"Seriously?" Mason deadpans. "I heard you were smart. Read the room."

"He's my chem tutor," I blurt.

Mason grins. "I thought I was your trig tutor."

Cade rolls his eyes. "Seriously, Rissa. You need to fucking focus."

I kick my brother in the shin and don't give a shit that I'm wearing Doc Martens. "Shut up."

Cade winces.

Mason grins. "Hey, I knew it was a stretch, but you can't blame me for trying. You can still come over and meet my chickens."

I feel another yank on my scalp. "I didn't know you were into farm animals. I'll introduce you to Addy's cows. You can feed them all the molasses you want."

"I'm not into farm animals," I say under my breath. "And quit pulling my hair."

It's not like Mason's perpetually-happy grin, but Levi smirks.

That's when a crack echoes through the cafeteria, breaking through the collective hushed chatter around us. I jerk and look to my left at the next table.

Fuck.

It's Isla Perry, in all her Angel-esque beauty, with her long black hair, sultry eyes, and perfectly proportionate curves.

Of all the people who I didn't know to wish some sickness on—like the flu or mono or head lice that necessitates a school absence—it's Levi's ex-girlfriend. She's standing one table away, leering at me. And if I could read minds, I bet she's manifesting every illness, curse, and tumble down the stairs that would be my official demise.

Her tray, which no doubt was the crack heard 'round the world, has been tossed in front of her, the remnants of her lunch spilled and splattered on everyone around her.

She proves she doesn't care, if her constant glare has anything to say about it.

Who does that?

I realize I'm caught in her trance when I feel fingertips pressing into my shoulder. "Let's go. I'll help you review before your test."

No matter how hard Levi tries to gain my attention, I can't look away from Isla as she glares at me one more moment before flinging her backpack over her shoulder as she does that whippy-like catwalk turn.

"Who's that?" Cade asks.

Mason mutters, "Can you say after-school rumble?"

A new voice, one I've never heard before, enters our fray.

"Dude. Whatever the fuck you're doing, I'm here for it. Your big-dick energy just sent Ursula down the tunnel to her lair where she belongs. But I have a feeling she's not gonna stay there long."

I flip my head around, but I doubt it has half the dramatics that Isla's did. A guy is standing at the end of the table where our weird foursome is huddled. He's as broad as Levi, just not quite as tall. If Levi is broody, this guy is comically wolfish.

I look at Levi and panic. "I thought her name was Isla."

Levi doesn't move away from me and glares at the guy who parks his ass on our table and props his feet on a chair. "Everyone, this is Jack. He's a likable asshole."

"That I am." Jack punches Levi in the shoulder but doesn't look away from me. "Who the hell are you and why has no one told me—the most important fuckin' soul in the school—that my boy here has come out from hibernation?"

"This is Carissa Collins." I get another hair yank. "Her brother, Cade, and Mason."

"Schrock," Mason adds. "Mason Schrock."

Jack spears us each with a friendly smile. "If this isn't *The Breakfast Club* remake, then pinch me and make me a priest."

This guy acts like he and Levi are BFFs, but I can't get over how different they are.

Levi proves I might be right, and they really are polar opposites. "I'm helping Carissa with chemistry."

I turn to Levi. "Not everyone needs to know I'm flunking chem."

Jack barks a laugh. "Fuck me, it's a student-teacher romance! How very taboo of you, Mr. Hollingsworth."

"I'm done," Levi announces and stands. Just when I think he's had enough of me—because I really am more trouble than I'm worth—he grabs my overstuffed backpack with his in one hand and holds the other out for me. "I'll help you review before class."

"Yeah, you will," Jack agrees.

"You're such a dumbass," Levi mutters, but I can't concentrate on the love-hate bromance being carried out for all of us to witness.

Because Levi grabs my hand.

My hand.

In his.

And if Ursula really is the antagonist, I hope she stormed off into some dark crevice of the building, because having the rest of the lunchroom witness my hand engulfed in Levi Hollingsworth's is too much.

There's no way I'm going to be able to focus on my test now. I thought stinky Mr. Stance would be the one to do me in, but no.

The hot, lacrosse-playing brainiac will be my demise.

Academically.

Socially.

And maybe sexually.

Because right now, I'd be down with Levi working out more parts of my body than just my brain, which is the last thing I should be thinking about right before taking a test that I really need to pass.

12

LITTLE JAILBIRD

Levi

The day blew up.
    I knew it would happen. After the drama that played out between Isla and me two years ago, I always knew if I got involved with someone else, it would get people's attention.

I met her Monday.

It's Friday.

And I wonder what's wrong with me. Why I worked so hard to steer clear of anyone and everyone this long, only to open my eyes and actually look at someone now. Like my dad said last night, I'm close to the end. In six months, I'll be gone.

College.

A fresh start with new people.

A do over.

But it all changed. All of a sudden, I'm not thinking about any of that.

The last two years have dragged on to a point I never

thought high school would end. But since Monday, the days have flown.

Then today...

From the moment I staked my claim for the whole damn school to see, it's been a fucking whirlwind. Not that I've ever given a shit what anyone thinks of me or what I do, but the last two years have made me hate attention more than anything.

And I did it for the sole reason that study hours after school weren't enough time together. I need to find a way to break her out of her grandmother's house. I don't know if she'll go without Cade, so if I want time with her, it's going to have to be during school hours for the masses to witness.

Even Isla.

That was funny. I enjoyed it more than I should've.

I really hope I didn't fuck up Carissa's test. I should've picked a better time to claim her, but when I saw her sitting at lunch with that kid, I didn't think it through. I barged in.

The rest is history.

Recent history, that is. As in the last five hours of history.

My phone hasn't stopped since. Everyone I've managed to ignore for the last two years wants to know who she is, how I met her, and what the hell I'm doing. And all I want to do is talk to the new girl who I threw in front of the school bus in front of the whole damn school in the lunchroom, where drama breeds about as fast as a stomachache from the shitty pizza.

I waited outside of Stance's chem class. Carissa looked slightly tortured after her test, but at least she didn't look like she hated me, which was the most important thing at that moment.

We had a study session scheduled after school, and even

though it was Friday, I wasn't about to cancel it and she hadn't either ... at that point.

That's why I was surprised when I got a text from her right before last period, saying she was going straight home with Cade.

I texted her about two million times asking if she was okay, then another two million more apologizing for what I did at lunch.

That's when she stopped answering.

She went as cold on me as the front blowing through the valley of our county, no matter what my dad said about the weather forecast for Sunday, it's fucking cold and we're supposed to get snow tonight. Mother Nature doesn't give a shit that the calendar indicates spring and outdoor lacrosse practice starts soon, no matter if we're in the mud or not.

I hit the gym hard after school. Getting ready for the season had nothing to do with it.

Aggression, frustration, and something else were my only motivators. Jack gave me so much crap for the first half. That is, until he realized I was not in the mood for his shit.

Yelling at him while telling him I wasn't in the fucking mood might've had something to do with his realization.

Then I texted Carissa another half-million times, but this pathetic string of text messages might as well have included me on my knees in a grovel. I looked so desperate, I wanted to slap myself for turning into a main character in the movies that Jack's mom makes him sit through.

Now I'm sitting at home, where I usually am on a Friday night unless Jack wears me down enough that I make a very rare appearance at a party or school event. I realize no one around me recognizes how fucking miserable I am since this is probably how I always look.

Dad got takeout. It didn't matter how tortured I was, I

inhaled dinner. Emma didn't say two words, and the three of us shared a silent meal eaten out of boxes. She was escaping to her room, but I was following her lead when Dad reminded us that Sunday was family day, and we'd better be ready to have some fucking fun and actually speak to him.

That was three hours ago.

Three hours.

I've got a basketball game on mute as I scroll through my phone, not comprehending any of it. I made myself stop texting her an hour ago.

So when the notification pops up on the top of my screen, I shoot to my ass from where I was sprawled on my unmade bed.

Carissa – Sorry.

Sorry? She leaves me hanging for hours, wondering what happened to her, or if she'll ever speak to me again after putting her under a microscope at school, and all I get is *sorry?*

What the hell?

Me – It's cool.

Fuck. When did I become so lame?

Carissa – It turned into sort of a day.

Me – I get that.

I don't get it. I have no fucking idea what she's talking about.

But now that I know she's alive and not ignoring me, I can start groveling again.

Me – About today. If you're pissed... Well, I don't know what to do to make it better since I fucked up you flying under the radar. But I'll make it okay. I swear.

I have no idea how I'm going to do that, other than beat anyone's face in who makes her eat shit. If that happens to be Isla Perry, I'll have to deal with that another way since I'd never hit a girl.

But if I did, it would be her.

Still, I'd never.

Carissa – When I said it was a day, I didn't mean that. That was A LOT, but it's not that.

Oh. Thank God it's not me. That was a long fucking night, though.

Me – What is it?

Carissa – My family. So messed up.

Me – You okay?

Carissa – No. Not really, no. I feel trapped, and there's no end in sight. Today proved that.

My thumbs hover over the screen. It's late. Not that I have a curfew. Dad's cool and there's no reason since I have no social life.

Me – You need to get out of Louise's house.

Carissa – Tell me about it.

Me – Can you? I'll come get you. Cade can come if he wants.

Carissa – Cade won't want to go. He doesn't do spur of the moment.

Me – Then just you. Just for a little bit. It'll be an escape.

My gut tightens as bubbles bounce across the bottom of my screen.

Carissa – I don't know... Louise is asleep.

Shit.

Carissa – Okay. But don't come to the door. I'll come out. And turn your headlights off. And, text me when you're close. Actually, stop at the road.

My feet barely hit the floor before I'm stuffing them into a pair of tennis shoes. I grab my keys, an extra hoodie, and I'm out the door before I can text her back.

Me – I'm coming for you, little jailbird. Be there in ten.

Carissa

"All I'm asking you to do is cover for me. Louise never gets up so it'll probably be a moot point. But if she does, just tell her I had cramps or something and went to bed early."

Cade sits in front of his computer screen with more tabs open than I can count. He barely glances at me. "Where are you going?"

I tell him the truth. "I don't know, but I need to get out of here. Levi is picking me up."

This gets his attention, and his gaze focuses solely on me. "You're sneaking out?"

I shrug. "You were invited. You can come if you want."

His expression twists. "No way."

"Then all you have to do is tell her I'm asleep. That's it. She won't get up anyway, so it won't matter."

"When will you be back?" he demands.

"That's the beauty of sneaking out—there is no curfew. I'll have my phone if you want to check on me."

His eyes narrow. "What are you doing, Rissa?"

I pull a black cardigan up my arms and flip my hair out. "I'm doing whatever the hell I want. From now on, we'll be accountable to each other. If you want to sneak out, I've got your back."

He looks back to his screen and mutters, "Whatever."

"It's not like I haven't had your back with Louise since we've been here. Just do this for me, okay? I really like him."

He returns to his keyboard and doesn't look up. "I wasn't kidding when I told that guy Dad will be all over him when he figures out you're into him. Levi doesn't seem like a dick, but there is the drama he had with Ursula, that's bound to come up."

I put my hands to my hips. "How do you know about that?"

"Mason." His answer is simple and clipped, before he goes on about what he seems to feel even stronger about. "He's nice, I guess. But I'm not going to meet his chickens."

"Yeah, I really like Mason."

"But not as much as you like Levi."

"Since I'm not sneaking out to see chickens, you're right. Who knew our only friends in Virginia would be a brainiac freshman and a brainiac jock?"

"And you're the only one in the weird foursome who's not a brainiac. So, yeah, who knew."

"It's not my fault you hogged all the brain cells from the womb."

He tosses me a glance and a half-smile. He knows I'm right.

"Remember, if Louise should happen to wake from the dead—"

"Lie, lie, lie. Got it." Cade waves me off. "Don't be stupid and get human trafficked."

"I'm not going to get human trafficked. Wish me luck."

"You'll need it. After today, we'll be here 'til we graduate."

I have a feeling he might be right.

13

DESPERATION AND STRENGTH

Levi

I barely roll up to the gates and flip off my lights when a body comes out of the woods toward me.

I climb out of my Jeep and meet her halfway. She's dressed in black from head to toe, her hair is pulled back, and she's hugging herself around the middle since the wind and flurries whip around us.

"You don't have a coat. Did you forget where you are?"

Her body trembles with a shiver. "I didn't want to mess with one since I was making a break for it. It would've slowed me down."

Since I seem to take any opportunity to touch her, I don't pass up this one and bring my hands up to her shoulders and pull her flush to me before running my hands up and down her back to create some friction.

Damn. She feels good.

And I should not be thinking about friction.

"Where do you want to go?"

She tips her head to look up at me. "Anywhere. Nowhere. I don't care as long as we leave."

I hold her tight for one more second before letting her go to claim her hand. "Let's get out of here."

I open the passenger door and help her up. When I'm sitting beside her with the heat blasting as we buckle, I put it in first gear. "How's Cade?"

"I asked him to come, but he didn't want to. I knew he wouldn't. He agreed to cover for me if Louise wakes up, but I don't think she will. She's old school. She doesn't have a security system or cameras or anything. I literally just walked out the back door."

I wait to get past her grandmother's property before flipping my lights on again as the snow glistens in the beams ahead of us. "It sucks you don't have a car." That's a lie. If she doesn't have a car, she needs me.

She leans back in her seat and stares ahead, appearing mesmerized by the flakes. "I know. Most things suck right now."

I come up to the intersection, stop, and decide to take her farther out of town. "I don't know. I hear your tutor is the shit."

"Mason." I hear a smile in her tone and look over at her through the dark. She bites back a grin. "Mason is the best tutor ever."

I narrow my eyes before focusing back on the road. "We'll see about that when the grades are reported for your chem test."

"I'm trying to temper my hopes with all my grades, Levi. I had a shitty start, and it's hard to come back from that."

I make a couple more turns before we bounce along a dirt road. When I get to the middle of the long old bridge over the river, I come to a stop, throw it in park, and kill the engine.

"Where are we?" she asks.

I leave my headlights on so she can see. "Nowhere. Anywhere. It's what you wanted, right?"

She leans her head back against the seat and exhales. "This is exactly what I want. Thank you."

"There's nothing open anyway in our sleepy, little town. And people wonder why teenagers are always doing shit they shouldn't be doing. There's nothing else to do."

She rolls her head my way. "But not you."

I shake my head and unbuckle. "Not me. You know all there is to know. The only thing interesting about me is my GPA and field stats."

She unbuckles, hitches a leg, and easily turns her small frame to me fully. "I highly doubt that."

I reach for her hand. "What happened that fucked up your day besides me claiming you in front of the entire school?"

Her brows shoot up. "You claimed me?"

I tip my head to the side. "If you think I'm going to let your other tutor have you, you're crazy."

She shakes her head and looks back out at the snow. "I'm no one's, Levi."

"After today, the whole school thinks otherwise," I argue.

She rolls her eyes back to me and pulls her hand away. "My gut tells me you're not a human trafficker, which is why I'm sitting in the dark on a snowy bridge over a frigid river with you. I trust you. Don't make me second guess myself."

"You *can* trust me." I claim her hand again, and she allows it. "What happened today that made me think you dumped my ass before I got the chance to kiss you?"

This time she rests the side of her head against the seat. "You think you're going to kiss me, huh?"

I lower my voice. "I know I'm going to kiss you. I'm just waiting for the right time."

"And when would that be?"

"You'll know when it happens." I shrug. "It'll rock your world."

She threads her fingers with mine. "If I didn't know better, I'd think you were a player, Levi Hollingsworth."

"I'm the farthest thing from a player you'll ever meet," I tell her the truth. "I'm also not a human trafficker, so you're safe."

A small smile touches her lips. Lips I want to claim the same way I did with her today in the lunchroom. "This kiss ... I guess I'll just have to look forward to it."

"Are you really not going to tell me what happened today?"

She sighs so dramatically, I wouldn't be surprised if she wilted on the spot. "My dad called this afternoon. We haven't heard from him since we left Phoenix. Not once. Not to let us know Mom is okay. Not to check on us. And especially not to say he's sorry for tearing our family apart and doing it on the nightly news."

"Did you answer?"

"Not at first. But he called and called and called. He wouldn't stop. When I refused to answer, he started in on Cade. Cade can't stand not to answer his phone, so he did. And he demanded to know where Mom is—how she is." Carissa's brown eyes start to glass over, and my hold on her hand tightens. "Because we deserve to know. And no one is telling us."

"He didn't tell you?"

She shakes her head, and a single tear escapes. "No. No one will tell us."

My words come out low and guttural, because I can't take seeing her like this. "Then why did he call you?"

She sniffs, swipes her cheek, and looks down at our hands that are now one. "He's up for election this year. His primary is coming up, and with the shit between him and Mom, he needs us to make some appearances with him."

Something stirs in me. I refuse to believe it's panic. "Are you leaving?"

It's almost a violent act when she scrubs her face with the back of her hand and wrist as she shrugs. "I told him no. It's the last thing Cade wants to do. His Chief of Staff has always been so short and impatient with Cade. He's fine in most situations as long as he knows what to expect. Spur of the moment stuff and quick changes gives him anxiety, and her end goals never included what was best for Cade. Yet she always expects us to stand there like wax figures and pretend we're supportive and agree with what he spews. We don't want to be a part of any of that."

Emotion bleeds from her—so much, she's hemorrhaging with it.

"You know, life really sucks when your only choices are to help your asshole dad's campaign or stay with Louise. We have a short time until we're eighteen, but it's not like either of us will have a high school diploma. It's why graduating early was so important to me in Phoenix. With my grades now, I'll be lucky to graduate from high school on time."

I pull her hand to me, holding it tight, and rest it on my thigh. "You'll graduate early. I'll make sure of it. Can your dad make you go to his political shit?"

She looks up at me, and for the first time since she

started talking about him, she doesn't look like she's about to lose it. "He'll try. But he also knows what he'll get. Cade and I are both worried about Mom, and I'm downright pissed at Dad. If he wants us at his event, he's taking a chance. We're not ten anymore. They can't boss us around and make us plaster a fake smile on our faces. I told him that. I'm not sure he's willing to take a chance on us being loose cannons."

"He might deserve a loose cannon," I note. "Not that I'm anxious for you to go anywhere. Though I guess that's selfish of me. I can tell how miserable you are here."

She sighs and looks out the windshield. "I don't hate it here. I hate living with Louise. I hate that she's not good for Cade and I hate that he's miserable." She looks back to me, and her tears have almost dried up. "And I hate chemistry."

"But you lucked out with your tutor. It all balances out."

Her lips tip on one side. "I guess so."

"That sounds less than convincing. You really know how to wound a guy."

She tugs her hand back but doesn't let go of mine. She pulls it to her, holding it in both of hers. My blood instantly warms when she flattens my hand to the center of her chest. She's got a thin tank on under her chunky sweater. It dips so low in the front we're mostly skin to skin. The palm of my hand is between her tits. They're not big but my hand is. I feel the small swell on either side of my palm and have to fight my cock from growing in my pants.

Now is not the time.

"Do you feel that?" she whispers.

My pulse throbs, coursing through my body as I sit here and feel her life beat rhythmically. Right now, I bet my heart could bounce circles around hers—that's how fast it's racing. "I feel you."

She presses my hand tighter to her chest and lowers her voice. "What do you feel?"

I don't look away from her eyes as my Jeep warms despite having killed the engine as the snow falls outside. The heater is nothing compared to what our bodies are collectively doing together.

My answer is firm. "Desperation."

She swallows hard but doesn't speak.

"And strength," I add. The strum of her heart picks up a beat when I utter that last word, and I bring my other hand up to frame the side of her face. Her gaze never wavers. But her heart ... I feel its anguish as it thrums under my touch. "You're strong, resilient, and protective of what's important to you. Of *who's* important to you. Most people don't think desperation and strength go together, but they do. They need each other. Take away one, the other goes haywire. They keep each other in check."

Her fucking heart...

I swear, it's singing to mine.

She manages a small nod.

"You have to fight for that strength to fucking eat up the desperation. Am I right?"

Her voice is thick with emotion. "Yes."

"But your desperation, that's what makes you beautiful."

Her brows pinch.

I keep talking. "It's what makes you *you*. It drives you to protect your brother. To keep going no matter what shitty circumstance your parents throw you into. You're desperate to move on, past them, and their shit."

Her breaths become deeper and labored, but I don't give her any space. If anything, it makes my grip on her tighten.

"Am I right?" I press.

Her chest heaves under my touch, and together our

bodies create a heat that no chemistry textbook could explain.

She nods.

I lean in and lower my voice. "Together, they make you beautiful."

Tears well again, and she shakes her head.

"They do," I insist.

I feel the shake of her voice vibrate through her chest. "I don't feel like it. I've never felt more alone. I feel like I'm going to lose it."

"You won't," I argue. "You're too strong. I feel it every time I'm with you."

She shakes her head, and she might as well tear my fucking heart out when she pulls away.

"Carissa—" I start to call for her, but she turns away from me.

Before I know it, she's gripping the handle, and a cold rush of winter air floods the red-hot energy coursing between us. I rush to follow as her despair pushes her from my Jeep.

I'm faster and tag her wrist when I reach her, the snow creating a wintery filtered sheen through my headlights. I swing her around, and her front collides with mine.

I wrap one arm around her back, and my other hand goes to the back of her head. Her hands land on my pecs, and she fists my sweatshirt, looking up at me through her big brown eyes. The spring snow is wet and melting the moment it comes into contact with us.

I can't speak for her, but I'm not at all cold.

I'm fucking hot.

For her.

"Why are you doing this?" she begs with her tone. "Why

me? You said yourself you didn't want anything to do with anyone after what you went through."

"Don't fuck this up and don't pretend you don't feel it," I growl. As my hold on her tightens, her body melts to mine. I tip her face, wet with melted snow mixed with her tears. "Don't pretend you don't feel this. What do you want? Tell me what you want. I'll do anything but ignore what's happening between us."

14

SURVIVAL

Carissa

The snow is cold on my heated skin, but that's not what I feel.
All I feel is him.
Rock hard muscle and white-hot emotion.
"Tell me what you want," he demands.
"I want the hurt to go away," I admit and give my head a tiny shake. "I want to know where my mom is and if she's okay. I want to erase the stress for Cade. I thought I wanted to go home, but everyone knows us there. They know who our dad is and what he did. The thought of going back and facing that in high school is ... I just can't. It's so messed up. I don't know what I want, Levi."

He drops his forehead to mine as his hazel eyes bore into me. I don't know if it's the headlights, the glittery snow raining around us, or the emotion that seems to thicken the longer we touch each other, but his emerald flecks shine bright through the night.

"Do you trust me?" His words are heavy, and every taut

muscle in his body is pressed against mine. His arm hitches me up his body, and the tips of our noses brush intimately.

I'm surprised our breaths alone don't melt the snow in a five feet radius. I tell him the truth, because I wouldn't be here if I didn't. "Yes."

His gaze drops to my parted lips, our heavy breaths dance in the air, swirling between us. When he looks back up to my eyes, he says, "I don't know if I can fix your problems, but I can stand next to you so you're not alone."

I barely have a chance to exhale at his words when his lips hit mine.

It's not sweet or gentle or even slightly romantic the way made-for-TV movies depict first kisses.

He wasn't wrong when he said he could see my desperation. It's simmered inside me since this nightmare started. But I'm not alone.

I feel Levi's possessiveness through his kiss. It travels down to my toes that are hovering over the earth. I'm off my feet and pulled up his body as his tongue spears my mouth.

I've been kissed a few times.

But this.

This isn't a kiss.

This is so much more.

This is life changing.

The shit with my family has knocked me off my axis, but being in Levi's arms with his mouth on mine, I am righted.

Steady.

And I can't get enough. I can't get close enough.

I drag my legs up his sides and wrap them around his waist. My action elicits a groan from Levi.

I feel it on my tongue, through my chest, and now, between my legs.

I've never had anyone between my legs.

He turns, and backs me into the grille of his Jeep. His hand grips the back of my leg so close to my ass, I gasp.

He breaks our kiss and sears me with a heated gaze. If I weren't already warmed all over, I'd combust.

"I've wanted to do that for days." His words are hot on my skin. "Tell me you've thought about it too."

I nod, and bring my fingers to his face for the first time. I trace his jaw until I reach his chin and stare at my fingertips as they touch his bottom lip. His head dips just enough to press his lips into my touch, and I shift my eyes back to his.

So close.

He's beautiful.

Beautiful and haunted by deception, just like me. It's in a different way, but when someone you trust breaks through your faith with a wrecking ball, it does something.

"I trust you," I whisper through the night wind whipping around us.

He brushes the hair from my face and pulls me to him. My arms circle his neck and his body presses into mine.

Everywhere.

My moan is more like a little hum that makes Levi deepen his kiss, and just when I thought things were winding down, Levi's big hand slides farther up the back of my leg and squeezes.

I bury my hand in his thick soft hair.

I wish this would never end. I wish the world would melt away, and my family shit would swirl down the drain with it. This is utopia, and I never want to leave.

He lets go of my mouth and runs his lips across my cheek to my ear. "When do you need to be back?"

"I don't know." I shrug. "Never?"

He looks up at the sky before turning back to me. "If we

get back in the Jeep, are you going to run away from me again?"

I give his hair a little pull and shake my head.

"As much as I don't want to move from this spot, you're going to freeze if we stay out here. We don't need to leave, but let's warm up."

"Okay."

He presses his lips to mine one more time before moving away from the nose of the Jeep with me still wrapped around him. He has my door open and my feet never touch the ground as he places me in the passenger seat. When he's sitting next to me again, he cranks the engine and turns up the heat. Then he reaches into the back seat and tosses a sweatshirt at me. "Spring snow is a slushy mess. We're soaked. Put this on, it's dry."

I hold out the huge sweatshirt he tossed at me, but I can't look away when he reaches for the hem of his hoodie and pulls it up and over his head. His T-shirt is taut across his chest, and the short sleeves hug his muscles in a way that makes me jealous.

He tosses the wet hoodie in the back, and I shiver for the first time since I jumped out of the car in an emotional haze. It's either the adrenaline fall or the lack of Levi's touch, but I'm cold to the bone.

I drag my wet cardigan down my shoulders, leaving me in my usual uniform of a cami and leggings. I'm about to pull the dry sweatshirt over my head, but I'm stopped by the expression on Levi's face.

He's not even pretending not to look, and there's nothing cold about his gaze. It's hot and intense dragging down my body.

I smile. I like it more than I should. I've never wanted anyone's eyes on me like this.

I shiver again and feel my nipples pucker, from the cold and Levi's heated gaze.

His eyes shift to mine, and his tone is low and rough. "Put the hoodie on, Carissa."

My next shiver isn't because I'm cold. Still, I pull the sweatshirt over my head. It's soft and warm and smells like him. It also swallows me whole in such a delicious way, I hope it's not one of his favorites, because he may never get it back.

I barely have it pulled down to my waist when he reaches for me. I'm up and twisted, pulled across his lap as he reaches for the lever and reclines his seat as far as it will go.

Then I'm engulfed in his thick arms and held tight to his rock-hard chest. I rest my head on his shoulder and kick off my wooly boots that are wet from the snow before I curl my legs into both of us.

He rubs my back and shoulders to warm me. "You okay? I'll leave the heat on for a few minutes, but I don't want to poison us with carbon monoxide."

"You and science," I mutter against his soft tee. His hand lands high on my thigh, and mine goes directly to his bicep. I don't know how, since it's so cold outside, but his skin is warm to the touch, so I slide my fingers under the band of his sleeve and leave them there.

I feel every word and emotion through his chest when he huffs a single laugh. "That's not science. It's survival skills."

"I guess when you grow up in the desert, you don't have to learn how to survive stranded in the cold. I could use some survival skills with real life."

His hands are still on me. "You don't miss it? You don't want to go back?"

I let my fingers trace circles on his skin. "There I'm Cillian Collins' daughter. Legit, some people don't even know my first name. And since Cillian Collins has been fucking his Chief of Staff, I know what I'd face—what Cade would face. Louise is no party, but the only other option at this point seems a lot less fun."

He says nothing and keeps rubbing my back. He's deep in thought as the quiet hum of the engine rumbles below us.

I like the quiet. I always have. My mom was always the one who felt the need to fill every space with random and worthless words.

I never needed that. Maybe it's because I'm a twin, and Cade isn't a talker. There aren't many times I don't know what he's feeling, and he's usually in tune with me.

Long minutes go by before Levi holds me to his chest as he reaches forward to click off the engine. He must be done with the silence, because his hand lands on the side of my head, and I find out what he's been mulling over. "I have a feeling I fucked up your unknown status after what I did at lunch today."

I think back to Isla trying to murder me by shooting daggers through her witchy eyes. "Yeah, that's not lost on me. It was nice while it lasted, I guess."

He moves abruptly, and I'm atop his body, front to front. He bends his knees and parts my legs forcing me to straddle his thighs where he holds me tight. "No one's going to give you shit. I'll make sure of it."

I try to get used to our new position and try not to think about the lunchroom on Monday. "It's high school, Levi. You can't control people talking shit behind my back."

"I can," he argues, staring up at me. My damp hair curtains us as his hand molds to the side of my face. "And I will. Mark my word, Carissa. No one's going to give you shit about anything."

He pulls me to him, forcing my lips to his as his other hand grips the back of my thigh.

Promises and declarations...

I don't know how he can assure me of anything. But right now, he's pretty persuasive that he can make it happen.

Levi

My Jeep looked like a sauna, and my dick was beyond painful by the time I cut things off. We were both breathing heavily, and it was all I could do to keep my hands in the safe zone.

So many things to think about...

I just met her.

I'm not that kind of asshole.

She's still seventeen, even if it is only for a short time.

She's emotional about her family.

There's also the fact this is the first person I've touched since Isla.

And, it's worth repeating, she's new and still seventeen.

Especially that last part.

It's after one in the morning. I just texted Dad to tell him I'd be home soon. His simple response was a firm *very soon*. I also need to get her home so Louise doesn't wake up and freak out on her. That's the last thing she needs to deal with right now.

But she's asleep.

On my chest. In my lap. Sprawled over me.

And other than my dick, I'm pretty fucking comfortable.

I'll wake her soon.

Until then, I need to figure out what the hell I'm going to do to fulfill my promise that she won't eat shit at school because of me. I might be able to ignore the entire student body, but I can't expect her to have to do the same.

And if Isla even thinks about fucking with Carissa...

15

COMMOTION

Levi

"Levi! Come here," my dad yells from the patio where he's talking to his friends and coworkers.

Cayden is crawling over my shoulders onto the back of the sofa. He's three and only mildly irritating. I'd rather be with Carissa than anyone else I've been forced to spend time with today. At least I'm not stuck coloring like Emma. That would be a cruel form of torture.

"Levi!" Cayden laughs and squeals when I grab hold of him and stand, before tossing him back on the sofa like a small bag of rocks.

Since I know he'll follow me, I suggest, "Go ask Addy for some candy. I'll be back."

"Okay!" He scrambles off to the kitchen where the wives are making dinner. Maya is married to Grady, and Addy to Crew. Both men work with Dad. Addy also owns Whitetail Farms Vineyard, and that's where we ended up after family time.

Maya, Cayden's mom, is a health freak. But we're at Whitetail, and Addy always has candy around.

I slide my phone into my pocket and head for the men. I've been texting Carissa ever since *family time* wrapped up. Or at least I thought it did, but I was very wrong and am feeling as pissy as Emma was when Dad dragged us here for dinner.

Family time consisted of six muddy miles through the Shenandoah forest, Dad grilling us on every fucking thing —thanks to weak cell service, he had our undivided attention—and Emma complaining under her breath the whole time. It was so little fun, I'd rather challenge myself to another go at getting a perfect score on the SATs.

After all the fun, Dad announced family day wasn't even close to being over, and we were going to Whitetail for dinner with our other family.

Our found family—the one we're closer to than anything our parents gave us by blood—the group of men my dad works with and their families.

Crew Vega and Grady Cain have been a part of our lives for as long as I can remember. They're like the honorary uncles we don't have through blood.

They also did what Dad did before they all retired. Now Crew and Grady are both married, have kids, and are working with Dad to train others to contract and kill for the CIA.

I step over Emma who's sprawled on the floor, half-assing her page in a coloring book with her own small human, Crew's daughter, Vivi.

Dad was right, the weather warmed up today. The sun is setting, and it's crisp, but Crew has a fire going on the patio of their centuries-old farm house that's so big it's like a mini-mansion.

I fall into a chair next to Crew. "What's up?"

Dad looks to his friends and then back to me. "We did a little digging on the senator from Arizona."

"Yeah?" I look around at the group and take in their expressions. "I know he's an ass. He cheated on Carissa's mom and has the sex scandal to prove it."

"He probably should've experienced more than this one scandal," Grady mutters. "Rumors are rampant."

"Rumors," Dad confirms. "I'm talking cold-hard facts. They prove he plays dirty to get what he wants and dirtier to block what he doesn't want. I'm not saying this will fall back on you. But I am warning you that he is not a good guy. However you proceed with his daughter, you shouldn't trust him or anything he says. There's always an ulterior motive. He won his position in congress because he gets shit done for his party, but from our research, it's rarely on the up and up. And when I say that, I mean worse than any regular politician."

I look him in the eyes. "But you're good?"

Crew speaks for everyone. "I appreciate the concern, Levi, but we're good. We all are, but we're concerned for you."

I shrug. "You've seen me the last two years. I spend more time hanging out with toddlers here than I do my own friends. I got an almost perfect score on my SAT and have a full ride to Hopkins. What the hell is he going to do to me?"

"You underestimate what a man will do to keep his daughter safe," Grady deadpans before rolling his eyes. "Or his sister, for that matter. And in my case, sisters."

"That's what we're concerned about," Crew says.

I spear them all with a look like they're crazy, because they are. "I'm into her, and I'm not afraid to admit it. But it's not like I'm ready to propose."

"You'd better not be," Dad mutters.

My phone vibrates, and I pull it out of my pocket.

Carissa – Mr. Stinky posted grades from our test on Friday. Any guesses on what I got?

Me – 100%.

Carissa – Wow, you really do think a lot of your tutoring skills, huh? I'm not Cade or Mason. Or you for that matter. Seriously, take a guess.

Me – Idk. 80%?

Carissa – A seventy-fucking-eight! Can you even believe it?

I try to fight my smile, but fail.

Me – I believe it. Nicely done, new girl.

Carissa – Thank you! I owe you. I'll Uber Eats you some coffee.

Me – I don't drink coffee.

Carissa – What are you, some kind of monster? And here I trusted you...

Me – You can trust me with everything.

"Fuck." I look up and all three men are staring at me, amused. But it's Grady who speaks, and he's talking to my dad. "When did he meet her? And what's the world record for being whipped by a girl?"

Crew picks up his beer. "Pretty sure you hold that record with Maya, since you were stalking her on the surveillance system before you spoke two words to her."

Grady doesn't look like he gives a shit and shoots back, "Says the guy who goes to farm auctions to buy his wife orphaned cows."

Crew shrugs. "Vivi likes them too."

I stand, not at all interested in sitting here for this. "Thanks for the warning."

"Don't take it lightly, Levi," Crew stresses. "Addison had

her run in with crooked government officials. It was bad, and I almost lost her."

I'll never forget that. "I don't take it lightly."

"He'll keep me up to speed," Dad assures them.

He's right. I will ... to an extent.

I head back inside and barely hear Dad start to tell Crew and Grady about some idiot on the side of the road who didn't know how to change a tire.

I go back into the house and am about to flop down on the sofa to give Carissa my full attention, when Addy comes out of the kitchen. "Dinner's about ready, Levi. Will you grab the kiddos for me so they can help set the table?"

I stand up as fast as I sat down. "Sure."

Her deep brown eyes smile. "Thanks. They'll do anything for you."

I take a quick look at my phone before having to wrangle the kids.

Carissa – I think Friday night proved how much I trust you. Looking forward to you busting me out of jail again soon...

I wanted to bust her out last night, but I worked all day at the golf course. And since I knew Dad was getting us up at the ass-crack of dawn for family time, I couldn't be up all night. Hell, I'm itching to break her out tonight, but I have a test in AP stat tomorrow.

Cayden leaps at me and hangs onto my leg. "Addy wouldn't give me candy before dinner."

"Imagine that. Dinner is ready. Let's set the table."

I type out one last text.

Me – Soon, Carissa. Very soon. Until then, we have a study room reserved at the library after school.

Carissa – I guess that'll have to do.

Yes. Being shut in a room along with a window for anyone to walk by and see us will be a different kind of hell.

I might need to think of another place to go. Even if I have to push my way into Louise's house.

Carissa

WELL, I figured it would be bad, but I had no idea it would turn out like this.

It went from bizarre on Monday, to uncomfortable on Tuesday, to downright eerie on Wednesday. I was a bit perplexed on Thursday, and now, on Friday, I'm just plain ... confused.

There's no flying under the radar anymore. Everyone knows Cade and I aren't some random Collins kids from some random family from the deep woods of Virginia.

None of this is good. Cade is upset enough about being cut off from our mom and having to live with Louise. Change is especially miserable for him. The attention isn't good.

Cade hasn't come out and said it, but my twin intuition tells me he likes the fact that, here in the middle of nowhere, he can go from class to class and no one knows who he is. That he's the son of Senator Cillian Collins. Or Mariann Collins, the darling of Arizona, who sits on more philanthropic boards than anyone else in the state. That he's a quiet kid who doesn't like to engage in conversation and thrives off a ritualistic schedule—for today to be like yesterday, and for that one to be like the one before that.

No, he'd never admit it.

But I can tell he likes it.

I, on the other hand, never minded being anyone's

daughter, and probably used it to my advantage more than I should have.

Until the scandal.

And the breakdown.

That was when I appreciated Cade's philosophy.

Being invisible is nice.

That was before.

Before the broody, popular, brainy jock claimed me in front of the whole school.

Before he made sure everyone—and when I say everyone, I mean Isla Perry—knows we're together. The student body might've given him a six-foot-wide berth before, but now I get one too.

Pretty much Cade does too.

All because Levi said I wouldn't eat shit for being with him.

Am I okay with this new turn of events?

I mean ... no.

It's weird. Cade and I have gone from nobodies to somebodies in the matter of days. No one has given us shit because of Levi, but what's more odd is that no one has given us shit about the scandal. And we're practically a neighbor of Washington, D.C.. Even high school kids, who are only into themselves and their instant gratification, have heard about the Cillian Collins getting caught fucking his Chief of Staff.

Those are actually the news stories that capture the attention of teenagers.

"What's wrong?"

I dump my half-eaten apple on the tray in front of me. We've quickly gone from the most ignored table in the cafeteria to the most watched. I can't take a bite or say a word without knowing half the school might be staring at any given time. Cade is across from me and Mason, who is now a regular, loves the attention.

And Levi...

Levi has sat at my side every day this week. He just pushed his tray to the middle of the table and is reclining in his lunchroom chair with an elbow propped on my seatback.

I turn to him, because we've talked about this a lot since last week when I snuck out of Louise's house, and we spent most of the darkest hours of the night together. If my experience with guys could be compared to a swimming pool, I've barely waded in the shallow end. I've certainly never snuck out to be with a guy I just met, and never, ever have I fallen asleep with one.

Let alone wrapped up with one.

It was the most intimate experience I've ever had, and it was hardly intimate.

"Carissa," he calls for me when I don't answer. Mason and Cade are talking about some mumbo-jumbo technical network stuff I cannot begin to understand. They lost interest in Levi and me about two days ago.

I wish the rest of the school would too.

"What's wrong?" Levi presses.

When I turn to him, he's close like he always is when we're together, no matter where we are. I lower my voice. "I can't get used to this. Everyone is staring at us. You're the guy who came out of hibernation, and I'm the new girl whose dad is living out his affair on the evening news."

He reaches up and steals a lock of my hair to twist around his finger. "But no one's giving you shit about it, right?"

"No," I stress. "How weird is that? It's very un-high-school-like. I'm used to bullies and mean girls and people whispering behind my back loud enough that they mean to be heard. This isn't natural."

He lifts his shoulders as his gaze drifts from me to his fingers in my hair. "Maybe it is."

I shake my head quickly to get his attention. "It's not. I know it's not, and I'm waiting for the other shoe to drop. Or the cleat. Or the..." My eyes wander to the left where Isla sits with her groupies, all of them with perfectly smoothed hair and so much makeup on it looks like they're hardly wearing any. They must spend a lot of time practicing. "Or the strappy heel. What did you do?"

"I have a secret weapon."

That's it?

I nudge his leg with my knee, which only prompts him to wrap his hand around the top of my thigh. "Levi. What did you do?"

He looks the opposite way of Ursula and her crew. His friend Jack is sitting on the table again, leaning forward on his knees, talking to a huge group of guys with some girls sprinkled in here and there. The guys look like they were built to be founding members of the jock club and the girls look only slightly less intimidating than Levi's evil ex. When Jack makes eye contact with Levi, he sits up straight and pounds his chest two times before pointing at my newest obsession.

He mouths *I love you, man.*

Then his gaze turns to me, and he winks.

Levi's grip on my thigh tightens, and he lifts his other hand to flip off his secret weapon.

Jack laughs and goes back to being the center of attention in his own kingdom.

"He's a piece of work, but you can thank him for your current state of peace. No one has the pulse of the school like Jack Hale. When I told him what was going on, he said he was so happy to see me among the living, he'd take down the entire school if it meant I'd quit frowning. You and Cade are off limits."

"That's crazy."

"That's Jack. Are you really complaining about people leaving you alone?"

I catch my lip between my teeth, because when he puts it that way, I do sound crazy.

"You have a quiz after school," he says.

My lip stretches between my teeth. "Ever the tutor."

Levi lowers his voice and leans in so his lips are close to my ear. "And the guy who will look for any reason to be alone with you. Where are we studying?"

My required study sessions with my tutor have multiplied, even though Levi started practice this week for his last high school season of lacrosse. Even with his full schedule, I apparently need more time than three days a week, even if they're not after school. It turns out having a tutor and a school-required study schedule is the perfect excuse to get out of Louise's house, so I'm taking full advantage. Our study sessions consist of actual homework and studying, interrupted by other things.

Delicious things.

Yet, all very innocent things.

Levi likes to touch me, but that touch has barely roamed.

When we're together, he leads, and I'm here for it. The anticipation of where it might go every time he kisses me is real and electric. He gives me a ride home every day after we study and knows all the private country roads. Louise glares at me when I walk in the door, but I've found she's easier to ignore when I'm floating in a post-Levi haze with swollen lips.

Levi sits up straighter in his seat. "Emma."

A girl stops in her spot when Levi speaks. She glares at him before her gaze shifts around the room, but she finally comes our way when he motions for her.

But she doesn't look happy about it. And I thought I was irritated with high school.

"What?" she snaps.

Levi spears her with a quick glare before motioning to me and our table. "This is my sister, Emma. Em, this is Carissa, her brother Cade, and Mason."

Cade barely gives her a glance and a wave.

"Schrock," Mason adds as he pushes his glasses up his nose. "Emma and I have been in the same grade for, like, ever. But in different circles."

"Yeah, well, I'm not in any circles anymore," Emma mutters as she shifts on her feet like she's about ready to race off into the deep, dark corners of the school where no one can find her. It was not too long ago I felt that same exact way. I need to ask Levi what her deal is.

"Hey, Emma," I greet her, but she barely glances at me. "Nice to meet you."

Levi motions to a chair. "You want to join the living?"

Levi's sister is a little bit taller than me and has Levi's thick wavy hair, though hers is long and pulled back into a messy pony. She's makeup free and looks like she cares less about her appearance than I usually do. "No, I've got to go. I've got a geometry test to..." Her eyes fall shut, and she pulls in a big breath. "Review for."

"I know the feeling," I say, if for no other reason than to try to make her feel better.

"I told you I'd hel—" Levi starts, but doesn't finish when his younger sister interrupts.

"I don't need your help," Emma snaps. "I told you. Dad is torturing me enough."

"Are you sure you don't want to join us?" I try.

She shakes her head but doesn't have time to turn me down, and Levi doesn't have time to irritate her further.

There's a commotion at the front of the commons, which doubles as the cafeteria at lunch. But it's not the commotion high school students are used to seeing. At least not at this high school.

It's not a fight or an altercation or even a made-for-TV drama-filled teenage break up.

It's adults.

A shit ton of them.

All dressed for business.

Or, more specifically, politics.

Anxiety races through me.

"Cade," I bite.

He doesn't look up from his iPad. "What?"

Levi tenses beside me. "What's wrong?"

"Yeah, I'm out of here," Emma mutters, and I can't focus on her taking this time to escape. I can't focus on anything at the moment other than the army of adults marching toward us.

"Cade!" My twin's name tumbles from my lips in a hissed whisper.

I don't know if it's my flustered tone or the fact my boot connected with his shin under the table, but my big brother sits up straight, and his gaze shoots to me. "What?"

"Look," I stress.

He looks.

"Fuck." Unlike my freakout, his curse word is unemotional, just like most things Cade says. But his posture is wired and frenzied, proving our twin connection is strong.

Or, maybe, the fact we haven't seen our father in person since the night Mom kicked him out of the house when all our phones lit up with notifications of viral pictures of him cheating on our family.

"Carissa?" Levi's big hand becomes one with my leg.

But I'm numb.

I can't take my eyes off Dad.

And he can't take his eyes off Levi.

16

POWER

Levi

I follow Carissa's gaze across the room.
 Well, fuck me.
 It's the Senator from Arizona surrounded by more people than any one person should need, being led straight to us by our principal, Mr. White.

Getting straight A's means I'm good at research, and I've done my fair share on Cillian Collins. The Irish-American might've been born in New York, but he relocated to Arizona with his family when he was in high school. That's where he became an attorney, then one of the youngest district judges ever before he ran for Senate.

I understand power. Everyone wears it differently. My dad has so much of it, you could wring it out of him on a humid day.

But you'd never know it if you passed him on the street.

Cillian Collins wears his power like a gaudy tie—front and center—to label yourself for everyone to grimace at.

Yeah, I know the difference of how people throw their power around.

Cillian Collins not only wears his power, he owns it and makes sure everyone around him understands what it means.

For example, me, since that's where his heavy stare is directed.

I stand and shift in front of Carissa. Her twin is already up and moving toward the cheating asshole. I feel her shift behind me, her hand fitted to my arm, a place I very much enjoy it.

Who am I kidding? She could touch me anywhere, and I'd enjoy it. Especially when she's wrapped around me in a way I know she doesn't want to let go.

Her father does not enjoy it. The way he's glaring at me is more than problematic, but I file that away to worry about later.

Cade stalks to his dad and puts a hand up to stop him from coming farther. "What are you doing here?"

Cillian stops in front of his son, grips Cade's shoulders, and plasters a fake smile on his rubber face. "I missed you, son."

Cade's entire frame is tense, and Cillian's gaze turns to his daughter who's partially standing behind me.

Then to me.

And back to his daughter.

He turns back to Cade. "You and your sister are hard to get a hold of. I wanted to see how you two were getting along at your new school."

"Great," Cade deadpans before lowering his voice so much, I can't hear what he says next.

But I can hear Cillian's response. "Your mom is okay. She's working through some stuff, but she'll be okay."

Carissa's grip on me tightens when she hears her father talk about their mom, as if it wasn't his fault they're in this mess.

Cillian turns to Carissa and me and makes his way around Cade. When he holds his arms out for his daughter, I realize there's a photographer in his entourage.

Shit.

I reach back and take her hand in mine. She holds tight as her dad walks to us and pulls her in for an awkward hug. I cringe but hold my ground as the photographer clicks away.

Carissa jerks away as if he burned her skin. In the short time I've known her, I've seen her indifferent, wounded, and a little happy. But I've never seen her like this.

Incensed.

"What are you doing here?" she hisses.

Cillian's smile swells with a fake chuckle as he looks around the wide space. Everyone is staring, and a number of cell phones are pointed at us. The Senator doesn't look like it bothers him in the least. If I had to guess, I'd bet he might even enjoy it, despite the anguish he's causing his kids.

That is, until he settles his sights on me. His smile doesn't change, but his eyes do. They're so far from a smile, they're not even in the same universe. "I see you're settling into your new school, Carissa."

Cade flanks his sister, and for the first time, it's evident she's not the only protective twin. Cade is cut and dry about everything and has been since I met him.

But not now.

"If you're not here about Mom, then leave," Cade bites. "Or tell us where she is and then leave."

I'd think a U.S. Senator visiting his school would be a wet dream for a principal. I'm not sure what Mr. White thought would happen, but I doubt it's this. His smile is tense and not as practiced as the politician standing before us under such circumstances.

Our principal holds out a low hand and tries to deflate the situation. "Why don't we move into my conference room? You can speak to your son and daughter where there aren't as many eyes on you."

Carissa's grip on my hand tightens, and she gapes at Mr. White. "No. We don't want to talk to him. We don't want anything to do with him—especially now."

Cillian reaches forward and brushes a strand of hair away from Carissa's face before smiling at Cade as if he didn't just tell him to get the hell out of here. It's all I can do not to yank her to me, and if we were on the field, I'd gladly sit in the penalty box for a chance at cross checking his ass.

Cillian lowers his voice. "I missed you both. It's been too long."

Carissa takes a half a step back and leans into me. I gladly take her weight. She looks over her father's shoulder before her body presses into mine tighter. "You have some nerve showing up here with *her*. Get her the hell away from us."

Her father doesn't miss her reaction and the fake-ass smile disappears from his face. "Let's move this to the conference room. This wouldn't have happened if either of you would've taken my calls. We have things to discuss."

Yeah. I'd take a whole day in the penalty box to lay this fucker out cold.

Carissa is about to argue, and Cade takes a step, inserting himself between his father and sister. "Call me later. I'll talk to you, but don't do this—not here."

I wrap my hand around Carissa's hip and regret the fact we're still in this fucking prison where I can't pick her up, run to my Jeep, and drive her into the mountains where her fucking father can't find her and her grandmother would be a distant memory.

Cillian is done pretending and glares at me. "Get your hands off my daughter."

Offering a hand to introduce myself would mean letting Carissa go, and I'm not willing to do that. Instead, I lift my chin. "Levi Hollingsworth. I'm a friend of Carissa and Cade's."

"I bet you are," he growls, and puts a rough hand to Carissa's upper arm. "Conference room. Now."

No one has a chance to argue further because the damn bell rings. The cafeteria, which turned eerily silent from the drama, comes to life. Students move and shuffle around us like we're an island in a brewing storm.

"Fine. You want to talk?" Carissa rips her arm from her father's hold and glances at her brother before glaring back at Cillian. "We'll talk, but you're not going to like what you hear."

"Carissa." I give her a squeeze. "Neither of you have to do this."

"I'll be fine. We'll be fine. I'll text you later." She turns to Cade. "Let's get this over with."

And then she moves away from me. Cade follows, and Cillian shoots daggers at me through his eyes once more.

"Get to class, Hollingsworth." I look over, and Mr. White is spearing me with his own glare.

What the hell did I do to him?

I move back to our table and grab my backpack. Mason is still standing here watching the Collins twins march off to the office with a trail of suits following. "Their dad is an asshole."

"Yeah," I agree. Mason doesn't know the half of it.

"They're lucky to have us," he adds. "Between you and me, we'll make sure Carissa passes trig and chem. Cade is a genius on his own and is going to teach me how to hack into networks."

I frown. "Seriously?"

He lowers his voice and shrugs. "Yeah. I figure, it might be a good thing to know, right?"

I think about Dad and Crew and all the shit they do on a daily basis. Most of it has to do with information others don't want them to have. "You're probably right. Just remind me not to piss you off."

"I got your back." The freshman, with about as much meat on his bones as a stray who can't hunt, straightens his spine and grins from ear to ear. "This is so cool and weird. Never thought I'd be friends with Levi Hollingsworth. See you Monday."

Since I wouldn't consider myself a friendly guy after Isla fucked me over and tried to trap me in the worst lie ever, I'd say it's weird that I'm friends with anyone. "As long as you don't hack me. Have a good weekend."

"I'd never hack my homies." He starts for class but does it walking backward as he yells through the sea of people more ready to start their weekend than ever. "See you Monday at our table!"

Then he's gone.

I head to class, but don't think about the test I'm about to take. All I can think about is what the fucking politician is saying to the girl who is consuming my every thought.

And if I'm honest with myself, it's not just my thoughts, but my choices and motivations too.

This is not what I had planned for my last couple months doing time. I planned to focus on lacrosse, finish my classes strong, and flip everyone off on my way out the door.

Carissa Collins has thrown a wrench in my exit plan, and she did it in a way I'm not ready for her to wiggle her way out yet.

Carissa

I'M HALFWAY into the conference room and spin on my heel when I hear the door click behind us. Cade stopped short of me, and I've never loved him more. And since I love him more than anyone else, that's saying something.

Cade thrives in a routine. He's focused to a fault, so much so, the world can pass him by. It's why he's beautifully brilliant, and I'm merely average.

Okay, I used to be average. Now I'm playing party host on the struggle bus.

Between his epic brain and my basic one, Cade and I couldn't be more different.

And he loves me as much as I do him, but for our entire lives, it's usually me having his back. Whether it's kids at school, political events we're expected to be perfect for, or even Louise who just doesn't get him, no one will fuck with my brother if I'm around.

But when it comes to Dad, I'm the picture perfect, easy kid. Some would think being a favorite would translate into a cushy childhood.

It didn't.

It *doesn't*.

Cillian Collins is demanding of me. Protective of me. *Possessive* of me. My experience stepping out into social circles isn't on this side of nil because of my own doing.

It's because of my father.

If I've ever led anything close to a normal, American teenage girl's life, it's because I've snuck around to do it.

Or it's because Cade had my back. He's either stood up to our father or covered for me.

Best.

Brother.

Ever.

Now we're in the privacy of this musty conference room, and all the fake personas have evaporated.

Dad stalks toward me—anger etched in his plastic face and medium frame. He ignores Cade, and his blue eyes are lasered on me. "What the hell are you thinking?"

It's weird how Cade is a mirror image of our father when Cillian wants nothing to do with his son. Even so, Cade does what he always does, and steps between us. "You don't get to do this. And Carissa hasn't done anything wrong."

The fact that Dad ignores Cade isn't new.

And the fact I take shelter behind my big brother like I always do isn't anything new either.

My father's face turns a shade of red I'm familiar with. He raises his hand to point at me as he raises his voice in tandem. "He had his fucking hands on you!"

"Well, since you're fucking someone other than our mother, I thought we were all free to do what we want."

"Watch your mouth, Carissa."

"Cillian," Frankie utters in a low tone. "We're not alone."

I glare at her. "Heaven forbid there be witnesses, right? You, of all people, know the ramifications of *witnesses*."

Frankie narrows her eyes.

Francesca Daley.

My father's Chief of Staff. She used to only be his campaign manager, but when you're fucking your boss, that apparently broadens your career options.

Levi

"Get them out," Dad hisses, not shifting his glare from me. "I want to talk to my children. Alone."

Frankie hikes a brow at me and turns to our principal, and the dog and pony show that follows Dad everywhere he goes—just in case there's a photo op he dare miss exploiting—exits.

Mr. White looks like he doesn't know what to do. He's being kicked out of his own conference room.

What an idiot. I bet he thought this was going to put him on the main stage, front and center on the nightly news to highlight him as the leader of the school a senator chose to bestow his presence upon.

He was so wrong.

Like the idiot he is, he allows Frankie to usher him and everyone else out of the room.

It's just Cade, Dad, his mistress, and me.

You'd think it was July in Virginia. The air is just that thick.

I step forward to position myself behind Cade and peek around his arm. I shouldn't use him as a shield, but today I'm desperate. I need my brother, and he's here for me. "How dare you come here and make a spectacle after what you've done—and with her?" I point to the woman who's torn our family to shreds. "We don't even know where Mom is, and you parade *her* through our school?"

Frankie crosses her arms.

Cade tenses.

I think I might throw up.

But my father...

He straightens his spine and an expression settles on his face that looks like he just killed his own dinner. "Pictures can be deceiving. Assumptions are for morons. And rumors..." He lets that word trail off into the tense air that has found its way into my lungs. It feels like poison. "People get bored. Fresh, new scandals find their way to the small screens. Rumors eventually die." He pauses, never taking his eyes off me. He takes a step and moves closer, lowering his voice. "We did nothing wrong, Carissa. It was a misunderstanding. The media ... they might spin their conclusions as truth, but then it all dies out." He holds out his arms. "And we're all still here. Breathing. Living." Dad looks between us and tosses a hand out coolly. "Thriving."

I barely recognize my own voice. "Thriving?"

Cade reaches around and grasps my wrist. But instead of the tone I'm accustomed to with my brother, his voice is strained and tense. "Where is Mom thriving?"

"She'll be back. I'm sure of it. I've spoken with her a few times. She needs some time to—"

"To what?" I demand. "To get used to the fact her husband is a cheating asshole? Do you expect her to assimilate to that new lifestyle?"

Dad narrows his eyes. "She was mistaken."

I grip the back of Cade's hoodie, about to lose my mind, but he's the one to say something. "But you admitted it."

Dad tips his head before giving it a small shake.

"Cillian—" Frankie whispers, but there's no way I'll allow that woman to say anything in my presence.

"You did," I confirm. "You begged Mom for her forgiveness. You begged us for forgiveness. Now you're denying it ever happened? Like you're trying to convince us you're not Santa or the Tooth Fairy? We're not idiots. You freaked the fuck out the day the scandal broke. Cade and I spent Christmas Day in our rooms listening to you beg Mom to forgive you. Don't fucking tell me that's a misunderstanding."

Dad's expression hardens. "Watch your mouth."

Frankie shifts her weight from spiked heel to spiked heel.

"Cade," my dad starts. "Let me talk to your sister alone."

My grip on Cade tightens.

But my brother—I love him so much—he bristles, "No way. I'm not leaving her."

I don't let Dad demand anything else, but make my own demand. "Tell us where Mom is."

Dad shakes his head. "She's safe. She's healthy. And she'll be home. Sooner rather than later, if I have anything to say about it."

"If she's in a hospital, she's close," Cade says. "We need to see her."

Dad lifts a shoulder encased in his custom suit jacket. "Trust me, she's fine."

"Tell us where she is," I demand.

Dad shakes his head, and his tone turns into a fake jab to my side. What, does he think we're three? "Don't worry, baby. She'll be back soon."

"Then why are you here?" Cade crosses his arms, and his laser focus turns on Dad. My brother is still standing sentry in front of me, and I can tell by his twitchy muscles, Cade is ready to get this done and get back to the things that will challenge his mind. "What do you want?"

Frankie opens her mouth, but I'm quick to shut her up and stare at our father. "If you don't get her out of here, you can say goodbye to your children for good."

Dad looks to Frankie. The silence is infuriating, but like the asshole he is, he lets it drag out longer than it should before he softens his tone, "Give me a minute with the kids."

Frankie has the nerve to stand her ground and hitches a foot. "No. The campaign needs them, Cillian. You cannot walk onto that stage next week by yourself. Not after what the media has done to you for the last two months."

My eyes widen, and I move beside Cade, but he grabs my arm when I exclaim, "What the media has done to him? He deserves it. You deserve it. And if you think we'll step anywhere close to a campaign event to support him after what he did to Mom, you've lost your mind—more so than when you turned into a homewrecker. I can't look at either one of you."

Frankie perches her hands on her hips. "You don't have a choice."

Dad puts a hand up to his Chief of Staff, and now, mistress. "Enough. I'll handle this. Wait outside."

Frankie doesn't move her glare from me and Cade as a shrewd smirk pulls at her red lips. "Okay, baby. But take care of it."

I'm not sure who I hate more, her or Dad.

Dad waits for the door to shut, and we're finally alone with our father. I lean into Cade who hasn't let go of my arm. We haven't been alone with Dad since he told us to pack, because Mom made threats to harm herself after his scandal hit the news. That was when he told us we were going to live with Louise while Mom got the help she needed, because he had to be back in the District after the new year.

It's amazing what this short amount of time has done to harden my heart against one of my parents. As much as I hate living with Louise, I can't imagine going back to Arizona now. I'm not sure it would feel like home anymore. That's where everything fell apart.

This time, it's Cade who stands up to Dad. "We're not going to your event."

Dad narrows his eyes. "You are. You're a part of this

family, and it's time for you to step up."

Cade shakes his head and starts to argue, but I interrupt. "You can't make us go anywhere."

Dad points at both of us. "You're not eighteen yet, and I'm your parent. I can damn well make you do anything I want. You're going to the event. It's next Friday night in Tucson. The arrangements have been made. My staff will contact your grandmother, and a car will pick you up Friday morning. You'll return to Virginia that night."

My lungs beg for air as the noose around our necks tighten. My tone is hoarse and my voice is weak, betraying me and laying my emotions out raw. "That will be the ultimate stab in the back to Mom. Don't do this."

"Do what?" he snaps, and looks from Cade to zero in on me. That's when his expression darkens to something between anger and disgust. "Expect my children to support me? Expect my children to show a little bit of dignity in public? Especially my daughter."

Cade's grip on my arm loosens, only to wrap it around my shoulders to pull me close. "Like you're one to talk. Leave her alone."

"You'll regret this," I whisper. "If you didn't like what you saw today, I dare you to put me on stage in front of thousands of people. If you think you can order us around to be your puppets, think again. I might just be the nightmare that will bury you for good."

Dad steps forward so fast, I flinch. Cade holds me tighter and puts a hand to Dad's dress shirt and gives him a shove.

But Dad is mad.

No, Dad is livid.

He pushes Cade's arm away and sticks a pointed finger in my face. "You'll be there. You'll smile. You'll do as I say, and you'll handle him." Dad tips his head to Cade, talking about him as if he isn't standing here protecting me. "And I'm going to find out who that kid is who had his hands on you. He'll regret the day he ever looked at my daughter."

Dad turns on his Italian loafer and heads to the door. Without looking back, he barks one last order. "And answer your fucking phones when I call you. I pay for the damn things."

The conference room door slams.

Cade and I are alone.

But neither of us utters a word.

Cade wraps his other arm around me and holds me to his chest.

Honestly, I wish I knew how to be a loose cannon. I've been the good girl for far too long.

But I know this, we are not getting on that plane next Friday.

We won't step foot on that stage.

And we will never, ever again, support Cillian Collins in any way.

17

BE PREPARED TO BE KIDNAPPED

Levi

Me – *Seriously, are you okay?*
Me – *Practice is over. I can come and get you.*
Me – *Or I can ring the doorbell, like a normal fucking human, and Louise will just have to deal with it.*
Me – *Dammit. I'm this close to causing drama with Louise.*
Me – *Now I'm just pathetic. Please answer and let me know you're okay.*

I toss my cell next to me on the bed and continue tossing a basketball in the air and catching it.

Up, down.
Up, down.
Up, down.

"Hey."

I look up when a knock on my door pushes it all the way open. Emma is standing at the threshold with her arms crossed, hugging her middle, in her big-ass hoodie. "What's up?"

"What's up?" She frowns. "Like you and the new girl

weren't the talk of school before, now I heard you have a target on your back because her dad hates you."

I hold the ball and fold at the waist to sit up. "Where the hell did you hear that?"

She rolls her eyes so hard, I'm surprised she doesn't pull a muscle. "Only everyone is talking about it. Dude, look at anyone's social media from school. It's all over. When they zoom in, it's clear—Senator Daddy hates you."

I grab my cell and skim through apps I hardly ever open. When you hate pretty much everyone at school, avoiding them on social media is the number one goal right behind avoiding them in real life.

But fuck.

Emma's right.

"Told you," she quips. "What are you going to do?"

I check my text string with Carissa one more time. Nothing. Not even a fucking bubble. I flop back to my bed and start tossing the ball again. "I'm going to do exactly what I've been doing."

"What is it with her?" Emma asks.

"She's different. What is it with you?"

"Never mind," she mutters and reaches for my door.

"Hey." I sit up, and Emma turns to glare at me. "For real. What's up with you?"

She shakes her head. "I just hate high school, okay? Nothing is the same. It's stressful. Not everyone is like you, able to bury themselves in a textbook and ignore the world. And now it's worse than ever. Dad is meeting with my teachers and Ms. Lockhart. It's horrible."

"I told you I'd help you. It'll be better than Dad nosing around at school."

She swipes her face with her hand that's still buried in her sleeve. "I don't know. Maybe."

Levi

My cell vibrates next to me, and I unlock it faster than I ever have. I don't look up from the screen as I say, "The offer stands. Until then, have fun with everyone talking about you at parent-teacher conferences."

Emma groans and slams my door.

Carissa – I need to warn you, my dad is officially the biggest asshole on earth.

Carissa – All I want to do is run away.

Bubbles.

Me – What are you asking me, Carissa?

Carissa – IDK...

Me – Just a reminder, I'm eighteen and you're not. Me helping you run away would be kidnapping. Kidnapping = felony.

Carissa – I mean, it wouldn't be a felony if no one knew I ran away and you brought me back. You know, eventually.

Shit.

Why does this girl make me stupid?

Me – I'm bringing you back tonight.

Carissa – That sucks, but okay.

Me – Is Cade coming?

Carissa – I'll ask, but I doubt it. He deals with rage toward our dad differently than me.

Me – Okay. Prepare to be kidnapped.

Carissa

It's odd ... how another person can hold power over you.

How it just happens. Whether you want it to or not. And sometimes, despite how much you will it not to, that power is even stronger.

Only a few people in my life have ever held me in such a snare.

Three to be exact.

Cade, in the best way possible, is powerful because I'll do anything for him. Our connection makes me desperate to protect him from our peers, the public, the world.

Dad. Fucking Dad. The power he wields over me is strong enough to make me cower to his demands. It always has. I might talk a good game—I sure tried to today in the conference room—but I have no idea what to do about his campaign rally. Today was worse than normal, and I have no clue how I'll get out of it.

And then there's Levi.

He's a new development.

The power he has over me is unlike anything I've experienced.

I'd call it chemistry—but not the textbook kind. The nervous-butterfly kind that makes me want things I never have before.

The moment I climbed into his Jeep, he leveled those hazel eyes on me and asked, "How long do I have to keep you before it's an official kidnapping?" And we took off.

My lips couldn't move fast enough. I told him everything that happened in the conference room.

Everything.

And then I told him how, when we got home, Louise was equally flipping out about us making a public appearance with our dad. But she wasn't upset the way a rational mother should be when her daughter has been cheated on by her husband of almost twenty years.

No. She was ecstatic.

I'd go so far as to call her gleeful.

She droned on and on during dinner that this was our

chance to fix things, bring our parents back together, and move on.

Put it all behind us.

As if.

Levi listened to every drama-filled word I spewed. He didn't even bristle when I told him how Dad basically threatened him if he touched me again.

That made me wonder if he was a masochist or the bravest, most brazen man-boy on the planet to not give a shit about threats from Cillian Collins.

I decided to go with the latter.

Which is why the moment Levi threw the Jeep in park, I flung my seatbelt to the side, and I climbed over his console.

The pull.

The attraction.

The pure, unadulterated magnetism.

I was desperate to be close to him. To touch him. For him to touch me.

It's a different kind of power. One I'm more than willing to fall victim to whenever he'll allow it.

His hands wrap around my hips. His long, strong fingers dig into my flesh, while his fingertips tease my butt. I'm straddling him in the driver's seat, very differently than we were the last time we were here.

He holds me from him. My hips are in a vise, and he's not allowing me to … touch him.

Where I want to touch him. Press into him. Even through our clothes, I want to feel him. I can't stop thinking about it.

For days.

But he won't let me.

Besides my legs flanking his thighs and our locked lips, Levi is controlling me.

Power.

So much of it. But, in this case, he won't let me do what I want.

"Carissa." He breaks our kiss and my name is an exhale across my skin. He battles for restraint.

I just battle for him.

"Baby, stop."

Goosebumps prickle my skin, but it's not from my body heat mixing with the cold night. And certainly not from Levi trying to restrain me.

No one's ever called me *baby* before.

I lift my face far enough to look into his eyes through the moonlit, clear night.

His strong hold on my hips flex as he pulls in a deep breath. "You're upset. Doing anything while you're upset isn't good. I'm not going to let you."

I run my fingertips across his stubbled jaw. "I'm fine."

He narrows his eyes. "You're not fine."

"You don't know what fine looks like on me," I try. It might be a desperate move, but I am. I've been desperate since Christmas Day when my family blew up.

Levi shakes his head, and the smallest of smiles touches his lips.

That's when I lose one of his vise-like grips. His hand comes to my neck, and he pulls my mouth back to his for a kiss deeper and more searing than I've given him since I climbed over the console. His other hand splays low on my abs to keep me where I am.

I drink him in, and my butterflies soar.

I'm not the only desperate one.

The roots of my hair sting when he pulls my head back. "You're so not fine."

I don't have a chance to argue. He twists me in his arms, and I'm sideways in his lap with my cheek pressed to his pec.

I pull my head out of his hold and look up to him. "What are you doing?"

He swipes a hand down his face. "I'm saving my balls from bursting into a million pieces."

My eyes widen. I'm speechless.

"Yeah," he agrees with himself. "You're gonna do me in."

He reclines his seat all the way back, and I put a hand to his chest to lean up and look at him. "Is this because of what I told you about my father?"

He brushes the hair from my face, and his gaze follows the trail of his fingers for several beats. When he finally looks into my eyes, he admits, "No. It's not like I want a senator on my ass, but I really don't give a shit about him either. This is about everything else, and the list is long. It's about mistakes I've made in the past that I'll do everything in my power to not repeat. How we haven't talked about it, but it feels like this is all new for you. But in the end, I'm eighteen and you're not. I have a future that I don't want to fuck up. So I'm putting you first, my future a close second, and your dad at the very bottom of the list of things I give a fuck about."

My chest tightens, and I try to pull away. "What are you saying?"

He pulls me right back where I was, and this time drags my thigh over the very firm bulge in his pants. My breath hitches, and all my blood whooshes south.

He's hard. Oh my gosh, *it's* so hard.

I wanted him to be, so badly. I wanted to feel it—feel him—between my legs.

My thighs immediately tense as wetness pools in my panties.

He presses the inside of my thigh into his erection, rubbing it up and down against his length.

His eyes heat, and his voice drips with something I'm not familiar with.

Lust?

"I'm saying this is what you do to me—when I'm with you and when I think about you. When I'm not with you, I can't get you out of my head. So, yeah, Carissa, I feel like I'm in a constant state of blue balls when it comes to you. And since I've pretty much ignored anyone and anything for a long fucking time, I'm about to go crazy."

I'm not sure if I should be happy or embarrassed about that. I'm actually both, but I think happy wins.

"Don't smile at me like that," he growls.

I bite my lip, but it doesn't do a thing to erase the bliss coursing through me. "Sorry."

"For some reason, I don't think you are."

"You're right. I'm not."

His tongue sneaks out to wet his bottom lip right before he hauls me up his body.

And this time he doesn't restrain me.

He grips my bottom in both hands and pulls me to him.

Into him.

I gasp into his mouth, the sensation shoots to my core like a shock of electricity. "Levi."

"Damn, you're going to be the death of me. I'll die at the ripe age of eighteen," he growls before taking my mouth again.

He lifts his hips, grinding into me, meeting me as I do what I can only say feels right—shift up and down his erection.

Oh.

I do my best to pull in a deep breath, but it's never been this hard to breathe.

I keep moving, and Levi brings one hand to the back of my head and the other slides down between my legs from behind. I thought his grip on me was tight earlier when he was preventing me from doing what he's now guiding me to do.

"Does that feel good?"

I can't speak. My jaw goes slack as my brain tries to fight the unfamiliar feeling while my body searches for more.

"Carissa," he demands, and wraps my messy hair around his fist. "Answer me."

I nod once and rock again.

When Levi cups me between my legs and presses into my sex through my leggings, I groan.

"Fuck," Levi hisses. "Don't stop, baby. Do what feels good."

I tip my forehead to his, and we never lose eye contact. I finally manage a couple words. "I've never..."

"I know," he cuts me off. "We won't do anything else, not tonight. If I had more room, I'd flip you and make you come on my tongue."

My eyelids fall, picturing that in my head.

Imagining how that would feel.

"Next time," he promises, but his hand between my legs squeezes me tight, and he stops me from moving. "Baby?"

My eyes fly open, and my brows pinch.

"You ever had an orgasm before?"

I close my eyes again.

"Answer me," he demands, the tips of his fingers finding my clit and pressing in through my clothes.

My head spins, but I manage to shake my head.

A satisfied and sexy expression settles on his handsome face. "Good. Your first one is mine."

That's hot.

And embarrassing.

My head falls to his shoulder, or at least that's what I try for so I don't have to look him in the eyes. But he won't allow it. He pulls my hair, and I have no choice but to face him with all my inexperienced virginal anxiety.

His eyes sear into me, and they're so hot, I'm surprised I'm not branded. "You want to come?"

I try to breathe as I give him the truth through a whisper. "Yes. Please."

His gaze drops to my mouth before he nods and lifts his hips again. "Move, baby."

When he realizes I'm frozen with apprehension, he takes over.

He moves me.

Guides me.

Teaches me.

Levi, ever the tutor.

The feeling builds again ... one I want more of and one I am equally terrified of.

I can barely focus on the fact Levi's tone becomes strained. "Fuck, what I wouldn't do to feel this with nothing between us. Keep going. Come on my cock, Carissa. Fall apart in my arms."

His cock.

Oh my.

I rock, up and down his hard length, as I take in his face, his expression becoming more and more pained by the second. It's building. I'm not sure I could stop if I wanted to.

I lose all sense of timidity. All sense of who I'm expected to be.

I do what I want.

What feels good.

My hips move on his cock faster.

My eyes fall shut.

Stars.

It's all I see as my lungs beg for air.

Moans fill his Jeep, and I try to stop, but Levi isn't having it. He rocks me, up and down his cock, dragging it out longer and deeper, until I shatter at my core.

I throw my head back and press my sex into him, wanting more and needing it to stop all at the same time.

Levi stops, but he doesn't let me go. He holds me tight, every muscle in his body tense and taut. He lets go of my hair, and I fall to his chest—spent and gasping for air.

"That was..." I pant. "That was unreal."

Levi reminds me where I am and who owns my first orgasm ever, because his hand between my legs squeezes. "That was very fucking real, Carissa."

That's when I realize...

I lift my head and drag my tired eyes open. "Did you...?"

He gives his head a terse shake. "I'm not losing my load in my pants."

"But—"

"That doesn't mean I didn't enjoy the hell out of that. Watching you come will be burned on my brain forever. It'll be the only thing I think about when I take care of myself later."

"You-you will?"

"Nothing but you." He pulls me in for a searing kiss before pressing the side of my face to the center of his chest. "But we need to chill for a bit. There's no way I'll be able to drive home like this."

I feel and hear his heart race below me. And I feel the evidence of him needing to chill between my legs.

"Levi?" I call.

He still hasn't let go of me between my legs, but his other hand lands on my head. He sounds like he's concentrating when he answers. "Hmm?"

I bring my hand up to his biceps and give him a squeeze. "Thank you."

He exhales unnaturally fast. "Please and thank you. You are going to kill me."

I let my sated body sink into his and enjoy the feel of him.

No, I love the feel of him.

If I'm honest with myself, I'm becoming obsessed with the feel of him.

I think I'm just becoming obsessed with him.

Levi and me.

As long as I don't focus on my drama-filled family, I'll be good.

I mean, what else could go wrong?

18

SNAKE CHARMER

Levi

I grab my gym bag and jog down the stairs.

I'm almost out the door when Dad comes up from the basement. Sweat is dripping down his chest from working out.

For a dad, he's no slouch.

"Dad, I'm out."

He reaches in the fridge for a bottle of water. "What're your plans?"

There's no way I can tell him my plans include kidnapping my new girlfriend out of her grandmother's estate, introducing her to my favorite Thai food, and maybe giving her another orgasm, depending on where the night goes.

Dad is cool, but I don't think he'd be down for those plans.

"Headed to the gym with the guys, and then some of us are getting together at Jack's." Jack's mom is out of town, and he's throwing a party tonight. That'll cover my kidnapping.

I have to tell him where Jack lives since he's new to the

whole full-time parenting thing. I turn for the door but he stops me one more time. "Will Carissa be there?"

I turn back. "Yeah, she'll be there."

That makes me feel a little bit better about my lie.

He puts his hands on his hips and spears me with a glare before giving in and asking, "You need money?"

I shake my head. "I just got paid. I'm good."

"Home by midnight, bud."

We'll see about that. He'll give me extra time if I want it. "I know. See ya."

We move our separate ways, him to the stairs and me to the garage. I toss my gym bag in the back that doesn't have anything in it for the gym, and drive around the corner before I park. I hit go on Carissa's number.

She answers in two beats. "Um, hey."

She sounds off, and I don't bother with a greeting. "What's wrong?"

She says nothing, and if I couldn't hear her shuffling around, I'd think I lost her. "I don't think I can escape. At least not for a while."

Shit. "Why?"

"It turns out Louise has friends. I had no idea."

"She has people there?"

"Yes," she whispers and shuffles around some more. "And I guess they've been friends for so long, they know my mom. So we're supposed to, I don't know, be around. The whole thing is bullshit. Louise told us to be polite, but Mom is off having a breakdown, and we don't even know where she is. We're supposed to act like everything's great. It's miserable."

"How many people are there?"

"Four up-tight, crabby women in addition to Louise. No wonder they're friends."

I stare out at the street, lined with houses that are all as new as ours, but don't really see anything.

"Levi?"

I snap out of it. "I'm on my way."

"No!" she hisses. "I told you I can't leave right now. I'm expected to be present. Cade is miserable. They're all trying to get him to talk. This whole thing is stupid."

I throw my Jeep in drive. "No kidnapping tonight. I'm coming to the front door."

"What?" Her tone is higher than I've ever heard it. "You can't."

"Worst case scenario, Louise will tell me to leave. But I doubt she will."

"How do you know that? She's never said we could invite anyone here."

"Trust me, Carissa. I have a way with old people."

Carissa

CADE and I have been tormented for almost two hours.

Dinner.

Dessert.

Coffee.

And as if it couldn't get any worse...

Small talk.

Kill me now. Levi thought he might die with a set of blue balls last night, but I'll die having only experienced one orgasm. And I wasn't even naked for the event.

More importantly, Levi wasn't naked for it either. And I have a feeling that's something I need to experience in this lifetime.

Soon.

I'm not ready to die having only had one orgasm.

Don't get me wrong. It was amazing. Epic. And it was delivered by Levi Hollingsworth.

Okay, fine. It was a team effort. But Levi's a team player. He has the full-ride scholarship to prove it.

"Carissa!" Louise barks.

I snap out of my orgasmic daydream from last night. "Hmm?"

"Mrs. Sheffield asked you a question."

I look to the lady with blue hair. "Sorry. What?"

She takes a sip of her coffee held over a matching saucer with pink and yellow flowers. "Where do you want to go to college?"

My foot bounces in my black and white checkered sneaker. "Anywhere."

"Anywhere?"

"Yeah." It's been more than ten minutes since I snuck out of the room to take Levi's call. He should be here any minute to blow this party up and send Louise's head spinning in an out-of-control merry-go-round. "I don't care. As long as I'm out of high school, out of here, and on my own. The sooner the better."

"Carissa." Louise glares at me.

"And Cade, what are your plans after high school?" the blue-haired biddy asks in a slow drawl, as if my big brother has a difficult time processing words.

My foot stops bouncing. In fact, it lands on the floor with a harder thud than it should when I uncross my legs and lean forward in the stiff chair I've been forced to sit in way too long. "Cade is brilliant. Not only will he go to college, he'll probably be accepted to the Ivy League of his choice."

Cade's irritated glare turns to the biddy who just offended him and me. "MIT."

"Well." The biddy with blue hair flushes as she tries to backpedal that one. "I'm sure Mariann is very proud of you both."

That wasn't the first time one of the ladies spoke to Cade like that, and now I wonder what Louise told them. Between this Saturday night rave, waiting on Levi, and dealing with the condescending-geriatric crew, I've had it.

"She should be, but we don't know where she is." I sit back in my chair and cross my arms as Louise gapes at my words. "Grandmother won't tell us."

All nosy eyes turn to Louise.

She shakes her head, trying to act like it's normal for a mother to disappear and her almost adult children to not know where she is. "Mariann is taking some time. She'll be back, and everything will be back to normal." Louise throws her hand out to Cade and me, and keeps on like this isn't the enormous deal it is. "The children are flying back to Arizona this week to support Cillian. It's primary season, you know."

My head might explode.

I'm about to show my true colors and turn into the youngest biddy in the room, but I'm saved by the bell.

The doorbell.

Louise frowns. "Who could that be?"

I jump up and run out of the room calling, "I'll get it."

I'm through the hall and down the long entryway when I realize Cade is on my heels.

I pull open the massive door that's more than a century old.

Levi is standing there in a pair of sweatpants that hug him in all the right places, reminding me of what I'm missing out on right now because of this damn dinner party from hell. I never knew I'd want sweatpants for dessert, but here I am. I think I deserve Levi in gray sweatpants for having to listen to a red-haired biddy talk about her thyroid, blood-sugar levels, and cholesterol for most of dinner.

I drag my gawky stare up his long, muscled body to his arms which are crossed over a hoodie. When I finally get to his lips, they're turned up in a smirk, and I want to throw myself at him and beg him to kidnap me for the rest of time.

I state the obvious. "You're here."

"Why *are* you here?" Cade asks, because the answer to this is much less obvious.

"What's up?" Levi lifts his chin to Cade. "I figured if I want to see Carissa and hang out with you, it was time to rip off the bandage. This is easier."

"Easier than what?" Cade asks.

Levi hikes a sexy brow and drops his arms, walking through the door uninvited. "Every other way we've been doing it."

"Who are you?"

I turn to see Louise standing in the wide hall that runs from the front to the back of the house, stretching to the third-floor ceiling. It doesn't matter how long I'm here, the echoes still creep me out.

I'm about to open my mouth, but Levi proves he isn't always broody and intense. He apparently can be charming and charismatic when the situation demands it.

Cade and I part like the Red Sea as Levi strides forward. He holds out his hand to Louise. "Mrs. Boyette, it's a pleasure. Carissa and Cade have told me so much about you."

That's the truth.

Louise places four fingers in his hand for the most stupid, feminine shake in the history of time.

I try not to roll my eyes.

"Of course they did. And you are...?"

The guy who encouraged my orgasm and made me blush at the word *cock* bows his head like he's the main hero in a Regency romance novel who wears couture sweats. "Levi Hollingsworth. I'm a friend of your grandchildren."

"Well!" Louise exclaims on a huff with widened eyes that shift to me and Cade. "I didn't know you had any friends."

"They're quite popular," Levi adds.

Cade frowns. I do my best to bite back a smile and wonder if Levi is as good at creative writing as he is chemistry.

Louise's hands clasp at her chest. I haven't seen anything make her this happy since we landed in the commonwealth. "Popular? I had no idea!"

"Yes, ma'am. We eat lunch together every day. I thought I'd stop by to see if they wanted to go get some ice cream."

Louise beams.

I'm simply in awe.

"What a lovely young man, you are. I have ice cream. And pie. Would you like a piece of pie?"

No.

No, no, no, no!

Levi smiles like nothing could make him happier. "Thank you. I love pie."

"Follow me. You can meet my friends from our local garden society."

Levi gives his head a shake. "Horticulture is a dying art. We all need to do better."

Louise's shoulders rise and fall with a sigh so content, I wonder if she'll invite Levi to live with us. I can think of worse things, but I'd never wish that on him. Keeping up this dog and pony show has to be exhausting.

"Follow me." Louise beams. "I'll warm your pie and serve it à la mode."

Levi lays it on thick. "That would be wonderful. I appreciate you."

"Well!" Louise exclaims again. "I do hope some of your manners rub off onto my grandchildren."

With a pep in her step I've never seen, Louise disappears around the corner.

"Who the hell are you?" Cade asks with the same frown plastered to his face that's been there since I opened the door for Levi. Cade shakes his head and returns to the formal living room, leaving me alone with Levi.

He turns to me in his perfect sweatpants. "Told you I was good with old people."

I look up at him and fall a little bit farther into the black hole that is Levi Hollingsworth. "You're crazy."

"But I'm here." He takes a step closer to me. "And I bet I can come back anytime I want."

I lower my voice. "Maybe your good manners will rub off on me."

He takes a step closer, though it's a small one. That's all it takes to plaster his front to mine. His hand wraps around my waist pulling me tight to him before it drops lower to my butt.

My hands land on his chest as his fingers slide between my legs for a delicious grope. His lips come to my ear where his tongue sneaks out for a taste of my skin there. His words are hot on my skin. "I was hoping to rub off on you in a different way tonight, but I don't see anything in my future besides pie."

I tip my head, and he takes advantage, brave and cocky with the horticultural club waiting for us in the next room. His lips hit the skin below my ear where they give me a quick suck. I try to catch my breath. "You're like a snake charmer with Louise."

His hand between my legs dip farther, and he presses his fingertips into my sex through my leggings. "It's a means to an end. I'd rather be charming you."

"Carissa! Pie is served!"

Levi doesn't move and only presses into me farther. I turn my head to look at him. "This is dangerous."

His lips land on the corner of my mouth. "Seems like I'm willing to push boundaries for you—boundaries I haven't stepped close to in a long time."

"I'm not sure what that says about me," I admit.

"It says I'm willing to eat pie à la mode when I'm knee deep in training and haven't had dessert since Christmas. It also means I'm going to have to pull some botany science vocab out of my ass so I can make small talk with the garden society just to be close to you."

I want to climb him like a tree and wrap myself around him until the end of time. "That's like sexy talk to me since I'm forced to live with Louise."

He bumps the tip of my nose with his. "I'm here for you."

"Carissa!" Louise yells again.

I get one more squeeze between the legs before he lets me go and puts a hand at the small of my back. "Lead the way to my pie."

I wrap my arms around my chest for the sole fact my nipples are threatening to cut through my shirt.

And I lead the way to the garden society and more snake charming.

19

RANDOM MY ASS

Levi

I slam my bedroom door and hurl my backpack across the room.

Two years. Two fucking years. Have I not done my time?

I've barely stepped out among the living for a minute, and this happens?

Drugs. Planted in my locker.

Pills, weed, and syringes.

They were all found during a random drug sweep. But there are two facts that made today more fucked up than anything.

One, the drugs aren't mine.

Not. Fucking. Mine.

And two, they were planted in my locker on the same day a *random* drug sweep was scheduled.

Random, my ass.

I'm a senior and can count on one hand how many

random drug sweeps there have been since my freshman year, which makes today's not fucking random at all.

A lot has happened over the last couple days. Some good. Some unbelievable. And others that are about as bad as it gets.

One thing I never thought I'd do is be an honorary member of the garden society, but I am. I killed it Saturday night. They fucking loved me, and I won myself a place at Louise's dinner table anytime I want.

I was riding the high from the thought of seeing Carissa anytime I wanted to.

When I got home, Emma cornered me and flipped the fuck out. Apparently Dad is into our school counselor—in a big way from what she described.

Don't get me wrong. Ms. Lockhart is cool. Some kids at school—mainly Jack—think she's the queen MILF, and when she walks by, he won't stop talking about her ass.

But she's a widow with two little kids. Though I heard she and her dead husband were on the outs when he bit it. Everyone knows this.

Everyone but my dad.

Emma described how he dragged her to Ms. Lockhart's house unannounced, took her and her kids to dinner, and hung out with some goats afterwards.

Emma said she had to school our dad on the way home about Ms. Lockhart's background.

Just when you think your single dad might be cool as shit, he goes and makes a fool of himself with your hot high school counselor. But if he did hook up with Ms. Lockhart, good for him. He's never been with anyone—that we know of—since our parents divorced when we were little. Not in front of us, anyway.

And Jack's not wrong. Ms. Lockhart is hot ... for

someone her age.

Then, today, to top off my drama-filled life, the woman my dad is into dragged me out of class during the drug sweep.

A drug dog hit my fucking locker.

I thought I was going to throw my chair through the conference room window while I was being interrogated by the police, the principal, and my dad while the whole thing was going down.

I'm no druggie and never have been. Dad was a cop before he quit to contract with the CIA. He's drilled the *Just Say No* shit down our throats for as long as I can remember. Then there's the fact Mom hovers over us so close, we're constantly tangled up in her maternal propellers. If there were any reason not to dabble in the illegal shit, keeping our parents off our backs is a decent one. Of course, followed by not losing my scholarship to Johns Hopkins.

Plus, that shit'll make you stupid.

Today started out as a shock. Then it sunk in.

The anger ... it settled in my bones like an unwelcome virus.

In the end, it was Ms. Lockhart who got me off the hook. She made them pull the surveillance video that runs constantly in the halls. Someone swiped the master key and dumped the drugs in my locker—the evidence was clear as day.

To top it off, Emma's childhood friend—who turned into the preeminent mean girl when she got to high school—stood as a lookout.

What the fuck did I do to either of them?

Nothing, that's what.

Not a damn thing.

Dad pulled me from school to settle my ass down. Then

I went back for practice and took my aggressions out on the field.

I went hard and pissed some people off in the process.

I checked someone. They checked back.

I hit hard. They hit back.

They might've tried to take me down, but I'm the biggest and strongest on the field. Had it been a game, I would've spent a considerable amount of time in the penalty box.

My phone has been blowing up since Ms. Lockhart pulled me out of AP stat. If anyone knows how fast rumors can spread, it's me. I've ignored every single one, but I'm going to have to face it since there's only one person I want to talk to.

I unlock my phone and scroll until I get to our thread.

Carissa – Um, are you okay?

Carissa – I'm hearing things. The rumor is a dog hit your locker. I didn't believe it, but Mason knows someone who's in stats with you. What happened?

Carissa – You're not answering...

Carissa – Now I'm freaking out.

Carissa – Shit. Text me.

Carissa – Mason just told me some other guy was arrested, and you're MIA.

Carissa – Louise just asked if you were coming for dinner. I did not tell her about the drugs in your locker... Seriously, CALL ME.

Carissa – It's Monday, and we're supposed to study. There's no way I'll be able to focus until I hear from you.

I don't respond.

I go straight to my bathroom and strip off my sweaty, dirty practice uniform. If only the hot water could wash away my wrath. Hell, I don't even know who to direct it at.

I don't do what's become a habit since I met Carissa.

Despite being hard as a rock, I don't take my dick in my hand with thoughts of her wrapped around me. Grinding down on me. Her pants. Her moans. Fucking daydreaming of that shit happening with nothing between us.

That can't happen. Not yet. I'm not taking any more chances.

But that doesn't mean I don't want to see her.

And that can't happen soon enough.

Carissa

I'M NOT sure if I'm relieved or more worried than ever.

Levi didn't call. Nor did he text.

But he showed up. If he keeps doing this, I might become in tune with the doorbell like Pavlov's Dog. If it rings and Levi isn't on the other side from now on, I might fall to my knees and weep.

But it seems I'm not the only one obsessed with the man-boy from school. Without asking if he wanted any, Louise fed him left-over meatloaf, mashed potatoes, mushy green beans, and has refilled his water so many times, it's as if she's looking for a tip.

He ate everything but the green beans, and I'm pretty sure he's downed a half-gallon so far.

She finally left us alone, but it took me complaining that I couldn't concentrate while she was hovering.

Now we're sitting at the dining room table—Cade, Levi, and me—text books open, papers strewn, and a stack of note cards that Levi found time to make sit in a pile in front of me.

But no one has studied. I'm sitting here, staring at him,

and can't believe what he just told Cade and me.

"Who would've done that to you?" I whisper.

"Are you dense?" Cade asks, in the same tone he'd ask if I could pass the salt.

My eyes widen when I turn to my brother. "There's no way."

"After what happened Friday? You can't deny it's a possibility," Cade says.

"Wait." Levi's hand lands on my thigh and squeezes to get my attention. "You think your dad did this?"

"He threatened to. And he doesn't make empty threats. Why wouldn't he be your main suspect?" Cade says.

Levi drags a hand down his face. "Great."

Panic bubbles within me like lava, burning me from the inside out. "I'm sorry. I don't know what to say—"

He shakes his head and claims my hand. "It's not your fault. And it's fine now. I had no idea I needed to watch my back, but from now on, I will."

"But you shouldn't have to, not because of me—"

"I have an idea," Cade interrupts.

We both turn to him. "What?"

"Dad can't do anything on his own. He orders everyone around him to do his dirty work." Cade focuses on me. "Maybe we should find out once and for all."

"How are we supposed to do that?" I ask.

A slow smile spreads over Cade's face. "I'll hack him."

My expression couldn't be more opposite of my brother's when I hiss, "No! He's a United States Senator with top-level security clearance. Even if you are good enough to do it, you'll get in so much trouble if they catch you."

Levi doesn't share my freak out. He's just impressed. "You can do that?"

"Yes." Cade turns his smile on me. "I'm not an idiot. I'm

not going to hack into his official shit. He wouldn't be stupid enough to run his shady antics from there anyway. I'm going to sneak into his private laptop. Maybe his personal cell. If he had anything to do with today, it'll be there."

I sit back in my seat to mull it over. "I don't know..."

"Hell, yeah. Do it," Levi says. I turn my glare on him. "As long as he doesn't get in trouble, right? But he sounds pretty sure of himself. You said he was brilliant. Let him do his thing."

"Who knows what we'll find? We might even find out where Mom is," Cade adds.

"I didn't think about that," I admit.

"You know what? I'll ask my dad to look into your mom. He..." Levi pauses before it seems like he chooses his words carefully. "Finds people for a living."

"He's a bounty hunter?" Cade asks.

"Sort of, but not really. It doesn't matter. I'll ask him, and you do your thing. Together, we might solve all our mysteries."

Cade flips his notebook shut and collects his things. "I'll get started. I might be good but I've never done anything this illegal before."

Levi smirks. "Are there different levels of illegal when it comes to hacking?"

"Cade, I don't think this is a good—" I call for him as he heads out of the dining room.

My brother turns back one more time. "This is something I can do, Rissa. It's not something you need to handle for me. Or handle me, so stop trying. I've had enough of Dad. I'm doing this."

With that, he turns and leaves. I can't look away from the hall he just disappeared into. I'm alone with Levi and my feelings.

"Hey," Levi calls for me.

I turn my empty gaze to his hazel eyes. His gold flecks are warm.

"You okay?"

"Do I really handle him?"

"I don't know." Levi shrugs. "Maybe?"

"I thought I was helping him." My throat clogs, and it's hard to swallow. "I've never wanted to do anything other than protect him."

Levi reaches for my hand and turns it in his. "I'm sure he knows that."

"I just don't want anything to happen to him. Or for him to get in trouble." I pull in a breath. "But if my dad was the one to orchestrate today and tried to frame you…"

Levi looks around the room and then gives my arm a yank. Before I know it, I'm up, pulled between his spread legs, and perched on his thick thigh. "I'm not going to lie, today sucked. I'm on someone's radar, and I don't know why. My dad is as angry as me or more, if that's possible. We'll figure it out. I can't lie, I'm grateful for Cade. I want to know what I'm dealing with."

I hope Louise screams for me before coming in, because I frame his square jaw in my hands, but he doesn't let me make the first move.

He pulls my lips to his.

The thrill of him…

I relish in it as it warms me from the inside out.

If my dad tried to hurt him in any way … I don't know what I'll do.

What I do know, I won't stand by and let Cillian Collins railroad me like he always does. Not this time.

I might've just found the first and only reason I'd be willing to stand up to my father.

20

BIG, FAT, BURNING LAVA PIT OF DRAMA

Carissa

I used to despise lunch.
There's nothing more telling about where the social lines are drawn than a lunchroom in high schools across America.

I lived in Arizona my whole life. I went to school with the same kids from preschool up until we were dragged away to live with Louise.

Am I popular there?

Maybe.

I mean, I guess I was, but it's also because of who I am in Arizona. Cade has friends there, even though his circle is small. Very small. I didn't eat lunch with him every day. But on the off day I noticed he was alone, I'd ditched everyone else to be with my brother. We didn't even have to talk. I guess it's the twin thing. We've never needed to.

And being Cillian Collins' children, we've learned that popularity isn't something to strive for.

It seems popularity and infamy tend to go hand in hand.

And being the latter just because you're the child of a senator isn't fun.

I'll take being a nobody any day over either.

But being the sole focus of Levi Hollingsworth, especially when his last focus was years ago and ended in a teenage soap opera, epic enough for a thespian award, leaves me straddling the line of popular and infamous.

And *sole focus* is an understatement. When we're alone, he can't not touch me. When we're not alone, he still finds a way to touch me.

Like now.

We're back to how it all started. His leg is entwined with mine, and his eyes rarely move from me.

And most eyes in the lunchroom are focused on him as he focuses on me. Specifically, Levi's last drama.

Isla Perry.

Which makes me feel completely infamous and not at all popular.

"She won't stop staring," I whisper.

"Everyone is staring, but I bet it has more to do with my shit from yesterday," Levi states.

"I'm sure that's true for most everyone else in here, but not her," I refute. "This is different."

"I'd say we could get a study room in the library, but the rest of us need to eat, and they basically frisk you for food in there. Ignore her."

I stare down at my fingers, because if I look up at him, she's just beyond him in my direct sight. "It's impossible."

Mason leans forward in his seat across the table next to Cade. "I think Isla is trying to murder you with the daggers she's shooting our way. I'm worried for all of us."

Levi stiffens, and his expression goes hard. Before I can say anything else, he untangles our legs, grabs my hand, and pulls me to meet him in a standing position. Then he grips me low on my hips and turns one-hundred-and-eighty degrees, taking me with him.

"What are you doing?" I hiss.

"Sit," he demands, pushing my booty in the still-warm chair from his large frame. I have to right myself to catch my balance when he takes the seat he pulled me from and tangles our legs together again. When I look up, it's his turn to glare over my shoulder. "There. I dare her to fucking stare at me."

"Holy—" I start.

Mason interrupts me. "That did it. She's not staring anymore. She's stalking out of the lunchroom."

Levi tries to reassure me I'm not being thrown into a big, fat, burning lava pit of drama. "Don't worry."

"You say that, but she still does that every chance she gets," I say.

Levi shrugs. "She needs to get a life."

"Dude, that was badass." I look up, and Jack is rounding the end of the table we've made ours. He yanks out a chair, sits, and turns his wolfish grin on me. "You just keep stirring up the shit, and I can't love it more." He leans back and props an ankle on the table before crossing his other over the top. "I'm really pulling for you youngins. Especially you, bro. You deserve your HEA."

I bite back my smile, and Levi rolls his eyes.

"Whadoya know?" Jack asks the table at large.

"I'm getting ready to hatch a new brood of chickens. They're in the incubator," Mason explains.

"Cool," Jack says, and shockingly he sounds like he really means it. "Whatcha working on over there, Cade?"

Mason answers for Cade. "Research." I turn my sights on my freshman friend and give him a shake of my head, but he's too focused on the charismatic senior. "He's stumped and can't break through the last firewall of their dad's—"

"Whoa-whoa-whoa," Levi interrupts before he looks to Jack whose brows are raised after the words *breaking through a firewall* were spilled. "That's not what he meant. It's a project he's working on. That's all."

Jack tips his head. "Why do I feel like the chump at the table who was left out of a secret?"

Levi shakes his head, but it's Mason who mutters, "Sorry. I thought he was in the group."

This time Jack crosses his arms and his happy-go-lucky persona takes a donkey ride to the bottom of the Grand Canyon. "There's a group, and I wasn't invited?"

Levi exhales.

I shake my head, "No, it's nothing—"

"Yeah," Mason refutes my answer. "A group. Like homies."

"Well. Fuck me." Jack drops his arms, frustrated. But the thing is, I don't think he's making fun of Mason. That would piss me off. I think he genuinely feels left out. "I want to be a homie too."

"I might've figured it out. I think I know what I was doing wrong," Cade mutters to himself. He looks up and glances around the table. He was so focused, he wasn't paying any attention to what's going on. "What?"

"What?" Jack boomerangs. "You're hacking your dad?"

"Of course not." I untangle my leg from Levi's and stand, grabbing my bag as I do. "I'm going to get to chem early. You know, suck up while I can."

Levi stands. "I'll walk you."

"Romantic as fuck." Jack gives Levi a fist bump. "Don't let anyone burn a hole in her head from glaring at her. She needs all her brain cells."

I look to Cade and Mason. "See you later."

Levi doesn't give them a chance to say anything and wraps an arm around my neck. Levi turns me and presses his lips to my hair the moment we're away from the masses. "Between my practice and Louise watching over us like a hawk, I need to kidnap you again."

He claims my hand, and I glance up as we walk. "I can sneak out whenever I want. You're the one who lives in a technological fortress."

He sighs. "I know. I can disable the whole thing, but there's no way I can do it in the middle of the night without my dad knowing. And I can't do anything tonight after practice. If you can believe it, I have to go to dinner at Ms. Lockhart's house. Dad told me this morning."

I stop in my tracks. Levi told me his dad took her to dinner this weekend. "Your dad is really hooking up with your counselor?"

"I guess." He gives me a little tug, and we're on our way again, but not to the science wing. He turns toward the gym. "All I know is there's a meeting of the families at her house tonight, and I'm expected to be there. He informed Emma and me on our way out the door this morning."

"Where are we going?" I didn't really want to be early to chemistry, but I did want to get out of the lunchroom.

"Here." Levi reaches for the knob of a supply closet.

He turns to me and smiles when it clicks under this touch. The next thing I know, we're enclosed in a small room that smells like high school. Balls and equipment from every sport line the walls from floor to ceiling. The scent of must, sweat, and rubber are thick, but what's thicker are Levi's arms when they pull me to him.

"Fuck, I've missed you," he growls. Our backpacks hit the dusty floor at the same moment his lips land on mine.

I've seen him almost every day, but not like this. His hand slides down my side until it lands on my butt, pulling me to him. His hips pin me to the metal door, pressing into my lower tummy. My hands slide up his sides and every muscle in his back tenses under my touch.

Wetness pools between my legs, and I'm one-hundred percent sure this will not be good for my chemistry grade. There's no way I'll be able to focus on Mr. Stance while recovering from this.

I wonder if he feels the same way, because he tips his forehead to mine as his breath caresses my face. "The bell will ring any minute. I'm not sure if I'll be able to get out tonight after this dinner thing. My dad was out late last night, but I'm going to talk to him about your mom. See what he can find out."

Desperate to steal every last moment with him, I lift to my toes for one more connection, because it feels like the best gift anyone could give me right now. Levi is the only good thing that's happened to me since I left Arizona. "Thank you."

He leans down to take my mouth once more as the bell rings, indicating the end of lunch.

"Shit," he mutters against my lips. "I'll walk you to class. If I can't make tonight happen, then tomorrow. I'll pick you up for a study session." A small smile forms on his full lips. "And other stuff."

He bends to pick up our backpacks and I reach for the door. There are a few people in the hall, but Levi doesn't care and grabs my hand. My phone is going crazy with notifications all of a sudden. Levi pulls his out of his pocket at the same time.

"You've got to be kidding me," he mutters.

"What?" We get to my class, and I stop to dig my phone out of my pocket. I've got a gillion texts on one text thread.

"Looks like you've officially been baptized by Jack Hale. He has a way, and you can't deny he's likable and loyal as hell." He leans in and his lips brush my ear. "Tomorrow night."

And with a heated look that says a million words, he leaves me.

I take a seat near the back. No matter how much I'm struggling in this class, I have no desire to be anywhere close enough to smell Mr. Stance. I open my texts.

Wow.

Levi was right. I've got a million texts and most of them are from Jack, who I haven't given my number to.

Not only that, Jack Hale started a chat group between Cade, Mason, Levi, and me.

He named it *The Homies*.

Jack – Exciting times. Senators, planted drugs, Louise, and a new brood of chicks. I've always got my boy's back. Levi knows I'll do anything to take down Ursula, the queen sea monster. Thanks for the invite. Homies for life.

Homies for life?

"Ms. Collins, do you need to deposit your phone into cell phone jail?"

My head pops up and I slip my cell under my desk. "Sorry."

Mr. Stance glares at me.

At least he's out of smelling distance.

Levi

It's late. Emma and I left Ms. Lockhart's house hours ago.

I feel like the roles are reversed. I've never seen my dad like this. Ever. We were like a big fucking Brady Bunch around the dinner table. Me and Emma, Ms. Lockhart's two little kids, and our single parents. The sexual tension between my father and my school counselor was off the charts.

I don't know if I'm happy for him or want to throw up. What I do know is when Jack finds out, he's going to be jealous as hell.

Because not only is my dad gone for her, I'm pretty sure she's into him.

She put her kids to bed before we left. That was hours ago. I'm happy for him, but he told me to stay with Emma since she's having a mid-teen crisis, and he insists on watching her like a hawk.

I could've kidnapped my own obsession tonight. Who knew when I finally found someone I wanted to be with, my father and I would be competing for time with our new girlfriends.

If it's possible, Emma is more withdrawn and ghostlike than ever. I tried again on the drive home to get her to talk to me, to pry it out of her. After hours of texts and FaceTimes with Carissa, it occurred to me that Emma might be acting this way because Mom moved. I've got one foot out the door, but she's only fifteen.

When this thought knocked me over the head on the way home, I wondered if this is how Jack's brain works since he's apparently emotionally in touch with females in general, while I've cut them off for two years.

So I asked her.

And by her reaction, I'm either so far off the mark it's not funny, or I hit it on the head. There is no in between.

Levi

Emma flipped the fuck out again. My Jeep was barely in the garage when she jumped out and slammed my door. I haven't seen her since.

I can't believe it's come to this, but I might need help from Jack.

Either that, or I need to start watching the Hallmark Channel.

And I'd rather gouge my eyeballs out with an ice pick than have to sit through that shit.

That reminds me that I might've given Carissa her first orgasm, but I have no clue what she likes when it comes to mindless TV.

I guess I need to figure that out. That seems like something an emotionally-connected, touchy-feely guy would do.

My thoughts are interrupted by the garage door. Dad's home.

I jump off my bed and jog down the stairs. He's dumping his keys and phone on the island and shrugging off his jacket.

"It's after midnight," I say.

He smirks, and I do everything I can to not focus on his rumpled shirt. I put that out of my mind because when I come home looking the same way, I certainly don't want to be called out on it.

He crosses his arms and leans a hip into the counter. "I didn't realize I had a curfew."

"I've just been waiting to talk to you, that's all."

He lifts his chin. "What's up?"

I get right down to it, since I have no desire to talk about him and my counselor. "I need you to find someone."

Whatever easy and happy expression he had on his face when he walked in is gone. "Who do you need to find?"

"Carissa's mom."

His eyes narrow. He also says nothing.

"Mariann Collins," I elaborate.

"I know who her mom is, Levi. She was front and center in most of the documents I got when I did a background on her husband."

"Carissa doesn't know where she is."

Dad frowns. "What do you mean?"

"Mariann Collins dropped Carissa and Cade off to stay with their irritable grandmother and they haven't seen or heard from their mom since. She told them she was checking herself into a facility. Their grandmother won't give them updates, their asshole dad won't tell them shit, and they're worried."

"And you want to wade into her family drama?"

I stuff my hands in my pockets. "No. But Carissa's upset. Her brother stresses over it. If I can help, I want to."

"You want to help," he echoes.

I take a step back. "Look, her family is messed up, and she hasn't seen her mom since New Year's Day. If I can make her feel better I want to. But if you don't want to mess with it, just say so."

Dad shakes his head and mutters, "I guess I can't talk. I'm pretty sure I just signed myself up to shovel goat and donkey shit."

My frown deepens. "What the fuck?"

"Watch your language," he says, but his heart isn't in it. He turns to look out the windows into the black night. "Seems you haven't fallen far from the tree. I can't fault you for that."

This is dragging on forever, and I have to lift before school tomorrow. "So?"

He pulls in a deep breath and looks back to me. "I'll see what I can do. I'll nose around myself and call Carson."

I give him a chin lift. "With the CIA at my back, I'll prove to her she chose well."

Dad smirks. "I'll work on it tomorrow morning."

"Good luck with shoveling all the shit."

He waves me off. "Goodnight. Love you, bud."

I back myself out of the room and try to keep the smile off my face. "I'll still love you when you smell like donkey shit since you're going ape shit over my counselor."

He picks up a kitchen towel and snaps me with it. "Get out of here."

I take the stairs two at a time, and despite how my week started with someone planting drugs in my locker, I'm looking forward to school tomorrow.

21

FUCK OVER LEVI HOLLINGSWORTH

Carissa

I barely get the back door open, and he slips through. I mentally give Chuck a high five for keeping Louise's home a well-oiled machine. Who knows how old this door is, but it's as quiet as a mouse coming out of the woodwork for crumbs in the middle of the night.

And it's practically the middle of the night.

But Levi is no mouse.

When his body hits mine, he's hungry for more than crumbs. His energy seeping through me is new, electric, and red hot.

He just left me an hour ago. I've hit the Levi jackpot tonight. It's Wednesday, and Levi was here all evening to study. But that also meant Louise hovering, serving cookies and lemonade, and creeping in the corner like it was nineteen fifty and not the twenty-first century.

I wonder if she did this to my mother.

Honestly, I wonder if she just does this because of Levi, the snake charmer. Who wouldn't want to be around him?

We're in Louise's potting shed off the back of her house. The hours sitting next to each other as Levi quizzed me on the nuclear and electromagnetic energy at Louise's dining table only created a different kind of energy. It built and festered and simmered below the surface. When he said goodbye to me an hour ago without a touch, I thought I might come undone.

The door barely shut on his muscled back and beautiful behind when I texted him and told him to come back in an hour.

I didn't have to beg.

"Baby." He breaks our searing kiss and the whispered word against my lips sinks into my bones. "Are you sure Louise sleeps like the dead?"

I nod against his lips. "I bang around at night and she doesn't budge."

That's all the convincing he needs. His hand snakes up the back of my shirt, hot on my skin. When he teases the side of my breast, I sink into his chest. He turns us, and my back hits the bench, causing the stacked pots that are being stored for the winter to rattle.

The quiet noise is shrill through the dark, quiet night, causing us to freeze. His hand flexes on me, but doesn't move.

Until it does.

His thumb.

A firm swipe over my nipple.

I tremble.

Through the room lit only by the moon, Levi's eyes darken, and my body heats.

"This is pure, fucking torture," he whispers. "I've never wanted to be with anyone more. And I don't only mean like this." He gives my nipple another swipe, but this time adds a circle. The tips of my fingers press into his firm muscles, and I wish I could glue myself to him. He keeps whispering. "I mean in any way. When I'm not with you, you're all I think about. I've never been desperate for anyone or anything. I don't know what to do with myself."

"There was nothing worse than having to pack up and leave Phoenix. That killed me—not just leaving my home and my friends and my life there, but knowing when we returned, it would never be the same again because of what my dad did. Virginia held nothing but resentment for me. Every waking minute is a reminder of what happened. But now, I'm dreading the moment I have to leave on Friday. What will happen when I have to leave for good?"

"I can't think about that. I feel like a selfish asshole, because right now, I think I'd move heaven and earth to keep you here. It makes me crazy that you're going back for even one day." He lifts me until my bottom hits the top of the bench, pulls my legs wide, and fits himself to me. Then he drags me forward until my core hits his abs. His hands sneak up my sides again, taking my T-shirt with them. The hem catches below my breasts, and the chill of the space mixed with his hot touch sends goosebumps up my spine. "We need to find a warmer room."

I wrap my legs around his waist and hold him to me. I love him between my legs. The feel of him, strong and warm, makes me greedy when it comes to him touching me.

I want things. I want more. And I've never, ever thought about more with anyone.

"Take your shoes off," I say between kisses. "Bring them with you and come to my room."

He pulls back and his hands drop to the tops of my thighs. "You sure? Louise might sleep like the dead, but what about Cade?"

"Cade has thrown himself into hacker mode. We share a bathroom, but I can lock my door. I haven't even heard or seen him since you left the first time. He might be asleep. As long as we don't have a rave, we'll be fine. Plus, Cade likes you."

He narrows his eyes. "There's likes me and then there's finding me in his twin sister's bedroom. Those are two very different things, Carissa. I have a sister. I know."

I do my best to be provocative. Sexy. Tempting. Even though I'm none of those things.

At first Levi was a distraction from the hell of Virginia.

But now he's so much more.

I'm desperate for him.

He's a lifeline.

I press my lips to his jaw and press my sex into his abs, remembering my orgasm that resulted from being in this exact position.

Well, just a little lower down his body.

When his cock was fit to me perfectly. Where I loved it.

And ever since, I've daydreamed about it ... in the flesh.

I start to rub myself against him, when we're interrupted.

Tap-tap.

I yelp.

And the only reason I don't jump out of my skin is because Levi's touch on me changes. His arms cage me, one hand lands on my head and the other on my bottom. I'm pulled off the table and his entire body tenses against mine.

"What the fuck?" Levi hisses.

Tap-tap.

Tappity-tap-tap.

I turn in his arms and jerk again when I see two faces in the window. One is mortified, and the other is sporting a grin bigger than the waning moon hanging in the sky.

Levi doesn't put me down and growls under his breath, "What are you doing here?"

Jack moves, grabbing Mason by the sleeve, and pulls him to the glass door where Jack points to the knob.

I release my hold on Levi and try to calm my nerves as I slide down his body. Levi goes to the door and yanks it open and repeats, "What the hell are you doing here?"

Jack crosses his arms and looks between Levi and me. When he speaks, he doesn't lower his voice one tiny bit. "I thought I was coming to be moral support for a hacker, but it turns out I'm here to be a chaperone."

Levi pushes me behind him and gives Jack a shove in the shoulder. "Lower your voice."

"Cade texted us in the Homies chat." Mason whispers. "You didn't see it?"

Jack does not lower his voice and motions to Levi and me but looks down at Mason. "Young Skywalker, do these lovebirds look like they notice anything in the world besides each other? They didn't even hear us walking up, and I'm pretty sure I stepped on every dead leaf and fallen stick in northern Virginia dragging my ass across acres of land." Jack looks to me. "I feel like I'm on a field trip to a civil war battlefield. Please tell me this place is haunted, Carissa. That'll just elevate the night to a level of epic I've not yet experienced in my short lifetime."

I ignore all of what he just said and move to Levi's side. "Cade asked you to come here?"

Mason winces, but it's Jack who speaks for the duo. "Yes. After we invited ourselves."

Levi wraps an arm around me, and I can feel the irritation rolling off him in spades. "You're a fucking idiot. You're going to get us caught."

Jack reaches out and gives Levi's shoulder a squeeze.

"Blinded by love. It's okay ... I'll look out for you from here on out." Jack turns to me. "Lead us to the hacker."

Mason's face lights up with excitement.

Jack has never looked more pleased with himself, and that's saying something.

And Levi...

I wonder if Levi was this angry when the dogs hit the planted drugs in his locker.

This is crazy.

Levi

I'M NOT sure how I thought this would play out, but this isn't it.

When Carissa told me to come back in an hour and meet her in the potting shed off the back of the estate, I knew I'd have to control myself. Willpower was going to need a new definition in the dictionary after tonight.

Or so I thought.

I knew I was going to have to control it, but this isn't what I intended. I could've cock blocked myself just fine.

At least, I think I could've.

And I knew the *Homie* text thread was going crazy, but I muted those notifications about five minutes after Jack created it.

Cade announced to the group he was on the verge of sliding his way into his own father's hard drive. That was two hours ago. I had to text Dad and tell him I was staying the night at Jack's house to hit the gym together in the morning and hope he trusts me like I think he does, because I know he can track me anytime he wants. I think he's too obsessed about Emma, and now my counselor, to worry about me.

Carissa talks about how smart Cade is. I've always taken her word for it. But being on the verge of breaking into the private files of a U.S. senator started over two hours ago.

Mason is asleep on Cade's bedroom floor.

Jack is pacing while squeezing a stress ball he found in the corner and has been since we got here.

I'm sprawled on the floor, shoulders to the foot of Cade's bed.

Carissa's head is on my thigh, and I'm doing what has become one of my favorite pastimes – touching her. But since we're with the fucking Homies, I'm only running my fingers through her hair.

And Cade is typing away on his computer as if none of us are here. My grades are perfect, and valedictorian or not, I wish I had his kind of focus.

It's almost three in the morning. I'm not sure how much longer he can be on the verge of success when we'll be fighting the sunrise and Louise waking up.

That's when it happens.

The clicking of the keyboard comes to a halt.

"Holy shit," Cade hisses.

Jack stops pacing.

Carissa's head pops up.

My hand drops from her hair. "What happened?"

Cade doesn't answer. The tips of his fingers hover over the keyboard and he stares at his screen.

Carissa pushes to her ass. "Cade. What is it?"

Cade turns slowly in his chair, but only has eyes for his twin. "I'm in."

Carissa scurries to her feet. I follow.

Jack kicks Mason in the ass. "Wake up, my Jedi in training. We broke into Darth Vader's Death Star."

Mason looks confused for about two seconds before joining us where we stand behind Cade.

"What do you see?" Carissa asks.

As if his keyboard might singe his fingerprints off, Cade hesitates before he slowly starts to maneuver through the system. "His files."

Jack bends at the waist to read over Cade's shoulder. "You think there will be a file titled *Fuck Over Levi Hollingsworth?* Go straight to the Fs. It's the most used key."

"Actually the spacebar is the most used key," Mason corrects him. "And, logically, vowels would follow."

"Not if you're an asshole who tries to fuck everyone over all the fucking time like the fuckwad he sounds like. For fuckers like that, it's the F key," Jack explains in a way that I almost believe his logic given who we're talking about.

"No," Cade mutters as his fingers move so fast, they look like they've come out of hibernation. "We're going to go to his most recent history. Hang on, I'm downloading as much as I can while I'm here. If I get kicked out, I want to be able to study it later."

"Do you think he'll know?" Carissa asks.

Cade lifts a shoulder as he focuses. "I'm in and don't see any other activity. I bet he'll be asleep another couple hours. And his firewall is shit."

Carissa glances up at me before looking back to the screen. "I don't want you to get in trouble, but we need to know everything, Cade. Everything."

"I'm looking at his recent activity." Cade scrolls and scrolls. "Hang on, let me go back another couple days."

I drag a hand down my face as we stand here on bated breath.

"Hell, he's got his phone linked," Cade mutters. "Dad is an idiot."

"You know, after I was inducted into the club, I have to admit, I looked up your parents," Jack says. "Your mom is hot, and he still cheated on her. He is an idiot."

Everyone turns to stare at Jack.

He holds his hands up defensively. "What? It's true. Can't women of all ages be hot?"

Now is not the time to tell him about my dad and Ms. Lockhart.

"There's nothing that shows it could be him. No talk of drugs, Levi, or us," Cade says, distracted as he keeps skimming. He stops and scrolls back. "Wait. What's this?"

We all lean forward and look at what he's pointing to on the screen.

"John Chester ... do you recognize that name, Cade?" Carissa asks.

"No." He turns to look at his sister. "Do you?"

Carissa shakes her head. "Never heard of him."

"Well, whoever he is, he wants his money," Jack deadpans.

"And he's pissed," Mason adds.

I wonder how I can ask my dad to look into someone else without telling him I might or might not've been an accessory to hacking into Cillian Collins' private computer.

"I'd be pissed, too, if he had my money," Jack retorts.

I give him a shove. "You're the least helpful person here."

"You're just mad that my mini-me and I showed up during your episode of *Love Island*. Get over it," Jack says.

"Can you do a search for him in his files?" Carissa asks.

Cade types at the speed of light.

"Wow." It's the collective feeling of this weird-ass group we've created.

Cade rolls away from the desk, and the rest of us give him the space he needs.

"That's a lot of money," Carissa whispers.

Cade spins in his chair to look at his sister. "Mom has a shitload of money from her trust, but I have no idea where these payments are coming from. I doubt she knows about this."

"Aren't politicians crooked and shit? I mean, maybe he's getting the money from the mob. Or a gambling ring. Maybe he's a Mac Daddy," Jack says.

I turn to him. "You literally say the worst things."

Carissa holds up a hand. "No, it's okay. Politicians can be shady. We know it. But that..." She points to the screen. "He might not have had anything to do with framing you, Levi, but this isn't good. It's definitely not on the up and up. It's more than crooked. But we still don't know who framed Levi."

I turn my attention to Cade. "How much deeper can you dig? We need to follow the money."

"Well, shit," Jack hisses, way too loud for sleeping grandmothers.

We all shush him as Mason asks, "What?"

"I've always wanted to say *follow the money*. That was probably my only chance."

Cade ignores my idiot best friend and looks up at his sister. "Do you want to go to Arizona on Friday to Dad's bullshit event?"

Carissa stiffens in my arms. "I would rather sit and have lunch with Isla, if that tells you how badly I do not want to go."

"I don't either." Cade does something he rarely does—he smiles. "I'm going to fuck up Dad's week so bad, he'll be forced to cancel that rally."

"Fuck, yeah, you are!" Jack is now Cade's official wingman. "We got your back, dude."

Carissa gives me her weight and looks up. "I'm not getting on that plane with my father."

I give her a squeeze, even though I'd rather be doing so many other things with her right now. "Yeah. You're not getting on that plane."

22

SKIP

Carissa

We should be dragging ass since the guys didn't sneak out of Louise's house until after four in the morning. I guess I can't speak for the rest of them, but ever since I got the news alert during third period, my nerves are frenzied. I can't stop refreshing for updates.

The headlines vary, but in the end, they all say the same thing...

Senator Cillian Collins has been funneling money to the same account for years—the identity of the receiver is being kept confidential for now. A special investigation has been ordered by the FBI.

As the years progressed, so has the amount and frequency of the payments. Apparently the price of parking isn't the only thing affected by inflation over the years.

I didn't know what Cade had in mind when he said he was going to ruin Dad's day, but this wasn't it. Not that I care about any of Dad's days, but in the matter of hours, this has blown into a national scandal that rivals cigars and interns. Being his second scandal in the matter of months isn't helping Dad's cause.

He's done everything he can to let the affair with his Chief of Staff evaporate into the wind like a trendy shoe from last season, but money is different. Payments like that are different when you hold a leadership position in the Senate, especially as finance committee chair. And unlike the sex scandal, there's no gray area or hearsay.

The proof is in the numbers in the form of bank records. Nothing is more official than bank records, right?

We might be going on little-to-no sleep, but our diverse and eccentric little group is not using the lunch hour to catch a nap. We're all focused on our phones.

"Fucking-A." Levi tenses. His chair is glued to mine, and our bodies are one from my shoulder to my knee. He looks up and spears my big brother with a sly grin. "Dude. You're a genius. You did it."

Even Jack has the decency to show a little discretion. He sits up straight and hisses. "Really?"

"Here it is," Mason whispers. "I want to be you when I grow up, Cade."

I grab Levi's phone to see what he's reading.

I knew Cade was a genius, but this makes it official. I read the headline aloud. "*As the office of Cillian Collins reels from this morning's news, they have canceled their campaign rally in Tucson tomorrow.*" I look up at Cade who sits across the table from us and lower my voice. "Are you sure this was completely anonymous? You'll be in so much trouble if this comes back on you."

When I see his face, I realize I've underestimated how angry Cade is with Dad. He's been upset since we arrived here, not angry. I assumed it had to do more with Mom being in a facility and being separated from her.

But as well as I know my brother, I missed the anger element. He leans forward with more emotion than I've ever seen from him. "I don't give a shit. If they find out it was me, I'll stand up and take credit. But until they do, I'm not stopping. I'm going to find out where Dad is getting the money and who the hell John Chester is. Because as far as I'm concerned, Dad didn't just fuck up our family for the shittiest Christmas present ever, he's been doing it for years—maybe our entire lives."

The bell rings. Lunch is over, and so is our time together.

"You're the shit, Cade," Levi says before giving my hair a tug. I look over and a contented smile settles on his lips. "You're staying here."

The way he says that, it feels like he's talking about more than tomorrow.

Cade, Mason, and Jack get up and leave us, but Levi doesn't move. He leans so close, his lips brush my ear when his tone dips. "You think Louise will forget to reverse your excusal from school tomorrow?"

My head jerks and my gaze meets his. "Why?"

He hikes a brow. "You want to spend the day together?"

Anticipation bubbles inside me. "Like skip school?"

"You're already excused."

"But you're not," I point out. "You're going to tell me the perfect, four-point-oh-plus Levi Hollingsworth is going to skip class?"

He shakes his head. "If I skip class, they'll call my dad, my mom, every emergency contact on the list, and probably my dog—if I had one. I'm not stupid. I'll get Jack to call in to excuse me. He's basically a professional."

My teeth sink into my bottom lip, if for no other reason than to control my erratic heart. "What are we going to do?"

His gaze drops to my mouth. "Whatever we feel like doing."

I look around and realize the lunchroom is almost empty. "We need to get to class."

He makes no move to get up.

"Levi. I can't be late to chem, even though my grade is now a solid D, thanks to you."

"Think about it." He doesn't give a shit that we're in school—he leans in close to press his lips to mine. It's so fast, I don't get a chance to reciprocate.

He stands, reaches for our backpacks, and offers me a hand. "Ready?"

I let him pull me to my feet, as desperation nags at me. I don't know what we'll do, but I know if I don't take advantage of an entire day with Levi, I'll regret it.

"Yes."

He frowns. "What?"

"If Louise doesn't un-excuse me, yes. Yes to whatever we feel like doing."

A satisfied smile spreads across his rugged face.

Wow.

I can't wait for tomorrow.

Levi

Sucking up to Louise might go down as my smartest move during my entire high school career.

She let me pick up Carissa and Cade for school. I was honestly worried that Cade would say something about me playing hooky with his little sister all day, so I invited him along.

I wasn't kidding when I said Cade was the shit last night. I like him. He's dedicated to his sister and might be smarter than me.

But when he didn't look up from his phone and muttered that he likes school and would rather spend the day with Louise than be the third wheel with us, I was relieved.

Cade must be cool with me, too, since he doesn't give a shit if his sister skips school to be with me all day.

Alone.

Fucking finally.

Since Dad insists on spending as much time with Emma as possible and takes her to school, it was just the three of us. We said goodbye to Cade at the edge of the parking lot and were out of there.

After a stop for breakfast and coffee for her, we literally left the state. We had an hour's drive, but it was worth it. Away from school, grandmothers, scorned exes, and asshole politicians.

I brought her to West Virginia.

Not deep into West Virginia. Not that I wouldn't want to go farther—I would in a heartbeat if we had the time. Today we barely crossed the state line.

"I can't believe in all the time I've spent in Virginia, I've never been here."

I claim her hand. "The Appalachian Trail?"

She steps over a rock. "Definitely not the Appalachian Trail, but not Harpers Ferry either. Do you hike a lot?"

We're over two miles up the trail. Skipping school is not my MO. No one gets to be in consideration for valedictorian by skipping class, no matter how smart they are. When I suggested skipping, all I could think about was spending time alone with her. I didn't think past her being here and not in Arizona.

That thought had me...

Hell, there was a moment I didn't recognize myself.

"We've always hiked. My mom has backpacked portions of the Trail. When we lived with her, she'd make us go all the time—no matter the weather or the time of year. We've traveled everywhere with Dad. If we're near a trail, he drags us on it."

"That must feel good—having parents who want to spend time with you, not just manage you. And they're divorced, but it doesn't sound like it's that bad."

"It's never sucked. It's just the way they are."

"Everyone acts like it's the end of the world for their parents to get divorced. But given what mine have done the last few months, I wonder if we all would've been better off."

"Come here." I pull her to a stop when we reach a fallen tree across the trail. Instead of stepping over, I straddle it and sit. I turn her and pull her down in front of me. I unzip my jacket to pull her to my chest. "You cold?"

"I'm okay." Despite her words, when she fits her back to my front, she shivers. It makes me wonder if it's because of the weather or the fact her ass is tucked tight to my cock. Since Mother Nature isn't cooperating with our skip day, and the weather is cool and overcast, it could be either.

Even though I'm anything but cold.

I wrap my arms around her. I've been kicking my own ass since I picked her up this morning about how to tell her this, but it's time I spit it out. "My dad thinks he might know more about your mom later today."

She jerks in my arms and shifts to look up at me. "Really?"

"Yeah." I pull her back to where she was and wrap my jacket around her shoulders. "His contact at the CIA has been out of town, and he doesn't trust anyone else. But he did have his contact who's a local detective in DC check the hospitals."

No matter how hard I try to keep her where she is, she pulls out of my hold and turns again. "And?"

This is what I've been dreading all day. But I can't keep it from her any longer—my conscience can't take it.

I shake my head. "They've checked everywhere in the area. Every psych facility and treatment center. Unless she checked herself in under another name, which could totally be the case, Mariann Collins is not being treated anywhere near us."

She doesn't move, besides her eyes that shift to the side, as if she's staring at something across the Potomac.

"But he's supposed to have a report from the CIA by the end of the day. They have access to so much more."

Her head lands on my pec. But that's it.

Fuck. Maybe waiting to tell her now wasn't the best idea.

"Carissa, baby. Are you okay?"

She shakes her head. "I don't know."

"Your mom wants privacy. I'm sure that's it. She probably checked herself in under another name. She needed a break from reality. No one can blame her for that after what she went through in the media."

"I guess." Her breaths become shallow and erratic. I feel it against my chest. "I just want to know where she is. I want to know that she's okay. Cade and I deserve to know that much." She looks up at me and something transforms on her expression. She's gone from desperation to anger. "We're not toddlers. Louise won't tell us. Dad won't tell us. A detective can't find her at any medical facility in northern Virginia. What the hell?"

I tip her chin to angle her face to mine. Her dark eyes are as stormy as the spring sky leering over us. "I'm sorry. I feel like I ruined our day, but I've kept it from you for almost two hours. It was killing me. I knew you'd want to know, even if it wasn't good news."

She pulls herself from me and stands. I'm about to get up and run after her, but she turns and straddles the trunk, facing me, her legs draped over my thighs. I grab her ass in both of my hands and pull her tight.

"Thank you," she murmurs against my lips after she frames my face with her hands. "Thank you for being exactly what I need right now."

I look her in the eyes and yank her even tighter into me. "Do you know how selfish I feel? Hoping like hell your brother could fuck up your dad's week so you wouldn't leave? You were only supposed to be gone for one day. This isn't even your home, but I don't want you to leave."

Her hands slide around my neck and she presses her tits to my chest. "No, it's not."

My fingers bite into her ass, giving away the unease that's been building in me for days. "And you hate living with Louise."

She nods, and the two little words are exhaled across my face like a slap. "I do."

My dick grows harder by the moment.

I've never felt so out of control. Not two years ago when Isla dragged me through it. And not this week when someone planted drugs in my locker.

Because I know … it's only a matter of time.

I'll lose her.

I'll graduate and go to college.

Her parents will eventually take her back.

I have to stop my brain from sprinting into the future, roadblock after roadblock thrown in my way. In our way.

She presses into me—grinding her pussy into my cock. "Levi."

"You're not mine to lose." I hardly recognize my own voice—gruff and desperate. "But it sure fucking feels like it right now."

I tangle my fist in her hair and meld her soft lips to mine.

Everything in life has come easy to me. Grades. Sports. Friends. I've never had to fight for anything.

I've never felt like something I needed so much was slipping through my fingertips, about to fall into a deep, dark abyss, and I'd never taste it again.

My hand moves up to dip into her joggers.

Fuck.

Skin to skin.

I squeeze her ass cheek, making her press into me even further. She wraps her legs around my waist and the heels of her shoes cut into my back.

If there's a bright spot in the storm, at least her despair matches mine.

That's when the sky rumbles above us.

Neither of us breaks the kiss. If anything, it becomes more intense.

Lightning.

Closer this time.

My hand slides south.

For the first time, I feel her.

I actually feel her.

"Fuck, you're wet," I mutter between kisses.

She nods, breathing through her parted lips, her heart racing to match mine.

I reach farther, straining her pants, just to see.

And I slide my middle finger inside her.

"Oh my ... Levi."

Her eyes close. Her head falls back.

I give her another pump.

This time her eyes fly open, and all I see is red-hot desire on a cold, spring morning.

That's when it happens. Rain drops.

Huge ones. They cut through the thick, humid air and land heavy on our skin.

As I slide my hand out from her pants, the rain comes harder. We don't look away from one another as we're pelted with sheets from the sky.

I blink the water away. "We're going to have to run for it. Who knows how long this will last."

As if she finally woke up to the world outside of Carissa and Levi, she looks around squinting, as her blond hair darkens in the cold rain. She climbs off my lap and we stand.

"Where are we going to go?" she asks.

I grab her hand. "I'm taking you home."

23

GAUNTLET

Levi

I pull her into my bedroom and kick the door shut, even though we're here alone. I turned off every alarm and camera Dad has on the place before we got here, so I'm not sure why the door needs to be shut, but it feels right. I've never had a girl in my room.

Driving an hour with the heat on high did nothing to dry us from running two miles in the pouring rain. We're still soaked to the bone.

"Wow, your room looks like it could be featured in a magazine. But, you know ... lived in."

"That's basically what it is. Dad pulled up a website, told us to pick a room we liked, and it was delivered. He's simple but generous." I peel off my sweatshirt and tee, dumping them on the floor. "Let me get you some dry clothes."

I pull out drawer after drawer and produce dry T-shirts and fresh hoodies. I'm contemplating raiding Emma's room to find her some pants that fit when I turn.

All thoughts of pants flee my brain like one of Jack's field parties that just got busted by the cops.

Her pants are gone.

I don't know where they went.

I don't care.

Her sweater clears her head of wet hair and is tossed to the floor. She rubs her arms for friction as she stands in the middle of my bedroom in nothing but a tank and pair a of panties.

The tank is wet.

And tight.

And see through.

Her snug panties leave nothing to the imagination.

She's wearing a bra, but I'm not sure why. It's not doing much as far as I can see.

And there's a lot to see.

I state the obvious. "You're cold."

She pushes her damp hair from her face. "It's not even fifty degrees, and we're wet. You're not cold?"

I'm anything but cold right now. In fact, I'm pretty sure I'm numb everywhere but my dick.

It, on the other hand, is hotter than the desert where she's from on a summer afternoon. A place I want to do everything in my power to keep her from going back to.

I decide to tell her the truth, but not about keeping her here. "No, I'm anything but cold right now."

She looks like she's physically swallowing over a boulder when she whispers. "I'm jealous."

I drop the dry clothes that would no doubt warm her, but there's no way I'm giving them the opportunity when I'm here to do it myself.

Three big strides is all it takes. She tips her head back to look at me as her hard nipples brush my bare skin through her thin, wet clothes. My hands land low on her hips and feel their way up, catching the hem of her tank on their way. I lift them, peeling the damp material up and up and up, away from her fair skin.

I look down, and her tits are on full display through her thin, wet bra. She's not big, and they barely swell above the low-cut material. I can't help but drag my hands up the bare skin of her sides, stopping just in time to brush the underside of her perfect swells with the rough skin of my thumbs.

My words mirror my thoughts, but it sounds like I'm talking to myself. "You're perfect."

She gives her head a shake. "I've never felt perfect."

I slide one hand to the middle of her back and pull her cold body flush to mine. "You couldn't be more perfect."

Her eyes follow her hands, down my chest as the tips of her fingers catch on my nipples.

My cock thickens against her stomach.

Fuck.

I need to lay it out there for her. For us. If I don't say it aloud, I'm afraid where things will go. And they cannot go there. Not today.

"We can't have sex."

She blinks and her dark eyes widen. "What?"

I shake my head and feel like kicking my own ass. "Not today."

She bristles in my arms and tries to push away on my chest. "Um ... okay."

I don't let her go and hold her tighter—one hand in the middle of her back and the other one lands on her still-damp panties. "It's not that I don't want to. Fuck, do I want to."

She says nothing, and her cheeks tinge pink as her fingertips press into my skin.

"I don't want to fuck this up. You're a virgin. I don't take that lightly. And you're seventeen—"

She's quick to interrupt me. "I'll be eighteen soon—really soon."

I don't tell her I'm counting down the days. "I know. But no matter how much I want to, it hasn't been that long. And there's the fact I don't have a condom. And you're seventeen and a virgin."

"Would you quit saying that?"

"Baby, I'm basically chanting that shit to myself silently. If I don't, I'm afraid of where I'll let this go. So I'm laying it out the way it needs to be right now—no sex."

"Then why are we standing here like this?"

I lean down and press my lips to her forehead.

Her temple.

Then the corner of her mouth.

But I don't take her mouth.

I drag my lips to her ear, as if I need to keep a secret from the universe. "Because you're cold, and I'm going to warm you up from the inside out. I can't do that if you're dressed."

Carissa

My bra goes slack with one snap of his fingers, as if he practices the nimble move for hours a day.

He could probably get a triple scholarship—lacrosse, grades, and stripping bras off willing females.

I'm just glad I'm the only recipient.

I exhale in his arms and find it difficult to pull in a fresh breath. Aggressive goosebumps spread over my sensitive skin, sending a wave of ... something through me.

Want.

Heat.

Lust?

Is that what it is?

I've never experienced lust before.

I really thought today would be the day. But then Levi laid down the no-sex gauntlet—like it was a new bill passed by the House, approved by the Senate, and signed off on by the President himself.

His lips land on mine as he eases my bra straps down my shoulders. I'm forced to drop my hands from his chiseled chest for far too long to get rid of it. And now I'm standing in nothing but my panties while he's still wearing pants.

His kiss deepens as his hand engulfs my breast. I've never felt smaller, more vulnerable and...

Safe.

When he took my hand on the overlook we hiked to and told me he was taking me home, I'm sure the comment was literal. This is his home, after all.

But, for some reason, it felt like so much more. I had to push those feelings away as soon as they crept in.

Levi is only eighteen. I'm not there yet. I'm not even from here. I'll have to go back to Arizona eventually, and he'll go to college. Some girl will snatch him up. Maybe they'll live their best college lives together. Parties, games, shacking up. Then, when the time comes, and Levi is ready to settle down, he'll make it official and they'll live happily ever after.

I'll be a distant memory ... that messed up girl from his senior year, who he had to tutor through chemistry, and then she flew home when her mother finally surfaced to take her back.

But for now, I'm here.

The one he took home.

I'm the one in his arms.

And the one who let him strip her down to almost nothing.

With one arm low around my back, my feet leave the floor. I'm up, and my legs wrap around his narrow hips where his pants still hang low like they were meant to sit there forever. Feeling him for the first time like this, skin to skin, my heart wants to beg him to never let me go.

I'm all of a sudden jealous of the one he'll ultimately choose.

When my bare back lands on his messy, unmade bed, he presses his cock between my legs. I moan into his mouth as he rocks against my sex. My panties are soaked and it has nothing to do with the rain.

His touch slides down my side and catches at my hip. He breaks the intensity between our lips to look down at me.

But he doesn't say a word. Instead, he lifts his hips just enough while never tearing his burning gaze from my eyes as he drags my panties down my legs.

No matter how much I want everything with Levi, the need to close my eyes to escape is strong. But the expression on his face is demanding and possessive. My fingers dig into his strong bare shoulders, and I hang on for dear life.

He tosses my panties over his shoulder and cool air hits my sex when he hooks me under a knee to lift my leg.

He finally breaks the heavy silence. "I'm not sure I could be more obsessed with you, Carissa. I want to memorize every inch of you. Learn your every secret and give you everything you want. I want to fill your heart with nothing but me. Fuck, I want to make you mine and never give you back."

My chest heaves with emotion. "Don't say things you

can't follow through on. Please. That will make this so much harder in the end."

"The end," he mutters and shakes his head. "I can't think about that right now."

I draw my knees up his sides and feel my sex open wider. "I don't ever want to think about that."

His eyes angle back to mine. This time they look determined. "I don't want to think about anything but you—right now, right here."

His head dips, and his lips land on mine again, but they don't stay there long. His hand slides down the back of my thigh, and my heartbeat is so erratic, I wonder if a healthy almost eighteen-year-old can die from sexual tension. When his fingers find me, wet, open, and ready, I gasp.

Two fingers.

And a thumb.

My jaw goes slack—I can't take it when the rough skin of his thumb circles my clit.

His lips move down my neck, across my collar bone, until they wrap around a nipple.

This time I call out when he sucks. His tongue and fingers are a lethal combination, causing me to fist his blanket below me.

He catches my nipple in his teeth for a soft nip before letting go. When I open my eyes, he's pushed up on one arm, looking down at his other hand where his fingers are buried deep in me.

Mortified, I immediately fold my legs together, trapping his hand, and cross my arms over my breasts.

One corner of his lips turns up, and he shakes his head. "Don't, baby. You're beautiful. If you only knew what this does to me." His heated gaze returns to his hand, as he nudges my legs apart. On an exhale, I allow my knees to drop to the side. "I crave everything with you—there's nothing too intimate, Carissa. I want it all."

"But no sex?" I breathe.

"Not today." His thumb keeps at my clit, and I think my heart skips a beat or three when his tongue sneaks out to wet his bottom lip. "But we can do other things. Let me see you. Move your arms."

I try to focus on even breaths. In, out, in, out. "Why?"

"Because I want to memorize you. Arms, baby."

The moment I drop my arms, his lips land on mine, but this kiss is quick. He pulls away completely, leaving me wanting more—my mouth, my breasts, and between my legs.

But what he does next...

"Oh... Oh, my—" and I gasp.

With his hands on the back of my thighs, he opens me. Wide.

Then he's kissing me again, but in a whole other way.

"Levi." His name is a desperate exhale on my tongue, which is fitting. Desperation seems to be my motto lately.

He licks and laps, all while holding my thighs firmly in his grasp. This is like nothing I've ever dreamed. His tongue ... wow. I think every muscle in his body is honed to perfection.

He sucks and licks and sucks some more. Pushing me to the edge before reeling me back again.

"Please," I beg.

His grip on me tightens.

He's done teasing.

He pulls my clit between his lips and with his tongue ... finally.

I fall and call out and struggle against his hold, but he doesn't let up until I'm spent.

My legs fall to his bed, and Levi crawls over me. He leans in to take my mouth and rolls, pulling me with him. My thighs fall on either side of his waist, I'm sprawled on his wide, bare chest.

His heart races as fast as mine beneath my cheek.

"That was..." I turn my head to press my lips to his pec. "That was amazing."

He sounds like he just went for a run. "Baby, I don't think there's anything I won't do for you, but when you say please, especially when I've got my mouth between your legs, I'll gladly face death to give you what you want."

"This is so new. Everything is new. The naked thing..." I pull in a breath. "Is very new."

His heart slows to a healthy, steady pace. He leans up and presses his lips to my forehead. "Fucking thrilled to be all your new experiences."

I'm about to ask what we're going to do. I've lost track of time. I need to be back at school to go home with Cade, and Levi has practice.

Levi's stomach growls under me, making me laugh out loud. "I was just wondering what time it is. I guess it's time to eat." I lean up far enough to look down at him, but not so far that I expose my breasts. "And I need to get dressed. How am I the only one naked?"

His smile from where he lies beneath me makes my stomach flip and flop. "Carissa, I need a layer of clothes between us. Like I didn't jack off enough to the thought of you, now I know what you taste like. We cannot be naked at the same time right now. That's going to have to wait."

I give my head a shake. "You need food, and I need my clothes. What time is it?"

He lifts his hips and digs his phone out of his pocket.

When he looks at the screen, he doesn't tell me what time it is, he frowns.

He starts to flip through his screen.

"Levi, what is it?"

"A message from my dad." His eyes cut to me, and he hikes a brow. "Apparently when I'm with you, you make me blind and deaf to the rest of the world."

I tense, and even though it's the last thing in the world I want to do, I scramble off him and reach for the first thing I see—a dry T-shirt. "Do we need to leave?"

He sits up in bed and doesn't pretend to look away, so I turn my back to him and yank the shirt over my head. The world is right again when it falls to the middle of my thighs. I turn. He's sitting there, smiling, not at all worried his dad might come home in the middle of my naked state. "Cade fucking up your dad's day might be the best thing that's ever happened to me."

I cross my arms. "I take it your dad isn't on his way to bust you for skipping school?"

He shakes his head. "But if it makes you feel any better, we can get dressed and leave. We still have time to grab a late lunch."

I pick up my joggers. "This is going to be like putting on a wet swimsuit."

He climbs out of bed and pushes his pants down, leaving him in a pair of underwear that are straining in all the right places. I was right when I said he was a man among boys. His cock is long and hard, and my mind is taken straight back to when he said he jacks off to thoughts of me. Every inch and bulge is visible, leaving very little to my imagination. His boxers are the kind that hug his thick muscular thighs, and now there's very little I want in the world more than to watch Levi on the lacrosse field. He's a powerhouse.

I bet he was frustrated having to wait for me when we were running down the mountain in the rain.

He walks over to me and wraps a hand behind my neck to pull me in for a kiss. I don't hesitate. I want to feel him—feel it.

I press into him, his cock long, hard, and a reminder of what we just did. His current state proving he liked it as much as I did.

Well, I'm not sure if that's possible. He's still standing here hard. I wish I had the nerve to do something about that.

I'm trying to decide what that should be, or at least work up the nerve to ask him what I can do for him, when he drags his lips from mine and looks at his watch and frowns. "Got an email from my dad. His friend Carson from the CIA sent him a report."

All thoughts of working up the nerve to touch his cock jump out the window. "Did he find my mom?"

He pulls away from me again and disappears into his closet for two seconds. When he comes back, he tosses me a fresh pair of joggers. "Here. Wear these for now. You can cinch them and roll them over."

I pull them up my legs and don't even care that I'm going commando. He does the same, and I go to him when he sits on the foot of his bed to look at his phone. "Levi, what does it say?"

His brows pinch as he reads and scrolls. Then his free hand reaches out and pulls me between his legs, but he never looks away from his phone.

"Holy shit. How long can it be? Did he find her?"

He scrolls up and back down again, as his other arm wraps around my waist and pulls me down to sit on his thigh. He might as well torture me in a whole new way, because I feel every muscle in his body tense as he slowly turns his hazel eyes on me. "I ... I don't know how to tell you this. Fuck."

I take in his hesitant expression, like he's warring with himself to share what he just read.

Well.

If he thinks he can keep something from me just like everyone else in my life, he's in trouble.

"Tell me," I snap, and reach for his phone.

Levi is quicker, and tosses it on the bed. But at the same time proves I can trust him with not just my body, but also my emotions.

Those green flecks bore into me, and he shakes his head, like it physically wounds him to speak. "Mariann Collins' passport was scanned at Reagan International on New Year's Day."

He holds me tight when I jerk. "What? There's no way."

Levi's intense stare never leaves me. "Baby, it was documented. Carson even had video pulled showing her going through security. She flew first class on a redeye to London. From there she went to Greece. Her passport hasn't been scanned since she entered the country, and her credit cards have been hitting in Santorini ever since. Her last charge was yesterday."

"But ... she was a mess." I stare unseeing at him for the second time today. I shake my head when I realize he's pulled me in tighter. For the first time since we walked into his bedroom, I wish he was wearing a shirt so I'd have something to hold onto. I need something to hold onto. "She threatened to hurt herself. She said she needed time, but that she needed help. That she was afraid of what she'd do if she were left alone. It was the only reason Cade and I didn't throw a massive fit when she moved us here and left us with Louise."

His square jaw goes taut, but his eyes soften. "I'm sorry. Carson went through her credit card charges. She has a house rented through May."

"The end of the semester," I mutter.

He pulls me in tighter. "I don't know what to say."

"What is there to say? She lied to us. We're used to that with Dad. He'll say and do anything to get his way. But Mom?" I shake my head. "She's never been like that. Or we didn't think she was. Cade is going to freak. She hasn't even called to check on us. Not even on him. She just dumped us and left."

"She could be calling Louise to check on you. You never know."

Resentment, anger, and hurt battle it out in my chest. I'm not sure which will come out the victor. Right now they're whipping up a storm that makes me want to rage and cry at the same time.

"That doesn't matter, Levi. We've worried about her for months now. Months," I stress. "Who would do that to their children just to vacation on the Mediterranean to escape the media and drama? And I know this because Santorini is her favorite place on earth. She's been so many times. Some with Dad, others with friends, and a couple times by herself to stay at a spa. She dumped us without a second thought to escape her life. It's as clear as crystal."

Levi glances at his watch before he pulls me closer. "We need to go if I'm going to get you back on time. I'll pick you up after practice. I swear, even if we have to sit with Louise, I'll spend the whole weekend with you. I promise."

I bring my hands to his jaw and can't help the tears that burn my eyes. "Thank you."

He presses his lips to mine once more. "I'll get you something to eat before we go back to school."

The more time that passes here in Virginia, the more Levi is becoming a crutch. As the days pass, my parents are proving to be more and more toxic, selfish, and doing everything they can to tear our family apart. And like the teeter-totter of ups and downs that is becoming more of a normal than I care to admit, there's nothing I want more than Levi.

Nothing.

In Levi's clothes, I'm back in his Jeep. He only pulls over long enough to re-arm what he explained is a security system that could protect a small country. But I can't focus on anything. Not the passing cars, not the bag full of tacos Levi stopped for, and when he dropped me off at the edge of campus, my insides hurt from having to say goodbye.

24

BULLETS

Levi

"So." Jack knocks me in the side, breathing heavily from running drills. "Did the bear come out of hibernation? Did you give the Senator one more reason to take you down? Did you rock her world?"

I check him with my stick. "None of your business, asshole."

He checks me back. "I'm the one who put his neck on the line pretending to be Daddy Asa, and you're not going to share? I just want to know if it was worth it."

I adjust my helmet and pads and wait for my turn. We're doing midfield drills, which Jack hates. He's a goalie for a reason—he can stay put in one spot. "It was worth it, for all the reasons you'll never know. I'm picking her up after practice."

"As long as my work is for the greater good, then I can rest well tonight. Though lunch was interesting today. As much of a commotion as you two made when her dad reared his ugly head earlier in the week, I'm not sure anyone but one person gives a shit that both of you were absent on the same day, doing the dirty."

As if I care. I move up in line and mutter, "Yeah, who's that?"

He taps my helmet with his stick like he's my fairy godmother. "Who do you think? Ursula, the teenage witch."

"You must be off your game. You're getting your cartoons mixed up."

The whistle sounds, and I go. Running to the middle of the field, I catch the ball, twist, jab, and spin before shooting it into the net. Jack follows, but the ball hits the post and ricochets off.

He jogs over to me and looks like he'd rather be taking a nap. "And that's why my lacrosse career will be over after high school. Anyway, it got around that the sea bitch wanted to know where you and your new main squeeze were. She even had the nerve to come up to me at lunch." He jabs my shoulder again. "*Me*. Can you believe it? If anyone has your back and isn't going to blab your secrets, it's your preschool-to-now-best homie. Fucking octo-witch."

"Like I care what she thinks. I'm just glad Coach didn't give me shit for being at practice after missing school."

"Of course he didn't give you shit. He's already sweating next year when he doesn't have his ace on the team."

I'm about to complain about the prison walls of high school, when the whistle squeals right before the coach yells across the field. "Hollingsworth!"

Jack and I both turn.

"Fuck," I hiss. "What is he doing here?"

"Fuck is right," Jack agrees. "Daddy Asa has always scared me."

Dad is standing next to Coach, who's motioning me over, and all I can think about are Carissa's panties that I'm pretty sure are still laying on my bedroom floor. She was so upset when we left, we realized we both forgot her clothes after we got to school. It was too late to go back and get them.

"If he found out I pretended to be him with the attendance secretary, I'll for sure die. Like, literally. I will be found dead in the forest. We've surpassed the Hallmark channel and gone straight up rogue to an HBO original series. My life is over—"

I hit him in the chest. "Shut up. They don't look patient. I've gotta go."

I start out in a jog across the field and don't look back when Jack hisses, "Don't you dare sell me out, Hollingsworth."

I don't make it all the way to them when my coach says, "We'll see you tomorrow, Levi."

I look from him to Dad, not at all wanting the answer to the question I'm about to ask. "What's going on?"

I don't think I've ever seen my father look so serious.

No. Not just serious.

Dangerous.

I've never seen him so angry and agitated and about to bust out of his own skin.

I brace.

"There's been an incident at home. Crew and Grady are already there. We need to go. Now." He pulls in a breath and I relax a fraction, confident this has nothing to do with Carissa's panties. "Levi, it's fucking bad."

Holy shit.

He wasn't exaggerating. When he told me what

happened, I knew it would be bad, but this is worse than I ever imagined.

Dad had a meeting after school with Emma's teachers since my sister can't get her shit together. I guess Ms. Lockhart offered to give Emma a ride home.

What happened between then and now, I have no fucking idea.

I followed my dad home as he sped through the sleepy roads of small-town Virginia, screeching to a halt in front of the house he bought so Emma and I wouldn't have to switch schools. I barely have the chance to throw my Jeep into park before I'm out the door and running up to pure chaos.

It wasn't even two hours ago that I had Carissa here. And now ... this.

Ms. Lockhart's minivan is sitting in our driveway and looks like it's been through the streets of a civil war, pelted with so many bullets, it's sitting on its rims. Every window is busted out.

The house is peppered too. Every window on the front of the house is shot out. Glass is everywhere.

And so are the cops. So many cops.

They're swarming the place. Two ambulances are parked front and center.

My gut turns when I see the driver and passenger doors standing open to Ms. Lockhart's van.

Fuck.

I catch up to my Dad. "What the hell happened?"

His grip on my shoulder is tight and desperate. "I don't know, but I promise you, I'm gonna figure it out."

My eyes jump through the crowd. When bodies part, I see Emma. She's with Grady, and besides her tears, she looks shaken but okay. Thank God. Beyond them, Crew is standing in the rubble talking to an officer. I move straight for him.

When Crew sees me, he steps away, and I move him to the side. "Are they okay? Where's Ms. Lockhart?"

Crew leans in and lowers his voice. "She was grazed but refuses to be transported. They've got her in the back of the rig getting her stitched up. Levi, we've never had an attack, never had blowback on us for what we do. We won't know until we can study the surveillance. Until then, we need everything out of this house. Every file, gun, piece of electronics, and anything that could connect your dad to our organization. It's what your dad would want."

I pull in a breath. "I can do that."

"You and I need to get that done while your dad deals with Emma and Keelie."

I look back, and Dad is climbing into the back of an ambulance.

"Fast, Levi. I'll get the guns and pack your dad's office. You get everything else. And pack a bag. I'm not sure where your dad will want to go, but you can always come to Whitetail."

I look back at the man I've known most of my life. "Yeah, let's go."

Crew goes to the office off the front of the house that's now littered with broken glass and bullets. I head straight for my room.

Fuck.

More glass. All over the floor. My bed. Where I just had Carissa not too fucking long ago. I drag a hand down my face and go straight for my closet for every bag and suitcase I can find.

The first thing I pack are Carissa's clothes.

Then I do exactly what Crew told me to do. I rid the

house of any evidence that my dad was a paid assassin for the CIA.

But the whole time, I can't believe this is tied to Dad. He wasn't lying when he said his shit is tight.

So who the hell shot up our house?

And if they did it because I wasn't at school today and thought I was here...

This is really fucking bad.

25

RHETORICAL BULLETS

Carissa

Louise stands in front of me and my twin, twisting her wrinkled fingers as if they were one of the stress balls that litter Cade's bedroom. Anxiety is set deep in her face. She has no idea how to respond.

"How did you find out?" she cries.

"It doesn't matter," I spit. "She lied to us. Dad lied to us. *You* lied to us."

I grip Cade and hold tight. When I came home today and told him what I found out about Mom, he straight up did not believe me. Then I showed him the report Levi sent me. When he saw the flight records and credit card charges, all from places we know Mom loves, he went silent.

Then learning it all came from the CIA, he was convinced. Cade might've been able to hack into Dad's laptop to access files, but getting this kind of information is out of his league. Even he knew that.

He's gutted—as much or more so than I am.

"Was it all a lie?" Cade demands. "Thoughts of hurting

herself? Did she really leave us here thinking we might lose her like that and run off to Greece just to avoid the media?"

"I don't know." Louise shakes her head, and an actual tear falls from one eye. I had no idea she was capable of that kind of emotion. "I don't know! When she called me on Christmas Day and told me what your father had done ... I didn't know what to do. And then the media, they were brutal. Mariann was mortified."

In all that's happened since Dad's scandal broke publicly, nothing has been as devastating as this. "So everyone let us think she was on the brink of a breakdown? Suicide?"

"You can't judge her. Please. You don't understand what your father has put her through all these years. Do you really think this was his first infidelity?"

Her words silence me, but not Cade. "I'm not surprised. But why wouldn't she leave him before?"

Louise's expression falls, mortified by his comment. "She couldn't! Then everyone would've known."

"Are you serious? You're telling me he's cheated on her before, she knew about it, and looked the other way? And you knew about it?"

She throws her arms out. "What was I supposed to do? She didn't want that kind of attention. What would people say?"

I drag a hand through my hair. "I cannot fucking believe this."

"Watch your mouth, Carissa!"

Cade takes a step forward. "Don't yell at her."

"How did you find out?" Louise demands. "If you know where she is, surely the press will find out soon. Do you know how bad this will look? Especially with this new debacle your father got himself into with those payments?"

I ignore the payments. I don't want to touch that subject and need to keep the focus on Mom dumping us here. "What, that she left us with you, lied about suffering from a mental breakdown, and is nursing her ego on a beach in the Mediterranean? Yeah, that doesn't look good. And guess what? We don't give a shit."

"No!" Louise panics. "You can't tell anyone. I'll call her, convince her to come home. She'll take you back to Arizona if that will keep you quiet. But this cannot get out. She just needs time."

"She needs time," Cade deadpans.

"I'll call her. Please, don't tell anyone. I'm sure she'll talk to you."

But now it's my turn to panic. "I'm not going anywhere with her."

Cade turns to me. "You're not staying here."

I back away from him two steps and cross my arms. The thought of leaving is ... I don't know. I've been living in the moment with Levi. Literally. Hell, my bra and panties are still back in his bedroom. The only reason Louise isn't freaked out about what I'm wearing is because we hit her with this as soon as we got home.

I ignore Louise and focus on Cade, afraid to utter the words aloud. We've never been separated for more than a couple days. "I don't know what I want."

"You'd stay for him?" Cade's question comes out like an indictment.

I hug myself tighter and don't answer.

"I haven't said shit to you about him because I thought he was a distraction you needed. Hell, we all need a distraction. But you'd stay here?" His judgmental glare bores into me as he motions to Louise. "With her?"

"You can stay as long as you want," Louise says. "I'll try. I promise to try harder. I've never been good with kids, not even with your mother. She was so difficult. But I'll do better. Please, stay."

It's like she's not even in the room with us. This is one of those moments between me and my twin.

When we don't need to verbalize what we're feeling.

We just know.

Though, most of the time it's me being in tune to him.

But right now, I think he sees me clearly. Maybe for the first time.

I will myself to speak, but my tone is pained. It kills me to say it, but I think right now I'd die a slow death if I had to go back to Arizona and deal with the fallout of what our parents have done. "If I can pass chemistry, I can still graduate a semester early. I can go to college here."

There's a tic in Cade's clenched jaw.

"You can stay too," I try. "Just think of the freedom we'd have if we had our cars here. There's such a short time until we turn eighteen. No one can tell us what to do then."

He shakes his head and seethes, "I can't believe you."

His shoulder brushes mine as he stalks past me and out of the formal living room where we cornered Louise when we got home.

"I'll try," Louise whispers. "I'm sorry I lied to you. Your mother made me promise not to tell you. I didn't know what to do."

I look at my grandmother and tell her the truth. "I can't speak for Cade, but the next time you speak to my mother, tell her I don't want to talk to her. I don't want to see her. I don't want anything to do with her. Adults suck."

I turn and follow in Cade's wake, needing to find my brother and make things right with him.

Everything is wrong. The last thing we need right now is

a wedge between us. I run up both flights of stairs to the third floor and am about to bang on his door that I know is probably locked, when my cell buzzes in my pocket.

It's from Levi.

When I read the text, I freeze.

Holy shit.

And I thought what just went down here was bad between Louise, Cade, and me.

Our bullets were only rhetorical.

But his were very, very real.

26

PAROLE

Levi

"I'm not going to California," I seethe. "Mom's called a million times. Emma's the one who was in that car, and she doesn't even want to leave. If I have to pull the *I'm eighteen card*, I will. But you need to make this stop."

Life was fucking fantastic for about two minutes before it blew up into the epic shitshow we're currently in the middle of.

Carissa found out her mom isn't in a medical facility, but instead dumped her and Cade to lick her wounds in the Mediterranean.

Emma and my school counselor were almost killed in a drive-by shooting in our own driveway.

We still don't know why our house was targeted, but I think it's safe to say at this point, it was not random.

If possible, Emma is even more of a mess than she was before. But after being shot at, I can't blame her.

We've basically moved in with my school counselor—

who insists I address her as Keelie—and I'm positive my dad has moved into her bed.

All that, and the most pressing issue of all is that I haven't seen Carissa since I dropped her off after skipping school two days ago.

Dad shut our shit down and hasn't let me go out on my own all weekend. We went to Whitetail yesterday since it's probably as safe as the Pentagon, but that's it.

Crew's people have set up surveillance on Keelie's property that makes our security system look like we dug it out of the bottom of a cereal box. My dad is not fucking around. There will be no sneaking out, no shutting down this security system, and no sneaking into Louise's mansion in the middle of the night.

Which all means no time with Carissa.

I've never looked forward to a Monday in high school more than tomorrow.

Dad pulls in a frustrated breath and drags a hand down his face. He went out last night with Jarvis after getting a tip about the car the shooters were in. I was able to breathe easy when he came home and told me it was most likely linked to the planted drugs in my locker, which don't seem to be tied to a certain politician I'd very much like to punch in the face.

All this combined has given my mother reason to hover all the way from California and keep me away from Carissa. Both are developments that piss me off.

"You're not going anywhere, and neither is your sister. Like you said, you're eighteen. When it comes to Emma, I don't want to take your mom to court over this, but I will. I'm going to fix this. After last night, I'm one step closer, but I need your help, Levi. It might be the worst possible time for this to happen, but I've made a commitment to Keelie, and that means her kids too."

I take a step closer and lower my voice. "How long are you going to hold me hostage here? It's not like I don't like Keelie and her kids—I do. I don't even mind being here, but I want to see Carissa. I had to cancel our plans for the weekend. This is bullshit. Not to mention, it's embarrassing."

"Lower your voice. Give me a few more days. As of last night, I got a lead on the car, but I need more time." He turns a pointed glare at Emma, who he dragged in here when I complained again about the hostage situation. "Until then, I have no idea why it happened. Before I let you loose again, I need to figure out who's targeting my family and why."

"Can we stay here?" Emma begs. "I don't want to go back home. I don't think I can."

Fuck. Moving in with my counselor isn't ideal, but at this point, I only want one thing—to see Carissa.

Dad and Emma go back and forth about him and Keelie being a thing. I'm done.

"Dad," I interrupt. "When do I get parole?"

He turns his glare on me, and it's very different from the one he just used on my sister. "If you do your best not to look miserable today, Carissa can come over later. You can introduce her to the goats."

That's all I need to hear. I turn to leave Keelie's office that we holed ourselves up in so Knox and Saylor couldn't hear us. I have one priority right now, and it's the girl I'm aching to see in more ways than one.

Carissa

I LUNGE for my phone across the bed and don't even greet him. "What did he say?"

Kids are playing in the background, along with other commotion. Maybe a ... donkey? "He said you can come here. If that's the only way I can see you, I'll take it. I'll pick you up after brunch. I don't care what he says, I'm leaving to come and get you."

I roll over and stare at my ceiling. "We'll go back to Ms. Lockhart's house?"

"Keelie is cool. Her entire family will be here any minute, and we've been warned to not mention the shooting. If I'm good with old people, it's because of my mom. Dad, on the other hand, has lived the last decade of his life not giving a shit, but he picks today, while we're in the middle of a crisis, to want to make a good impression. It's like I don't even know him anymore. There's no way for me to guess what will happen next. The Rock could show up at this point, and I wouldn't be surprised."

"Well, if The Rock is going to be there, then I'm definitely coming."

He pauses before his tone dips. "I haven't seen you for two days. Don't make me jealous."

"Thank you," I say seriously. "Cade still won't speak to me—I gave up trying last night. He only comes out of his room for food, but otherwise keeps his door locked. We still haven't heard from Mom, and now Louise is sucking up to me and Cade. It's so weird. I don't know how to feel about it. I'm not used to her being nice. And I miss you."

"I miss you, too, baby. I'm sorry about Cade. He's upset about your mom, but he'll come around. I'll call when I'm on my way to pick you up."

"Levi?" I call for him, almost desperately before we say goodbye.

"Yeah?"

"I need to buckle down with school. The last thing I want to do is study when I haven't seen you all weekend. But, after the last few days, there's nothing I want more than to graduate early."

An exhale comes across the phone. A relieved one. Or maybe one of approval. "You graduating early is my first priority."

"See you soon."

And for the first time in days, a smile spreads across my face.

Now I need to make things right with my brother.

27
MEMORIES

Levi

"This is killing me," I murmur against her lips. "If I'd known you were in my future, I would've asked for a bigger car."

"We shouldn't be here. Your dad barely let you take me home by yourself."

I slide my hands up the sides of her thighs, and they land on her ass. "We deserve it. We just studied for hours. You're going to kill your test tomorrow. I told you I'd make sure you graduated early."

She rubs up and down on my hard on held hostage in my jeans. "I hope you're not this invested in everyone you tutor."

It's easy to slide one hand between her legs since she's straddling me. I barely threw it in park on our country road when she didn't hesitate. She climbed over the console and was on top of me before I could extend an invitation. "Baby, I've never been this invested in anyone."

She trails kisses across my jaw. "Your mom is nice."

I can't complain about my mom, not when Carissa still hasn't heard a peep from hers. "Her barging into Keelie's house unannounced today was over the top, even for her. So much for Dad making a good impression with Keelie's family."

"You're lucky."

"Hey." I frame her face with one hand and look into her eyes. "At least you know your mom's okay. She'll be back."

"I'm done making any assumptions about my parents."

"Even though my mom hopped on a red-eye and surprised us, we still have to go to California next weekend. There's no getting out of that. Maybe it will be good for Emma. With the way she's been lately, I need to go just so she's not traveling by herself."

Her pussy rocks against my cock again. "Do you know how hot that is?"

I'm not sure if it's the two days of separation, but there's nothing shy or timid about her tonight. Even so, that statement is confusing. "Since I was talking about my mom and sister, you'll have to explain that."

A small smile settles on her lips. "That you're protective of your sister. That you're sweet with your mom even though I can tell she annoys you. That you love your family."

"If that's hot to you, then you're definitely not like anyone I've ever met before. But it makes sense given how you are with Cade."

She shakes her head. "If he would only speak to me, I'd feel like a better sister."

I tell her the truth. "I wish I could bring you to California with me."

"Louise might've been kissing my ass all weekend trying to make up for lying to us, but I'm not sure she'd agree to that."

"When I get back, we'll have something to celebrate." I slide my hands up and dip them inside her shirt. The need to touch her when we're together is overwhelming. "Eighteen."

She grinds down on me, and I can't help but lift my hips and meet her. "Your obsession with my age is as over the top as your mother."

"If there's one way to soften my dick, it's to talk about my mother when we're like this."

She smiles. "You know what I mean. Your protection of my virtue is maddening."

"Your virtue was very much in question when I had you stripped naked with my mouth between your legs. I'm no saint, Carissa."

Her lip catches between her teeth, and she looks like she's mulling over her words.

"What?" I ask, wanting nothing more than to know what she's thinking.

She runs her fingers through my hair. "I'm ready."

My hands on her freeze, and my body tenses.

"I am," she keeps going. "You have a list of reasons to wait. And after what you went through with Isla, I get it, but—"

"That's not why," I interrupt. "She has nothing to do with us or me. Don't ever think that. This is a big fucking deal. I didn't take it seriously before, but I do now. And there's something about you. I'm taking this more seriously than ever. More than I ever thought I would."

"And I've never thought about this before with anyone. I'm not being flippant or emotional. I know what I want—I want you."

My chest rises and falls below her. Where she's pressed

into me in every way I want. And I've never wanted anything more than her.

But with all the shit up in the air right now...

"I want to be yours," she blurts.

"Fuck," I hiss.

My chest, it feels like it might burst or seize or implode. I bury my hand in her hair to pull her mouth to mine for a searing kiss. If I could meld our lips together until the end of time and forget about politicians, planted drugs, and drive-by shootings, I would.

I want her to be mine, and not just for the rest of the semester. Not just for my last summer before college.

I don't know when it happened, but I know when I'm with her in any way, all the other shit in the world doesn't matter.

And when I'm not with her, I feel desperate and out of control. I'm not sure how to fix that.

Or if I even want to fix it.

All I know is when I do make her mine for the first time —for her first time—it's not going to be in my fucking car.

My phone vibrates from where I threw it in the cupholder, reminding me of our shitty reality. I'm forced to break our connection.

Her breath is hot and heavy on my skin as she burrows into my chest. I reach for my phone and unlock the screen.

"Shit. It's my dad."

Dad – I see your location. Do I need to assume you're broken down on a dark, desolate road that's out of your way and need to come get you?

Me – No.

Dad – Then your car had better be moving on my screen pretty damn fast.

I pull in a breath and wrap my arms around her. "My

dad is tracking me. I'm not surprised after the shooting, but that sucks because he's never done it before."

She presses her lips to my neck. "He loves you."

I lift her face to mine. "He's tracking every single thing that comes across Emma's phone after what happened. I heard him tell Crew. If he's willing to do that to her, I can only assume he threw me into the mix. Don't text or message me saying anything you're not willing for him to read."

Her brown eyes widen.

I lean in to kiss her again when my phone rattles.

Dad – Pretty damn fast means now, bud.

I hold my phone up for her to read the text. "See?"

"I guess that means I need to climb off you." Despite her words, she doesn't move.

I don't push her off and get moving like I should to keep my dad from freaking out on me. I cup her face in my hands and make her a promise I'll die before breaking it. "You'll be mine, Carissa, in every way. And I can't wait to make that happen."

Carissa

Louise might not have a security system, but that doesn't mean she leaves her doors unlocked. So when my key doesn't catch the deadbolt and the knob turns, I frown.

It's not that late, not even ten. But Louise is always in bed by now, and since Cade has cut himself off from everything and locked himself in his room, I'm surprised every light is on from the entryway to the door leading to the back gardens.

Until I hear voices.

Not just voices.

Her voice.

My heart races as fast as my feet that take me to the commotion in Louise's formal sitting room. When I come to a halt at the wide threshold, my brain has trouble catching up.

"Carissa."

She's here.

Standing in the middle of the same room in which I've sat pretending to study with Levi. A room I hated when I first moved here because all it did was remind me how stuffy and non-grandma-like Louise has been our entire lives. But now...

Now I have different memories.

And I'm not ready to let them go.

"What are you doing here?" I seethe.

"Rissa," Cade mutters and shakes his head. "Don't."

I look from my brother to Louise, whose fingers must be a mangled mess from the stress of twisting them into knots lately.

She doesn't look happy to see her daughter.

Mariann Collins sure knows how to play the part of a politician's wife. Despite having gone missing for months, she's the picture of perfection, just like always. She has a way of demanding attention when she enters a room, no matter if she's on my dad's arm or alone.

I've always wished I were as tall as her. I might've gotten her blond hair and fair skin, but she stands four inches taller than me. It's always made her seem so extra—and me so ... not. If she's been traveling the world to get back here, no one would ever know. She looks like she just had a blow out and applied a fresh face of makeup.

Levi

I look back at Cade but motion to our mother. "Don't? She decided to come back after we found out she lied to us about where she's been all this time? And, even worse, her mental health?"

"Carissa," Mom clips as she starts to move for me but stops when I retreat. "Your grandmother told me how upset you are, even though no one will tell me how you two found out where I was. But I've had time to process what your father did. I'm in a better place."

"You mean you were caught in a lie, and now you're forced to face us?"

She puts her hands on her hips. "No, I'm forced to face reality. We all are. And the reality right now is your father's campaign is in trouble. All our lives will change drastically if he can't overcome this. It's time to move on."

Louise holds out a low hand and tries to be a voice of reason. "Mariann, let's talk about this. The kids have struggled. And now with Cillian's new ... political challenges, it might not be the best time to take them back."

I look from Louise to Mom. "Wait, what?"

"We're going home. It can't wait another day. Your father is in full-on damage control. He needs a united front."

I turn to Cade. "You can't seriously be considering going back."

"I'm not—"

But Mom cuts him off. "It's not a choice, Carissa. I have a charter booked. We're set to take off in less than ninety minutes. Get your things."

"Mariann, please—" Louise tries.

"You're going back to him?" I blurt, my words are an accusation. "He cheated on you, and you're just going to take him back like it never happened? You expect us to forgive him for that just because you want to live your fake life and all the bells and whistles it comes with?"

Mom's expression bristles. "I expect you to step up for your family. As of this morning, Frankie has been fired. She's no longer on your father's staff. As soon as this special investigation sham for the on-going payments gets buried, we can all get back to normal. Your father is working on a deal to make it go away as we speak. Pack your things. We only have thirty minutes if we're going to make that flight."

"No." I cross my arms and take a step back. "I'm not going."

"Rissa, we can't stay here forever," Cade says.

The thought of forever stirs a panic inside me. "I'm not leaving."

Mom narrows her eyes. "If this is about the boy your father told me about, get over it. And make it twenty minutes—I can't get out of here fast enough. I'll wait in the car with Chuck."

"Mariann, please." I've never seen Louise desperate. "Stay the night. We'll talk about it in the morning when everyone is rested."

Mom tucks her clutch under her arm. "I don't have time for this. Make sure they're packed."

Our mother stalks out of the room, leaving the three of us shocked and rooted in our spots.

I turn to Cade. "How can you just go along with her?"

"How can you not? We don't have a choice, and I don't have anything here."

"You don't have anything there either," I blurt.

His expression falls. "I can't believe that you, of all people, just said that to me. Like I need the reminder. The world reminds me every day that I'm different, Rissa, but never you. Not until right now. Thanks for that."

Tears well in my eyes, and I can barely speak over the lump in my throat. "I'm sorry. I didn't mean it like that."

But he's already on his way out, his shoulder bumps mine on the way as he mutters, "Hurry up. You know she'll be in a pissier mood if you make her wait."

I'm stuck in my spot and stare at Louise. I can't believe I'm about to do this but I beg, "Can you talk to her? Please, do something."

"I'm sorry," Louise whispers, feelings pour from her. "I know I'm not a good mother. No matter what I did or how hard I tried, I've never been able to reason with her—or please her, for that matter. I probably shouldn't have tried. I don't know where I went wrong."

Her words.

The look on her face.

I've never seen her like this.

"Go on," Louise croaks, trying her hardest to control her frayed emotions. Emotions that look like they have taken years of abuse. "If your mother wants you at home, you can't stay here. I'm sorry, Carissa. So sorry I've failed you both as a grandmother."

She turns to leave, too, but I see her swipe both cheeks on her way out.

And I'm left alone.

With absolutely no options.

28

YES

Levi

I thought I knew what anger was when Isla lied to me about being pregnant.

I thought I knew what it meant to feel powerless.

I had no fucking idea.

This...

This is what having no control over the one thing you want more than anything feels like.

It happened in a blink. I kissed her goodbye in Louise's elaborate circle drive and thought I'd see her today.

That today would be a normal school day.

But she's gone.

Just like that.

When she texted me last night to tell me what was happening, that she and Cade were on their way to the airport with their mom and had no choice, my mind went to places I'm not familiar with.

Real, legitimate kidnapping was one of them.

And not the *I'll bust you out of your grandmother's house*

for a couple of hours kind of kidnapping. No, I'm talking the *screw stupid titles, my scholarship, and future to take her somewhere no one would find us* kind of crime.

Regret was another. She said she was ready last night. It would've been so easy to make her mine, take her virginity, and beg her to stay with me forever. Because the thought of her being with anyone other than me, pushes my thoughts to an even scarier place.

And finally, my brain started making plans. Plans that, if I shared them with anyone other than her, would sound ridiculous to the society we've been conditioned to buy into. I'm eighteen. She's seventeen—even if it is only for another week. People like us in America don't make decisions like this. We graduate, go to college, fuck around for a few more years, and then make moves that include words like *forever* and *until death* and shit like that.

No one makes plans like that in high school.

Before last night, I was selfishly trying to figure out a way to keep her in Virginia so she wouldn't be across the country from me next year. Two hours I can handle. But an entire continent?

No fucking way.

Her mom showing up out of the blue and Carissa literally disintegrating into thin air was not on my radar.

This is what desperation has done to me. The shit going through my mind might sound asinine to the rest of the world, but right now, there's nothing I want more.

She'll be mine.

I'll get her back. There's no other option.

I'm sitting in the high school cafeteria, and she should be with me. But instead, I'm staring at her on my phone as she stands on stage with her family. The scene playing out isn't unlike the hundreds of images on the internet I found during my searches.

But this one is live.

She and Cade are standing next to their parents. Her dad is the picture of a consummate politician—polished, fake, and spewing shit that's been practiced and rehearsed. They're actually at a foodbank, one her mom apparently started years ago.

I can't take my eyes off the girl who's got my insides tangled into a messy knot. She looks nothing like my Carissa. Her hair is perfect, she looks like someone rolled her around in a drugstore makeup aisle, and she's wearing a dress that might be conservative on the hanger, but fits every curve of her body in a way, I know for a fucking fact, will have every set of eyes glued to her. Men of all ages are probably peeling that dress off her in their minds, fantasizing about things I've already done to her.

And other things I haven't gotten to yet.

Yeah.

I thought I knew what rage was before today.

Today can go down in the history books as the day I learned what possessiveness feels like.

I'm fucking flooded with it.

She's standing next to Cade with her hand on the back of his arm. Every once in a while, she'll push up on her spiked heels to whisper something in his ear and direct a small smile at him. Besides that, Carissa has played the part. Her expression isn't happy, and it's not pissed. She's perfectly bland.

I've never hated anything more.

Cade, on the other hand, looks like he's in hell. It hasn't even been twenty-four hours since Mariann Collins snatched her kids to take them home, and Cade has had a makeover. His hair is short and clipped, he's been stuffed in a suit, and shoved on stage in front of who knows how many people. Between the booming sound system and cheering crowd, it's evident for anyone to see—anyone willing to look, that is—that this is not good for Cade.

It shows. His expression isn't bland like his twin's. It's tight and tense. To anyone else in the crowd, he might come across terse. But I know him, and my gut turns for him. The rest of the world might think Cade Collins is curt, but I know his anxiety is through the roof.

And his parents don't give a shit. That pisses me off for my new friend.

"They look miserable," Mason says, watching the same shit play out on his phone.

"Look, I know Carissa is hot ... but man. Nicely done, my friend. She's fucking smoking in that tight-ass dress. No wonder she's front and center while Cillian lies to his constituents. Every cameraman is probably sporting a woody and has lost focus."

I tear my eyes away from the bullshit playing out live from across the country, and glare at Jack. "Say that one more time, and I'll come across this table and rip your balls out through your throat."

"Whoa, cowboy." Jack gives me a palm. "I'm just saying, those frumpy-ass sweaters she wears really hide the goods, if you know what I mean."

"Shut the fuck up, asswipe," I clip and look back to the twins.

"I can't believe they're gone. We didn't even get to say goodbye," Mason adds. "It won't be the same."

"No, things are definitely not the same," Jack clips and glares at me. "You're living with the hottest school counselor on earth. If your new obsession hadn't deserted you on *Love*

Island where you can't touch her twenty-four seven, I'd say you were the luckiest bastard on earth. Still, your dad is porking Ms. Lockhart. He's officially the luckiest man on earth. You could use a little of that luck to rub off on you, because the way I see it, you're going to be rubbing your junk solo from here on out."

"I'm into older women too. But they're hard, you know? I didn't take Carissa for the kind of girl who'd be into broody guys. Is that common?" Mason asks. "No offense, Levi. You're cool and all. I just don't get it."

"You don't have to be broody. I'm an asshole—all I have to do is snap my fingers, and I'm hot tubbing with an entire dance team. You've got the boy next door thing going on. Use it to your advantage. You have a lot to learn, but you're lucky. You have us. Watch and learn, young man. We can teach you our ways."

"I never thought high school would be this exciting. Thank you," Mason says, and sounds like he means it from the bottom of his genuine heart.

I ignore them both and focus on Carissa.

Cillian-fucking-Collins is at the climax of his bullshit speech, pointing to the crowd, lifting a fist in the air, making promises that are impossible to fulfill. When the crowd erupts, Cillian turns to his wife whom he screwed over, and she happily goes straight into his arms for a hug and kiss, like he didn't just get caught cheating on her a few months ago. Together, they turn to their children who do not fake happy.

Carissa and Cade are stiff and apathetic. I stare at her as long as the feed lets me, until it finally cuts off. I close the app when the news starts to pick apart his speech and focus on the scandals he's doing his best to squash like a pesky gnat. That's the shit I don't care about.

I toss my phone to the table. "I've got to find a way to get her back."

"Dude, you're in high school. She's just a junior." Jack reminds me of my miserable existence. "You're not some badass who can just pick up, take off around the world, and rescue your damsel in distress from the creepy King. What the fuck do you think you're going to do? Not to mention, you have to go to your mom's this weekend."

I drag a hand down my face and lean back in my chair. "You don't need to remind me how miserable life is right now. I've hardly had a chance to talk to her today. Carissa said her mom channeled her beauty pageant days and had them in hair and makeup for hours this morning. They're expected to start back at their old school this week."

"So you're going to do nothing?" Mason exclaims.

I grab my phone and bag, swinging it over my shoulder. "No fucking way. I might not be able to do it alone, but I know who might help me."

"Daddy Asa?" Jack asks.

I shake my head. "My dad might be powerful, but he has enough shit on his plate for two lifetimes right now. I'm counting on someone else—someone who's way more powerful than she thinks she might be."

"Your future step mom? The ultimate MILF herself, Keelie Lockhart?"

"Stop it with the MILF talk." I cringe given the fact my dad moved his shit into her bedroom. "I'm going to Louise. She loves me, and I'm going to capitalize on that in every way I can."

Carissa

Levi

THE MOMENT we're out of sight from the crowd, I storm through the backstage area.

Dad's new Chief of Staff—who's a man and old enough to be our grandfather—is waiting by our things. Mom said that from now on, she'll have final say on who's hired to work with Dad on a daily basis. She said it was part of their agreement for her to return from Greece early.

I rip my shoes off and throw them on top of my mother's exploding Louis Vuitton suitcase. I'm exhausted. Cade and I hardly slept last night, and the time change has messed with me. I'm hungry, exhausted, and emotional.

And, on top of everything else, I got my period late last night.

All I want to do is cry. I miss Levi so much and want to strangle my parents in the same thought.

"Carissa," my mother hisses from behind me. "Did you smile even once?"

"Mom, leave her alone," Cade demands.

I ignore them both and reach for my jeans that are laying in a heap on my backpack. I yank them up my legs, shimming up the damn dress Mom forced me to wear as I go.

Of course, Mom does not leave me alone. She grabs my arm and swings me around to face her. "We have enough problems, Carissa. We don't have the time or energy to deal with your attitude on top of everything else."

"My attitude?" Not giving a shit who sees me standing here in my bra—not even Grandpa Chief of Staff—I rip my arm from her hold and reach for the dress bunched at my waist. I struggle to get it up and over my head, because it's just that tight. My earring catches, and I'm in a pretzel, standing here in my jeans and bra. Once I finally get untangled, I throw it at my damn mother. "You mean you want me to forget how Dad cheated on you, and how you lied to us about where you were the last few months? And then being dragged back here for this bullshit rally, and all we want to know is who or what Dad has been sending millions of dollars to over the years?"

My mom turns red in the face. I'm surprised she doesn't combust from her body heat setting off her hair spray. That has to be some type of chemistry phenomenon. I should ask Levi. "We're all doing what we have to do."

"No. You're doing what you're desperate enough to do. Cade loves you, so he's here. I'm doing what I'm being forced to do. You think I give a shit if he wins?" I reach for my tank and drag it over my head. "I have days. Literally days until you can't force me to do shit like this ever again."

"Lower your voice." My father rounds the corner. Just like I've been accustomed to my whole life, he's a different person when he gets off the campaign stage. It seems the damage-control stage isn't any different. He looks me up and down. "Why did you change? I told you we're making another stop on the way home."

I pick up my purse and dig for my phone. "Because I'm done. I'm not going to stand next to either of you any longer and pretend we're some happy fucking family when we clearly are not. It's bad enough I let you force me to do this one." I turn to Cade. "Are you coming with me or staying with them?"

Cade threw a mild fit this morning when Mom had someone come to the house to cut his hair. It took less than twelve hours, but she turned us back into the puppets we've always been. Now it's his turn to stand back and watch me throw a fit. I'm usually the amicable one. He's not used to this. He reaches for his tie that was already loose, since he can't stand it choking him, and gives it a good yank. "Where are you going?"

"Home, until I can figure out what to do from there."

"You're not going anywhere," Dad snaps. "Get to the bathroom and put that dress back on."

I tip my head and lower my voice. "If you think I was uncooperative at this rally, I dare you to make me go to another one. I am not in your corner."

Mom looks at her watch and then to Cade. "We're going to be late. If your sister won't come, it will look odd with just one of you. Go with Carissa." Then she turns to me and narrows her eyes. "But we're talking about this when we get home. This is uncalled for."

I slip my feet into a pair of plastic flip flops. "I think the last few months have been uncalled for. There's already buzz about Dad firing Frankie. It would be a shame if the press found out where you've been and how you, as an unelected nobody, are in charge of the hiring and firing of the staff for the Senator from Arizona."

Mom's tone turns lethal. "Don't threaten me, Carissa. I will cut you off from your life faster than you can throw your attitude. We're all drowning here—it's not just you."

"Cade and I would be fine if you two weren't pulling us under. Call us a car. We want to go home."

Cade has untucked his dress shirt and tossed his tie on the floor with my dress and shoes. "If I never go to another one of these, it will be too soon."

"Let them go," Dad growls. "We'll talk about it tonight. We're going to be late."

Grandpa looks up from his phone, and I'm happy to see he's at least technologically savvy, unlike Louise. "Wait out front. A car will be here in ten to take you both home."

"Stay at the house," Mom warns, as her heels click on

the concrete floor in a quick clip, following Dad out of the building and to their limo.

I look at Cade. "I'm sorry. I can't keep up this charade. I'll hate myself more than I already do. I feel like I'm as much of a fraud as he is by just being here."

Cade hasn't said much to me since we left Virginia. Then again, I haven't said much to anyone until my tirade just now. "You want to go back, don't you?"

I cross my arms over my chest. "From the moment we got to Virginia, I didn't want to be there. But being back here doesn't feel right, either."

"But you want to go back ... for him? Tell me the truth, Rissa. I just need to know so I can prepare."

"I miss Levi already." My throat thickens and my eyes sting. "I feel foolish for saying it. And I feel selfish for wanting to go back whether you come with me or not."

He frowns. "It's not your job to take care of me."

"I know it's not my job. But I love you. We've hardly ever been apart. You're my crutch, too, you know. Are you happy to be back?"

He runs a hand through his short hair that I hate, but I'd never tell him that. "Let's wait for our car. I'm tired and have some shit to catch up on."

"I was supposed to have a chem test today. If I can somehow make it back to Virginia, I'll be even more behind." I move to him and bump his shoulder. "Maybe you can hack into the school's network and change my grade. That would be so helpful."

"I'm hacking into enough shit lately," he mutters.

I grab his hand and pull us both to a stop. "Wait. What's that supposed to mean?"

He pulls away from me and keeps going. "It means I'm still snooping."

I skip to keep up. "On who?"

"Who do you think?"

I put a hand up. "No. You need to stop. I'm afraid you'll get caught, and you're close enough to eighteen, they'll hit you hard. It'll be on your record forever—or worse."

Cade rolls his eyes. "You have no confidence in my skills."

I rush after him when he starts to walk away from me. "I know you're good—too good. That's the problem. You're going to find something you can't backpedal from. We did what we wanted to do, but we're back with them anyway. Please promise me you'll stop."

He sighs. "Fine. I'll stop even though I don't want to."

We get to the door and push it open. Despite it being spring in Arizona, the heat and sun assault us. I slide on my sunglasses and pull my phone from my bag. I have a million texts, most of them are on the Homies thread.

But there's one more.

Just one.

And it's from Levi. I texted him as I cried all the way home on the flight last night, and more this morning. But he sent this one while we were in the stupid rally.

Levi – You're fucking gorgeous. I'm pissed and jealous. You're there. I'm here. And there's nothing I want more than you. If you want to come back, I'll come get you. If not, I'll find a way to come to you. I'll drop my scholarship if I have to. I'll find a school close to you. I'll even deal with the wrath of Cillian Collins if it means being with you. Tell me what you want, baby. I'll make it happen.

The message was sent twenty minutes ago. My fingers start to type, because my answer is easy.

I want him.

I want to go back.

"Here's our car," Cade says. A car from the limo service my parents use turns the corner.

I look up at my big brother and wonder if he'll come with me. I wonder what it would be like to live without him across the hall. I knew it would happen eventually when we left for college, but not now.

Cade opens the door for me and I climb into the back of the car for the two-hour drive to our house. When he sits next to me, I put my fingers to my screen, because I know my answer without a doubt.

Me – Yes.
Levi – Yes to what, baby?
Me – Yes to everything.

29

LONG WEEK

Carissa

Cade makes a half-turn in his chair. "You're really going back?"

I give him a little shrug, because I don't know how to handle this. "I knew I wanted to go back the minute that door closed on the jet leaving Virginia. And now that I'm actually home, it doesn't feel right. I miss him. What do you want to do?"

He hikes a brow and spins back to his computer. "Does it matter?"

"Yes, it matters." I get up from where I'm sitting and go to him, forcing him to look at me. "It matters to me. Besides Louise not knowing what to do with us, and Mom and Dad's drama, did you hate it there that much?"

He shakes his head and turns back to his computer. "We're not the same, Rissa. People don't flock to me like they do to you. I mean, thank goodness. I don't want them around me anyway. Does it really matter where I am?"

My heartbeat speeds. "I care where you are."

He drops his hands from his keyboard and turns back. "It doesn't matter what we want. Not right now, anyway. We're here. You think Mom and Dad are going to let us pick up and go anywhere before we graduate? You need to get used to it, and we need to make the best of it. Not that it was great living with Louise either."

"We're almost eighteen," I point out.

"Right. Mom and Dad will get us each something stupid ridiculous, and we'll move on. It's just a day. Nothing changes other than we can vote against Dad, if we even decide to bother. But we have an entire year of high school to go. Even if you can manage to graduate early at this point, you're not going anywhere anytime soon."

I cross my arms to hug my middle and announce, "I want to go back."

He looks at me like I'm dense after all the reasons he just explained why I need to suck it up. "There's no way."

"I'm working on it," I admit.

He narrows his eyes on me. "Working on it how? Running away?"

I say nothing, but my eyes do shift to the side.

"Rissa," he bites. "What are you going to do?"

I pull in a big breath and brace for his reaction. "I'm thinking about leaving. This weekend."

He pushes to his feet, and I have to take a step back to make room. "You're just going to drive across the country?"

"That's actually not a bad idea. I'd at least have my car there."

"We don't turn eighteen until next week. Mom and Dad will go apeshit."

I shrug. "I stopped caring what they think. Come with me, Cade."

"You want me to run away?"

"You make it sound like it's illegal or a crime against nature. Might I remind you, you're the one hacking into private networks," I say, trying to defend myself.

"Where are you going to go? Do you think you're going to live with Levi? Because if so, you're crazy. And did you forget he's living with the counselor?"

"There's always Louise. I feel like she was coming around. And if we had a car, it might be better."

"So you are going to drive across the country," he deadpans.

"I told you, I'm still figuring things out. I want you to come with me."

He leans back in his chair, shakes his head, and turns back to his screen.

He says nothing.

"Think about it. Please," I beg. "I know we'll go our separate ways after high school, but I'm not ready yet."

His jaw tightens and he stays silent.

"I'll let you know my plans so you can make a decision. But start thinking about it now so you can prepare."

This isn't the first time he's blocked me out, and I'm sure it won't be the last. But at least he knows. If I have to beg him more, I will.

I leave his room and go across the hall where my room and private bath is and go straight for my phone.

Levi picks up on the first ring. "What did he say?"

I sigh. "He didn't say no."

Levi pauses. "Is that good?"

"I don't know. It's not bad. I might be able to talk him into it. If I were to guess, it's the uncertainty of what our parents will do once they realize we're gone. He doesn't deal well with that."

I hear a door slam in the background, and my mind goes

back to our time in his room. Levi lowers his voice. "Have you changed your mind?"

I pull in a breath. "No. Not at all."

"Fuck. It's going to be a long week."

"Tell me about it. My parents are in salvage-the-campaign mode while still hating each other. At least Cade and I got out of the last two stops for the day, but ever since my parents got home, it's either been a screaming match or the silent treatment—nothing in between. It's miserable. Worse than the misery we had at Louise's house."

"I think she was actually happy to see me. I ate five cookies while we talked."

"At least she likes you," I say.

"I have a feeling Louise is complicated. What are you going to do for the next week?"

"It's not like I have a lot on my plate."

"If there's anything else on your plate other than me, I'm gonna be pissed."

I lay down on my bed and roll to my side. "I can't handle anything else besides knowing I have a plan. Last night at this time I was crying my eyes out."

"When I get you back..."

I say nothing and wait, but he doesn't finish. "When you get me back, what?"

He exhales. I wish I were there to feel his chest rise and fall as his heartbeat strums under my touch. "Let's just put it this way, I can't wait. My fucking brain is so consumed by you, I can't think straight."

That's an understatement.

I can't wait to be back in his arms where I belong.

30

UNSAFE

Levi

I've been to a lot of places, but never Phoenix.

My mom wasn't happy when I told her what I wanted to do. At first, she flat out said no.

Then she asked why I was the one who needed to get involved.

I told her I couldn't stand by and let Carissa be miserable. That she wanted to go back to Virginia to finish high school. And that she wanted to live with her grandmother.

Then I might've told Mom that Carissa is already eighteen.

Not a big deal, it's only a few days.

I might've left out that her parents don't know I'm coming for her.

A minor detail.

I have a plan and the support of Louise Boyette. What else do I need?

In the end, I convinced my mom she needed alone time with Emma anyway. She finally handed over her keys.

I pull my mom's Expedition to a stop and throw it in park. Damn. Career politicians must do really well. I'm sitting in front of a miniature mansion. Contemporary, gated, and surrounded with cameras that are not at all hidden. Whoever is inside wants those outside to know they're being watched.

Great.

The drive was just under six hours, and I'll turn around to go straight back. Emma and I got to Los Angeles yesterday and will fly home tomorrow. This is a long day, but one I'm more than willing to take on, because in the end, I'll have her back.

Me – I'm here, parked on the street in front of your house.

Carissa – OMG. They're fighting.

Me – Are you okay? I'll come in and get you.

Carissa – No. You can't do that.

Carissa – Holy shit. He's on a bender. He has been since last night when he found out the FBI investigation into the payments wasn't dropped.

The house sits far back from the road. I can barely see the front door for all the landscaping. It won't be ideal, but I can scale the wall.

Me – Baby, are you unsafe?

Bubbles dance on the bottom of the screen and then disappear. It happens two more times, and I'm about to climb a wall when the gates part.

I don't think twice. I pull into the circle drive. I hear it the moment I climb out of the car at the massive double front doors. Yelling from inside the house. And not just the Senator.

It's Carissa.

Fuck the doorbell or knocking. I'm about to reach for the handle when the door bursts open.

Damn. I feel like it's been a whole year, not just a week.

She's in a pair of short shorts, a tank, and flip flops. The only time I've ever seen her close to looking like this is when I had her stripped naked in my bedroom.

I can't think about that right now, because she's also crying.

Two duffle bags that are about as big as her weigh her down. I hold my hand out to take them when her dad follows her through the door and grips her upper arm with so much force, I see his fingers bite into her bare skin.

Rage takes over my brain.

The bags fall to the ground at her feet when he yanks her back, whipping her around.

Carissa screams.

"Get your hands off her," I demand and reach for her.

Cillian pulls her to his side and glares at me through glassy eyes. He looks nothing like he does in public. He's wearing a dirty T-shirt and a pair of shorts. He's barefoot, his thick hair is disheveled, and his words are slurred. "Get the fuck off my property, you little prick. Lay a hand on my daughter, and I'll take you down. No one fucks with me and gets away with it. And no one fucks with my daughter."

"Cade, come back!" A woman's voice rings from inside the house right before Carissa's twin comes to a halt at the threshold.

Cade has a bag of his own and two backpacks slung over his shoulder. But the minute he sees his sister, he drops them all and puts his hands to Cillian's side, giving him a shove. "You're hurting her, you fucking drunk!"

Cillian's vehement gaze shifts to his son. He pushes Carissa, and she goes tumbling to the side, landing in a rock garden.

Fuck. The only thing I want right now is to get the hell out of here with the Collins twins.

I pull Carissa to her feet and guide her toward my car.

Cillian is drunk and sloppy and has forgotten about his daughter. He puts his hands to Cade, fisting his shirt at the neck and slams him against the side of the house. "Son of a bitch, don't ever fucking touch me like that again. You two have been nothing but a pain in the ass since you came home."

"I hate you," Cade spits and tries to push Cillian away. "I hope they take you down for all the shit you've gotten away with."

Cillian's expression hardens.

"Dad, stop it!" Carissa cries and tries to move to them. But there's no way I'm letting her close to her dad again and hold her back.

"Cillian, let him go!" Real life looks very different than the fake picture they put out to the world. Mariann Collins is frenzied, her eyes frantic when she sees her husband's hands on Cade.

Cillian doesn't listen to either of them. I can see it coming, but I can't get to him with Carissa hanging on my side before it happens. The Senator might be drunk, but when he pulls an arm back, his fist connects with his son's jaw with some power behind it.

"No!" Carissa screams.

"Cillian, stop!" Mariann begs.

The moment my feet move, Carissa lets me go. In three long strides, I reach him.

I grip Cillian's forearm and pull him off his son. Cade moves instantly, and I growl, "Hold her back."

I can't look back to make sure Carissa's okay, because her dad comes for me next. All I see is a fist coming for my face.

I don't flinch.

"Dad, don't!" Carissa calls again.

His fist catches my jaw. "You're not going anywhere with my daughter, dammit."

I push him. He stumbles back a step, and I follow. "You think I'm going to leave her and Cade here? You just committed battery on both your children."

"They're mine and they're staying here." He swings for me again, but this one is sloppy and grazes my temple. He looks around me to Cade and Carissa. "Get back in the fucking house."

Mariann is crying behind him. "Don't leave. Please, don't leave."

"Get in the car," Cade bosses Carissa.

"Levi," Carissa cries through tears.

I can't look back for her because Cillian charges.

I'm done. I've done what I needed to do, and we need to get the fuck out of here.

I catch his forearm before he hits me this time and twist him. His back is to my front, and the smell of stale alcohol rolls off him. He struggles to get away but I hold tight while Cade moves in front of us to get their bags.

"Let me go!" Cillian grits. "I'll have you charged with kidnapping and assault. You can't touch me. No one can touch me!"

"You should've thought about that before you laid a hand on Carissa and Cade. You do that all the time? Hit your kids? Your wife? Your fucking mistress?"

He says nothing, but I hear a car door slam. I don't let Cillian go and turn to see Carissa sitting in the passenger seat and Cade standing sentry in front of her. They're both staring at their father. I wonder how often this shit happens.

Their bags are loaded. They're ready to get out of here, and so am I.

I push Cillian to the side and he lands on his ass. "Leave them the fuck alone."

"Cade, no. Don't go." Mariann cries for her son.

Fucking bitch. She just dumped her kids a few months ago to lick her wounds on an extended vacation.

When I get to the car, Cade climbs in the back. No sooner does his door slam, closing out their Mom's pleas, and we're down the driveway and on the road.

I glance over at Carissa. She's leaning on the door, cradling her face in her hand. The only sound in the car is her crying. I turn the corner and look into the rearview mirror. "You okay, Cade?"

He's trembling, staring unseeing out his window. Blood is dripping down his chin from his busted lip, but he doesn't move to look at me.

Fuck.

I drive another couple miles before I find a parking lot to pull into and stop. I dig through the console until I find my mom's stash of napkins and wipes.

"Here." I thrust them at Cade. "You're bleeding."

It's like I woke him from a trance. His breaths are shallow when he turns to look at me first and then his sister as he touches his lip. He takes the napkins and wipes the blood.

"Can you download any footage from any of those two million surveillance cameras?" I ask.

"Yeah," he wheezes. "I should be able to."

Carissa turns in the front seat to look at her brother. "You brought your inhaler, right?"

Cade drops the bloody napkins to his lap and digs through one of the backpacks he threw in the backseat until he finds it. He shakes it, takes a long puff, and leans back to close his eyes. "I'm fine. Give me a second, and I'll check the feeds."

"Download whatever you can and keep it in a safe place. If they try to take you back again, you'll have that as leverage."

I turn to Carissa. Tears stain her beautiful face, but she's here. She's got one hell of a mark on her arm and her leg is scraped from where she fell. When I reach out to touch her face, she mutters, "He hit you. I can't believe he hit you."

I shake my head. "I'm fine. No matter how much I wanted to pummel his face, there was no way I was going to give him the satisfaction of having that on video and hang that over my head. It was all I could do to not lay him out flat."

She unhooks her seatbelt and leans across the console. I don't make her go far and bury my hand in her hair to bring her face to mine in a searing kiss. I don't give a shit her brother is sitting three feet from us.

I have her back, and I'm never letting her go.

"Thank you," she murmurs against my lips. "Thank you for coming all this way for us."

"Fuck, baby. I would've driven across the country for you."

"I got it." Cade breaks into our moment, and when we look back, he's holding up his phone. The crisp, clear picture of the U.S. Senator pulling his arm back and clocking his own son in the face dances across the screen. "This is worth the bloody lip."

I look from one twin to the other. One who I like a lot, and the other who I'm feeling things for I've never felt before. I've never been so pissed and relieved at the same time. "That's your golden ticket—your leave-me-the-fuck-alone-for-good ticket. If they try to force you to do something or be where you don't want to be, you've got that in your back pocket."

I pull Carissa to me for one more kiss before settling back in my seat. "Turn off all your location services, just in case."

Carissa reaches for her phone, but Cade says, "Did that before we left the house."

I put my fingers to Carissa's chin once more and turn her face to me. "He'll never do that to you again. If he ever lays another hand on you, I swear, I'll take him down."

She presses her lips into a thin line and gives me a small nod.

I pull out of the parking lot and press go to a landline I've called way more than I ever thought I would. She doesn't have a cell, so a text is not an option.

She answers over Bluetooth. "Hello?"

I glance at Carissa as I speak. "Hey, Mrs. Boyette."

"Levi." She sounds tense. "How did it go?"

"I've got them, that's all that matters. I'll let Cade and Carissa fill you in. We're on our way back to L.A."

She sighs, and it sounds like pure relief. "I'm sure I'll hear from Mariann soon enough. It won't be pretty, but I'll deal with the consequences. Chuck will meet you at the airport tomorrow night. Please tell them..."

Silence hangs through the SUV so thick, I could cut it with a knife.

Since she has no clue she's on speaker, I give the old woman a break. "I'll tell them you're looking forward to seeing them."

"Yes. Yes, I am. I'll do my best, Levi."

"See you soon."

"Goodbye."

I disconnect and reach over to claim Carissa's hand as we settle in for the drive. She scoots down in her seat to settle in. "I'm lucky you're good with old people."

"Louise and I are tight now. She wants to make it right," I explain as we get on the highway. "She just doesn't know how. But she didn't hesitate buying your plane tickets and promised me things would be different."

"She's never gotten drunk and hit us, so there's that," Cade mutters. "She's too worried about her white carpet."

I have a feeling things will be different from here on out.

I'll just have to explain to my dad why I helped a Senator's kids run away from home, and took them across state lines days before their eighteenth birthdays.

Carissa

Levi's dad is intimidating.

Not in a way my dad tries to be intimidating.

But when we walked through security of Reagan International tonight and he laid eyes on his son holding my hand, it was very clear Levi didn't fill him in on the weekend's events.

Mr. Hollingsworth was surprised to see me. And surprised, in this case, equates to not happy.

I'm not sure if he thinks I'm going to turn into another Isla-slash-Ursula nightmare.

Levi's dad doesn't know me. If he has a reason not to want Levi to have anything to do with me, it should be because of the drama anyone close to my father has to deal with, not because of me. I might be totally and utterly obsessed with Levi, but it's in a way I'd never want any harm to come to him. Seeing him physically attacked by my father yesterday was bad enough. I'd never do anything to hurt him.

Levi informed me on the flight home that he wasn't worried about what his dad would say about him driving all the way to Phoenix to get us. He said he might be mad for about two minutes, but knew he'd be able to make him see why he did it. And he knew if his dad were in his position, he'd do the same thing.

Chuck pushes the big front doors open and motions for me to enter first. Cade follows, but I only move inside far enough for Chuck to bring our bags in and say a quick goodbye.

He's gone in a flash.

And we're alone with Louise.

Again.

She says nothing, but wrings her fingers.

"We're back," I announce, as if it's not apparent that we are, in fact, back.

"Ah, hey," Cade mutters. It's going to take him a while to get over the whole our-grandmother-almost-killed-him-by-ignoring-his-asthma ordeal.

"Hello," she clips with a tight smile. It looks so uncomfortable on her face, I wonder if it's giving her a wedgie. "How was your flight?"

I glance at Cade and try not to frown. I've always thought that is the weirdest question to ask after a trip across the country in the air. We're here, alive aren't we? I mean, I think by process of elimination, that makes the flight successful.

"It was good. Thank you for buying our tickets," I say, because after yesterday, we're more than grateful.

"You're welcome. Have you eaten?" she asks, always concerned with food.

"We had pizza in Chicago at our layover," Cade pipes in.

Her smile relaxes a centimeter and she clears her throat. "Very well. Let's try this again, shall we? I'm not accustomed to teenagers, but I'll do better. No, no," she backs herself up. "I'll do my best. Here." She closes the short distance between us in her house shoes and holds up two fobs I didn't know she was fisting. "Happy early birthday. You'll have to share. It's not too big and not too small. Chuck picked it out. My only conditions were it was to be safe and American made."

We each take a fob and our gazes move from each other to her.

"What is it?" I ask.

"A Jeep Cherokee. It's red. I've heard red cars are good for teenagers. People will see you coming and get out of your way," she states, as if we drive into people every other day. We've never been in an accident—either of us.

I don't tell her that. I don't want to be rude, and I'm overcome by her gesture. She's actually trying. "Thank you. This is amazing."

I elbow Cade, and his gaze jumps to Louise. "Yeah, this is great."

"I do have rules. You're to tell me where you are at all times. Don't speed. Be courteous. I dislike rude drivers."

"I hate rude drivers too," I agree.

"And you'll have an allowance in exchange for keeping your rooms and bathroom clean. You can pay for your gas out of that. It's important for you to learn how to manage a budget. We'll address anything else that comes up as we go."

I look into her old, wrinkled eyes. The only other time I've seen her look remotely like this is when she got caught in her lie about where Mom was and remorse and guilt were etched in every inch of her expression. "This is really nice. We appreciate it."

"Well. That's done." Louise exhales as if she's been dreading this moment all day. "I made lemon bread. It's in the kitchen in case you have a taste for something sweet. It's late. I'm going to bed. I'll see you in the morning before school."

She takes two steps backward, and Cade and I both mumble, "Goodnight."

Louise turns on her slippers and shuffles off into the mansion, leaving us standing here with our haphazardly-packed duffels and loaded backpacks, as if we were escaping a third-world country on the brink of attack, instead of our childhood home and that of a U.S. Senator.

We wait another minute when Cade whispers, "She bought us a car and made us dessert. What the hell was that?"

"I don't know. But I do know it's good and we shouldn't question it." I turn to my big brother. "Are you happy to be back?"

Cade bends and picks up his bags. "A new car and dessert are cool. But Dad hit me yesterday while he was drunk. What do you think?"

He doesn't wait for me to answer. He heads up the stairs and disappears on his way to the third level.

I look around. It feels different than it did when we arrived here on New Year's Day. I'm not filled with dread and the walls aren't ominous. They're weirdly comforting tonight.

I finally allow my insides to loosen a bit.

My phone vibrates from the front pocket of my hoodie.

Levi – You home?

Home.

I don't know how I feel about that word right now, even though I know what he means.

Me – Yes. Louise bought us a car.

Levi – Wow. She must feel really guilty.

Me – I know.

Levi – Do the seats recline?

I smile

Me – IDK. I haven't seen it yet.

Levi – I can't wait to test them out.

Me – Same. I've got to unpack.

Levi – So fucking happy you're back, baby. A week is way too long. Makes me want to drop out of college and never leave you.

Me – I'm down for the never leaving me part. But your dad will hate me as much as he does Isla if you drop out of college. I'm not sure I can handle that.

Levi – He doesn't hate you. I talked to him on the way home. I told you he'd understand, and he does.

Me – That's a relief.

Levi – Go to bed, baby. I'll see you tomorrow, and all will be right with the world again.

I exhale and hold the phone to my heart.

I hope he's right.

31

BIRTHDAY GIRL

Carissa

I walk out of Mr. Stance's room after making up the test I missed last week. My teachers have been nice and given me a few days to catch up from being gone.

We might've only been gone a week, but it feels like a month. I doubt Cade will have any problem catching up. I'm not sure how he did it, but Levi scored a study room in the library every day at lunch and has helped me review.

Besides the normal footsie play under the table, he was all business and proved why he'll probably be valedictorian come graduation. When push comes to shove, he's disciplined and crammed that shit into my foggy brain until I could spew it back verbatim.

But on our way out of the library and before the bell rang, he'd pull me into the non-fiction section between technology and the arts. We'd leave that part of the Dewy Decimal System askew after he'd push me up against the books to kiss me crazy.

It's been like that for three days.

I barely finished the test on time and had to work well after the bell rang. If I get anything lower than a C plus, I'm blaming my tutor's hands, lips, and the minty taste of his tongue that were all in the forefront of my mind while taking a test.

I'm late to my next class and the halls have started to clear out when I come around the corner and someone almost bowls me over.

We both come to an abrupt stop, and a book hits the floor in a bang as papers go sliding.

"Sorry—" I blurt, but stop when I realize who it is.

Shit.

Isla Perry.

The Victoria's Secret Angel doppelgänger, in all her natural beauty and perfection. Her jeans fit like a second skin, and her sweater is cropped just enough for her not to get sent home for a wardrobe violation.

I'm caught wondering why I can't get my hair to be so perfectly imperfect when I realize she's glaring at me through her sultry, sexy—and when directed at me, callous —eyes.

"Sorry," I repeat and leave it at that. She doesn't move, so I bend to pick up some of her papers. "Here. Ah, sorry again."

She doesn't move. "I thought you were gone."

I press my lips into a thin line and shake my head. "I'm ... no. I mean, I'm not gone. I'm just..." I pause and sigh. "Back."

Wow. Her eyebrows are even more perfect when one is hiked above the other while frowning. "I had one week of peace without *you* being thrown in my face. It was the best week of my senior year."

Interesting. Last week was my worst week. I don't

mention the first semester of her senior year before she knew I existed. She must have a short-term memory.

"You came back for nothing, you know. I heard you're barely passing half your classes. He's going to forget all about you when he gets to Hopkins. Four years being a star for a lacrosse program like theirs? He'll have girls throwing themselves at his feet his freshman year." Isla loses the glare and a small satisfied smile settles on her naturally red lips. "You'll be nothing but a high school memory of a basic girl that he made into a last-semester project."

A few students who were rushing to their next class slow to take in the drama. This is worse than any day in the lunchroom with Isla staring at me sitting with her ex-boyfriend who dumped her faster than the trash from last week.

I realize I'm fisting her papers in my sweaty hand as she spews this shit at me. Do I think I'm Levi's last-semester project? No.

No fucking way.

But the rest of it...

The part about him going away to school, no matter if it is only two hours away. That's a given, and there's the fact that I'll still be here next year. The last two weeks have been too dramatic for me to even think about next month, let alone next year.

I push her papers toward her, but she shifts back, like I'll burn her, or rub off on her and make her merely ordinary and basic.

"Here," I clip, but she doesn't give me the satisfaction of ... anything.

She stands there, cool as a cucumber. I'm either going to have to shove the papers in her face, drop them at her feet, or rip them up and shove them in the trash.

I know which one I'd prefer right now.

"You and I have something in common, you know," Isla says. "He'll get tired of you eventually and be done. All those times he said it, I was convinced he loved me, too, but I was wrong."

I feel the color drain from my face as the papers in my hand crinkle tighter.

Isla's hand flies to her mouth, and her sexy eyes widen. She takes a step closer, lowering her voice without really lowering it. "Oh my God. He hasn't told you he loves you ... so sad."

I try to control my beating heart, but the bell rings.

I'm officially late to class.

Everyone who's paused their day to eavesdrop on our conversation doesn't move either. I guess Levi Hollingsworth's ex and current girlfriends are worth the tardy.

Isla smiles and says it in a sing-songy tone that makes me think even she's surprised. "So let me get this straight. He went all the way to Phoenix to bring you and your brother back, but there's been no profession of love?"

Damn. He hasn't, but why would I expect him to? I haven't said it, even though I've thought it. I've thought about it more than I care to admit ... even silently to myself.

But I don't know what to say or do. I don't do mean girls or drama well. I'm the kind of person who thinks of a good comeback two days later, so I stand here completely silent.

Isla looks surprised. "Hmm. I'm trying to process what this means for you. Other than you're exactly what I said—merely a project. Maybe Levi needed to up his volunteer hours and thought he could have some fun in the process. It has been a couple of years I hear. If rumors are true, and they usually are, the last person he's been with is me." Her smile is as bright as a nuclear explosion. "I hope you're not one of those *girls* who gets caught up in the comparison game." She leans in and lowers her voice. "It can really mess with your head."

"Well, fuck me."

I whip around and realize how impossibly fast my heart is beating. I'm a deer in the headlights, and Isla is doing everything in her power to leave me bloody, messy road-kill.

Jack glares at the mean girl I just can't shake as he walks to my side and casually drapes an arm over my shoulders. "Why the fuck is the bottom feeder making you late to class, Mrs. Hollingsworth?"

What? No! He needs to stop talking.

My breath catches, but there's no point in trying to speak. When Jack is around, he demands all attention.

"Fuck you, Jack," Isla hisses.

"See, Ursula wants to be in your shoes. So much, she was willing to trap a man with all those suctiony tentacles." I jump when Jack flails his arms around, even the one draped around my shoulders, as he makes slurping noises. "She's jealous of the new Mrs. and is willing to spew her venom to kill the love and turn everyone into seaweed for her garden."

Isla's face grows redder with every ridiculous word spewed from Jack's mouth.

Jack continues to speak to me. "Don't let her rain on your fairy tale, Carissa. When your boy toy finds out about this, he's going to come un-fucking-glued. I mean, he went all the way across the country for you. What do you think he'll do to a bottom feeder who's bullying you?"

I shrug and shake my head, but he grabs the papers out of my hand before I can think of a response. When he realizes they're Isla's, he drops them to fall at our feet, scattering between us.

Jack tags me around the neck and pulls me with him. "Let's get you to class. I can't wait to tell my boy Levi how I saved his heroine from the wicked sea monster."

I allow Jack to pull me along as people watch. I try to turn to him and whisper, "Please don't tell Levi. I'm surprised she hasn't done that before now. It's not a big deal."

"Carissa, you see all these people?" He points around us with the hand that's draped over my shoulder. "I'm not going to have to tell Levi shit. He'll know everything before practice. I feel sorry for the asshole who's scrimmaging against him."

Oh no.

Levi

I DON'T REMEMBER what normal was.

Not that I liked normal. I hated normal, actually. It was mundane and miserable. And I do not want to go back there.

But what I'm in now is this weird limbo universe where things are equally amazing as they are shit.

I met Carissa—good.

Someone stuffed drugs in my locker—bad.

Carissa proved that all girls are not psycho—all good.

Someone shot up our house—nightmare bad.

There was the time I got Carissa naked—like, wet dream good.

Carissa's parents dragged her and Cade back to Arizona in the middle of the night—really fucking bad.

I got them back—epic good.

Then, in the last couple of days...

My dad sorted out Emma's drama, but that won him a trip to the hospital and a shitload of stitches. Keelie isn't speaking to my dad, but we're still living there—which is fucking weird.

And I hear from pretty much everyone in the school that Isla tried to fuck with my obsession between classes.

So it's official.

I'm going to have to kill someone.

And, oh yeah, it's Carissa's birthday. But given all the other shit going on, I haven't seen her since lunch, and since the Isla encounter, she's barely returned my texts.

We had plans, dammit.

I had plans.

Me – She won't answer me. Can you let me in?

Cade – She's in the shower.

Me – I'll wait.

Cade – Cool.

Me – No, I mean, let me in. I'll wait inside.

Cade – If she doesn't want you here, she'll be pissed at me.

Me – Look. It's your birthdays. I have something for her. I even have something for you. Let me in. I'll make sure she's not pissed at you.

Cade – Fine. I'll meet you at the garden room door.

Fucking finally.

I grab my bag, lock my Jeep, and jog up the fucking hill to the back of the house. It's creepier than shit at night, standing three stories high with enough nooks, crannies, and doors to make for a killer haunted house.

Cade is already waiting and flips the simple lock before holding it open for me. "She's already in a pissy mood, and if she directs it at me, I'm holding you responsible. I don't know if she's on her period or what, but she's not a fun twin today."

I reach in my bag and pull out a box that's still in the plastic sack from the store. "Happy birthday. They're the best and newest on the market. Trust me, they're the best ones I've ever had. Keelie's daughter, Saylor, is as loud as a fucking siren. Wearing these is the only way I can focus. You put them on, the world will leave you alone."

Cade opens the sack and pulls out the noise canceling headphones. "Wow. Thanks."

Commotion and loud noises have a way of clawing at him. Carissa's explained it. He can deal if he has to, but why deal when you don't have to? "Hey, take it from one brainiac to another, these are the shit."

He looks from his gift to me. "This is cool of you."

I shrug. "You're an adult. You can officially tell everyone in your life to fuck off. Congrats."

Cade mutters as he skims the back of the box. "A half a car, the ability to shut the world out, and flip everyone off in the process. Not a bad birthday."

He moves, and I toe off my shoes and pick them up. It's been a hot minute since I've snuck in, but the house is as dark, silent, and eerie as ever. I told Dad I was staying at Jack's again. If Carissa kicks me out, I'll have to actually go to Jack's sofa or sleep in my Jeep.

"Good luck," Cade mutters when I get to Carissa's bedroom door. "I don't know if that's what's wrong with her, but Mason told me about Isla. I'm always the last to know shit. Don't let that happen again."

"That's never going to happen again," I promise. "I plan to take care of it tomorrow."

With that, Cade disappears down the hall. I shut myself in Carissa's room, lock the door behind me, and dump my bag on the floor by her bed. I have to wait another five minutes before the water shuts off and another two before the bathroom door opens.

She chokes out a mini scream before silencing herself when she sees me sitting on the foot of her bed. Her long hair is wet and dripping down her shoulders, and she's fisting the towel at her tits.

Other than the study room in the library, this is the first time we've really been alone since I brought her back to Virginia.

There's nothing more I've wanted than this.

I've craved this.

At this point, I don't care what happens tonight. I just want to be close to her.

"What are you doing here?" she hisses, and shuts the bathroom door behind her.

I sit up from where I was leaning back on my elbows and look her up and down. "It's your birthday. You really think I'm going to let the day go by and not see you?"

She tightens the towel around her and shifts her weight. "It's just a day."

I shake my head. "It's not just a day. You were brought into the world today, and now you're an adult. Birthdays are a big fucking deal and should be celebrated."

She leans into the door jamb. "I thought you were the broody jock who hated the world. When did you turn all balloons, streamers, and candles?"

I cringe because I should've gotten her a cake. I didn't think about that.

"I'm not a party planner, baby. If that's what you want, then you picked the wrong tutor to hook up with."

Her eyes narrow.

I hold my hand out for her. "Come here."

"You need to leave so I can get dressed."

I try to bite back my smile. "It's not like I haven't seen you naked before."

"The last time you saw me naked, there was a drive-by shooting an hour later. I don't need that kind of juju again."

I shake my head. "Nice try. But you know that's sorted out. It's the only reason my dad let me out of the house. I'm supposed to be at Jack's for an early morning workout."

"But you came here for a workout instead since I'm of legal age now?"

My smile dissolves into something else. Something I try to control, because it's her birthday, and I don't want to show her how much that pisses me off. "The last thing I want to talk about right now is Isla, but maybe we need to."

She finally moves and goes to her dresser. Drawers bang open and shut, and she's downright violent with a pair of panties and what looks to be a T-shirt. "I've had about enough of Isla today."

I want to move to her. Touch her. Rip her towel off, drop to my knees in front of her, and taste her again. I've been dreaming of doing that and more for weeks.

But I don't. I sit here and watch her shimmy a pair of panties up under her towel and I barely get a glimpse of her bare ass in the process. A tight-ass tank is pulled over her head as she finally tosses the wet towel to the floor.

She might be covered by very little clothing, but I can still see everything when she turns and leans her ass on the dresser across from me.

I only focus on her dark eyes through the dim room. "After all we've been through, you think I'm here to fuck you since you're finally eighteen?"

Her lips press into a thin line.

"Isla's a jealous bitch. Put her out of your head." I

motion between the two of us. "She doesn't belong here and never will. This is you and me. And I know if you didn't trust me, you wouldn't be standing there barely dressed."

Her arms fall to her sides. "It wasn't fun. I don't do mean girls well. Like, next week, I might think of a good comeback."

And that's what I love about her.

"Baby, come here." I hold my hand out. "Please. I can't stand you being all the way over there. Come to me."

She pushes off the dresser and cuts the distance in her big bedroom. When she puts one hand in mine, I take advantage and pull her into my arms. The world feels a little more balanced.

She's barely taller than me, standing between my legs. I wrap one arm tight around her back and dip a hand into her wet, messy hair to pull her to me for a kiss. "Happy birthday."

She fingers the hair at my nape and sighs. "Thank you."

"I don't want to talk about anyone else. I want to focus on you, and I want to give you your gift."

She shrugs one bare shoulder and bites back a smile. "Now I'm curious."

I press my lips to her neck and run my hands down her sides, to her thighs, and back up to her ass where I give her a squeeze. "You're going to have to trust me."

She pulls back just enough to look down. "You say that a lot."

"But this time you're really going to have to trust me. Just know, this isn't my first time."

She tenses and tries to pull away.

I shake my head and hold her tight. "You won't be sorry. At least I hope you won't. I hope you'll love it."

She rolls her lips in, and her chest rises and falls against mine.

My smile swells, and I stand to look down at her. "Lie face down."

This time her eyes widen. "What are you going to do?"

I shake my head. "It's your present. It won't be a surprise if I tell you. Trust me—lie down and face away from me. You can't see what I'm doing."

I let go of her, but she doesn't move as I roll her desk chair over to the side of the bed.

She crosses her arms. "You're not going to try to give me birthday spankings or anything are you?"

I freeze and stare at her. "If you think you might be into that, we can try it later, but you'd have to be quiet. But now you've made me hard, and I need to focus. We can't talk about that right now."

Her eyes flit to my cock.

"If you want to check, you can," I offer. "But that won't help my focus. Lie down so we can get started."

Her arms fall, and she moves to the bed. She settles herself on her stomach but turns her head toward me.

I sit in the chair next to her and run a hand down her back to squeeze her ass as I lean in to kiss her. "Nice try, birthday girl. Turn your head the other way."

She rolls her eyes and turns. "This is a big deal for me, you know. I don't enjoy surprises."

I unzip my duffle and start setting everything on her nightstand. "If you look, we might have to revisit the spanking conversation."

"Shut up."

"Just don't look." I work fast because I don't trust her not to peek. "You'll break my broody heart if you look."

"You're not that broody, Levi. You just like to play the part at school."

I plug the machine in and slip on a pair of microscopic glasses. "I'm not pretending. I like very few people—you just happen to be at the top of the list."

She sighs.

I sit back, pull in a breath, and flex my fingers. I've done this once but never on an actual person. "Okay, whatever you hear, try and relax. Just remember, I came all the way across the country to bring you home. You trusted me then—you can trust me now."

She doesn't move, but she does talk. "You're not helping me relax. Just so you know, I'm the exact opposite of relaxed right now."

I look down her body and can tell. Her ass cheeks are clenched as they're peeking out of her panties.

Look away, Levi.

Focus.

Shit. I hope she doesn't hate it.

32

BONDED FOREVER

Carissa

He's banging around behind me. My heart might pound out of my chest.

I wonder if it's too late to get up and put on a pair of pants.

He swipes the hair away and pulls the pillow out from under my head. His lips come to my neck before I feel his breath on my ear where he whispers, "Close your eyes."

I do as he says.

His fingers press into the bed under my neck to reach through on the other side. I try to control my racing heart, but it's no use. He's wrapping something around my neck. "Levi—"

"Don't talk," he commands, and sounds just about as relaxed as I am right now. "Just ... be still."

"So much for cool and collected Levi Hollingsworth," I mock, since I have no idea what else to say.

More noises and movements are going on behind me,

but he talks as he goes. "How many atoms does it take to make oxygen?"

I pause. "Wait, are you really quizzing me on chemistry right now?"

He pushes my hair out of the way farther, and I feel something flat and sort of heavy on the back of my neck. Something tightens on my throat before it loosens again. "How does that feel?" I start to bring my hand up but he stops me. "Be still."

"Am I supposed to trust you or not? How am I supposed to know how it feels if I can't touch it?"

"I mean, does it choke you?"

"Spanking and choking. This is turning into the weirdest birthday ever. I'm still a virgin since we had that conversation the last time."

"You'd better be," he mutters. "I mean, is it uncomfortable?"

"Everything feels uncomfortable right now, but the noose around my neck, it's fine."

"Okay, back to my question." He moves around some more and a snip is louder than it should be since it's so close to my ear. "How many atoms does it take to make oxygen?"

"That's easy. Two."

"Right. O is the chemical element of oxygen. It's useless on its own. One element by itself just floating around doesn't do shit, you know? It needs to join another atom to make oxygen."

I jerk when something starts buzzing behind me. "What's that?"

His forearm presses into my back and down my spine. "Be still."

"Quit being so bossy."

"Quit being a difficult birthday girl," he mutters through

the buzzing. "Anyway, two atoms are necessary to create oxygen, the very thing that gives us life—or takes it away."

I fist the sheets by my face, trying to be still and control my breathing. "You're such a science geek for a hot guy."

"You love me for it," he mutters right as something zaps way too close to my head. "Baby, I'm not kidding. The last thing on earth I want to do is hurt you. You have to be still for me."

I exhale, overwhelmed by everything.

The unknown.

His actions.

His words.

"But together." I sense him, bent over me focusing on whatever he's doing. He keeps talking between zaps. "They make oxygen. It's colorless, odorless, tasteless."

Another few zaps, and I feel him blow on my neck. Then the machine clicks off, and he lays a heavy hand on the middle of my back. My room is silent. I don't move. Whatever he put on my neck to work, disappears.

Fingertips replace it, trailing across my skin, and his deep voice dips even further. "Together, those atoms are bonded forever to create something so essential, that without the product they create, we wouldn't survive."

If I weren't laying down, I might pass out from my heart bursting.

I hear something else hit my nightstand next to the bed. Then he presses his lips to the back of my neck right before I lose his touch.

"There. Happy birthday."

"Can I move?" I whisper.

His voice is gravely. "Yeah."

I push up to a hip and shift to my butt to face him. I don't look away from his beautiful green-flecked, hazel eyes as I touch the chain on my neck for the first time. It's so dainty, I hardly feel it on my skin. It sits at the dip of my throat, and as I finger the chain, a charm falls forward.

I feel it and frown because I can't see it. "What is it?"

"It's you ... and it's me." His eyes on me are heavy and intense. "O_2. It's bound around your neck as a reminder until you decide to break it. And I'm telling you right now, baby, it'll have to be you. You'll kill me in the process, but I won't be the one to break it." He takes my hand and lays it flat over his chest for me to feel his heart race, not unlike what I did in his Jeep a lifetime ago. "The thought of breaking it actually hurts. I don't care how old we are—or not old we are. I'm not fucking around when it comes to what I want. And I want you."

His heart pounds under my touch, but that doesn't stop me from doing what I want.

What I need.

My bare feet hit the floor before my legs circle his waist. I press my lips to his. His arms circle me, and I hear the desk chair roll back and hit the wall when he stands with me in his arms. One hand cups me from below and fists my hair, pulling at my roots as he kisses me deeper than he ever has. My back hits my bed, and I wonder how he concentrated if his cock was this hard while working so delicately at my neck.

He presses his erection through my thin panties, and now I regret putting any on.

My moan builds through my throat, and he drinks it up as he yanks my leg higher. "Fuck, baby. The things going through my brain right now ... they have everything to do with making you mine and none of it has to do with sex."

Oh shit. Because all I can think about is sex, but now I want to know what he's talking about.

"After what happened to you today, I feel like an ass thinking about sex. But you and sex pretty much go hand in hand in my brain right now. I can't help it."

"Oh, thank goodness."

He pulls away from my lips to look down at me and frowns. Instead of explaining myself, I reach between us and pull at the hem of my tank. His intense stare never leaves my face as I yank it over my head.

I toss it to the floor, and my fingertips go directly to the necklace he just soldered on me for good. I swallow over the lump in my throat before I say, "I've never felt so... Well, I'm not going to let anyone ruin my birthday. Especially not a mean girl trying to intimidate me. I want you, Levi. I've wanted you for a long time. Nothing has changed. If anything, it's intensified. I want to give you everything."

His eyes roam my face. I wonder if he's waiting for me to change my mind or yell jinx. I drag my hands up his side and bring his shirt with them, my nails dragging up his hot skin.

He shakes his head once, and the air surrounding us shifts. It zips around us with the same electric current he used to fuse the necklace on me as if he were branding me. He reaches behind his head and his shirt lands close to mine.

All of a sudden, I'm desperate for it.

For him.

My feet nudge at his joggers, trying desperately to get as close to him as possible.

"You're sure?" He's breathless, which is impossible. His body is a machine—I have the naked evidence in front of me.

"Please have a condom, Levi."

He looks down at me, and his lips tip up on one side.

My smile is bigger. "I'll take that as a yes."

He presses a kiss to my lips once more before pulling away from me. Standing, he stares down at my mostly naked body as he reaches into his pocket and tosses a condom on the bed next to me. He reaches down to yank his socks off before dipping his thumbs into his waistband.

Holy...

It's my turn to be breathless.

The bottom of his defined V is no longer a secret.

Nothing is hidden any longer.

And I can't stop staring.

He's long, hard, and thick. The head of his cock is swollen in a way I feel sorry for him. All this time we've been together, it's been about me. He's been neglected.

I lick my lips.

"Don't do that," Levi growls.

My gaze flits to his face. "Do what?"

He narrows his eyes, but he distracts me when he wraps a hand around his cock. Why is that so hot?

He pumps himself twice as his square jaw tenses. "I don't know how much more I could want you. I feel like I could explode." He pumps himself once more. "And not just like this."

He reaches for my hips and my panties disappear. I'm as naked as he is. But he doesn't slide the condom on, nor does he kiss me. But he doesn't waste any time either.

His mouth is between my legs again.

I throw my head back and gasp. I need to be quiet.

He does just what he did in his room. Licks, sucks, drives me mad.

But tonight it's not new. Tonight, I want it. I'm chasing it.

I thread my fingers through his hair, put my feet flat to the bed, and push up. I realize Levi might've been holding out on me. He's hungry and wasn't kidding when he said he wanted every inch of me.

His big hands cup my ass and his thumbs reach up to spread me farther.

That's when I tumble.

My jaw goes slack, and I turn my head to the side, doing everything I can not to wake the next county over. I'm gasping for air and realized I've lost his touch altogether.

A rip.

I open my eyes just soon enough to see him roll the condom down his thick cock. Wow.

I've thought about having sex for a long time. I dreamed about how it would go, what it would feel like, where it would be.

But I never gave a thought as to who it would be with. Not until I met Levi.

Now I can't imagine anyone but him. And we haven't even done it yet.

He bends at the waist and one hand rests on the bed by my head. His other hand finds my sex and starts to tease me again where I'm sensitive and wet from before.

His fingers move, leaving a trail of my own excitement up the middle of my body. He looks down at his touch on me, watching his fingers move between my breasts, until they land on the necklace around my neck.

"This might be premature..." His words trail off.

My hands glide up his shoulders. "What?"

"This might just be a necklace, but it's just the first thing I plan on marking you with forever." He looks from the piece of jewelry to me. "Does that make you anxious?"

I lick my lips. "Should it?"

"Yes." His answer shocks me. "Society says it should. Pretty sure my parents would agree. Given the way your dad treated me the other day, I'm sure he would try to kill me. I haven't even told you I love you."

I bring my hand to his jaw. "It doesn't make me anxious, Levi. It makes me feel ... safe."

His touch on me goes from soft to firm. His hand wraps around my neck before it slides down between my breasts, and this time he presses his hand to my heart.

Possessive.

Protective.

Mine.

Nothing has ever felt so good.

Besides maybe the orgasms he's given me.

But other than that...

He leans down to kiss me at the same time I feel his tip at my opening. "Relax, baby."

I close my eyes and allow my head to fall back. And that's when he does it.

He takes me, in one firm thrust.

"Oh." My eyes fly open. I see nothing but his fierce possession staring down at me.

"You're mine, baby. Forever."

I lift a leg and wrap it around his waist.

"You okay?"

I'm so full. I figured I would be, but to be this close to him, taken by him.

Owned by him in such an intimate way.

I love it.

I nod.

He pulls out a little before pushing back in. He does it again and again and again. Little by little, letting me get used to him. The more he does, the more I want.

"Don't stop," I plead.

He keeps moving. Deeper and harder. He finds a rhythm

—one that the longer he goes, becomes less and less rhythmic.

It becomes desperate.

He becomes desperate.

His forearms frame my face, our breaths are heavy, and the oxygen he talked about earlier is hot around us.

He reaches between us and his thumb finds my clit once more. The moment he puts a little pressure there, I lift my legs higher, wider, needing more.

"Baby," he grits, as if he can't last another minute.

His thrusts intensify.

I move with him. Our bodies are heated and our movements are out of control. When I come, his hand slides under my back and he slams into me two more times before he stays there, deep within me.

He rests his forehead on mine as we catch our breaths. "I'm staying until dawn."

I nod and ask something that just popped into my head. "Where did you learn how to fuse a necklace onto me forever?"

His eyes fall shut, and he shakes his head. "Baby, don't make me talk about my mom right now."

My body shakes with silent laughter. "Your mom taught you?"

His eyes look resigned. "She's taken on every hobby under the sun. When I told her what I wanted to give you for your birthday when we got to L.A. last weekend, she taught me how and sent the stuff back with me."

"That's so cool."

"That's also something we could've talked about later."

"I love it. Thank you."

There's that word again. It's been thrown around and

insinuated more tonight than ever. But never actually declared.

And I don't care.

Because I feel it.

And I've never felt more alive.

Levi
The next day

I CAN'T STOP STARING at her.

Do I always stare at her like this? I think I do, but today is different.

So fucking different.

I snuck out of Louise's mansion an hour before dawn and wonder how long our lives will be like this. Sneaking in and out to steal the time I crave with her so the rest of the world melts away.

I need to find a way to change that. Sooner rather than later.

I tuck her leg behind mine like I always do. It's second nature for us now. She drops a hand to the top of my thigh and gives it a squeeze never looking away from Cade and Mason across the table. Jack is sitting at the end with his feet propped on the corner as he schools Mason on how to charm a girl in his literature class.

Carissa laughs and talks, but the whole time she can't tear her fingers away from the chain I fused around her neck. It's thin, subtle, and twenty-four karat solid gold. It'll never turn and she can leave it there forever as far as I'm concerned.

Levi

I marked her in more than one-way last night. Both will be something I'll never forget.

I glance across the lunchroom and tense.

Carissa feels it and turns to me. "What's wrong?"

I untangle our legs and lean forward to put my lips close to her ear. "Stay here. I need to take care of something."

I don't give her a chance to say anything else.

I could've done this anytime, but I've been waiting for this moment. I might hate high school, but I know how it works. Isla made a choice, and tried to fuck with the most important thing to me. I'm not doing this shit in a half-empty hallway so it takes hours for rumors to spread. She's not getting off that easy.

Because this is no rumor, and the event will be laid out for seventy percent of the school to see firsthand.

I stalk across the lunchroom and know that with each stride, more and more eyes are on me. I don't look at any of them.

I glare at the bitch who tried to manipulate me.

Her fake-ass friend whispers something to her, and Isla's head pops up immediately. Her eyes widen with shock for a quick second before she straightens her spine and sets her witchy expression in place where it usually sits.

We don't take our eyes off one another as I approach, and I realize with all the shit she put me through, I've never hated her more than I do right now.

I place my hands on the table directly across from where she's sitting.

"Levi," she croons.

I don't croon anything.

My words are seething. "If you ever approach Carissa Collins again, there will be hell to pay. You see her coming, walk the other way. If you bump into her, you'd better fucking run."

She hikes a brow. "It seems I've struck a chord with the simple girl from Arizona."

"No, you've lit a fire under me. And with me comes Jack Hale. And with him comes the entire lacrosse team and half the senior class. I can ignore your shit when it's directed at me, but if you even glance in Carissa's direction, I will ruin you. I'll find a way for that to follow you to whatever shit college you manage to get into. I can make your life ten times as miserable as you made mine. It's time to get over yourself, tuck your tail between your legs, and move on." I stand straight and glare down at her. "That you're even playing these games two years later is embarrassing."

When I return to the table that has quickly become the oddest group of friends in the history of high school, I fall back into my chair next to Carissa. She's wide-eyed, staring at me. "Why did you do that?"

I yank her chair so she's glued to my side. "Why wouldn't I do that?"

"Because I can ignore her," she whispers.

I drape an arm over the back of her chair. "But now you don't have to."

Jack lifts his chin and leans over to give Levi a fist bump. "And now the whole school knows. She won't try to pull that shit again. We've got your back, Carissa."

Carissa sinks into her chair another couple inches, but I smile and wrap my arm around her neck and pull her to me. I press my lips to her soft, blond hair. "Now we just need to make sure you graduate early. I'm all over that."

It's not the only thing I plan to be all over.

When it comes to her, I can't get enough.

33

NO MORE LIES

Carissa
Six weeks later

I use every minute of the extended period and work until the bell rings.

I'm not brilliant or uber-focused or even an overachiever like Levi, Cade, and Mason. I'm barely above average in most subjects. Heck, I think I'll pull out a solid B in trigonometry, and that's a surprise. Something to celebrate.

Levi has told me for a week not to stress. We did the math, I'm going to pass chemistry no matter what. But if I do well, I'll pass with a C. A solid C, that I had to fight for, dammit.

I want it to be a solid one.

The last push of the school year has been a blur. If Levi isn't sneaking into my room a few times a week, then I'm sitting front and center at his lacrosse games. They made it to district and are expected to go to the state tournament.

When Levi isn't hot and sweaty from practice or games,

we're studying at Louise's dining table or sprawled in Keelie's living room, even though it's harder to concentrate there. Her kids, Knox and Saylor, are cute but that little one is rambunctious.

Mr. Hollingsworth is only a little less intimidating than he was when I first met him. Intense isn't a strong enough word to describe the man.

But, then again, Levi was, too, when I first met him. I guess he still is intense, but in the best way possible—completely focused on me.

Cade doesn't hate Virginia anymore. Since we've made the commitment to staying here through graduation, he's joined one club and is competing on a couple academic teams. They're all smart as hell. He found his people, and I'm thrilled for him.

He also doesn't hate Louise as much as he used to. I can't say I blame him after the night from hell we all spent in the hospital when she almost killed him. But Louise is trying, and she's trying hard.

She and I have actually fallen into somewhat of a ... dare I say ... nice relationship. Is she your typical grandma? Absolutely not. But she is kind, in a sort of not touchy-feely way.

Louise is palatable—plain and simple. And I think she likes having us around. So much so, she's acted as the barrier Cade and I need from Mom and Dad.

They, on the other hand, don't seem happy at all. At least as far as I can tell from the news and my dad's polling numbers, which look like jumping beans on the graph ever since his first scandal hit over the holidays.

He's up and down, depending on which poll you look at, which means one thing for certain—the primary is going to be tight. And it's never been a close race for him.

Cade and I refuse to speak to them. It took a couple of weeks, but they finally stopped calling after Cade threatened them with the video from that dark day when Levi came to get us. From what I can tell by stalking them on the news, they're back and forth between Arizona and D.C., doing everything they can to sprinkle magic fairy dust over his constituents—or maybe hit them with the memory zapper like a sci-fi movie.

It's what all politicians do during campaign season. Especially the creepy ones.

I still keep tabs on them every day. We might be eighteen now, but Cade holds the smoking gun—the video of Dad hitting Cade and Levi, and tossing me to the ground.

There's not enough fairy dust in the world to pull that kind of shade over child abuse.

The bell rings. I put my pencil down and sigh. I'm done with chemistry for the rest of my life. I'll choose a major that lets me get away with taking astronomy or something like that.

I grab my bag and drop the test into the file basket on Mr. Stance's desk. He barely looks up at me and still smells like onions from last month.

Just why?

I hope I never see him again.

When I leave his classroom for the last time in my life, I stop in my tracks.

Seniors have been done since last week. They take finals early because graduation is tomorrow.

I tip my head to the side. "What are you doing here? You're supposed to be spending the day with your mom."

Danielle flew in for graduation. She and Keelie are throwing a party for Levi. It was supposed to be small, but is quickly turning into the event of the year. I'm pretty sure it has nothing to do with Levi and everything to do with Jack.

Levi pushes off the opposite wall where he was waiting for me, and before I can stop him, he plants a kiss right on my lips. "What kind of tutor would I be if I didn't check on my number one student?"

I look around. "You can't kiss me at school."

He grabs my hand. "What are they going to do, suspend me? I'm done, and I'm valedictorian. The programs are printed. They can't change it now."

I give his arm a yank as we walk. "Yes, but I'm here for another semester."

He grins down at me. "You're welcome. I didn't think anything would make me happier than getting the hell out of here, but you getting out a semester early? I'm fucking giddy."

I smile. "You are giddy."

"You and Cade want to go to dinner with my big-ass, blended family tonight? It'll be a shitshow but you being there will make it tolerable. Louise can come if she wants."

"I'll check and see. That might not be enough time for Louise to do her hair, and you never know with Cade. I'll see if he's in the mood."

"But you'll be there," he demands.

"I'm not sure why that's even a question. You don't have to ask me twice to be anywhere."

He circles his arm to pull me tight to his side.

One more semester. I'm not sure how I'll survive it without him.

Levi

Levi

I'M OFFICIALLY DONE.

Graduation.

Valedictorian.

Party.

I'm fucking done.

I grab my keys and bag and jog down the stairs of Keelie's farmhouse. It's late—really late.

We cleaned up after Dad and his friends finally kicked everyone out after midnight. They said their goal was to make sure everyone was sober and not pregnant by the end of the night. My mom and step-dad fly out first thing in the morning. To say I'm ready to not be the center of attention is an understatement.

When I get to the kitchen, the lights are dimmed. Dad is standing at the island taking a drink of his beer, and Keelie is sitting on the counter with a glass of wine sitting next to her.

Dad's eyes narrow, but he doesn't move from where he stands between Keelie's legs. "I thought we sent everyone home at curfew? It's a little late, isn't it?"

I ignore that to say the next thing on my mind as I look at my counselor. "Thanks for tonight. It was really cool of you to throw the party."

Keelie smiles, and I'm instantly happy for my dad. "Graduating is a big deal, let alone Valedictorian, Levi. Things like this in life deserve to be celebrated. You deserve to be celebrated."

"It was bigger than planned. That's Jack's fault. Sorry about that."

"Don't worry. It was perfect. I'm glad you had a good time," she says.

I flip my keys around my finger. "I'm going to Jack's for the night."

"Speaking of Jack," Dad starts. "Tell him to stay away from Emma."

I frown. "Jack flirts with everyone and anyone who breathes. He'd never hit on Emma. Once you're friends, sisters are off limits—it's like an unspoken rule."

"From the way things looked tonight, I'm not sure Jack knows the rule. Or else he needs to be reminded of it."

There's no fucking way. "I'll remind him. But Emma isn't his type."

"If I had to guess, I'd think everyone is Jack's type." He pulls in a breath and exchanges a private glance with Keelie.

"What?" I ask.

Keelie bites her lip, but it's Dad who speaks. "We're getting married."

I knew this was probably coming, I just didn't know when. I'm genuinely happy for them—for our family. "Congratulations."

"We didn't want to overshadow your graduation. I know it's soon, but we want it to happen before you leave for school. I also want you to be my best man."

A smile spreads across my face, and I move to them. I get a man hug from my dad and a warm embrace from my former counselor and soon-to-be stepmom. "You guys have been through a lot. I'm happy for you."

My dad wraps an arm around his fiancée. "Thanks bud. I wanted to tell you first. We'll tell Emma and the little kids tomorrow."

"Sounds good. I'm out. We're hitting the gym in the morning."

"About that," Dad starts.

"I'm going to get ready for bed," Keelie announces quickly and leans in to kiss my dad before he helps her to her feet. "It was a great day, Levi. I'll see you ... later."

She takes her wine and leaves.

Before I have a chance to ask what that's about, Dad says, "You've been at Jack's a lot lately."

Shit.

By the look on his face, I have a feeling this isn't about Jack.

He doesn't take his eyes off me when he takes another drink. "I know I've been focused on your sister and her drama for months now. I've been tracing her every step, which hasn't been hard since she's barely been out of my sight unless she was at school. So imagine my surprise when I opened the app last week to find you were at a certain historic mansion all night instead of Jack's house. Unless Jack's mom recently upgraded from her two-bedroom condo to the Boyette estate, and no one told me."

I hold out a low hand. "Dad—"

"I'm just going to put it out there, if Louise Boyette knows you're spending the night there while I've been kept in the dark, I'm going to be even more pissed."

I shut my mouth.

"Levi, I can tell you're in deep, but what the hell are you doing?"

I pull in a much-needed breath before I lay it out there. "I'm not going to stop. I can't. I'm in deep. So deep, I can't see straight."

He shakes his head. "You're young—"

"Don't," I interrupt. "It's different. We're different."

He pulls a heavy hand down his face. "You'll be on your own in two months and will be able to do whatever the fuck you're going to do. Tell me you're being careful, son."

This is the last thing I want to talk about with my father. "I'm not an idiot."

"Never said you were. Hell, I've trusted you so much I

haven't checked to see if you were where you said you'd be. But you've lied to me. I'm not good with that."

"No more lies," I promise but add on that same thought, "But I'm still going."

"Levi—"

He can take it or leave it, but it's the truth. "I love her. I'm not going to change anything. I'm leaving for Hopkins soon. The thought of not seeing her whenever I want is hard enough for one semester."

He looks at the ceiling and shakes his head. "Shit."

I move for the garage door.

"Levi," he calls for me.

"Dad, it doesn't matter what you say. I'm going."

"I know you are." He's resigned. I see it in his eyes and hear it in his tone. "If I get a call from Louise Boyette, you can bet I'm going to pretend I'm clueless. I'll go apeshit on your ass, and you'll deserve it."

I bite back my smirk. "Got it."

"I've got four kids now. I'm not ready to be a grandfather anytime soon, especially before you get married."

"Deal."

"And don't tell your mother any of this shit. She'll take me to court to get Emma back."

"No way. I don't need that kind of drama in my life either, and Emma needs to stay here. I'd never do anything to jeopardize that for her or you."

He shakes his head. "I'll never sleep tonight. Just don't lie to me anymore."

"Promise."

He waves me off, and I can't get out of here fast enough.

I'd like to bleach that entire conversation from my brain.

34

DECLARATIONS

Levi

Skin to skin.

"Fuck, baby," I groan as Carissa sinks onto my cock. She looks into my eyes and rocks forward and back. "You're fucking heaven. I'll never get enough of this. Of you."

Carissa has come a long way since our first time together. Her first time. And tonight is another first. She wants to lead. I'm letting her do what she wants, and I fucking love it.

She frames my face with her hands and leans in to press her lips to mine. "I'm afraid to count days. But I'm counting days."

I shake my head as I cup her ass in my hands to help her move. "Don't do that."

"You graduated," she murmurs against my lips.

"And you gave me the best gift anyone could give me."

Tonight when we were sitting by the bonfire at the party, she snuggled between my legs and leaned in to whisper what she got me for graduation. The party couldn't end soon enough. And when my dad announced he found out I've been here instead of Jack's, there was no way I was staying away from her tonight.

Birth control.

She's been on the pill for a month and hasn't told me.

Until tonight.

That means no more condoms.

I haven't told her my dad announced he'd better not become a grandpa yet. She thinks he's intimidating as it is. Plus, the more I can do to tie Carissa to me forever, the better.

Those are thoughts I haven't shared with anyone.

I run a hand up her back and hold her tight on my cock with the other. "Two hours between us is nothing. It's only for a few months."

"I know, but—"

I shake my head and stop her. "Baby, I love you."

She freezes.

We've danced around that word for months, but not anymore.

I keep talking. "I love you. That's never going to change. As soon as you graduate, I'll make sure we're together. I'm not going to let anything keep you from me."

Her expression turns desperate. "Promise me."

My hand on her back presses in. "Never letting you go."

Her pussy spasms around my bare cock. I'm not sure how much longer I can sit here, buried inside her and not move.

"I love you too." Her words whisper across my skin, like a promise of her own. A promise I'll hold her to.

"Fuck," I mutter against her lips. "Baby, you need to move, or I'm going to have to flip you."

A small smile takes over her lips. "It's your gift, Levi. Do with it what you want."

I put a hand to the bed and turn. She's on her back, and we never lose our connection when I reach for her clit. My favorite thing in the world might be to make her come while I'm inside her.

To do that with no condom?

Fuck.

She's so wet.

So perfect.

I watch her breathing pick up, her tits rise and fall with her chest as I give her more pressure. When she arches her back, I can't take it any longer.

I move.

Thrust after thrust, I make her mine all over again as she comes. I try to hold on for as long as I can, but her tight pussy squeezing my dick with nothing between us is enough to make me lose all control.

I've been careful with her.

Built and added something new every time we've been together. But taking her bare?

I slam into her three more times, her small tits shake under me. It's the most beautiful view I've ever seen.

When I come, I imagine a day—probably farther into the future than I want—where there's nothing that will prevent us from coming together in another way. Taking her bare is one thing, but when I can plant my seed in her and know it will mean something more...

"I want everything with you," I groan, admitting the thoughts in my head as I come and come and come. "It might sound fucked up, but I'm ready to tie you to me in every way. Damn your last semester of high school."

I can tell she's biting back a moan. Her brother is in the

next room, but we've come to not care. He also doesn't seem to hate me during daylight hours, so there's that.

I give her most of my weight and press her into the soft bed. I know she loves it, because every time I do this, she wraps me up and holds me to her. I press my lips to the side of her head, leaving a trail of kisses on the way to her mouth.

"Love you, baby. So fucking much, it hurts more every day," I say.

She looks up at me and there are tears brewing in her eyes through the dimly lit room.

"Baby, what's wrong? Did I hurt you?"

She shakes her head as her tears flow and disappear down each temple. Her words are thick with emotion. "I'm just so happy and afraid at the same time. I've never felt so … settled in my soul as I do now."

I roll and take her with me. "We have all summer and only one semester to get through. It'll be okay."

I slide out of her, and she buries her face into my neck the way she always does when I sleep over. "I guess I'm the one who needs to clean up now, huh?"

I kiss her forehead. "I love you. I'm pretty sure that's going to be the answer to every question you ask me from now on."

"Then it's good I already passed chemistry. Your professions of love are amazing, but they won't help me graduate early."

I capture her chin in my fingers and tip her face to mine. "I love you."

"I love you too."

35

REINDEER GAMES

Levi
One month later

"You may kiss your bride."

I stand next to my dad and watch him reach for Keelie's tear-stained face. He pulls her to him, and it's not chaste or quick.

I've been by my dad's side all day. I've felt his intensity. His impatience. His sheer will for this to be done.

Not because of the wedding. It's small. We're standing in Keelie's backyard—no, our backyard since it's officially our home now too—and if there are thirty people in attendance, I'd be surprised. It's Keelie's immediate family and Crew Vega's entire organization, which is small. This is what they wanted.

Oh, Carissa, Cade, and Louise are here too. Carissa is rarely not by my side, and Cade feels like family now. Louise butted her way in—she still loves me.

But Dad wanted this to be done because he was desperate to tie Keelie to him forever.

And him to her.

I've never seen him like this. My father deserves this more than anyone.

I'm honored to be standing here.

I've also never been more jealous.

Dad found who he wanted and made it happen in a matter of months. He almost lost Keelie, which fed his desperation. Had Keelie not wanted a ceremony this size, I bet Dad would've been happy to tie the knot weeks ago in front of their goats and donkey.

I wish I could do that. Make Carissa mine and take her with me wherever I go.

I'm leaving her here, and I'm sick about it.

I look away from Dad and Keelie, and my eyes go straight to Carissa. She's sitting in the back row between her brother and grandmother. I catch her dark eyes instantly and don't look away. She fidgets in her chair as her teeth find her lip like she does so often.

At this point, I know her every mannerism like the back of my hand.

Every inch of her body.

Every desire in her heart.

And at this moment, there's nothing I feel more than red-hot jealousy of my own father.

I have to check myself when everyone claps. I look back to my father and new stepmom who's seriously the shit. Saylor, who Emma has had to wrangle for most of the ceremony, throws herself at the newlyweds. My dad tosses her up in his arms and turns to me.

I take his hand and he pulls me into a man hug with him and my new younger sister. Knox and Emma are next, taking turns with Keelie.

They're married.

And in a few minutes, Dad will sign the adoption papers to officially make Knox and Saylor his forever in the eyes of the law. Emma and I have gained a stepmom, a brother, and a sister.

They don't bother walking down the aisle. Their family and friends congratulate them privately before the big party at Whitetail, where they did invite everyone and their cows.

I look back to Carissa, who's standing off to the side with Cade and Louise.

I wonder how soon I can tie her to me forever.

Carissa

CADE AND LOUISE skipped the reception. Louise wanted to go home, and Cade was happy for the excuse to take her. Then again, he'll use anything as an excuse to get out of an event with so many people.

That was hours ago. So when Cade texted our Homies group, I could sense the urgency. Levi and I left the party and came right away. Jack and Mason were already here.

I kick my heels off the moment I walk in the door, but I'm still in my dress. Levi lost his tie and jacket a long time ago, and his dress shirt is thoroughly wrinkled, unbuttoned at the neck and rolled at the cuffs. If Cade wasn't so intent on showing us what freaked him out, I'd pull Levi into my bedroom and throw myself at him.

That will have to wait until later.

"Dude, you're never going to believe this shit," Jack says.

"Cade followed the money," Mason adds.

Cade points to his computer screen. "Look."

I look closer. "Who am I looking at?"

There's a driver's license pulled up on the screen, and we can read every detail. "That's John Chester."

"John Chester, the guy who Dad has been sending money to for years?" I pause and stare at the picture of someone who is clearly not John Chester. "But that's a woman."

"It's also not John Chester. It's Janet Chase. She lives in Ashburn, Virginia." Cade states the obvious since we can read what's in front of us.

"That's who Dad allegedly has been sending money to all these years?" I lean in closer to get a better look. As far as a driver's license picture goes, hers is fabulous. She's five-seven with red hair and blue eyes. Even in the tiny picture blown up on the screen, she's glamorous at the age of twenty-nine.

Then it dawns on me. This is huge, for so many reasons.

"The FBI finally dropped the investigation," Levi says. "Your dad's attorneys somehow proved the payments were tied to his real estate investments."

Cade doesn't look away from the screen and mutters, "Which we all know is bullshit."

"True, but there's no proof otherwise," I say, and then grab the back of his desk chair to swivel it toward me and address something more important. "Where did you get this? Please tell me you didn't hack into some government-secured network. I thought you agreed to quit snooping."

Cade crosses his arms and glares at me. "Do you really think Dad is innocent? That all those payments are legitimately connected to his properties?"

"Of course not. But that's not my main concern right now. Are you hacking into government servers?"

"I'm not that good or that stupid, Rissa." He swivels back to face his screen. "I'm still in Dad's email. I got curious when the investigation was killed right before his primary."

Dad won the primary last week, proving that politics is much like high school drama. If you're patient enough to wait it out, people get bored and will fixate on the shiny new scandal of the week. I mean, why beat a dead horse when there's fresh road kill to pick over for ratings? I could barely stomach the sight of our parents on stage the night of the primary, knowing everything they do in public is fake and contrived. I've tried to put it out of my mind.

"He has a mole who was feeding him information. This is who the investigation led to when they followed the trail of bank accounts," Cade explains. "But this was never officially added to the investigation. Someone in the committee buried it and kept Dad in the loop."

"You need to be careful," I demand. "They've left us alone. That's all we wanted. Can we not just let it be?"

"Can you find anything else on her?" Levi asks.

I give Levi an elbow to the abs. "Don't encourage him."

"I want to know who she is," Jack says. "Plus, look at her. It's no surprise she's on your dad's unofficial payroll—she's hot."

Mason winces. "She's old enough to be our mother. I mean, if she got knocked up in middle school."

"Which is even more impressive, right?" Jack leans in to get a better look. "That must take a lot of effort."

Levi ignores Jack and wraps an arm around my shoulders. "Don't you want to know who she is and why your dad's been funneling millions of dollars to her? Someone in the committee buried it for a reason."

"I do," Cade says. "This was easy to find since it was all sent to his private accounts. Now I just need to figure out who she is and why the hell Dad has paid her for years.

There are very few reasons anyone pays those amounts to another person, and none of them are philanthropic. Dad doesn't have a generous bone in his body. There's always a self-serving reason for everything he does. I want to ring her doorbell and find out who the hell she is."

I gape at my brother who would probably rather have his toenails plucked out than walk up to someone's door he doesn't know. "Seriously?"

He rolls away from his desk and turns to the four of us. "Not really. But if someone else wanted to..."

"I'll go," Jack offers.

Levi frowns at his best friend. "And what are you going to do when she answers the door? Hit on her, and then charm her into telling you why a sitting U.S. Senator has been paying her off for years?"

Jack shakes his head. "That would be weird. I'll think of a reason. Maybe I'll bring Mason. He's got the wholesome thing going on. She'll open the door for him."

"No way," Mason argues. "I'm not walking up to her door. I'll go for moral support because I'm a good friend like that, but I'll sit in the car and wait for you."

"What good will that do?" Jack says. "You don't even have your license. You're not legal to be the getaway driver. If anything, you ring her doorbell, talk about your chickens or some shit, maybe try to sell her some eggs like a good Boy Scout. I'll be the getaway driver."

Mason rolls his eyes. "Boy Scouts sell popcorn."

I need to put a stop to this before anyone else lands on my dad's radar. "No one's being a getaway driver or pretending to sell anything."

"You found this." Levi looks at Cade. "What else can you find on her?"

"Any of us could do a simple Google search," Cade says

before his eyes shift to me. "Or I could do something more thorough."

"Cade—" I start.

My twin keeps talking. "It's not a big deal. It's not like I'm going to hack into a bank or the congressional network. I'll just ... poke around."

"Poking around is something I can get behind." A wolfish grin spreads across Jack's face. "I like the sound of that. Definitely do that."

Cade spears me with a look I recognize all too well. It's one that comes from pure determination when he fixates on something. I also know there's no way I can talk him out of it. "Where exactly are you going to poke around?"

"Wherever the trail leads me."

I sigh. I don't need my twin intuition to realize there's nothing I can do to stop him short of taking a sledgehammer to every computer he owns. And since Louise just bought him a new one, that's out of the question.

Cade continues to speak to me as if we're the only members of the Homies club. "I know you're curious too. We can't just sit back and let him get away with this shit."

I lean farther into Levi and he gives me a squeeze, but I don't take my eyes off Cade. "If you get caught, I'll be so mad at you."

He gives me a rare smirk. It wraps around my heart like an embrace.

I jerk in Levi's embrace when a loud clap comes from my side. Jack's grin is big enough for the whole group when he rubs his hands together. "Let the reindeer games begin."

36

FBI, CIA, NCAA, ELVIS, OR THE RUSSIANS

Carissa
Two days later

"Levi, please."

He's behind me, and his words don't come low or whispered like they usually do when we're like this. "I could watch you like this for the rest of my life. I'm in no hurry."

Easy for him to say. He's not the one being tormented, pushed to the edge over and over and over, only to be pulled back again.

Levi leaves tomorrow for three days. He's got freshman orientation and a team camp at Hopkins. It will be the first time we've been apart for more than a day since Mom dragged me and Cade back to Arizona. I'm trying to prepare myself. This will be like a trial run for his fall semester.

I'll be miserable.

Levi just flipped me to my stomach. My cheek and knees are to the bed, leaving me exposed and desperate. So desperate, I can't even think about what I look like right now. The room is bright and sunny, which is a first for me.

For us.

Day sex.

Levi didn't sneak into my room at Louise's house. Instead, we're in his new room in what has become his home, too, where Keelie and Asa have created a new family together.

And we're here alone for the first time. Keelie and Asa left for their honeymoon yesterday, Emma flew out to spend some time with Danielle in California, and Knox and Saylor are staying with Keelie's sister.

It's just Levi, a brood of goats, a talkative donkey, and me.

And afternoon sex.

There's something very different about sex in the middle of the day, in a house all to ourselves, without the privacy that the dark of night offers.

Levi nudges my knees farther apart. "Spread, baby, and arch."

Because of desperation, I do as he says.

My clit loses his touch when his hands knead each globe of my ass, moving down the backs of my thighs.

"More," he demands.

"Levi," I mutter, pressing my face into his sheets.

"You can do it."

I slide my knees out, feeling myself open and spread for him. A hand slides back up my leg, over my ass, and presses down on the small of my back, forcing me to do exactly as he demanded.

"Good girl." He praises me, and then rewards me with his touch—just the tip of his finger. It's light, and starts at my clit before giving me a shallow dip into my sex.

But then it keeps going, and I jerk when it circles my ass. I can't seem to utter anything but his name. "Levi."

"Bring your feet together." I don't have a chance to move on my own. Levi puts me where he wants me. "Fucking beautiful. Don't move."

This is like when he fused the necklace around my neck all over again.

He flicks my clit as a reward, but talks as he does so. "I don't think you get that I crave everything with you. There's not an inch on your body that I don't want to be mine. There's nothing too intimate when it comes to you. I want every experience. Every memory. I want to burn them on my brain so when I'm not right here, I'll at least know you're waiting for me, and that you're mine. You don't know how impatient I am for the day when I can make this more than just a private commitment between us. I want the world to know."

His finger continues to torment me. I feel him move to his knees behind me, as a wet finger presses into my ass.

I groan as my muscles instinctively tighten around it.

"There you go," he croons.

I've heard of this. I've even read about it. But I never thought I'd like it.

And I'm not sure I do—not until my clit gets equal attention. When fingers from his other hand circle the most sensitive spot on my body, I instantly push back on his touch for more.

"Good, baby."

It feels so good, I rock again.

"Fuck, you're so beautiful. Keep your feet where they are. You can move on my fingers, but stay spread for me."

My breaths come as quick as my movements. My toes

never disconnect, and I'm getting so close to the edge again, I need more.

"Don't stop," Levi encourages.

I don't.

Every time I rock, his finger drives in and out of the last spot on me that was left for him to claim. His touch drives my orgasm deeper, higher ... its intensity is a level I've never experienced.

My moan is louder than it's ever been when I start to fall. He holds me where I am despite the powerful orgasm that shudders through me. I'm not sure I can stay on my knees.

But when Levi slides in from behind, it's so different. So deep.

His finger pinch into my hips, guiding me to meet his every thrust. "Fuck, Carissa. Don't stop, baby."

I couldn't stop if I wanted to.

I want it all too much. Like he said, the more intimate it gets, the better it is.

Levi pounds into me, over and over and over. His grunts aren't muffled like they normally are. The sounds of us coming together and our pleasure fill the room.

I realize I love it.

An added layer of freedom to look forward to.

His last few thrusts are not gentle, and I wonder if I'll have marks from his fingers digging into my skin. But every sensation builds on the other, and together, they're too much.

I come again.

Levi slams into me one last time and holds me to him for long moments before he bends at the waist, taking us both to the bed.

His hand covers mine as he threads our fingers. I press my lips to his jaw. "I love you."

He tips his head to press his lips to my hair. "Love you, too, baby."

"And I love afternoon sex. I hope Jasmine doesn't tell on us. I bet she could hear."

"She's loud as fuck, but only speaks donkey, so we're safe."

I pause and relish in this moment—naked and wrapped up in Levi.

"I'm going to miss you."

He pulls me to him, and his tone is tight. "It's only a few days."

"Can we hang out here the rest of the day?"

He slides out of me and moves far enough to roll me to my back. "You're not going anywhere even if you wanted to."

I smile up at him and try not to be a clingy freak.

He'll be home in a few days and we'll have the rest of the summer.

I'm only going to think about today.

Levi

"Dude, I'm handing in my cool-man card and actually making a fucking phone call like a Baby Boomer because I can't text this drama in case the FBI, CIA, NCAA, Elvis, or the Russians are tapping our shit. So if you could take a break from your smart-people convention long enough to answer your fucking phone, the rest of us average folk would appreciate it. But now I'm going to have to speak in code, so try to stick with me, smart guy. Your wife is having a conniption because your brother-in-law actually did something that is so far out of left fucking field, it's not even in the field at all. It's actually something she told him not to do. And

we think the Russians might be watching, which is no bueno. I'm here with Chicken Man, and so far we've got this shit under control, but we think there's a chance the Russians might show up. Your brother-in-law is ... concerned, and your wife is worried how Granny is going to react if the Russians do, in fact, knock on her door. Oh, also, and most importantly, I forgot to add that your father-in-law knows all. I repeat: your father-in-law knows about your brother-in-law's ... eh ... hobby. This is driving your wife's conniption to epic proportions that might blow the roof off the creepy, old mansion." He exhales and sounds like I just kicked his ass at the gym when he's hung over. *"I hope you're getting the classes you want since you're a fucking weirdo and get off on that shit. Call me back. Love you, man."*

I've listened to the voicemail twice. The first one I've ever gotten from Jack, and probably the longest I've ever gotten from anyone, including my mother, who enjoys hearing herself talk.

"Is everything okay, Levi?" My advisor is staring at me, waiting for me to pick bullshit study hall hours that are required by my lacrosse coach.

"Yeah," I answer, freaking out on the inside while I try to figure out how to get out of orientation early and not piss off my coach or the scholarship board. "Everything is great."

Fucking great.

37

LOUISE HAS A HEART

Carissa

I pace Cade's bedroom for what feels like the millionth time but stop when my phone rings again.

"Shit." I look up. "It's Mom this time."

"Send it to voicemail," Jack bosses. "I think it's a bad idea to talk to either one of them right now. You don't want to be an accessory."

"How can Carissa be an accessory?" Mason asks. "She was, like, eight when it happened."

I put a hand out to Jack. "We don't know for sure what happened."

"Oh, something happened," Jack argues. "Something had to have happened. Your father has been paying off his congressional intern for ten years. A whole fucking decade. And not with chump change, either. She rakes in over a mil a year. That's a lot of fucking money, too, when all you do is go to yoga, shop for shoes, and meet your friends for cocktails. No wonder her DL pic is smokin'. She spends her life stretching and drinking martinis. She's in a constant state of loose and happy. I doubt the woman is ever constipated."

Cade is sitting in his desk chair, bent at the waist, elbows to his knees, with his head in his hands. "This is bad."

"It's not bad." I try to console him. "Dad is back in Arizona, right? He's not down the street in D.C. At least there's that. Are you sure they found out who you are? I mean you kept telling me to trust you and how good you are and all that."

Cade sits up and glares at me. "I'm in high school and full of shit. At least I'm good enough to realize when I've been made."

Mason shifts from foot to foot. "If you really think the FBI or whoever watches government servers are going to show up at Louise's door, maybe I should go home."

"That might be a good idea," I agree.

"No one's going anywhere," Jack clips and looks at me. "I'm not leaving you here to deal with the wrath of your parents. What kind of best friend would I be to your lover if I did that?"

I wince.

Cade looks like he might throw up.

Mason mopes, but caves. "That's true, I guess."

"You're fucking right it is. Now, who's in?" Jack sticks his arm out, palm down, like we're supposed to huddle and yell "Team Homie" on three.

No one moves.

I turn to Cade. "Let's go over this again. What do you know for sure?"

Cade pulls a hand through his hair. "Janet Chase was an intern in dad's office ten years ago. She worked there for two-and-a-half months but was supposed to be there the whole semester. She not only quit the internship, she also dropped out of school."

"Your dad was porking the intern," Jack surmises. "I mean, it isn't the first time it's happened in American history."

"But, Frankie, the Chief of Staff, wasn't Dad's first affair," I say. "Cade found the archived emails to prove it, and he's not paying anyone else off. In fact, as shady as he is, he's not paying off anyone else through that account or any other. Just Janet Chase. It makes no sense. What's so special about her that she quit in the beginning of March ten years ago, only to be bankrolled for over one mil a year and never earn a dime of it. And where is he getting that money?"

"How do you know he's not still porking her?" Jack asks.

I cringe. "Can you please quit using the words *porking* and *our dad* in the same sentence? It's disgusting."

He actually looks remorseful, and now I feel bad.

"Dad's calling me again." Cade stares at his phone before shifting his gaze to me. "Sorry, Rissa. I fucked up."

"No, you didn't fuck up. Dad did. At this point we're in so deep, we need to figure it out. Don't answer his calls. Do you know how he found out you hacked into his accounts?"

Cade leans back in his chair. "On his first message when he threatened to *wring my fucking neck before shutting me down for the rest of my life,* he said his team hired an outside firm to monitor everything because of the leak to the media. When I logged back in, it was triggered, and led back to me."

"Carissa!"

The four of us freeze.

"The Russians are here," Jack whispers.

"The Russians?" Mason ricochets.

"Sorry, private joke," Jack mutters.

"Carissa! Cade!" Louise yells again. I go to the door, and

Cade follows. When we get to the hall and look down the two flights of stairs, Louise is standing in the hallway with her land-line cordless phone fisted in her hand.

I jut my thumb over my shoulder. "We're hanging out with Jack and Mason."

"We need to talk about your parents," she calls up to us.

"Well, we've ... got company," Cade says.

Louise ignores us both. "Your mother wants to speak to you. She said they tried to call you both and neither of you answered. Is that true?"

Cade and I both nod lamely.

"Well..." Her sigh is visible all the way from here. "Your mother was insistent. But for the first time—maybe in my entire life—I held my ground with her. You do not have to speak to anyone you don't wish to. It's a lesson I wished I'd learned before now. I didn't stop her from taking you back when I should have." She looks like she's working hard to school her features. "I'll never forgive myself for that."

Wow. Cade and I glance at each other. When we got back from Arizona, Cade showed her the surveillance video.

Louise is not a touchy-feely person, but that video affected her.

"Thanks," Cade says.

I'm about to run down the stairs. I've never once hugged Louise, but I think she could use one right now.

But I stop when she clears her throat and straightens her spine. "Anyway, I told your mother the same thing. This home will be a safe place for you, as long as you want to be here. And if you leave for college, you may always come back."

That's it. We don't have a chance to respond.

She takes her cordless phone and disappears into the formal living room, probably to do something she has to sit up too straight for. Even so, my feelings for Louise have softened in enormous proportions since we came back.

Louise Boyette might not be a cookie-cutter grandma, but she's trying.

And she's ours.

She's our Louise.

We turn back, and Jack is standing in the doorway to Cade's room. His arms are crossed over his wide chest. "I can't lie. That was really cool. Louise has a heart."

"Um, guys?" Mason is scrolling slowly on his phone. "Have you ever heard of a woman named Rae Lindstrom?"

I frown and turn to Cade. "I haven't, have you?"

"No. Who is it?"

Mason looks up and his eyes are almost as big as his glasses. "She was your dad's administrative assistant ten years ago."

I shrug. "There are so many people in and out of his office. They'd drag us onto a stage, tell us to smile, and then we'd leave. We never really knew who worked for him."

"What about her?" Cade asked.

"She died."

My eyes widen.

"Ten years ago," Mason keeps reading. "On March second."

"What?" Cade bites.

Mason nods and reads from the screen. "*Rae Lindstrom, twenty-eight, originally from Montpelier, Vermont, was found dead in her Chantilly, Virginia apartment. Her death is being investigated by the Chantilly Police Department. Because of the violent nature of her death, federal investigators have been brought in to assist. Authorities are not releasing any further information. Lindstrom worked at the U.S. Capitol as the administrative assistant to Arizona Senator, Cillian Collins. Collins put out a statement: Rae will be missed. We will do everything we can to assist authorities in bringing to justice the person who tore her away from us so brutally."*

"That's an odd coincidence." Jack gapes at us. "You never heard about this?"

I shake my head and try to defend myself. "No. We were eight. Mom might be a shit mother now, but she never exposed us to the news when we were little."

Jack shudders. "No wonder, with shit like this swirling around them. Your parents are drama magnets."

"Janet Chase officially put in her resignation on March third," Cade says. "It was in her file."

"That's..." I can't even bring myself to say the words.

"Rae's murder was never solved." Mason keeps scrolling his phone. "I'll keep looking, but I can't find anything more recent on the case." Mason throws Cade a glance. "But I'm on Google. You know, the legal way to search the internet."

"We wouldn't know this if it weren't for Cade's mad skills," Jack points out.

"Janet Chase killed Rae Lindstrom?" Cade asks.

"Or," I start and all eyes land on me. "Janet knows who killed Lindstrom. And someone wants her quiet."

"Fuck," Jack drawls.

"Yeah," Mason agrees. "This is not what I thought would happen when I became a part of the cool kids' table at lunch."

My stomach churns as my cell vibrates. I cringe when I pull it out of my pocket thinking it will be my dad again, but it's not.

Levi – Jack called and told me everything. I'm on my way home.

38

THE LOVE MACHINE

Levi

"We have her address. I say we head over to Ashburn, knock on her door, and straight up ask her what she knows about this chick who had her head bashed in with a bookend. I've researched body language. I'll know in an instant if she's the killer or the one blackmailing the killer."

I swear, there are two kinds of people in the world who will legit be successful in whatever they do—leaders and charmers. Jack will never be the first but will pave his way being the second. He'll for sure have a chance if he ever runs for president.

Even so, he has a long way to go.

We all stare at my idiot, yet lovable, best friend who will no doubt charm his way through life eventually, even if today is not that day.

I shut him down. "We are not doing that."

Mason nods, agreeing adamantly.

Yeah, Mason will definitely be a leader.

"I say we do nothing," Mason says. "I don't think the NSA is going to be knocking on Louise's door anytime soon. Your dad has more of a reason to keep this hush-hush than we do. We're just a bunch of stupid kids who were messing around on the internet, right? They'll find something else to focus on that's more threatening than us, and we can all go back to the cool kids' table in the fall."

Carissa tenses where she's leaning into my shoulder. "I can't forget about this. Someone was murdered—bludgeoned to death in her own home. And from the reports we read, there was no forced entry. It was someone who knew her, and I'd say there's a good chance Dad knows something. At the very least. I can't even fathom the idea that he's more involved than that, but we can't ignore that the pieces fit into the same puzzle. We have to do something." She turns to her brother. "Cade, are you okay?"

It's late. I hit rush hour traffic on the way home, so it took me longer than it would have otherwise. The five of us are sprawled on Cade's bedroom floor. We don't have to sneak in anymore. Louise has gotten used to us being here. She goes to bed, and tells the twins to lock the door when we leave.

I do, however, sneak out the back after staying the night—I do not want to tempt pissing off Louise.

Cade is staring at the ceiling. "I think he killed her."

Carissa presses in to me tighter but doesn't answer.

"I've been trying to spin it in my head trying to find a way that it isn't him." Cade turns his head to look at us. "When you add up his track record, his history of cheating, and bursts of violence ... it's all there. And if it is him, he got away with it. I bet he covered his tracks so well, he's got alibis standing in line, drooling to save his ass. If I could only get back into his files, I'd go back ten years. I was too focused on the bank records."

"No, you can't do that," Carissa says. "It's bad enough he knows what we did. Louise can only protect us for so long. We'll have to face Mom and Dad eventually. I agree we have to do something, but not that."

Jack jumps to his feet and cracks his neck. "I can't sit still this long. Let's just drive to Ashburn and sit outside her house. I've never done surveillance before, but how hard can it be? You just sit there and watch, right?"

Carissa looks up at me when I give her hair a tug. "I have an idea."

"Dude, it's my plan. Don't steal my thunder," Jack deadpans.

I shake my head at Jack. "No surveillance. I need to make a call, but you'll have to drive. I can't fit everyone in my Jeep."

Jack crosses his arms. "Okay, but if your plan sucks, we're moving on to a stakeout. We'll stop and get snacks and even pee in our empty Gatorade bottles if we have to. This is hardcore."

Carissa's eyes widen. I stand and pull her to me. "Don't worry. I'm going hardcore, too, and no one's going to have to pee in a bottle. But we are going to have to take the Love Machine."

Jack gives the room a chin lift. "You haven't lived a full life until you've taken a ride in the Love Machine."

Carissa

THE LOVE MACHINE is a Grand Marquis that's probably three times older than the sticky cold murder case we've tripped into like quick sand.

It's baby blue with a leather roof and rusted door handles. There's a bench seat in the front and the back was spacious enough for Cade, Mason, and me to buckle up and not even touch one another. It was handed down to Jack from his grandma, who he described as nothing at all like Louise. She handed him the keys the day she moved into a nearby assisted living facility, gave him a big smack on the lips, and told him it would keep him safe throughout high school.

She must have been familiar with his need for speed.

Jack drove us across the county like we were the main characters in a two hundred-million-dollar-budget feature film, and there were ten replicas of the Love Machine waiting offstage, so when we trashed this one, there'd be extras to get us to the happily ever after.

Only this is no feature film, and with an unsolved murder thrown at our feet, I don't see happy anywhere on our horizon.

But we made it in one piece.

It's a miracle.

However, should we have to do surveillance after all, this would be the car to do it in.

I don't let go of Levi's hand and stand tucked half-behind his thick arm. We're standing in another home that looks to be centuries old, but this one is less stuffy and way more welcoming than Louise's.

I thought Mr. Hollingsworth was intimidating. But he's Levi's dad, and I can tell he's so into his family, they're his first priority. He's proven it the last few months. That must soften his edges a tinge.

I've seen the two men standing in front of us at Levi's graduation party and Asa and Keelie's wedding, but I've never officially met them.

Crew Vega.

Grady Cain.

Both scary in their own right.

It shouldn't be possible for a human to be one-hundred percent casual and one-hundred percent alert at the same time. It defies mathematics.

However, the proof is standing in front of me.

Crew Vega is just that intense.

Grady Cain, on the other hand, wears a lazy smile as he takes in my family drama from hell.

What a freak.

And even though we dragged these men from their warm beds and families in the middle of the night, they seem completely alert and ready to take on adulterous politicians and unknown murderers.

"I remember that case," Crew states, after Levi explained my ugly reality. "It was never solved?"

"Nope," Mason pipes in and wiggles his cell phone. "I've checked."

Crew gives him a chin lift. "Nice work."

Mason beams.

"What I don't understand," Crew keeps going, "is how you know your dad has been paying off his old intern for years. Why would you assume she has something to do with a murder."

The five of us look at one another, and my gaze finally settles on Cade. He didn't want to leave Louise's house, but I think he wanted to stay there by himself even less. But when Levi announced his plan—a far stronger one than a stakeout—he agreed to join us.

The car ride over here didn't help his anxiety.

"We did a little digging and figured it out." Levi shrugs. "You know, technical digging?"

Grady frowns for the first time. "You have bank records that go back a decade. Bank records that aren't yours."

Jack nods.

Mason fidgets.

Cade exhales.

Crew looks straight at Levi. "I thought you had plans to go to medical school? Do I need to hire you, instead?"

Levi sighs. "It was a team project."

"We were there for moral support," Jack says.

"Like cheerleaders," Mason adds.

Jack turns to Mason. "Dude, no. We were hype-men."

Mason rolls his eyes.

Crew sets his laser focus on me, and my cheeks instantly warm. "You into computers?"

I shake my head. "My knowledge of computers is to turn it off and turn it back on if it freezes."

"By process of elimination, you're the hacker." Grady's smile is back and aimed at my big brother. "Nicely done."

Cade looks like he's never been less comfortable. "Thanks. It wasn't easy."

"I've got to admit, this is impressive." Crew crosses his arms and takes us all in before speaking to Levi. "Does your dad know about this?"

"This?" Levi throws a hand out to our group. "No. I promise to fill him in, but I don't want to bother him on his honeymoon. That's why we're here."

"Why *are* you here in the middle of the night?" Grady asks. "Let's get to that part."

"First, when *we*," Mason takes the initiative and looks

around for us to acknowledge our team project, "were furthering our investigation, *we* think that someone figured out who *we* were."

"You mean you got caught," Crew says.

"Maybe," Levi says. "We don't know."

"Who do you think caught you?" Grady asks.

"The government," Mason states, as he lowers his voice.

Crew finally shows a different emotion in the form of a hiked brow. "The U.S. government?"

Mason nods, but Jack adds, "Or the Russians. Though, I hope it's our government. I'm not going to be anyone's bitch in a work camp."

Grady scowls. "Yeah, that would suck."

"Look, I'm just going to shoot straight," Levi says. "We just need to know if we were caught so we're not sitting around waiting on a SWAT team to bust through our doors. Also, we want to know if Cillian Collins is a murderer."

Grady's eyes shift to Crew. "That's not a lot to ask, right?"

Crew looks back at Grady. "Fuck. Is this what it's like to have teenagers?"

"And you can't tell my dad," Levi adds adamantly. "You have to promise."

"Oh, I can't fucking wait to tell your dad, but I'll wait until they get home. If we tell him now, he'll rush back, and we can handle this shit." Grady turns to Crew. "Right?"

Crew looks like we're talking about picking up the groceries instead of solving a murder and pulling one over on Uncle Sam. "Of course we can."

Grady turns to me and Levi. "So she's the one, huh?"

Oh my gosh.

My eyes fall shut, as I will myself to be anywhere but here.

Levi clears his throat.

"I'm just saying ... her dad took a jab at you, and you're wading into a murder investigation for her. Kudos to you, man. You didn't waste the next decade of your life fucking around."

Jack motions to us. "It's like *Love Island*, I tell you."

Crew doesn't want to talk about *Love Island* or me and Levi. Thank goodness, he's ready to get down to business. "Let's get this done. Levi doesn't need to be messing with this before he leaves for college. Grady, call Carson. I want everything he can find on the Rae Lindstrom murder and Janet Chase. I need that by sun up. I know a guy at the Chantilly PD who's been there over a decade. I'll see what he has to say first thing in the morning." Crew turns to Cade and me. "Do you know where your parents are?"

"They were last reported to be at home in Arizona by the news," I say. "But they're never right, so who knows."

"I'll see if I can confirm that." Crew pauses a beat. "I'll call Levi when I get some answers—probably first thing in the morning."

Mason is impressed. "Wow, first thing. You're so fast."

"You guys okay to go home? You can crash here if you're really worried about the SWAT team," Crew says, but it's the first thing he's said that doesn't sound serious.

I think Mason is about to accept Crew's invitation to sleep over when Jack says, "Nah. We're good. We don't want to attract SWAT to your house anyway."

Crew lets out one single chuckle. "That's funny. No one steps on my property without me knowing far in advance."

Levi pulls away from my death grip and offers Crew a hand and then Grady. "Thanks. I owe you."

"I'll hold you to that," Grady quips. "When you're a doctor, and I get my head bashed in, you can sew me up."

Holy crap. What do these men do?

Jack turns to the four of us. "Alright, kiddos. Load up in the Love Machine, and I'll take you home."

39

YOU KNOW WHAT THEY SAY…

Levi

Jack cranks his window down. "It's been an experience. I hope the government doesn't find you, but you know what they say…"

Cade frowns even though I know he's happy to be home. "No. What do they say?"

Jack, for once in his life, doesn't have a comeback. "I don't know. I'm tired. See you homies tomorrow. And stay off the internet."

The Love Machine disappears into the night. Mason needs to get home before his chickens and parents wake up.

Louise was asleep before we left, and my Jeep is still parked out front. I take Carissa's hand, and Cade walks next to her. "I'll make sure you get in, then I'd better go. It's almost four. If I come up, I might sleep through my alarm."

Carissa bites back a yawn. "I feel so much better, even though your dad's coworkers are scary. Thank you for asking them for help." She turns to her brother. "We'll get it all figured out."

He sighs. "I know. I just feel like I fucked it all up."

"No way. I want to know the truth, no matter what it is. I feel like we've lived in this big bubble of nothing but lies. I say screw them, and let the world know what really happened," Carissa says.

We make our way up the hill to the back of the house where we left the gardening room door unlocked. "Crew will figure it out. He always does."

We slip our shoes off and make our way through the butler's pantry and kitchen, but stutter to a halt when we see a light peeking at us from across the main breezeway of the house. I look at Carissa and Cade and widen my eyes.

Carissa motions to the back door and mouths, "You should go."

No.

Something feels off, and it's not just that Louise is up in the middle of the night. I'm about to shake my head and tell her I'll take the wrath of her grandmother so she and Cade aren't alone when they get caught, but that's when it happens.

The dark kitchen comes alive.

I blink the bright light away, but only for a second.

Mariann Collins is standing at the opening to the kitchen.

And she's not happy.

Carissa

I SIT SANDWICHED between Cade and Levi on Louise's stiff settee. My poor, sweet Louise is a wreck. She's sitting on the other side of the room in her housecoat and slippers with rollers on the top of her head to keep her hair set while she sleeps. Her old face is etched with anxiety, not much different than Cade's next to me.

I don't know what's happened to our mother over the past few months. It's like a switch was flipped. How have we never seen this side of her all our lives? She's turned into someone I don't recognize.

She's a frenzied mess—pacing back and forth between us and Louise—ranting, arms flailing.

"What the hell were you thinking, Cade?" she screams. "Neither one of you will answer our damn calls. Are you trying to ruin our family?"

I reach over to grasp Cade's hand. He immediately white knuckles my fingers to the point of pain, but I hold tight. His breaths are coming quicker—he's bleeding anxiety. I can't imagine what he's going through, being betrayed by his own mother who used to be his greatest protector.

She's the one who taught me to stand next to my twin throughout life, no matter what.

Levi sits on my other side, crowding me more than necessary. His legs are set wide, he leans forward, and his thick arm covers almost half of my body.

He's shielding me from the barrage of my own mother.

And he looks like he's ready to pounce.

"Mariann, don't yell at him. Please." Louise's voice is strained, every year of her life can be heard—wobbly and weak. She's just as scared as we are.

Mom spins and yells at her own mother. "Shut up! I can't think. Everything is falling apart. This is not how it was supposed to be."

"What's falling apart, Mariann?" Levi asks. His voice is even and controlled with an edge to it I've never heard before.

Anger bubbles within me when she turns and screams at Levi. "Don't you dare say a fucking word. I came here to deal with them. When Cillian gets here, he'll deal with you in his own way. You'll regret the day you looked at our daughter. He'll have to add you to the long list of all the other shit he's dealing with."

"What else?" Cade asks. His tone is hoarse but brave. "What else are you here to deal with?"

Mom shakes her head and runs her fingers violently through her hair. She looks at Cade like he just struck her. "You. Why would you do this? You had to have known this would hurt me. I've done everything I could to protect you, Cade. I know your father got caught and started this whole thing, but when I found out it was you who took your father's antics and blew them up into this storm, that is what hurt the most."

"Don't put this on him," I warn.

The moment I speak, Levi shifts in front of me farther.

"Why are you even here?" I plead. "All you had to do is stay away. This is Dad's mess. Why won't you just leave him?"

"I'm stuck!" she cries. "It was fine—it's been fine—but now it's falling apart. All of it. Your father is losing allies left and right. The FBI investigation has been reinstated. That will probably hit the news today, along with everything else."

Holy shit. That's why she's here.

"Where's Dad?" I demand. He's the violent one, and the thought of him dealing with anything on his own is frightening.

Her arms fall to her side. Her eyes are something I've never seen before. Not panicked, not irritated, not even incensed.

No.

They're crazy.

"He's dealing with *her*, okay?" she screams.

Louise jerks at the outburst, cowering to make herself small. I've never seen anyone try to shrink so fast.

"Who is he dealing with?" Cade demands, even though I'm almost positive I know the answer.

"You know who!" she screams. "You're the one who led them to her!"

"Janet Chase," I whisper. Even though I would have put money on that answer, her expression confirms it

"What is he going to do?" I exclaim.

"He's trying to put out the fucking inferno you all started. She's been subpoenaed about the payments, okay? She's not going to keep her mouth shut. There's no reason for her to keep quiet now. She's going to do everything she can to save her own ass. He's trying to reason with her."

Holy shit. Reason with her?

Cade presses into me.

We've all bared the brunt of Dad trying to reason with us before.

Mom starts pacing again.

I've had enough.

I shoot to my feet. Levi is up next to me in an instant. He wraps an arm around my waist and pulls me to his front.

This time it's my turn to raise my voice. "Is he trying to reason with her the way he reasoned with Rae Lindstrom?"

Mom freezes.

Louise gasps.

Levi reads the room and pulls me back two steps.

Mom freezes. "What do you know about her?"

Cade stands and moves next to me. "Everything."

Mom's expression falls, and she turns a ghostly white. I

stare at my brother and wonder what the hell he knows that he hasn't told us.

"The poor woman who worked for Cillian that was murdered?" Louise is gripping the arms of her high-back chair. "What about her?"

"No," Mom whispers. "You can't know about her. There's no way."

Cade doesn't have a chance to answer, because there's a commotion from the front door. Levi turns me, pulls my front to his side, and holds tight.

And this is where we are when my dad stops in his tracks at the opening to the front hall.

He's not drunk like he was the last time I saw him months ago. His eyes are alert and agitated, his gaze shifts around the room before landing on me.

And then Levi.

"Cillian." Louise bites. "Get out of my house. You're not getting close to my grandchildren again."

Dad ignores Louise and turns to my mother. "What the fuck is the Hollingsworth kid doing here in the middle of the night?"

"Do you think I give a shit about him right now?" Mom exclaims. "Did you find her?"

I'd be worried about the way Dad is talking about Levi, but something bigger grabs my attention.

The gun dangling from his hand.

What the hell is he doing with a gun?

Our parents aren't gun people. At least I didn't think they were. But I also didn't think they were adulterous or murderous or blackmailers either.

I fist Levi's T-shirt as every muscle in his body tenses next to mine. I'm ready to beg him to kidnap me for good.

Dad's glare on Levi lingers before he turns to Mom. "No. She wasn't home and she won't answer my calls."

Mom runs her hands up her face and through her hair. "What are we going to do?"

"I'll find her," Dad seethes. "But right now, I need to deal with the kids. And him."

"Dad, put the gun away." I try to shift out of Levi's hold to move in front of him, but he holds me where I am. "Calm down. We were curious, that's all. Cade didn't mean to cause any harm."

"Yes, I did," Cade spouts immediately.

"Cade," I bite. "Stop it."

"They know everything, Cillian," my mom cries. "I don't know how. But they figured out about Janet and the payments. It's been under wraps all these years, but they *know*."

"Put the gun down," Levi demands and shifts me out of his arms to push me behind him. "We're not the only ones who know. Stop while you're ahead so no one else gets hurt."

Dad looks to Mom. "They know it was you?"

"What?" I gasp.

The electric current running through the room is so strong, Louise's old mansion might combust if there were a spark.

"Fuck," Cade mutters and stares at my mom.

"Mariann?" Louise looks like she was struck by lightning, and shifts nervously in her chair.

"This isn't happening," Mom mutters. Her chest heaves with deep breaths and looks like Cade when he's suffering from an asthma attack. "After all these years."

"You killed Rae Lindstrom," Levi states in disbelief.

This is ... this is so bad and nothing like I assumed.

Levi is holding me tight to his back. I do everything I can to keep my movements hidden as I slide my phone from my back pocket. I hold the buttons down long enough, press the red button on the screen, and say a silent prayer.

"I didn't mean to," Mom cries. "I was so upset. I made the intern give me the address so I could just talk to Rae. I begged her to stay quiet about the affair for the sake of my family. Janet got nosy and followed me. She knew everything, and we had to keep her quiet."

"We saw photos of the crime scene online." Cade doesn't sound like himself as his tone matches the energy in the room. "That's not the scene of involuntary manslaughter, Mom."

"It's his fault!" Mom screams, pointing at Dad. "I've ignored every mistress. Every hushed rumor. I've always looked the other way for our family and my own personal sanity. I had to. All these years I managed. But I can't manage when it's thrown in my face. And Rae wanted more of him than he was willing to give. She threatened to go public with their affair to ruin him. I can look away quietly, but there's no way I'd be able to deal with the world looking at me like I'm not enough."

"Shit," I hiss. This is why she actually left the country when the media reported the scandal.

Mom's tears come fast and furious as she looks across the room to my dad. "I hate you. I hate you more than the women you fuck and the lives you throw to the side like they're disposable."

"I've done everything I could to cover *your* fuck up for years," Dad hisses back. It's like the rest of us have evaporated and it's just the two of them. "Don't put this on me. You're the one who lost it in a jealous rage and bashed her head in until she was unrecognizable."

A whimper comes from Louise, but I can't tear my eyes off my parents.

And they go directly to my father's hand gripping the gun. His index finger flirts with the trigger.

Levi must see it too. Every muscle in his back tenses further.

"You aren't taking me down with you, Mariann. I'm not losing everything because you lost your fucking mind. I offered you a divorce more times than I can count." Dad raises the gun and points it at Mom. "Get in the car. We're leaving. I can't believe you dragged this shit here."

Mom shakes her head. "No! I'm not going anywhere with you. I should've stayed in Greece and never came back. I need to get out of the country. Janet will surely talk to save herself. You're not innocent in this, Cillian. You're the one who arranged to pay her off all these years. You cleared Rae's house of all the evidence. If I go down for this, I'm taking you with me."

"Fuck," Levi grits so low, I barely hear it. But I do feel it, just like I feel Levi's cell vibrate through his back pocket.

"I don't want to do this here, Mariann. Not in front of the kids. Get in the fucking car."

"No!" Louise cries. "Don't go with him!"

"Don't go, Mom," I beg. As messed up as this is, there's no telling what Dad will do to save his own ass.

Dad's eyes narrow on me, and he moves. But not toward us.

He moves straight for his wife.

Mom backs up two steps before she makes a run for the side door toward the back of the house.

Louise and I scream at the same time when Dad chases her.

Levi pulls out of my hold, and Cade follows.

I'm frozen to my spot when Levi tackles my dad from behind.

They both go down to the old wood floors with a thunderous crash.

Dad claws to get away. The gun slides. Cade lunges.

But so do Levi and Dad.

It's chaos.

I see a hand in the scrum reach and land on the gun.

Then...

A shot.

40

OVER

Levi

"Fuck!" Cade yells.

Screams fill the room.

I can't concentrate on any of it.

Cillian is face down on the floor. I have him pinned, but he was able to reach the gun that slipped from his hand when we went down.

That's when I see blond hair in front of me—in front of us.

"Carissa, get back," I yell.

"He's bleeding," she cries.

I've got Cillian's forearm pressed to the floor, but he's still white-knuckling the gun.

"Get the fuck off me," Cillian grits. The side of his face probably has antique wood grain indented into his skin. That's how hard I have him pressed to the floor.

"Drop the gun," I demand.

But he won't. If I let up on his arm, he could twist and turn it on me.

Or worse. The object of my obsession. My future.

There's commotion everywhere, but all I can focus on is him. I know the moment I let up an inch, there will be trouble. He's desperate.

Carissa disappears from my line of sight. I take the opening without anyone in the line of fire.

Keeping hold of his arm with the weapon, I let up with my other arm long enough for him to move.

He tries to headbutt me, but I'm ready and take the opening I need.

I wrap my arm around his neck and pull.

"Fucker," I mutter into the side of his face.

Cillian's eyes widen, and his serrating breaths are erratic. His body heaves to find air and to fight me.

"You'll never touch them again," I say.

He couldn't answer if he wanted to.

He gags and tries to gasp.

He needs something that only I can give him.

Oxygen.

And there's no fucking way he's getting it.

Not from me.

"Drop the fucking gun, asshole."

Cillian starts to shake in my hold and stops fighting me, but he won't let go of the gun.

His neck and the crook of my elbow become even better acquainted. The moment he starts to panic, I tighten my hold.

His face grows red and the veins in his forehead and temples pop.

Only when he starts to drool do I hear the gun clink on the wood floor.

In a faraway place in my brain, I hear Louise cry, "I have the gun."

But I don't let go. "Carissa is mine. You'll never see her or Cade again, do you understand? You'll never hurt them again."

Voices enter the room—deep ones—barking orders and calling my name.

It's only when Cillian's eyes start to roll back, do I comprehend what's going on.

"Fuck, Levi! Let him go."

I feel hands on me.

It's my turn to fight, because I'm not letting him go. I can't stop the visions of him tossing Carissa onto the rocks. Cade being slammed against stone, being struck by his own fucking father.

Cillian Collins doesn't deserve even stale oxygen.

"I can't pry him off." I vaguely recognize the voice hovering over me. "Dammit, Levi. I don't want to hurt you. Let him the fuck go."

Too many people have their hands on me. I can't keep hold of his neck. My arm is pried far enough, someone gets their hold between me and Cillian.

That's when I go flying through the air.

I land on my back with someone's arms wrapped around my chest.

"Let go!" I yell and fight.

I'm throwing elbows when the voice in my ear growls, "It's Grady. Stop fighting."

Grady.

I freeze, before I pull in a breath.

Shit.

Crew has Cillian on his back. Cillian's color is slowly coming back as his chest heaves, coughing on the precious oxygen he doesn't deserve.

"You don't want that on your conscience, Levi." Grady's

words rumble in my ear for only me to hear. "You're too young to live with that shit in your head. Trust me. I experience it every day. I'm not going to let you walk that road, man. We're here, so calm the fuck down."

I look around and Carissa is kneeling next to her twin with her mom sitting next to them. Tears run down her face.

Grady's arms constrict around my chest. "It's over. Are you going to calm down if I let you go?"

I nod, not able to find the words. All I see is Cade lying on the floor, blood seeping onto the floor below him.

I need to get to them.

"Let me go, dammit."

Grady's arms loosen in an instant. I scramble to my feet and move across the room to kneel by Carissa.

Cade is pale but alert.

"Is it bad?" I ask.

"I don't know." Carissa is as white as a ghost. Blood seeps from her hands where she's pressing on his shoulder. She speaks to her twin. "Look at me, Cade. Try to stay calm."

"An ambulance is on its way. They said they already had units called out." Louise stands over us in a mess of nerves. "He'll be okay. He has to be okay."

I look down at Cade, who's holding it together. "We won't leave you. I'll make sure Carissa rides to the hospital with you, and I'll follow. The bullet caught your shoulder. As long as it didn't hit a major artery, you'll be okay."

He swallows hard and nods. "Maybe you should actually go to medical school before telling me I'm going to be okay after my own father shot me."

"Since this will never happen again, this is my one and only chance to announce your prognosis. Cut me some slack."

Levi

Grady leads a small army of police officers to the room, followed by a team of EMTs lugging bags of equipment.

When they start to tend to Cade, Carissa doesn't budge. I lean in and put my lips to her ear. "Baby, let them work."

She lets out a strangled breath as I wrap a hand around her wrist to pull her away. I move her back far enough for them to work and pull her between my legs and into my arms where we sit on the floor.

"He's going to be okay," I promise her.

Her gaze shifts to me before it strays across the room where her father is being yanked to his feet in handcuffs. Mariann is sitting on a chair with her head in her hands as they Mirandize her too.

I put a hand to Carissa's chin and pull her face to mine. "Don't look at that. Focus on Cade. He needs you."

She plants her face in my chest, her tears seep through my shirt. Louise is kneeling on the other side of Cade, clutching her robe in her arthritic fingers.

I press my lips to Carissa's head. "It's all over."

41

JUST THE WAY YOU ARE

Levi
Two weeks later

I'm standing in the old farm house situated deep in the woods on the land next to Whitetail. This is where Crew, Grady, and Dad coordinate their work with the CIA.

It's also where it all started years ago, when the men standing before me retired from being merely assassins to train and manage others like them. Dad doesn't mince words, I know every part of his work. And since they retired, they do it differently than anyone has in the past.

They're growing, building ... diversifying.

I've been here many times over the last few years. I work out with the men in Crew's gym when I can. But I've never been the focus of their attention like this.

"What were you thinking?" Dad's expression is set to stone as he stands at the head of the table in the old dining room that acts as their conference room. Crew hasn't even bothered ripping the tattered, decades-old wallpaper off the walls. He has more important things to do.

Grady puts a hand out. "In all due respect, your boy handled the situation like a young badass in training—"

"He's not a fucking trainee, Cain," Dad bellows.

Crew steps in. "That's not what he meant. Levi did everything right. He came to us when it mattered. Because of that, we pinged the Senator's phone and were able to follow him. When we saw Cillian headed to the Boyette mansion, we figured it was bad news and went right away."

Dad's infuriated stare shifts between the three of us.

"Not that he didn't have it under control," Grady adds. "He did. It took both of us to pry him off Collins. He would've killed him had we not—"

"If you don't shut your fucking mouth, Cain, I'll come across this table and take you down right here. Put yourself in my position." Dad points to me but raises his voice to Grady. "What if this was your son?"

Grady tips his head. "My son is three."

"Just for your information, it doesn't matter how big and strong they might get. They'll always be three in your fucking heart." Dad exhales and drags a hand down his face.

Dad and Keelie got home from their honeymoon this morning. Crew decided it was best to tell Dad what happened right away and do it together. I argued that I could handle it myself, but Crew insisted, and Grady reminded me he got to be the one to tell him.

Now I'm glad I listened to them.

Crew proves he not only keeps his cool in every situation but will also put his foot down to keep the peace within his organization. "All that matters is it's done. Collins and his wife are being held without bond. Cade is recovering from surgery and will be fine. Carissa won't have to deal with her parents ever again. This isn't public knowledge yet, but Carson just informed me Collins was being paid bogus rent through his real estate investments in exchange for funding special interests. Some shell company out of Finland, if you can believe it. That's where he was getting the money to pay Janet Chase. His list of problems just got longer." Crew focuses his intensity on Dad. "And your son leaves for school in a week. He's fucking smart and made the right choices. He has plans for his life that don't include this." He motions around him. "It's all good."

Dad exhales and stares at the table between us. When he looks up, he speaks to me like no one else is in the room. "Do you have anything to say, or are you going to let them speak for you?"

I cross my arms and tip my head an inch. "I'd do it again."

"Levi. You need to slow things down with her. Go to school. Have fun. Act your age—"

I interrupt. "I love her. Told you that once. No skin off my back if I have to repeat myself. I tell her every chance I get."

"She's the one." We all look at Grady. His grin that is aimed at my dad might as well be an invitation to square off on the mat until someone taps out.

"Fuck you," Dad throws at Grady.

"Dad," I call.

He looks at me and hikes a brow.

"Would you want me to be any other way?"

Dad plants his hands on his hips and turns to look out the window into the woods. When he finally moves, I tense.

He walks around the table and comes straight for me.

But I know everything is okay when he tags me around the neck and pulls me into a dad hug.

His voice is low and hoarse when he admits, "No. You're perfect just the way you are, bud."

42

ARE YOU READY?

Carissa
Four months later

The bell rings.
The last bell of my last day of my last class of high school.

When Levi Hollingsworth was assigned to me as my tutor, he made me a promise. He said he'd make sure I'd get out of prison early.

And he did.

Levi might be as determined as I am for me to graduate early.

I've seen him every weekend since he left for Hopkins. He either comes here or I go there.

I'm surprised Louise has allowed it, but she's changed. She might not be all hugs and kisses, but she is caring, loving, and simply wants us to be happy.

I doubt she tells her friends from the garden society that I go to Maryland to spend the weekend with my boyfriend, but she's never tried to stop me. Sometimes I wonder if she thinks I'll threaten to leave, but I'd never do that.

I'm home.

The only other place I want to be right now besides the Boyette mansion—which isn't at all creepy anymore—is with Levi.

Home has a new meaning for me.

It's where you're loved and cared for. It's where the people are who you simply cannot live without.

I pack up my bag, turn in my test, and walk out the door.

Mason stands across the hall, leaning on the bank of lockers, grinning from ear to ear.

He pushes his glasses up his nose. "I can't believe you're done. At least I have Cade for one more semester. But after that, no more Homies. Next year I'll be by myself."

I grab him by the sleeve of his sweatshirt and pull him to walk down the hall. I'm so ready to get out of here. "If anyone could graduate early, it's you."

Mason shrugs. "I don't know. I've leveled up since last year. I'm popular, even if it did come by association. I want to ride this out as long as I can. Plus, I want to go to my senior prom."

Nothing sounds more miserable to me, but this is what I love about Mason. He's always optimistic. "You'll probably set a record for most titles. You're the perfect mix of Levi and Jack and will surely be valedictorian and crowned prom king."

We walk through the commons, and I start for the door that leads to the parking lot, but Mason stops me. "Wait, come this way. I want to show you something."

"But I'm meeting Cade at the car. He's waiting for me."

"This'll only take a second," he says. "Come on."

It's his turn to yank me by the sleeve. "Okay, but I need to let him know I'll be a few minutes late."

"He'll be fine," Mason says.

"I know," I concede. "It's a habit."

"Hey, you." I look over and Emma meets us at the end of the hall. "You're done. It feels like you just got here. I'm jealous."

I smile at Levi's sister. She's come out of her shell this year—a completely different person than she was when I first met her. She's not a full-fledged Homie, but she will sit with us at lunch every once in a while. She's sweet, outgoing, and people flock to her. It's like her troubles from last year never existed.

Mason gives Emma a nudge. "You have two-and-a-half years to go, Emma. Everyone wants to leave me."

"I can't believe I'm done," I say. "I can't believe Levi had to stay so long after finals. I'm ready for him to be home for break."

"Yeah," Emma mutters. "That really sucks."

It's a week before Christmas and snow is already falling on the mountains and valleys of Virginia. After growing up in the desert, I love it—even though I still hate wearing a coat.

We talk about our plans for the holidays. Jack has already been home for a few days—he's making plans to get the gang together again.

When we exit the front doors of the school, it's not lost on me this will be my last time doing so as a high school student. I didn't need a tutor this semester, which is good since my preferred private teacher is now away at college. I had Cade and Mason if I needed them, but I didn't.

I had a goal. And I was going to reach it no matter what.

"There," Mason says.

I stop in my snowy tracks before Mason has a chance to fully get the word out. A smile creeps across my face, and I warm from the inside out when I see him.

Levi is standing behind his Jeep, leaning on the spare tire. His hands are stuffed in his jeans pockets, and his legs are crossed at the ankle. His dark, thick hair is spotted with snowflakes, and I wonder how long he's been standing there waiting on me.

His expression doesn't match mine that's grown into an ecstatic grin. His hazel eyes burn through the winter air. If I didn't know he was here for me, I'd think he was posing for a commercial.

Levi's classes were over a week ago, but he had team practices. I turn to Mason and Emma. "You knew about this?"

Mason shrugs. "Yeah. And Cade knows too. He's probably already on his way home."

"You guys are really sickening, you know that? I've had to keep this secret for days." Emma grins as she rolls her eyes. "I should say, my brother is sickening. I'm just happy I like you so much."

I beam at both of them. "I'll see you both before Christmas, right?"

"Louise invited me over for Christmas cookies tomorrow. I wouldn't miss it," Mason says.

"And now that Levi's home, I'm sure I'll see you every day," Emma adds.

I glance at Levi and bite my lip. "I'll see you both later then?"

He smirks. "We're not looking for an invite, Carissa. Go."

"Tomorrow for cookies. I'll be there." I back up two steps and give them a small wave. "And I'll see you at home, Emma."

Mason looks over my shoulder at Levi and lifts his chin. Mason is at least two inches taller and has put on some weight. He's mastering his own cool, chill vibe but remains as sweet as ever.

Emma waves to her brother, and she and Mason head to the student parking lot.

Me, however...

I'm not feeling cool or chill right now.

I pick up my pace and can't get to him fast enough. His eyes never leave me as he catches me when I throw myself into his arms. "You're early. What are you doing here?"

His answer comes in the form of a searing kiss, before he says, "I'm here to kidnap you. Why else would I be here?"

I'm breathless. "I guess you can kiss me like this in the school parking lot now. I'm officially done too."

"Yeah, you are. How does it feel?"

"Now that you're here, it feels even better. No, it feels real."

He presses his lips to mine once more before pulling away far enough to look down at me. "Come on. I have a surprise for you."

"Another surprise? You being home early is plenty."

He lets me go and grabs my backpack from my shoulder. "You underestimate me, baby. You're done with high school and moving on to college. It's a big fucking day, and we're commemorating it."

I push up to my toes and press my lips to his for one more quick kiss. "Now I can't wait."

He walks me to the passenger door and holds it open for me, tossing my bag to the backseat. He could throw it away for all I care. I can't wait to start over next month.

We're in, buckled, and he's flipped the heat on high when he turns to me. "I never thought this day would come.

It's been the longest four months of my life. Love you, baby."

I don't care where he's taking me or what we're doing. I'm done with the building behind us, and after the holidays, I'm moving to Baltimore.

Levi

I PULL to a stop in the middle of the deserted, dirt road on the bridge where I brought her the first time I ever kidnapped her. Where she experienced her first orgasm—one I gave her.

And the last place I had her in my arms before her parents tried to steal her away from me.

"We haven't been here in forever," she says, looking around as I kill the engine.

"Where it all started." I unbuckle and sit back to look at her. "Where we started."

She turns and leans the side of her head on the seatback. "It feels like another lifetime."

It hasn't even been six months since that dark day at Louise's house with her parents when Cade was shot. Her parents are still awaiting trial for everything from murder to illegal possession of a firearm. Carissa, Cade, Louise, and myself are witnesses.

Cade handled the whole thing better than expected, especially given the fact his own father shot him. Whether it was accidental or not, that shit can't be easy for anyone.

We only talk about it when we have to. Carissa had trouble sleeping for weeks after it happened, which made it even harder for me to leave for school. I've made it a priority to see her at least once a week, but it's not enough.

I'm about to remedy that.

"Are you ready?" I ask.

She sighs, and a contented smile settles on her beautiful face—one I'm seeing more and more of the closer we get to spring semester. "I'm not sure I'm ready for calculus, but I'm so ready for everything else. And I'm ready to be close to you. Across campus is nothing compared to two hours. I might get to see you every day."

"Baby, come here." I reach for her hand and pull. We haven't had to be like this for a long time, but it only takes a moment for her to kick her boots off, climb over the console, and straddle my hips the way I'm obsessed with. I recline my seat farther, drag my hands up her thighs, and look up at her. "There's no might. Unless I'm traveling for games or you're visiting Cade and Louise, we'll be just like this."

"So you're telling me we'll both be in dorms, but we'll have to hide away in your Jeep still?"

I shake my head. "No way. I might have a roommate, but you don't. Remind me to thank Louise for springing for a private room."

"Louise is worried about me, but she's also worried about my privacy with everything going on with my parents. I'm grateful for that. And to your coaches who I have a feeling had everything to do with getting me through the acceptance process."

She's right, but I'll never admit it. I threatened to transfer if she didn't get in. And since I'm probably going to be a starter my freshman year, they made it happen. "You applied and got in. That's all."

Her dark eyes slide to the side. I have to bite back a smile—she knows I'm full of shit.

"Does it matter?" I ask. "You're in. It's what you wanted. What I really fucking wanted."

She leans in to kiss me. "No, you're right. It doesn't matter. And I've been thinking about my major. I'm not going to let you be the only focused one."

She enrolled as undecided. I told her it didn't matter and she'd figure it out eventually. "What's that?"

She fingers the buttons on my shirt as her eyes find mine. "Speech therapy."

"I like it. You'll help people. It fits you."

She lifts a shoulder. "Cade and I both went through therapy when we were little. We each had different issues, but we spent hours and hours with our therapist. I'll never forget her. She was kind and patient. We'll see if it sticks, but it's always been in the back of my mind."

"I bet you'll love it."

"It's not molecular and cellular biology." She rolls her eyes. "You'll be in med school before I can think about graduating."

I shake my head and stare into her dark eyes that I'm more than willing to get lost in forever. "I refuse to fit into anyone's mold. We'll do what we want, on our timeline. Fuck everyone else."

"We're sure trying."

"We need to try harder."

She frowns. "What?"

"Marry me." Those two little words have been brewing inside me for months. It's been all I could do to wait until today to say them. So much so, it's been painful.

Her dark eyes widen and she whispers, "What?"

"We haven't talked about when, but we've talked about it. Why wait? Why should I have to wait years to call you mine? I don't want to wait, Carissa. I want you ... forever. Tell me, baby, what do you want?"

Her eyes brim with emotion. I can see it—feel it in her body that's so close to mine. I know every part of her now. There's rarely a moment I'm with her that I can't read her.

Her chest rises and falls with deep breaths as she whispers, "I wish I were like you."

My chest tightens, because this is not the way I thought this would go. "Carissa—"

She shakes her head quickly and interrupts me. "My parents are awaiting trial for the worst offenses. I have Cade and Louise, but that's it. I love them—even Louise—but they're not enough. There are times I feel lost. But the only time I'm not is when I'm with you. You're my home, Levi. I don't know what I'd do without you."

My throat thickens. "It doesn't have to be tomorrow or even in six months. We don't even have to tell anyone for a while. But this part can't wait. It's gnawing at me to make it official, even if it is just between the two of us until we think people can handle it. I need to know the next step is imminent."

Tears fill her dark eyes. "I feel selfish. Like you're saving me, and I'm giving you nothing in return."

I shake my head. "Never say that again. You're mine, and that's not going to change. This only makes it official. Marry me, Carissa. Say you'll be mine forever. I want to be yours. More than anything. I'll always stand next to you and take care of you."

She falls to my chest. Her hands frame my jaw, and her lips land on mine.

I wrap my arms around her and hold her to me. One hand slides to her ass and the other to her soft hair. My desperation for her floods me to the point I might not be able to breathe if she says no...

I fist her hair and pull her head back a fraction.

"Say yes," I demand. "I don't want parties or bars or benders. I want you. We can be poor college students together. We won't know what we don't have. Marry me, Carissa. Flip off society with me and be mine ... now."

Tears stain her face.

But I can see it.

I can feel it.

I smile.

She shakes her head once. "Your dad is going to be pissed."

This time I'm flooded with relief.

And fucking ecstasy.

"He'll get over it." I reach up to press my lips to hers. Then I lift my hips enough to reach into my front pocket. I open the box I bought two months ago when I couldn't stop thinking about this moment and pull out the ring that was the best I could afford. I pluck it out and toss the box to the passenger seat.

"Oh my," she whispers.

I slide it on her left ring finger. "Someday I'll get you something bigger—"

"No," she interrupts, staring at her left hand like it's a cure to all the world's ailments. "It's perfect. I never want anything else."

The band is solid gold, but the diamond is small.

Small but perfect.

Like our beginning.

"Say yes," I demand.

She looks away from the ring that will show the world she's mine. "Yes."

"Love you, baby."

She falls to my chest once again, but this time it feels different. It feels final.

And I fucking love it.

"I love you so much, Levi. I can't wait to marry you."

I wrap my arms around her and pull her to me.

"I can't either, baby. I can't either."

EPILOGUE

Carissa

I'm sandwiched between Levi and Cade.

It's not lost on me this is exactly the way we were when our family, as we knew it, ended.

The day dark truths came to light.

The day Dad shot Cade.

We were sitting just like this when that nightmare began. Only now we have Remi.

Remi Louise.

Named after her great grandmother.

My Louise ... the grandmother I didn't have enough time with.

Five days ago, Chuck came to work, just like he does every Thursday morning. But that day he wasn't greeted with a cup of coffee and a list of to-dos. The house was quiet.

Eerily silent, as he described it.

He found Louise in bed, like she'd just rested her head for the night. She passed in her sleep.

"Chuck is to remain on staff at the Boyette estate for as long as he wants to work. He's to have a twelve percent increase in salary every year until he retires." Louise's attorney, Mr. Smythe—who has to be older than she was—reads from Louise's trust.

He said she updated it the day after Levi and I were married here on the grounds of her estate. It wasn't lost on us we took our vows on the same hill we ran up and down, sneaking in and out of the mansion so many times.

The attorney looks up and adds, "I just want you to know that I met with Chuck yesterday. Not only did your grandmother make her wishes clear about his employment, but she was incredibly generous with him as well. He's been loyal to her for over two decades."

"I'm glad. He made sure she was well taken care of," I say, swiping a tear from my cheek with the back of my hand. Levi pulls me tighter to his side and with one arm since he's holding Remi with his other, and Cade squeezes my hand. My little family is even smaller now. I'm flooded with grief and anger that we didn't have more time with her.

I blame that on Mom.

Levi shifts Remi when she stirs, but he gets her to settle. She missed her nap, and has been passed out on Levi's chest since we got back from the funeral.

We didn't wait to start a family after we got married. I was pregnant just a few months after we were married. And as I look at Levi and our daughter, who has my brown eyes and his thick dark hair, I wonder if it's too soon to think about doing it all over again.

Levi just finished his first year of medical school, and I graduated with my degree in speech therapy. Levi was right when he said we'd never know what we don't have. All we need is each other. And now Remi.

Cade is at MIT. If I thought my twin was smart back when he hacked into Dad's private accounts that led to uncovering their ugly truths, then he's a downright genius now.

"Are you okay, Carissa? Would you like a break or should we keep going?" Mr. Smythe asks.

I shake my head, needing this to be over. It's been the longest week. "Go ahead, please. We've kept you long enough today."

He looks back to the documents and continues to read. "*The estate, bank accounts, and investments within the trust will be split equally between Cade Collins and Carissa Collins Hollingsworth.*" He pauses and spears Cade and me with his light brown eyes through his reading glasses. "This is where your grandmother became incredibly specific. She was passionate that her next wishes be followed exactly."

I tense and glance at Cade. He frowns, and I wonder what we're in for.

Mr. Smythe continues. "*The Boyette home, and the land it sits on, will be funded through the estate as its own entity. This includes taxes, maintenance, updates as you see fit, and the caretakers' salary. The home and land may not be sold until your thirty-eighth birthdays.*"

What?

Cade's frown turns into a look of shock. When I turn to look at Levi, he shakes his head and shrugs.

"As I said, she was very specific. As much as I told her this was an uncommon stipulation for those inheriting a trust, especially given your young ages, she was adamant." Mr. Smythe continues to blow our minds. "This next part is specifically addressed to the twins... *Cade and Carissa, it's my biggest regret that I didn't fight to be a part of your lives sooner. I understand this big, old rambling house isn't your home ... but it could be. It's what your grandfather and I wanted to give your mother, but we failed somewhere along the way. You might wonder why I chose the age of thirty-eight. Well, thirty-five seems too young. And if you haven't fallen in love with this home and land by the time you're forty, then it's never going to happen. It's plenty big enough for two families. Live here full-time or don't, but come back. I want memories made here. I want your children to run and play on the grounds. I want the next generation to grow up knowing this land and every nook and cranny of this beautiful house I failed to make a home. You're lucky to have each other, and I want you to be here together as much as possible."*

Cade turns to me. "She wants us to live here, together?" He looks from me to Levi and back to me again. "All of us?"

I sniffle one more time and defend Louise. "I just learned this too. And I don't know what's wrong. I sort of like the idea." I motion around us. "I mean, it's huge. You live in a studio apartment, and we have a tiny two-bedroom. What's wrong with having this to come back to?"

Cade shrugs. "It's not bad. I just need to get used to it, okay? I like Boston. I might want to stay there after graduation."

"Well, you're coming back here for Christmas. Louise said so," I bristle and turn to my husband. "I don't know what to say. I hope you're okay with this. I had no idea."

His lips tip on one side, and he pulls me in close enough to press his lips to my forehead. "Like you said, we live in a two-bedroom apartment in the middle of Baltimore. There's nothing to be upset about, baby. To have this for Remi?" He looks around the house like he's seeing it for the first time. "It's Louise giving to us for years to come."

"I agree," I whisper.

"Yeah, I guess it's cool," Cade says. "Just ... odd."

"It is odd," Mr. Smythe agrees. "But it's also very Louise."

"I like it," Levi says, his voice low and thick. "This is where I met you—both of you. This is home."

I sink into his side. "It is. I'm glad she set it up this way. As far as I'm concerned, it's a gift that will last. Who knows, we might want to keep it forever."

Cade looks around. "Maybe so."

"Do you have any questions? I'll continue to work for you for the next year to make sure everything is transitioned. Beyond that, everything is up to both of you," Mr. Smythe explains.

Cade and I don't have a chance to ask any questions. Levi spears me with a knowing gaze and motions to our daughter. "A security system is going in right away. Cameras everywhere. And I mean *everywhere*," he stresses.

I can't help but smile.

Cade rolls his eyes.

Apparently, no one is going to sneak into this mansion to have their way with our daughter, like someone else I know.

Levi
Six years later

CARISSA THROWS her head back and gasps. "Oh, Levi."

She doesn't have to be quiet. The house is just that big.

I watch her come, her beautiful body sitting over me where her legs straddle my hips. The minute I got home from the hospital and showered, I came to bed to wake her.

It's our thing after I pull a long shift.

But tonight, I didn't need to wake her. She was alert and waiting for me. She ripped off her tank and panties and climbed on top.

She missed me as much as I missed her.

I'm halfway through my neurology residency. It's a grind. Not just for me, but for Carissa too. The hours are no joke, and I thought my sleep was jacked when we had Remi and Leo, but it turns out infants are nothing compared to the years required to make it in my field.

It's hard, but I love it. Not as much as I love my family and the life we've built here in small-town Virginia. Together, it makes the commute halfway to the District worth it.

We live at the Boyette estate full-time. It's crazy how it doesn't seem as massive as it did when we were in high school. Filling it with kids has something to do with that, but making it ours does too. The stiff furniture is gone and Louise's formal living room is full of toys. I've stepped on more Legos and Barbie shoes than any dad should have to endure.

Cade settled in Boston after graduate school and is killing it in his field. He comes home as often as he can, but it's still not enough to appease my wife, who's doing everything she can to live out Louise's wishes. We haven't even talked about it since I still have half of my residency to go, but we both want to settle here. I want to be close to Dad and Keelie, and Carissa wants to be here and raise the kids in the house Louise gave her.

This is home.

It's becoming more and more set in our souls the longer we're here.

There's nothing more we need than each other. And every time one of the kids reaches another milestone, does something funny, or breaks a bone in this house, the memories we're making are priceless. And when Cade is here, I can tell my wife is content.

"Don't stop, baby." My hands frame her hips as she rocks on my thumb while I circle her clit. "Fuck, I missed you."

She tips her head to look down at me. Her hair is a mess, her eyes hooded, and her jaw slack. It's my favorite look on my wife. As the years click on, I've become more and more obsessed.

She pushes up to her knees. I grip my cock, knowing what she wants. When she slides down, taking me inch by inch, it's my turn to groan.

"Yes," she moans, filling herself to the root. I lift my hips from the bed, and she moves. She rocks. She fucks herself.

Tonight, my wife is energetic.

I drag my hands to her tits and roll her nipples to hardened peaks.

She pulls in a shallow breath and utters the words, "I have something to tell you."

I try to concentrate on her words, but it's hard when she's moving in all the right ways. I drag my gaze up her body to her beautiful face, and mutter, "What's that, baby?"

"A baby," she repeats, breathy but definitive.

My hands come to her hips and freeze, holding her down on my cock. "What?"

Her fingers tease my abs as she drags her fingernails over my skin. "I took a test tonight. I'm pregnant."

I do a sit up, and we're nose to nose. The only thing in my world are her big brown eyes. "You're pregnant?"

Her teeth find her lip, biting the sensitive skin as she smiles and nods.

"No shit?" I ask again.

She brings her hands to my face and frames my jaw.

"Yes, Dr. Hollingsworth. If you want to do a thorough examination, I'll be your willing patient."

"Don't tempt me." A smile grows slowly across my face. "A baby."

"Yes. We wanted to make this house feel a little smaller, right?"

I bring my hand up to bury it in her hair, and pull her mouth to mine for a searing kiss.

"Third time around, and it feels like the first all over again," I murmur against her lips. "Knowing you're pregnant with my baby? Hits me in the gut, Carissa. I love you so much."

She rocks forward and back on my cock. "You've given me so much to love, Levi. I don't know what I'd do without you."

"Wouldn't change a thing about our story. Just when I think it's complete, life just keeps giving. Every moment with you is perfect, and this baby will make it better. Make us better."

She leans in to press her lips to mine. "This was a team effort, Levi."

I put my hand to the bed and flip her to her back.

I make love to my wife.

To celebrate.

To love.

To make more memories.

Cementing our family here.

At home.

Forever together.

Thank you for reading. If you enjoyed *Levi*, the author would appreciate a review on Amazon.

Read Crew and Addy's story in *Vines*
Read Grady and Maya's story in *Paths*
Read Asa and Keelie's story in *Gifts*
Read Jarvis and Gracie's story in *Veils*
Read Cole and Bella's story in *Scars*
Read Ozzy and Liyah's story in *Souls*
Read Evan and Mary's story in *The Tequila – A Killers Novella*

ACKNOWLEDGMENTS

When I released Gifts, Levi always intrigued me. I knew there was a story there—a story that went beyond normal high school drama, about normal high school kids, who were thrown into extraordinary situations.

That's what Levi is about.

As a mom, an aunt, a friend ... I think we don't give this generation enough credit. Not only are they destined for great things, they're empathetic, loving, and accepting.

It was my goal to write a new adult book that brought a menagerie of kids together of different ages and social circles for a common goal. I loved each and every one of them, and I hope you do too.

I'm not sure why I keep torturing myself by writing up to a deadline, but it seems I'm a masochist. Hadley Finn, my editor, is an angel. She encourages me, keeps up with my ridiculous self-imposed schedule, and never complains. All that, while perfecting and polishing my messy words. Working with her is seamless. I'm grateful to have her in my corner.

Layla Frost and Sarah Curtis, thank you for your daily support and putting up with my daily ramblings. I don't know what I'd do without your friendship and support.

Annette, you've become a part of my daily life, and I adore you. Thank you for always having my back, wanting the best for me, and working tirelessly to encourage me to always be my best. I couldn't do this without you.

Michele and Karyn, you read Levi chapter by chapter as I wrote. You read every raw error and put up with every dramatic emotion I laid at your feet. Thank you for pushing me, putting up with me, and loving my words as much as you do me. I could not have written this book without your support.

Adriana, thank you for your support and encouragement to write a character with a disability. I can't thank you enough for your time, the private chats, and your endless friendship.

Carrie and Beth, your eagle eyes are always my saving grace when it comes to my pesky, invisible errors. Thank you for your time, support, and desire to make my words perfect.

Emoji, you continue to be my hype man. I love you for making me laugh every day and loving me back endlessly, especially when I had to work on vacation to finish this book.

Lauren, drinking wine late into the night and plotting this book will always be one of my favorite memories. We plotted so much, I couldn't fit it all into one book, but I promise those kickass storylines won't go to waste. Look in future books! Love you to the moon.

Finally, to the Beauties. Not many people can say they have thousands of BFFs at their fingertips, but I do. Thank you for your support, reading an NA book for me, and pushing me to be my best. You will always be my favorite corner of the internet.

Until our next drama and HEA, thank you for reading.
BA xoxo

ALSO BY BRYNNE ASHER

Killers Series

Vines – A Killers Novel, Book 1

Paths – A Killers Novel, Book 2

Gifts – A Killers Novel, Book 3

Veils – A Killers Novel, Book 4

Scars – A Killers Novel, Book 5

Souls – A Killers Novel, Book 6

The Tequila – A Killers Novella

The Killers, The Next Generation

Levi, Asa's son

The Agents

Possession

Tapped

Exposed

Illicit

The Carpino Series

Overflow – The Carpino Series, Book 1

Beautiful Life – The Carpino Series, Book 2

Athica Lane – The Carpino Series, Book 3

Until Avery – A Carpino Series Crossover Novella

Force of Nature - A Carpino Christmas Novel

The Dillon Sisters

Deathly by Brynne Asher

Damaged by Layla Frost

The Montgomery Series

Bad Situation – The Montgomery Series, Book 1

Broken Halo – The Montgomery Series, Book 2

Betrayed Love - The Montgomery Series, Book 3

Standalones

Blackburn

ABOUT THE AUTHOR

Brynne Asher lives in the Midwest with her husband, three children, and her perfect dog. When she isn't creating pretend people and relationships in her head, she's running her kids around and doing laundry. She enjoys cooking, decorating, shopping at outlet malls and online, always seeking the best deal. A perfect day in Brynne World ends in front of an outdoor fire with family, friends, s'mores, and a delicious cocktail.

- facebook.com/brynneasherauthor
- instagram.com/brynneasher
- amazon.com/Brynne-Asher/e/B00VRULS58/ref=dp_byline_-cont_pop_ebooks_1
- bookbub.com/profile/brynne-asher

Printed in Great Britain
by Amazon